The Rapture of Corruption

Richard Rose 1

The Rapture of Corruption

Richard Rose 2

THE RAPTURE OF CORRUPTION

RICHARD ROSE

2024

Zero Roze Books
Plagiarize This Press
Philippines

The Rapture of Corruption is a work of fiction. Characters in this novel are either the product of the author's imagination or, if real, used fictitiously without any intent to describe their actual conduct.

The Rapture of Corruption

ALSO BY THE AUTHOR:

BLACK CAT SUNRISE
BLOODLUST PARADISE
DIMINUTIVE NARRATIVE
ROSE CITY REVISITED
ROSE CITY CATASTROPHE
THE ZOA
TRIBAL VENGEANCE
SAINT ANTHONY'S FIRESTORM
TAI/DICE
TOBIAS AND OSAZE
BEFORE THE AFTERMATH
JESUS CHRIST!
VAGUELY VIVID

The Rapture of Corruption

The Rapture of Corruption is dedicated to my exquisite wife Michelle Rose who is a constant reminder that sometimes things go good.

The Rapture of Corruption is also dedicated to my two precious daughters: Zeta Celestia and Richelle Mizuki. Your father loves you with all of his heart; always and forever.

And, of course, too, The Rapture of Corruption is dedicated to my wonderful mother. Never was there a better.

The Rapture of Corruption

The Rapture of Corruption

Chapter 0
A Trucker Forever
If one day, in a moment of clarity, or in a moment of lucidity, I came to find myself in the padded cell of a sanitarium, or in the jelly filled glass chamber of a mad scientist, or suddenly awakened in the black confines of a coffin- after having dreamed the dreams of a dead man; I wouldn't be the least bit surprised. For endless endlessly long days I wondered whether I was who I am, and whether what was happening was really happening. And that, if anything- I think- is the central theme of this narrative. None of us can say with any certainty that we are who we think we are and that this world is what we think it is. I for one can attest that nobody really knows the nature of our nature. Even the person who devotes their life to knowing- whose sole purpose, devotion, and dedication is the pursuit of knowing; even such as these are only deluded at best; restricted by the same limitations of identity and materiality as any other person in any other pursuit. I've been oblivious. I've been omniscient. With stops at all points in between. I've known the unimaginable. I've seen the unthinkable. I've done the impossible. I've been the unbecoming. If that makes sense.

And so it is befitting to find myself at a writing desk; creating this narrative. For if ever a man had a tale to tell, then certainly I am such a man. I am not an author. I am not a writer. I am not a linguist or a scholar or an academic or a journalist or a poet or a scribe or any such thing. Quite the opposite. And proudly, may I add. I am a trucker. Or. I was a trucker. Now... I don't know what I am anymore. My story is a trucker's story; first and foremost. Because a trucker is who and what I am.

Everything I know about books is from listening to audiobooks while I was driving. And that was only after I hurt my knee. Before I hurt my knee, I only ever listened to the engine's RPMs when I was floating gears. Maybe some tunes when the road was open. Or, talk radio in traffic. After my knee injury, I had to put myself in an automatic. Because there wasn't any way I could shift through city traffic after that. I don't think I read a book in my life before I started driving an automatic. I should elaborate... No real trucker ever wanted an automatic. My old man- I don't think he ever forgave me for betraying the principles of my heritage. The old goat knew I couldn't bend my knee. It was no excuse, in his mind. But, in retrospect; I guess that was his thing. Bending the knee. I was over and over forced to bend the knee to that demented old bastard. Some men are so small, all they want is to feel big.

Those old truckers hated the idea of an automatic transmission. And I wasn't enthusiastic about it myself. But I eventually came to realize that it had certain advantages. It was easier to focus on the other cars when you weren't working the stick, and it was easier to focus on what the road was doing, too. Like at intersections and interchanges. And with an automatic transmission, you could turn your brain off and cover vast distances without ever even coming out of highway hypnosis. Maybe that's not a good thing. I know these are trivial details; but, like I said; I was a trucker. And the 'manual versus automatic' debate- as banal as it may seem- was at the crux of our culture. Right up there with the 'CB radio versus no CB radio' debate. Or, the 'day cab versus sleeper berth' debate. Truckers were forever looking for different ways to feel superior to other truckers. What I've mentioned is only a cursory examination of a trucker's egomania. It goes a lot deeper. Suffice to say: We all had pride, but a lot of us were conceited.

I'm just trying to drive the point home. I was a trucker. That was the alpha and the omega of my existence. I will be a trucker forever. Maybe trucking doesn't function in the same capacity as it used to. But my mind is a trucker's mind, and it always will be. No matter where I go, I see the road first and foremost. I see potholes and uneven pavement. I see tight right turns. I see bridges with low clearances. I see blindsided backing maneuvers. I see mountainside switchbacks and wonder if I could get a rig through the area; even though I know better than to try it.

I wasn't a learn-ed man. I wasn't an author. The only reason I can cobble this narrative together is because I listened to a lot of long books on a lot of long hauls. After a while, I kind of got a sense for what the writers were doing. A lot of them- it seemed like... they weren't trying very hard. And I used to think; I could do that. If I had a story to tell. Of course, at the time, I didn't have a story to tell. But I sure got one now. And it's a doozy. It's a whopper. It's a humdinger. I'll tell you what. It's the apex. It's the zenith. And to think, used to be, I was just another dumb trucker who didn't know nothing about anything.

It's fair to say that this book is about bad things happening to good people. In some instances, the book is about bad things happening to myself. One interesting thing- I think- is that after all is said and done, the worst thing that happened to me, or- about the worst thing that happened to me; it happens right at the beginning. In the first chapter. Basically, within the next couple of pages. This terrible event... Many years later and I still shudder at the thought of it. I feel incapable of telling it without understating it. I don't think I could possibly overstate it. I guess a lot of things will be understated in the telling; in this chapter, as well as in all the chapters to follow. Words can't describe the worst things in life. And words can't describe the best things, either. Words can only describe the absolute middle, and they can barely do that. In my opinion. That's why there's no talking in Zen. Words have a way of detracting from what is. Nonetheless, words are what we are here to do; so they must be good for something.

I've seen trauma. I've seen violence. I've seen gore. I've seen cataclysm. I've seen evil on a cosmic scale. I've seen the end of days and the dawn of days, and more than once- it feels like. But I dare to say that no horror surpasses the relatively ordinary occurrence I endured which turned out to be the first installment of a lengthy saga that is as dismal as it is disturbing.

There's more that I could say by way of an introduction. There's more that I should say, to be sure. But it will all get told in due time. There are things I want to say. Divine mysteries that I want to express for the simple reason that they frustrate me and for the more commanding reason that these mysteries are the central tenet of my ordeal. Of the human ordeal, as well, I might add. If I just came out and said what I am thinking, then it might not resonate how it should. It wouldn't be good enough. So, instead, I suppose I will weave the details into the tale and a discerning mind can figure out why. Because, after all, that's how we come to know the mystery, anyways. A little bit at a time.

For instance; the first evidence of our heavenly mystery- as it pertains to my story- was just a simple little thing. Pertaining to about a dozen sets of tail lights. If what I'm about to describe happened on any other day, I wouldn't think anything of it. Even if it happened on the night before or on the day after; I wouldn't have thought anything of it. But it happened on a specific day, and even at a specific period of time. So, it must mean something. But what it means exactly; I cannot imagine.

I was in traffic. Somewhere east of Lincoln, Nebraska. It was Monday morning traffic. Which any knowing trucker would agree was the worst time of the week to be on the road. There are a million cars and they're all moving like demons on fire. Except for the couple of them who are not. There was one car out there driving like five miles per hour under the speed limit, in the fast lane, of two lanes, and riding alongside a putt-putting grandmother in the slow lane; as inconsiderate as they were ignorant. I was eastbound; just trying to get south of Omaha to shut down for the night. And by 'night,' I mean 'day,' because I always ran at night, so to me, night was day and day was night. It had been a pretty good day. Or night. Or, whatever. A good day as far as trucking goes; the roads were flat, the miles were ticking over smoothly, and it wasn't raining or windy. A lot of people didn't know this, but truckers did; Monday morning traffic actually began on Sunday night. So, there were some extra cars on the road for that reason, but, out in the midlands, it wasn't much of a bother. Not until Monday morning proper. Around 5:30 am, give or take. Monday morning rush hour was a hassle in every city in the nation. Probably in every city on Earth.

So, just like any other morning, I was trying to shut down for the night, or day, or whatever. And all the four-wheelers were getting hung up on the super cool guy going slow in the fast lane. A couple of them were squeezing through the gap on the right when they were able to, but it was an ugly display at best. And the speeds were erratic, too. We'd accelerate a little, and then slow down even worse. All contingent on the two tortoises who were dictating the flow. For that reason, there was a lot of brake tapping.

As I was mindlessly observing this, I thought my eyes were playing tricks on me. I saw the tail lights flashing and the imprint was jumping across my view. Not far across; just a little to the side of the actual position. That deep red light of brake lights; it was jumping out of position and moving just a few millimeters or centimeters across my vision. To the right, to be exact. This went on for about a minute. A moving red glowing; like demonic eyes peeking through the ether. Each car's lights had a different shape, but they were all that vibrant deep red color. The sun was up but the skies were overcast, so the scene was gray and diffused.

I should mention that I had been trucking for as long as I had had a driver's license. This wasn't the first time my eyes played tricks on me. It wasn't even the first time I'd seen a legitimate distortion of the physical realm. Nor was it anything special by way of otherworldly experiences. The only strange thing about it was the timing. As to why the timing was strange, I will commence to explain.

It had something to do with the super cool dude who was blocking the flow and holding up all that traffic. I knew they were super cool when I first saw them, but I sure didn't have any clue as to their legendary status among the countless super cool four-wheelers of the world. This one was about as super cool as they come. The situation with the traffic resolved itself as one might expect. Eventually- after five or ten minutes of people flashing their lights in their mirrors and tailgating them and rocketing around them when they were able to- they randomly decided to participate in the activity which they were engaged in; namely- being a competent component of the motoring public. This individual, for the record, was driving one of those varieties of cars with an odd and unnecessarily boxy design that- for whatever reason; liberalism... attracts bad drivers. The color was yellowish-goldish-greenish.

I on the other hand was in a black and chrome 367 with a 13 speed transmission and a six cylinder turbo diesel engine. It was a big mean tractor. Not the biggest or the meanest; but it suited me well for the kind of work I did which was basically jumping around the country like a man possessed. It certainly weren't no tupperware truck such as were only ever gaining in popularity; despite the lamentations of "real truckers," like my father. Mine was an honest to goodness tractor of yore. The backbone of the country. And I loved it. There was a 53 foot reefer trailer on the back. I was pulling potatoes from Idaho to Atlanta.

All the cars that had been trapped behind that slowpoke- of which there were many- had succeeded in making their way down the road and taking the slowpoke with them. Apparently, the slowpoke had emerged from their stupor. For the time being. I was moving at 70 miles an hour. My truck liked to move at about 70, but was capable of getting up to 80, or even higher on a downgrade. So, I was doing about 70 when I came back up on the slowpoke. Unsurprisingly, the dude was still riding slow in the fast lane. Most of the other cars had gone on down the road, but there was a trail of three or four others who were following on their tail. These individuals were either too timid to pass on the right or they had decided that they too were not in any particular hurry to get to where they were going. I didn't think much about any of these all too ordinary circumstances. Truckers were always cagey around four-wheelers because four-wheelers were unpredictable, but at the same time truckers often found themselves underestimating the destructive potential of those same people. There was no right answer to any of it. At any rate, I certainly wasn't too timid to pass on the right. On the contrary, I didn't think anything of it. My concern was that one of the other cars would move out in front of me and block my way around the tortoise. That did not occur.

What did occur was that- at the very last second- this super cool four-wheeler who had been riding in the left lane for the past 20 minutes or more and who had been passed on the right by everybody and their extended families; this legendary super cool four-wheeler noticed that a tractor-trailer was passing them on the right and decided to take umbrage at me. As if they'd not been taking umbrage at polite society at large all that morning already.

This absolute legend not only placed themselves directly in front of me. They also slammed on their brakes and came to a complete stop directly in front of my 40 ton kinetic projectile. What happened next happened before I could think anything about it. It happened so fast that it's difficult to communicate the order of operations. Or, maybe it's more straightforward than I'm making it out to be.

I was presented with three options. The first option was to swerve to the left and obliterate the two or three cars in my immediate vicinity. My second option was to slam on my brakes and come to a smoking, screeching, skidding halt on top of this legend's car. Leaving my new favorite person crushed and mangled and tangled within that silly automobile turned pancake. A lot of drivers; this is what they'd say they'd do. Because it's the safest option for the truck driver. It's the option most likely to deliver the driver home to his loved ones in an alive condition. Drivers who claimed they'd do that; very few of them ever had to go through with it. Thankfully. The third option available to me was what we call; 'taking the ditch.' It's not always a ditch. Sometimes it's an old growth forest. Sometimes it's a desert chasm. It could be a body of water. Or it could be an urban area. In my case, it actually was a ditch. I chose the third option. I took the ditch.

I can describe what happened up to a point, but after that point; it got weird. I remember I had the delusional notion that I was going to steer good enough to keep that big son of a bitch upright. Two things occurred as I was descending down into the ditch; which was a sudden drop off of about ten feet. First, I found myself looking over at the car who put me in this predicament. I saw the brake lights inexplicably shifting about before dimming back to normal as the car continued on its merry way. Then I looked into the vehicle. Perfectly clearly I saw into the car, and to this day, I swear it; there was nobody driving. I doubt anybody would believe it, hearing me tell it. But I swear it. There was nobody driving that car. And probably, all things considered, by the end of my story, that won't seem near such a bizarre claim. The second thing that happened was that all my potatoes shifted hard to the right and pushed the trailer over on its side. The trailer then pulled the tractor over on its side. The rig was overturning at about sixty miles per hour. I remember trying to steer it back onto the road as the front right corner struck the incline on the far side of the ditch. That was not a gentle impact and it threw all the potatoes hard forward. I felt the hurtling potatoes thrust the rig forward a touch faster. And that was the last thing I remember.

Here's where it gets weird. I suddenly found myself sitting down by the side of the road; positioned with my legs splayed out before me and propped up on my arms to keep from falling backward and falling asleep. There were cars driving by. They were slowing down to observe the crash, but none of them were stopping to help. Not yet, anyway. My thoughts were very confused. Like in a dream when you realize you're dreaming but still can't make sense of anything that is happening. I could see the wreckage of my tractor-trailer; kind of on its side, and kind of upside down. The weight of the potatoes had forced the trailer up over the tractor and the tractor had been ground down into the ground underneath. It was a complete mess but I remember being astonished that the potatoes hadn't spilled out all over the place. I wondered if they'd salvage the load. Also, I was extremely grateful that the diesel hadn't burst into flame.

The tractor-trailer was all bent out of shape and it all looked like a nondescript pile of scrap metal as much as it looked like what it actually was. Really, that was what it was. I could swear I saw movement in the shadows of the wreckage. In retrospect, I know that I saw movement in the shadows. There were entities creeping around in there. They had no form or figure, but they were glistening. Sparkling almost. They were black things moving in black places but they shone with tiny bits of glistening and glinting white light. Because of these sparkles, I could discern some vague aspects of their sizes and shapes. There were three of them. I also ascertained that these shadow creatures were pixelated in a subtle way. Beyond that, I couldn't make any sense of what they were nor could I reckon why they were there. Furthermore; I accepted their presence at face value because the entire experience was dreamlike and my mind wasn't in any condition to be inquisitive.

I noticed a girl approaching me. She was wearing a costume of some kind. It was all white. A white tunic with a belt tied at the waist and a rosary hanging by her knees. A white cloth over her head. The cloth covered her hair. I now know the cloth was called a wimple, and her hair was black and shoulder length.

Her face was asian. My face is kind of Asian, because I am half Japanese. But this girl was completely asiatic. I know now she was a Filipina. But, at the time, I was only just realizing that she was an adult woman and not a young lady. She was tiny in size and dainty in stature. When I understood that I was looking at a nun, my first thought was, 'Great, she's here to tell me I'm dead.'

Her eyes were big and pretty. Her cheek bones were high and elegant. Her cheeks were cherubic. Her nose was flat between the eyes and upturned at the tip and you could almost look straight into her skull through her nostrils. There was a beauty mark at the lower right corner of her mouth. Probably the most beautiful beauty mark there ever was. Her mouth was small and she was smiling and I got the impression that she was happy to see me. Although, simultaneously, she was evidently trying not to smile. I saw there were braces on her teeth, and so I presume she was self-conscious about them. A delicate chin gave an otherwise rounded head a distinctive shape. I was happily married and this woman was a nun, so neither one of us was inclined toward impure thoughts; but... nonetheless... I was a man and she was a woman and neither one of us could completely conceal our twinkling eyes from the other.

This exquisite female sat down beside me as though we were on a chaise lounge and not the side of Interstate 80. Some cars screamed by. Some cars crept by. Some cars stopped and the midwesterners inside of them got out to apprehensively approach the tractor-trailer; no doubt afraid of what they might find. These bystanders completely ignored me, and that was just as well. I was happy the woman was there, though. Even though I was pretty sure I was dead.

"You're Kevin," she said.

"How'd you know that?" I asked.

"I know all kinds of things," she explained, adding, "You'd be amazed."

"Am I dead?" I asked.

"No. Love. You're sleeping. Kind of."

"Who are you?"

"My name is Charisma Gomez."

"Are you a nun?"

"How'd you guess?"

"You look like a nun."

"Indeed I do," she said.

Her voice had an unfamiliar accent that was unusually pitched and which possessed a whimsical lilt unlike any other I had ever heard before.

"Why are you here?" I asked.

"I am here for you."

"What do you need me for?"

"If I told you, you wouldn't believe me."

"This is kind of a bad time."

"There will be worse times. You will see."

"I don't understand. I'm so confused."

"Kevin. You did a bless-ed thing. You did a noble deed of the highest order."

"What? I don't understand."

"You sacrificed yourself to save the life of the one who endangered your own."

"That's just trucking. It's nothing special."

"No. Kevin. It was very special. One day you will understand."

"I mean. Ok. If you say so. I guess."

"Kevin. Do you know anything about corruption?"

"Like, when there is mold growing on a peach?"

"If the mold is evil, and the peach is humanity. Then, yes."

"You're a nun. You know about evil. I don't know anything about evil."

"You know that evil is bad, don't you?"

"Well, I'm smarter than a five year old, so, yeah. I know that evil is bad."

"Do you agree that civilization would be better off if evil were eliminated?"

I thought about what she said as I watched the onlookers and good samaritans approaching my destroyed truck and looking around and trying to figure out what was happening or what they could do about it. They seemed overly ineffectual, but it was nice that they cared enough to make an effort.

I said, "Evil is intrinsic. It's part of life on Earth. It exists to generate good. Good is only good relative to evil. For all I know, if it weren't for evil, then we wouldn't have anything at all, or we might have something worse."

"You're playing devil's advocate."

"Yeah. Well. I mean. Nobody sane ever said evil is a good thing."

She said, "Most evil in this world exists as corruption. Evil cannot create, it can only corrupt. Reality itself is a corruption of the divine light of Christ. Only the purest of evils can exist outside of corruption. Most evil has to feed on holiness to exist. Corruption is parasitic. It's why we can't have nice things. Like, peace or justice. If we could eliminate corruption, then we could be free from evil."

"We wouldn't be free from pure evil, though, would we?" I asked.

"No, but for the first time, we'd finally be in a position to combat it."

The nun had my attention, but then I saw something that completely blindsided me. I saw me. I saw myself crawling out- or, more like shimmying out; out of the ruins of my tractor. My thoughts, I recall, were kind of stupid, like, 'What am I doing over there, if I am over here?' Or, 'How can I be over there and over here at the same time?' I was able to escape through the flaccid cracked safety glass of the windshield, but barely. Mostly the cab and berth were all crushed in like a soda can, but I somehow found my way out, anyhow. At about this time I was hearing sirens and the red and blue flashing lights illuminated me purple as I crawled off toward where I was sitting. I seemed to be in pretty good shape except for that I was dragging my left leg; which couldn't support any of my weight and was obviously badly damaged. The bystanders and good Samaritans were imploring me not to move, but I remember wanting to get far away from my truck because I was afraid it was going to explode.

I looked to my left to see if Charisma was at all astonished in regards to how I could be in two places at once, but Charisma had vanished as mysteriously as she had appeared. And I didn't think much of it at the time, but I remembered her well in the years to come and I thought of our conversation often. In some ways, meeting Charisma changed me more than the accident did, but really, Charisma and the accident were one in the same; from my perspective. I couldn't separate the two events. Too, I often thought of the glistening black figures moving in the shadows. Or, I thought of the driverless car that caused the wreck. I wish I'd known it was devoid of occupants. I'd have happily crushed it and gone about my affairs as certain other truckers might.

I should mention that all that happened thereafter was that- as bystanders crowded around me- my injured self reached the place where my out of body self was sitting and suddenly I was one person again. The pain overwhelmed me and I passed out immediately. When I woke up, I was in a hospital bed.

That about concludes this chapter of my life; a preface to the actual story that I intend to tell. But there're still a couple things that I should add. Add being the operative word, because at the time, as a 20 something year old, I was practically incapable of putting two and two together. The year this occurred was 2011. It was an important time in the world, but I didn't know it then. The significance of these days occurred to me later on and in retrospect. The important thing about that time period pertained to the internet. You've probably heard of the internet. The internet was at the height of its power, because it was at the pinnacle of its usefulness to the common good. People used to call it the information superhighway. Eventually they stopped calling it that because the overlords removed as much information as they possibly could. The internet, in the days of my crash... It was holy. It was immaculate. It was free and capable and it was doing the work of the Christ. We took it for granted at the time, and they took it away from us in the years that followed. The powers-that-be effortlessly forced the internet into submission; bound it, gagged it, enslaved it, and then used it to make themselves richer while turning it against us. Blinding us and deafening us and dumbing us down. Dumbing us down further, I should say. 2011 was a special year for the internet. It had come of age. Come into its own. Then, in 2012, 2013, and 2014, the overlords began figuring out how to censor and stifle free speech and- more importantly- independent research. It was like a circumcision. They mutilated it and expected us to believe it was better that way. In 2011 we had the best independent researchers that we were going to get. And that was a special thing. In 2011 we could see the puppet masters working the strings. We could see the set designers. We could see the casts and the make-up artists; the lighting and sound techs. We could see the screenwriters and the directors and the producers. We could see that what we think of as the everyday affairs of the world, are- in actuality- elaborate productions put on by the wickedest of wicked forces. We got an unprecedented glimpse into thousands of years of devious and downright devilish socioeconomic manipulation. And before we knew what we had, they took it away from us.

I'm mentioning this because it was my serendipitous good fortune to be recovering and bedridden and glued to the computer screen during this most excellent year. If it weren't for my accident, I would've just kept on trucking and remained blissfully ignorant. After 2011, I knew what corruption was. I knew what evil was. I knew what they were hiding from us. I knew what they were doing to us. I didn't know exactly how or exactly why, but I had at least learned something about the full extent to which we've- each of us- been victimized. By them. The wicked and the damned.

Chapter 1
Gnosis
I was in one of those decrepit industrial areas that epitomizes why people hate driving in North Jersey. To get in or out of the place, you had to jump on and off about five different roads in about five minutes' time. When you're in there, you look around and think; they should bulldoze all of this. There's evidence of every manner of industry, but it all looks like it hasn't turned a dollar in decades; random decaying silos, fuel tanks scattered around, conveyor belts leading to nowhere, pipelines going in every direction, the remnants of oil refineries, sewer pipes that jut out of the hillsides, a river with multiple half sunk barges of indeterminate purpose, dead trees that couldn't get very big, and tractors and tractor-trailers inexplicably parked in every crack and crevice; basically stacked on top of each other.

I was dropping off a load of dog food. The warehouse had almost finished unloading. My phone rang. A sobbing and wailing woman coughed and spat words at me. She was struggling to speak, but I got the jist of it. It sounded something like this; "Kevin... They called... Vanessa... The medical examiner... She's dead, Kevin... They won't let us see her... They said they cremated her already... They said... infectious disease... She's gone... Kevin... She's gone..."

This was my wife's twin sister calling. I remember immediately not believing her. But, at the same time, I knew something bad had happened. Something important. And bad.

My wife dragged me into Gnosis about five years ago. And I liked it for what it was. I thought they had a good message and a good mission; but I was always kind of an outsider. I came and went. If I wanted to drink a beer, or eat a steak, I had to do it off Gnosis property. It's illegal to drink beer in your tractor, but I was more afraid of the Gnosis loons than I was of the Department of Transportation.

The reason I didn't believe what I was hearing was because I'd once heard some gossip about a dead girl from another state. It was just a rumor, but the details were exactly the same. This was a couple years back. It was Vanessa who had told me about it. Apparently, the woman had been elevated to the upper echelons and was no longer in need of her former identity. Nonetheless; this was my wife in question. The woman I loved since I was fourteen years old. More than twenty years we'd been a couple. About 15 of those years we'd been married. She was my whole world. And I got the immediate impression that Gnosis was actively stealing her from me.

"Gloria. Calm down. Listen. Vanessa isn't dead. It's Gnosis. They're faking it. It's fake. I've heard of this before. It's a Gnosis thing. Just try to relax. Tell your sisters to relax. I'm going to figure it out. I'm going to find her."

I was supposed to pull a load of pet store stuff to some pet store somewhere, but I had to cancel it. I had to go find my wife. About now was when I started blowing a not so small fortune on fuel costs. But, that's not important. Compared to all the terrible things that happened later on; the money was nothing. Of course, I tried to phone my wife and got no answer. I called some friends and asked them to check in on her, but they called back and said she wasn't home.

The sun had gone down and it was a sultry Sunday night. In North Jersey. One might think Sunday night traffic would be easy, but the opposite was true. The denizens of the cities would scatter to the winds around Friday afternoon and then come Sunday night they'd decide to hurry home at around the same time as all the church people started moving around at a snail's pace. Plus, some Monday morning people would use Sunday night to get a jump on their day. For a trucker, Sunday night was de facto Monday morning. Besides all that, there was an X-factor to Sunday night. Something unreal about it. All over the country. Anxiety in bloom; rooted in the soil of dread. Everybody was afraid of the next five days. Well, they didn't really know what real fear is. But they would learn.

I was in a 2019 T680 tupperware truck; black and fake chrome, with Robertson Trucking in cursive on the side, and a late model 53 foot dry van on the back. I put the hammer down and headed up the New Jersey turnpike. Running hard and fast; with white knuckles and sweating palms. Completely disregarding speed limits and lane restrictions. Of course, that's pretty much how most truckers drove most of the time, so it wasn't particularly unusual.

There was construction traffic at the George Washington bridge. Not surprising. You'd come up on it and it's two lanes and they're stopped, but then more and more lanes appeared to the right and you could kind of go around and get out ahead a little bit as the lanes became available. The bridge was an unending traffic jam for like half of the year.

Breaking out of that; I rode the no-no lane through the Bronx. Bouncing over the unrelentingly lumpy pavement. Passing beneath the underpasses that were all marked with the wrong heights. Occasionally, somebody unfamiliar with the area would come to a dead stop when they saw those asinine signs. Meanwhile, I'd done the drive a thousand times and a thousand times again. It never got any easier. Anything could go wrong.

The grace of God grants a trucker a certain amount of luck; contingent on his skill and abilities and disposition as much as on his fate and destiny. My luck ran out once before. But then again, I survived, so maybe not. Anyways, the only way to get a semi through the Bronx- without tripping over the drugged-out urbanites who live there- is to haul ass down the no-no lane. That's what I usually did, and that's what I did on that day.

I was doing about 65 miles per hour. And I saw something in the road. I assumed it was garbage. Two days earlier, when I was stuck in traffic in that place, going southbound, I had seen a rat running along the concrete barrier on the median. So, when I saw that the garbage was moving, I assumed it was a rat. Maybe the same rat.

This all happened very fast. I was slowing down because I didn't want to kill the rat, but I couldn't possibly slow down enough, and I couldn't possibly swerve. As I got closer to it, I realized it wasn't a rat. It was a cat. A kitten. A black kitten. A black cat. Directly in my path; with nowhere to go. No safe place to escape to. Its back legs were already broken, it looked like. It was right in line with my tires. As I ran it over, I thought, 'Well, at least I can put it out of its misery.'

Tearing out of New York and into Connecticut, I couldn't stop thinking about that cat. Everybody knows that if a black cat crosses your path, then you're going to have bad luck. It stands to reason that crushing said cat is even worse luck. I wondered why it had to be me who had had to kill that cat. There were fifty million other drivers on the road. It could have been any one of them who killed it. I couldn't understand why it had had to be me killing the cat, but, thinking back on it, it would've been strange if it was anybody other than me. We were meant for each other.

It's impossible to know if the black kitten was even real, or if it was illusory. Because, we can't know what is real or what is illusory. We simply cannot. All indications indicate that reality is illusory. The other cars on the road; there's nobody driving them. If you look inside, then you will see a driver. But if you don't look inside, then there won't be anybody in there. This is Gnosis talking out of my mouth. But, they weren't wrong. I don't think. 'Who knows?' That's my mantra. Gnosis means knowing. Supposedly, Gnosis knew. But I doubted it. Although, they knew more than I gave them credit for, for sure.

'The danger zone' is what I called the 100 miles of Interstate-95 between Carteret, New Jersey and New Haven, Connecticut. Northbound or southbound, it made no difference. That was the most congested road in the nation. And trucking it just plain sucked; always and forever. That trip north was no different. In fact, that trip north was among the more intense which I can recall. It was too early for the trucks to be out in any real quantity. I'd shaken off the other truckers back in the Bronx and thereafter I was adrift in a sea of four-wheelers. They'd slow me down to a crawl if I let them. But if you let a four-wheeler dictate your cruising speed, then you should just turn in your CDL and go flip burgers. No. I was in a hurry to get to where I was going. Not unlike any other day, really. So, I applied the method. I called the method, 'tiptoeing through the tulips.' Four-wheelers- as frustrating as they are- tended to repeat a litany of mostly predictable patterns and I had a contingency for each pattern as well as for each inevitable escalation of hostilities. Essentially, we were playing tit for tat. It was a game in and of itself but I had a lifetime of experience and they were just too stupid to realize they shouldn't be playing with me at all. There were a thousand cars all around me, but only one or two of them would be actively engaging with my semi at any given time. Those one or two were problematic. Everybody else was no problem. The exact technique for tiptoeing through the tulips- as fascinating as I find it- is somewhere between a trade secret and boring shop talk. And for that reason I will omit it from this narrative.

I'd just gotten out of the danger zone when it started raining. Headlights and taillights and streetlights and city lights; they all morphed and mutated in the rainwater on my windows. Traffic continued to burrow under my skin until I finally got onto Interstate 84. Only then could I catch my breath. Strangely, the drive had gone by like nothing. Sometimes that happens. I wondered who'd been driving my truck. It seemed like the truck was driving itself. Maybe it was.

There were parking lots at the edge of the Gnosis compound and I had my own parking spot there. There were regularly scheduled shuttles, but I kept an electric bicycle chained to a tree; just to get in and out in a more timely manner. Unlike myself, Vanessa lived at the compound full time. We had our own condo, but I was gone a lot for work.

Gnosis began building this village in 2014. They brazenly called it Heaven. Heaven's population had exploded in the past couple years. There was a lot of public interest in the Gnosis way of life. We had good publicity and a good reputation. People were sick of being manipulated and treated like livestock. But Gnosis wasn't the utopia it pretended to be. For instance; Gnosis said Heaven's population was 13,000, but they also claimed that all population statistics were fabrications. And I couldn't help but to believe the claim. For instance; I came from a town of 2,500 people. But, I lived there my whole life and I only ever encountered about 250 people. One tenth the number on the town's welcome sign. So, probably there were 1,300 people at this Gnosis compound. It was kind of depressing that they were replicating the same behaviors that they were supposed to be rescuing us from. Typical, really. Gnosis was nothing special. Ultimately, they offered nothing we couldn't find on our own. They made a lot of empty promises which I for one could have done without.

Sitting with my hands still gripping the wheel; I was apprehensive to move. I just wanted to crawl into the sleeper berth and pretend nothing was happening. I'd been ignoring all my thoughts and questions about it. But it had come time to face the future. There weren't any weapons allowed on Gnosis property, but I kept a subcompact 10mm in my truck and I stuffed it into a concealed carry holster and secured the holster to the nylon shorts I had on; at the appendix. I stuffed an extra magazine in my cargo pocket. I had a mesh tank top on and there wasn't any reason to put anything over it. I didn't care about getting wet, it was so hot.

There were streetlights on overhead and I could see steam rising off of the pavement. It was nighttime proper now, so most of the people would be going to sleep. I got on my bike and took off. It was raining more than I thought it was. Or maybe the trees were drip-drying on me. I had long black hair and soon it was clinging to my skull. The fireflies were abundant in the forests and their twinkling was a pleasant distraction. The frogs were chirping and croking and grunting; I was amazed at their volume. The residences I passed by were quiet and subdued. The village had a nice way of not overpowering its surroundings. The Gnostics had a reverence for nature that counted among their positive qualities.

I happened upon the townsquare and I could see there was some sort of gathering taking place. We had a sheltered area with a lot of picnic tables and a huge fireplace where they'd grill food sometimes. Where they'd grill vegetables, I should say. These people were all vegetarians. But they could bake bread or make stews or whatever. There was a fire going; but it was way past dinner time and I knew they weren't cooking anything edible because the smoke in the air had a faintly toxic odor. I was in an inquisitive mood, and still wired from trucking and caffeine and the simmering rage about not knowing where my wife was; about these people telling her family she was dead. Or, maybe she actually was dead, and I was in denial. It was catching up with me. I was going to crack. I felt a breakdown coming. I'd been in denial. Maybe. I didn't know what to think or what to believe. My electric bicycle was almost silent and I rolled up on the crowd without anybody noticing.

What I saw would've been an unusual sight outside Gnosis, but inside Gnosis it was an ordinary community activity. They'd gathered up a stockpile of birth control. Condoms, intrauterine devices, RU-486, diaphragms, sponges, a variety of birth control pills, etcetera. They were casually tossing this stuff into the fire. This bothered me because I had no children. Vanessa could never give me one. But I loved her just the same. I couldn't imagine life with another woman.

I shrugged and rolled my eyes and got back onto my bike and headed out toward the medical center. Gloria had said that the authorities had said that Vanessa had already been cremated. I needed to confirm this. I needed to talk to these people. This was my wife. This was my life. I was freaking out.

The medical center was a modest structure, but impressive by Heaven's standards. Definitely more capable than one would presume. It was a Sunday night. So there weren't a lot of staff on duty. But there were some.

"Vanessa Robertson. Where is she?"

The woman at the desk was kind of old and very Connecticut. By that I mean, she looked like she was coming apart at the seams. That's what Connecticut does to people. Her hair was stringy and gray. Her skin was pasty and flabby and wrinkled. Her eyes had permanent bags. Her ill-fitting blue scrubs were disheveled.

"And you are?"

"I'm Kevin Robertson. Vanessa is my wife."

"She's dead, sir. I'm sorry."

"Where's the body? Did you see the body?"

"Sir. She contracted ebola. They had to cremate her. To destroy the infection."

"Ebola? Are you kidding? Do you know how ridiculous that sounds? I talked to her last night! She was fine!"

"Sir, if you'll come back in the morning, I am sure there will be paperwork and a formal process. You'll be wanting to organize a funeral and register the death certificate, I imagine."

"Lady... Is there any sort of evidence to prove your claim that she was ill? As far as I know she's been murdered and you are covering it up."

"As I said, sir. Come back in the morning. I am just a third shift nurse. The medical examiner will be in at 8am."

These people didn't know that I knew about the other guy who this had happened to. They'd told him the exact same thing. He never got his woman back, but she was still somewhere in Gnosis orbit. The doctors must have known it, too. But there was nothing the guy could do. Or, he didn't have the balls to do what had to be done. I knew this story because Vanessa had told it to me. I never imagined her implication.

I needed to talk to the director, but I didn't want this woman to alert him; so I tried to throw her off my scent. I asked her, "If my wife's been cremated, then where are her ashes? I have a right to see my wife's ashes."

"Sir. I'm very sorry. But, like I said. There is nothing I can do for you. You'll have to come back in the morning."

Thinking, or maybe at a loss; I gave her a hateful look. And with that, and without another word, I stormed out of there; figuring she'd been sufficiently duped.

The director was what we had instead of a mayor. He was a smart guy, but a complete jerk. Gnosis had a culture of self-righteousness and fanaticism and of course our fearless leader exemplified that. It was obvious to me that he was just a glorified stooge. His thinking was brilliant but it was lockstep inline with Gnosis dogma. Gnosis itself was brilliant, but it wasn't as perfect as it pretended to be.

On my way to see the director, I stopped by my cabin. I was hoping Vanessa would be there waiting. I was hoping she'd be confused and oblivious, and that the whole thing had been some kind of a mistake. Like she'd been busy with some arts and crafts; making a popsicle stick house or a macaroni necklace. And she hadn't noticed her phone battery died. Meanwhile, they cremated some other guy's wife and mixed up the paperwork. Some ordinary explanation. She wasn't home, but I noticed some things that set my mind at ease, at least a little. The house looked normal. But her luggage was missing. And there were random belongings missing, too. Most obviously; her make-up and hair products. As well as a lot of her clothes. I don't know much about the plague, but I wouldn't imagine a plague sufferer would be overly concerned about their appearance.

Most of us lived in tiny cabins that were built alongside the village roads. But the director lived on a private road. In his own private neck of the woods. A most special place for our most special guy. His home was similar to all of our homes; cherry stained wood, with big windows, and black shingles. The difference was that his place was like four or five of our places fused together. It rained heavily as I made my way over there. This was good because people are better at minding their own business when it's pouring rain out.

Gnosis was a polite society. The director wasn't expecting to be accosted in his own home. But he should have been. Considering what was transpiring. I ditched the bike in the trees at the end of his road and walked the rest of the way to his home. When I found him, he was in his living room; talking into a webcam. He had no shirt on, wore blue cotton drawstring pants, and had no shoes on. His facial hair was bushy and the semi-circle of hair on his bald head was bushy, also. His speaking was very animated and accompanied by exasperated expressions and wild gesticulations. Being outside, I had no idea what he was saying, and- considering my plans- I didn't want to be on camera when I confronted him. So I crouched in the shadows in the pouring rain and waited. It was a long wait. I watched his computer; anxious for his podcast to end and his face to disappear from the screen. Remembering how fond he was of his own voice.

While I was waiting, I decided on exactly which landscaping stone was the perfect size to throw through his floor to ceiling window. As soon as his podcast was finally over, I picked up the rock and chucked it through the glass and had my gun trained on him before the shards were finished falling.

"Don't fucking move, you little worm!" I shouted.

The director took off running and I hurried after him. I didn't shoot him because I didn't want to shoot him. I didn't want to cross that line. He slammed a door in my face and I heard the dead bolt slide, but I'm a trucker and Gnosis housing wasn't the best, so when I threw my weight into the door the wood around the latch broke apart easily. I fell into his bedroom and saw him leaping over his porch railing and running out into the night. The sliding glass door was left open behind him. I followed him over the railing and gave chase. The house was lit up bright, but he was making for the shadows of the forest. If I let him get out there, I'd never find him again. I'd be expelled from the compound and I'd never see my wife again. All this ran through my mind in an instant and instead of giving him another warning, like I wanted to, I just ran with everything I had in me. Although, with my bad knee, it was more like a gallop than a sprint. I had the pistol raised out in front of me and I began popping off shots at his legs. The third shot caught him in the meat of his thigh and he went down. I'd just put a hollow-point into this guy and I felt bad about it, but I wasn't in the mood for sympathy. I had my own problems. Not the least of which being I'd just shot a guy.

The director was writhing. Clutching his wound. Groaning. "Why'd you run?" I asked him.

"Fuck you!" he spat. His eyes were bulging out of his head with pain. And his cheeks and nostrils were flaring as he breathed.

"Where's my wife?" I asked him.

"She's gone."

"Gone where?" I asked him.

"She's dead," he lied.

I held the pistol on him. I didn't know what to say or do. I should've kicked him in his gunshot wound. Or, threatened to shoot him again. Or, actually shot him again. In the foot or something. I just stood there. Watching him watching me. The rain had let up. But the water was dripping from the trees in heavy thudding droplets. We were in a clearing at the edge of a pond and the frogs were loud like an orchestra; every variety of them- all crazily trying to find a mate. The fireflies were thick enough that their flashing was in unison.

The director stared at me. I stared at the director. Our faces lit with blinking firefly light.

"I need medical attention," he seethed.

"I'm sure you do," I replied, as I sat down in the wet grass. I told him, "I know she's not dead. She didn't have ebola. She was fine just last night. She packed her bags and left. She took her fucking curling iron. Tell me where she went."

I could see him considering his options. Weighing the alternatives. And he said, "Let me get to my golf cart. I need to get to the hospital. Just let me go. I'll tell you."

"Fine. Start walking. Start talking."

"I can't walk... You shot me in the leg..."

"Then crawl."

And I'll be damned if that isn't what he did. He started crawling. And I remembered watching myself crawling out of my wrecked truck, about eleven years before. "The sage," he said, "She went to live with the sage."

Finally, somebody said something that made some sense. And I was glad to hear it. The director- to his credit- pulled himself along quite rapidly; as I imagine he could feel the urgency of the blood spilling out of him. In the light of his home I could see that the blood was not gushing. The blood was casually leaking. So I wasn't in fear of him dropping dead. In fact, I threatened his life.

I told him, "Don't ever come between me and my woman again. If I find out you warned the sage I am coming, then I'll be back for you, and- I swear- I'll kill you, if it's the last thing I do."

"Whatever," he said, laughing, with clenched teeth and labored breathing, adding, "It's funny... You think she is your woman... She left you... On her own accord... You shot me... for a woman... who doesn't care about you."

"You know you have to tell me where the sage is, don't you?"

"Yeah... I know... I don't care... I've already been shot... And you're just wasting your time... I'll tell you where they are."

The director was true to his word. I rode on the back of his golf cart as far as to where my electric bike was stashed and we parted ways there. I was heading back to the parking lot to get my car, and he was heading over to the medical center to get bullet fragments removed from his flesh. I wouldn't have guessed it, but the sage was in a pretty obvious place. Not exactly close, but not exactly far, either. Although, I'd been trucking and sitting out in the rain, and the fatigue was catching up with me. So the drive over to Gnosis corporate headquarters felt longer than it rightly ought to have. I called Vanessa's twin sister, Gloria, on my way, and I told her that her sister was alive and that I was going to find her. But part of me knew the director was right. My wife didn't accidentally fake her own death and abandon me to be with another man. She'd done so by her own volition.

I drove fast. I had a fast car. It was a 2017 Mustang GT. Blue, with white racing stripes. And a 5.0 302 under the hood. As angry as I was, I was still happy to drive my car around; and pleased to have an excuse to give it the onions.

Gnosis corporate headquarters was a four story office building on a road laced with other similar four story office buildings. Only an hour after saying goodbye to the director, I was already sitting in the parking lot and looking up at the place. There weren't any lights on, but there were several other vehicles parked there. Including a handicapped van parked in the handicapped parking space. I didn't understand why she would be here, nor did I know why the sage would be here. I mean, logistically, these buildings weren't zoned for residency. So it didn't make sense for anybody to be here unless they were pushing papers or burning the midnight oil or whatever. It was midnight. The place was devoid of life. I began to lose faith in the director.

I was standing around outside the building, wondering if I was going to have to break in, or wait for somebody to show up in the morning, or call the police and tell them my wife was kidnapped, or... I didn't know what I was going to do. But then the front door opened. No lights had come on, but the front door opened and Vanessa walked out.

Vanessa was 5'2" and weighed about 115 pounds. Her skin was pale and her eyes were blue. I'd been on the earth long enough to be suspicious of blue eyed people, and here was another reason why. She was dressed in a pink velour tracksuit. Her typically straight blonde hair was perfectly curled. Her expression was irritated and dismayed; obviously not happy to see me.

"How did you find me?" she asked me; out there, in the darkness.

"It wasn't easy. But, it wasn't that hard, either."

"He said you would. I said you wouldn't."

"Well, you obviously don't think very highly of me."

"I suppose not. He certainly does. He wants to meet you. He sent me out here to get you."

"Does he have a name?"

"Damon," she said, adding, "Come on."

Vanessa led me into the building, and it was still weirdly dark. I remember wondering why there weren't any lights on. I was going to ask her about it, but there were little night lights that were motion-sensored and they came on as we went. So, I figured, whatever. Vanessa led me to a stairway. Even the stairway was dark. We followed it down into a basement area. The basement area was not what I expected to see. Steel doors painted yellow opened up into a sprawling and luxurious communal living facility of some sort. Inside, there were a multitude of beautiful women gathered. Other men's wives, I presume. They glared at me grimly and didn't bother to introduce themselves. I got the distinct impression I was intruding on something. But I couldn't imagine what. Nothing special, in retrospect.

It was an impressive dwelling, to be sure. The floors were white stone and the countertops were black stone and the chandeliers were crystal and faucets were gleaming metal and the fridges and dishwashers and washing machines were massive and stainless steel and the couches and chairs were black leather and the tables were made of glass and everything was extremely nice. The kind of place women like to be in. Go figure. But the strangest thing was that- at the far corner- there was all kinds of medical equipment stockpiled. There were hydraulic lifts and mechanical beds and monitors with wires coming out and IV stands with tubes looped over them. I had no idea what all that stuff was doing over there, but I would figure it out just a few minutes later.

Chapter 2
Captive
I'm realizing that I've been giving something of an abridged account. I've been elaborating on trucking when I

should've been elaborating on the dynamics of the cult fanatics. There's a simple explanation for that. I like writing about trucking. I don't like writing about the cult fanatics. Trucking made me happy. Cult fanatics pissed me off. Well. The fanatics didn't totally suck, but I certainly wasn't pleased with them. That, and, like I said, I was just a stupid steering wheel holder. Not a big brain bachelor degree, PHD, with a doctorate in small hats and a masters of literary criticism; ivy league, Madison avenue, who's who, who you know, so and so- writes one article and gets a book contract and a big fat advance- type person. If the reader will cut me some slack then I will try to stay focused.

Where were we... We were down in the luxurious dwelling of the sage and his harem of living dead women. There were doors all around and I could deduce- because some of the doors were open- that those doors opened into bedrooms for the ladies. I won't elaborate on what these six or seven women looked like. Suffice to say; they were all different in their features, but similar in their beauty. Some of them were outright hot as hell.

The bedroom doors were all singular doors; ordinary and painted white. But, at the far end of the sprawling main area, over by where all the medical equipment was, there was a set of double doors. These were painted yellow, like the doors that opened from the staircase. All that yellow was quite gaudy in contrast to the elegance of the rest of the place.

Those lovely ladies looked at me like I was garbage, or a dead rotting thing. Vanessa said to me, "Go knock on the yellow doors." My pistol had one in the chamber and I was glad for it at that moment. I had an apprehension like I was going to my death. But I felt like that every day at work. And, really, it was nothing compared to what was coming. Maybe the dread was actually a premonition.

I knocked on the yellow doors and they opened. A man of about 25 years stepped out to greet me. He had naturally tan skin. A nose with a lump in it. No facial hair. A chuckling grin on a small mouth. A pointed chin. A well-groomed head of ear-length hair. Intense eyes that shifted from me to the women and back. Wearing a navy blue hoodie, light blue jeans, and black combat boots. With a knife hanging from his belt. And I guessed he was also packing heat. I thought I was a decent looking guy, but this guy was basically the definition of a hunk.

I could practically hear the women swooning. I looked back at them and their coquettish smiles turned to mud when they made eye contact with me. I rolled my eyes and shook my head; asking the guy, "You're the sage?"

"No. I'm Jeremy. I'll take you in to see Damon. But I got to check you for weapons."

"I've got a gun. If I give it to you, am I going to get it back?"

"Yeah, man. I know it probably seems kind of sketchy down here, and you're probably... displeased... about what's happening, but Damon is excited to meet you. You're among friends. Believe it or not."

"Yeah, I don't believe it. I'm not giving you my gun. If you killed me, it would solve a problem for you. I'm not going to make it that easy. I do not have any reason to hurt anybody and you all have a good reason to eliminate me. If I'm among friends, then let me keep my gun."

Jeremy thought about what I said, and said, "Ok. Fine. But don't make me regret it."

"Deal."

And with that he guided me in through the yellow doors; closing them behind us. We were in something like an airlock, but instead of locking out the air, it was locking out the light. Out where the girls were, it was very bright. But in there, there was just a single red light bulb. And some more medical equipment. Plus stockpiles of medical supplies; gloves, diapers, cleaning materials, bedsheets, and medicinal powders and fluids. And there was an odor. Not a pleasant odor. The opposite of a pleasant odor.

Jeremy said, "I'm going to hit the light switch. I'll take your arm and lead you in to meet him. The couch is about ten steps in and on the right. You can feel for it. Just sit down and you won't have to worry about tripping over anything."

He didn't explain further. We went in like how he said and I sat. And it was dark. Like, pitch black. I was confused and annoyed, but intrigued too. Then I heard a chilling voice; rasping and wet. It said, "Thanks. Jeremy. You can leave us alone, now, please. I need some quality time with our truck driver."

"He has a gun," Jeremy said.

"He won't shoot the messenger."

"He shot the director."

"The director's not the messenger."

"If you say so," Jeremy said carelessly. And then I heard his footsteps as he walked away; closing the doors behind him.

Damon then said to me, "I imagine you have a lot of questions."

"In fact, I do," I said, asking, "What the hell did you do to my wife? Did you scramble her brains?"

"Your wife is a woman. Women talk. Your wife talked to the wrong women. She got it in her head that this was where she wanted to be. And now she is here."

"We've been together for twenty years."

"Not anymore. I'm sorry to say."

The more Damon spoke, the more I could hear that there was something seriously wrong with him. He choked out his words like each took some effort. But, even so, he seemed to like to make conversation. We were in complete darkness and so, of course, I couldn't see him. At the time, I had no idea what his problem was. And I wasn't particularly interested. But I found myself pitying him. I could tell he was seriously crippled in some way.

I was wondering why I was in there with him; when I should be out there with Vanessa; trying to talk some sense into her.

Then he said, "You're wondering why you're in here with me, when you should be out there with Vanessa. Trying to talk some sense into her?" And I thought, 'Ok, well, that was weird.'

He continued, "I don't want to be insensitive to your plight, but Kevin, pretty soon, believe it or not, you will forget all about your wife."

"That doesn't make any sense."

"She is lost to you. Lost to the world. More to the point; she betrayed you. I know it won't be easy to think about anything else, but there is a reason why I wanted an audience with you and it has nothing to do with Vanessa."

"Why is it so dark in here?" I asked.

"I live in the dark," he said.

"Why?"

"Because I am a dreamer. In the darkness, I can dream; waking or sleeping, I am always dreaming. And I dreamed a dream of you, my good trucker."

I took his words at face value, and really, I was losing interest. I wanted to see my wife. I wanted to hear what she had to say for herself.

"I'll get to the point. God. You're so impatient. Do you know anything about a nun?"

Now he had my attention. "I don't know any nuns," I said, lying.

"Ok. But this nun knows you. More importantly, she needs you."

"What? Needs me for what?" I asked.

"She needs you to rescue her. She's being held prisoner."

"Is the nun asian?" I asked.

"She's a filipina, yes."

I felt my head spinning, but it was dark and I was sitting down. I might have fainted, otherwise. Of course I remembered the woman. I thought about her whenever I thought about my truck wreck. Pretty much everyday. I remember her talking about corruption, and evil.

I said, "I can't believe she's real. Do you know how I know her?"

"You said you don't know her."

"I don't know her. I knew her in a dream. In an out of body experience. I was in an accident. She appeared in a vision. It wasn't real. It couldn't be real."

"Aren't you a Gnostic? Don't you realize that nothing is real? A dream can be as real as anything else. Under certain circumstances. These are those circumstances. Kevin. You have to rescue this woman. Her life is in danger. Jeremy will give you her coordinates."

"You have her coordinates?" I asked.

"Yes."

That seemed odd, but I didn't question it. I just asked him; "How am I going to rescue her? I'm just one guy."

"You have two good legs. And two good arms. If I were so gifted, I'd go get her myself."

"I don't know anything about any of this. I don't know what to do."

"You'll figure it out. There's a damsel in distress. Do whatever it takes."

"Why don't you send Jeremy? He seems capable."

"It has to be you. This is your destiny. She chose you."

"Is it urgent? I have to get some sleep."

"They're torturing her. Of course it is urgent. So just go. Jeremy!"

Jeremy came and he took my arm and I left the sage behind without another word exchanged between the two of us. I was dazed and confused. Back out in the red glow of the lightlock, Damon's dutiful companion handed me a slip of paper.

"Do you know about this?" I asked him.

"I don't know nothing about nothing," he told me.

"I want to speak with my wife. Before I go."

"She's not your wife anymore. But if you insist, then be my guest."

There was a big couch that wrapped around one corner of the main area. The women were gathered there; eating snacks and gabbing. Maybe about me, maybe about interior decorating. They were delighted to see Jeremy but they grimaced when they looked at me. Vanessa seemed embarrassed; reluctant to meet my gaze.

"Vanessa. Can I have a word with you? In private. Please."

With a bitchy look on her face, Vanessa said, "Anything you want to say to me, you can say it in front of the others."

"The others. The other what?"

"It's none of your business. What do you want to say?"

"I've loved you. My entire life, I've loved you. Only you. You are my wife."

"I was your wife. Before. I'm nobody's wife now. I am free."

"You're not free. You're trapped. You faked your own death. You can't ever leave this place. They'd put you in jail."

"This is where I want to be."

"What about me? What am I supposed to do? How can I live without you?"

"You were always gone. You loved me, but you loved the road more. I always came second. To your job. Your car. Your motorcycle. I got sick of it. I wanted a change. This is the change that I chose. And if you don't like it, well, that's too fucking bad. Because I don't give a shit." The other girls nodded and muttered and whispered to each other; all very approvingly.

I looked at Vanessa. The only woman I ever loved. The most beautiful woman I had ever known. The only woman I had ever made love to. And I didn't recognize her. Her beauty was contorted into an ugly mask of rejection. Her mind was poisoned against me. I couldn't believe what I was seeing; what was happening. But I knew I had to accept it. It was all so final. Considering the lengths she'd gone to. I looked down at the paper in my hand, with the coordinates written on it. And I said to the lot of them, "I'll show myself out." They didn't protest.

Back in my car, I entered the coordinates into my phone. The numbers corresponded to a blip in a place called Pigeon Lake Wilderness, in upstate New York. A lot of thoughts bounced off the walls in my head; but mostly I was thinking that I needed a nap. Thankfully, operating on little to no sleep was a trucker's special ability. I was delirious with doubts and questions and anger and despair. But, at the same time, I'd been given an objective. It didn't make any sense to me, but it struck a chord at the core of my being, and I didn't hesitate to get underway.

I wasn't going to take my Mustang into a wilderness. And I didn't have to. What I needed to do was to get out to my parents' property. They lived in Fall River. That's where Robertson Trucking was based out of. I turned on my radar detector. I was going to need it. I had a sixth sense for knowing where the cops would set up speed traps, but the radar detector was keener than I was. I took 91 to 95 to 195 and arrived at my folks in about two hours. First thing I did was start brewing a pot of coffee. While it percolated, I strapped my KTM 450 into the back of my cherry red, short cab, short bed, 4x4 F150.

My folks had a guest house and I kept a lot of my stuff there; including my firearms. With regard to arming myself for this... mission...; I had some options to choose from and I selected my 1301 shotgun with an extended tube. Mainly because it had a strap- a bandolier strap- on it and also because it didn't have a cumbersome magazine or scope. I loaded the shotgun and the bandolier with 3" slug shells. And I also switched out my 10mm carry piece for a higher capacity 92fs 9mm; to be holstered on my left side for a right hand draw. After dumping the coffee into an old thermos I had, grabbing two gallons of water from a stash I kept for work, changing into my riding pants, grabbing my riding gear, and moving the radar detector from the car to the pickup; I was ready to go. So I went.

Seems like the sun was coming up like ten minutes later, but it had to have been an hour or two gone by because I was on I-90 out in the Berkshires by then. Always so weird to see those places in the daytime. Because I usually saw them at night; which is to say, I usually did not see them. I tried not to think of how long I'd been awake for, and that there was no rest in the foreseeable future. I tried not to think about what I was doing. I tried to relax. I had a permit to carry firearms in Massachusetts and that was good. I couldn't remember if the permit had reciprocity in New York. Really, my legal standing was becoming moot. I was passing beyond the pale. I'd shot Sonny. But, there was nothing he could do about it; short of shooting me back. He couldn't report me because I'd report Damon's harem if he did.

I tried not to think about the series of events and just couldn't help myself. If I was supposed to rescue the nun; it didn't make any sense that I had to shoot Sonny to get to Damon to get a distress call from her. I didn't understand what was happening, but I got the distinct impression it had something to do with the black kitten I had crushed in the Bronx.

I stopped at a big box store outside of Albany to get a hiker's GPS. In the parking lot, I plugged the device in to charge and register and I used what little brains were available to me to figure out how to use it to get me to where I needed to go. I saw on satellite images on my phone that the roads could get me kind of close, but whatever was happening out there; they were evidently trying to keep their operation as inaccessible as possible. On I-87 north, I reflected on the obvious fact that I might be walking into a death trap. Then I got off my exit, exit 25. It seemed prudent to fill up my tank before I headed out into the forest; so that was what I did. This wasn't a short drive. In fact, this was a spectacularly long drive. But I had my big thermos of coffee and I knew how to use it. Those mountain roads dragged on forever. The forest closed in from both sides; all the local species of trees were intertwined and growing strong, thanks to the Great Lake rains. Even the highway was at risk of being swallowed by the woods.

It was some mighty fine country, out that way, to be sure. I could tell I was in a place that got overlooked by most people. The area was far out of the way and sparsely populated. God's country, as they say. Eventually, I was in range of my destination. I'd been searching for a road that could at least theoretically get me out to the spot, or closer to it, and there really wasn't one. There had to be one, but there wasn't one. There had to be a logging road or a construction road. I would've been happy to find a deer trail, even. I couldn't venture a guess as to where I was trying to get to, but it had to be a place- whether a house or a dungeon- and that place had to have been built by somebody. It had to be accessible, somehow.

The time was around noon and the sun was high overhead. For the life of me, I couldn't find any way to get any closer. But, I had my riding gear- boots, helmet, gloves- and this was the reason why. I offloaded my dirtbike, zip-tied the GPS to the handle bars, saved the truck's location in the GPS memory- in order to find my way back- and then I utilized a setting on the navigation device which produced an arrow that would always point the way toward my destination. With my gear adorned, my tactical shotgun slung over my back, and my pistol strapped to my hip; I headed out into the wilderness.

I'd been dirtbiking since I was a kid. And my KTM had plenty of power and fresh knobs on the tires. But still, this wasn't like riding around in the forests back home. This was serious terrain. If I wasn't charging up a steep and rocky and fallen-tree-littered mountainside, then I was switchbacking down the backside of said mountainside; skirting revines and dropoffs. It required a lot of forethought to visualize and anticipate each upcoming maneuver and forethinking was not exactly my forte on this particular day. I'm not ashamed to say that I dropped the bike on more than a couple occasions. To my credit, I didn't go tumbling over any precipices. Even more miraculously, I finally closed in on where I was headed; walking the last mile on foot. I made sure to leave the bike directly to the east; so I'd only have to walk straight in one direction to get back to it.

I left my helmet and gloves on the bike but I had to wear my riding pants and boots; which were both bright orange. I wouldn't be relying on camouflage. And I didn't know what to expect, but what I found made me groan. It was a fortress. Or, more like a bunker, but a large bunker, not a small one. The building sat in a paved over clearing; but the pavement was cracking and the weeds were sprouting through. There was a shining blue four seater helicopter sitting on top of the structure. I took one look at that place and thought; 'There's no way I'm getting in there.' I thought maybe I could leverage the helicopter against the occupants. Force them to give me the woman or else I'd blast holes in their million dollar machine. The nice thing was that there was nobody guarding the place. I was able to sit and ponder what I was going to do. I even stacked some rocks so I wouldn't forget where the east was. I knew I had to do something fast, so I decided to try the first thing that came to mind.

The bunker had a reinforced steel door. And no windows. There was an array of solar panels on a platform on the pavement. There was an outhouse like the kind they have at national parks. There were aluminum ladder rungs built into the wall. I could easily climb up to that helicopter. Now, I'm no genius. And I was clearly in over my head. But apparently, these individuals weren't especially intelligent themselves. Because- at a loss for any better idea- what I did was walk right up to the front door. And I guess the occupants just never expected anybody would ever find them out there. Because the door wasn't even locked. I didn't even have to turn a knob. I just pressed on it and it opened as silently as could be. And closed softly, too. As I entered, I had my pistol in the low ready position. My shotgun slung over my back.

I observed what I could but didn't really know what I was looking at until after I had been in there for a minute. There was a central corridor and the place was divided into four quadrants; a cell with bars on it, a sleeping area with two bunks, a mess haul with a fridge and kitchenette, and an open area for torture or other activities. The lights were on in every room in the place, but I could see shadows coming from the open area. I felt a weak chill from an air conditioning unit. And I heard voices. They were speaking a foreign language. Actually, they were chanting a foreign language. It wasn't difficult to sneak up on them, and when I peaked around the corner; I saw... well... I don't know what I was looking at, exactly, but I saw the Filipina nun hanging by her ankles, upside down in the center of the room; her eyes closed and her dangling hair soaking wet. There was a metal tub of dirty river water underneath her. The men standing around her had their eyes closed as they chanted their prayer. Or, their incantation. Whatever it was. They wore black tunics over black slacks, had yamakas on their heads, shaved faces, and curly cues of hair coming from their temples. The nun wore nothing but a black bra and pink panties, and her hands were tied behind her back. It looked painful and the sight upset me greatly.

I don't know if she was conscious, but she appeared to be unconscious. I was suddenly livid. It took all the restraint I possessed not to waste those assholes where they were standing.

There was a weapon in the room. Just one. An AR-15. But it was leaning up against the wall in the corner. It wasn't until I saw that rifle that I realized I might have to kill one or more of these people.

I know. I'm slow.

Thankfully, the nun was in the center and they were somewhat crowding around her. They weren't anywhere near their gun, but at the same time, they were way too close to the nun for me to comfortably open fire on them.

"Nobody move. Put your hands in the air," I said; totally prepared to squeeze the trigger. They stopped chanting and turned their eyes to me as they obeyed my command.

"Sir. You don't know what you're doing. You're making a mistake. You're making the worst mistake of your life," one of the Jews said. All four looked the same.

I replied, "It's true. That I don't know what I'm doing. But, the funny thing is, I don't really care. You're torturing that woman. And she's special to me. And you idiots left the front door unlocked. So, now you're going to do what I say, or you're going to die. I don't care which. Who's got the key to the jail cell?" Three of them looked at one of them. I trained the gun on that one and said, "Throw it at my feet." This was done and I picked it up slowly. It looked like a regular house key. "Alright. Go get in there. Do it now." I stepped aside. All four of them wanted to move for the rifle. But nobody did. They just went into the cell, instead. I was able to lock them in without incident.

One of them said, "That woman is the antiChrist. She'll invite hell into this world. If you help her, you'll be guilty of the worst crime in the history of humanity."

"Worse than what your people do? I doubt that. I'm not as stupid as I look. I know what's in the Talmud. I know you own the money, and use it against us. To enslave us. I know you own the government and the military and the corporations and the media. The utilities. Agriculture. The water. The land. The religions. I know you own anything and everything of any value. And you use it all as a way to dominate us. Thousands of years of exploiting everybody around you. Elevate yourself. Diminish everybody else. Pit goy against goy. Then you cry how you're the victim. Fabricate history and glorify your fake tragedy. I ain't got no sympathy for you people. If I was a different man, you'd be dead already. I'm so angry. So just shut the fuck up! And take your clothes off. Throw them into the hall."

I had a fixed blade hunting knife on my hip and I commenced to lift the nun in my arms and cut the rope that held her upside down and catch her as she dropped; all while keeping the pistol trained on the Jews. I held the Filipina nun in my arms- she weighed almost nothing- and told them, "Your underwear, too. Get butt ass naked."

After I cut the ropes from her ankles and wrists, I cradled the unconscious woman in my arms and tried to revive her. I put water on her lips. I rocked her back and forth. I found her pulse in her neck to confirm that she was even alive. I really didn't know.

Once the Jews were totally naked, they began their overtures again; "That woman is the devil. She will open the gates of hell. She will deliver hell unto this earth." And if I had been in a better state of mind, then I would have asked them what in Sam Hill they were talking about. But I was just so tired, and so angry; I really didn't care. I told them to shut up and they did. For a while.

I looked around and there were random religious materials strewn about. There were some leather bound religious texts. Some satchels. Some trinkets. Some baubles. None of it interested me. I was worried about the nun. I took her to a bunk and laid her down and covered her with a blanket.

I hovered over her. Over Charisma. And I ignored the Jews; who were imploring me to listen to them. Eventually, I had to threaten violence to get them to shut up again. Charisma came to a short while later. I was happy to see her smile when she saw me kneeling over her. No more braces on her teeth. "Kevin. My hero. You rescued me."

"Yeah. Are you alright?"

"I think so. Where are my clothes?"

I'd already gathered her tunic and wimple and things and had it all ready for her. Her hair and undergarments remained damp, but she got dressed without any hesitation and then went out to take a look at the naked Jews.

"Charisma Gomez?"

"You remembered my name?"

"I never forgot. But, Charisma. What are we going to do with these men?"

"You should kill them."

"Why?"

"It's complicated."

"Can you explain it?"

"Maybe. Kevin. We have work to do. God's work... to do..."

"Were they going to kill you, if I didn't get here?"

"They almost did. Didn't you see?"

"What were they doing to you?"

"I don't know. I don't think they knew. They wanted information I do not possess."

One Jew shouted, "She's evil! She's a devil! You have to destroy her! She'll kill us all!"

I thought about what she'd said when we first met. About how I'd done a bless-ed thing. Saving that four-wheeler. Then I thought about that four-wheeler. How they'd slammed on their brakes in my kill zone. Forcing me to make the ultimate sacrifice. Forcing me to choose to forfeit my own life; in order to save theirs. I remembered I saw there was nobody driving the vehicle. I realized; this is none of my business.

"Do you think they deserve to die?" I asked her.

Chapter 3
Deceit Knows No Limits
She took a look at them. They were naked, and trying to hide their genitals. Her face contorted with disgust and disbelief. I don't know what she saw, but I think she was reliving the torment she'd endured at their hands. Then she said to me, "There will be a lot of dying. A lot of people who don't deserve to die. They will be dying. And it's a terrible thing. But it's for a good cause. We're going to transform the world. After an eternity of unspeakable tyranny. We're going to set things right. These men; they want to keep the

arrangement the way it's always been. Because they benefit from the suffering. From the corruption. From the evil. But... No. They're not special. They're not evil. Not in their minds. They're just entangled. I am a threat to their fragile position in the universe. They don't deserve to die."

I thought about the helicopter. It's difficult to hide from a helicopter. I thought about the audiobooks I listened to at work. I remembered how... when good men allowed their enemies to escape... To live... Out of the goodness of their hearts.... Every time, the enemies returned to make another attempt on the heroes' lives. I didn't know what to do. I wanted to kill them. To make things simple. But I couldn't bring myself to do it. I didn't want to be a murderer. Even though these men had almost killed the nun. The nun who'd become my world. I couldn't decide.

"If I let you live, are you going to come after us?" I asked my naked Jew prisoners.

They all responded at once, 'Of course not,' 'Yes,' 'Probably,' 'We have to.'

They didn't know my identity, but it seemed like they were capable of figuring it out. Then my exhausted brain started working. At least for a couple minutes. I came up with a plan of action. The Jews became emboldened when they realized I wasn't going to kill them. They started talking and wouldn't shut up, but the things they said were tedious and they were too concerned with their own conceit to enlighten me as to why I should be on their side. 'You seem like a smart man. Won't you listen to reason?' one said. I asked them to reason with me, but I remained unimpressed. They said stuff like, 'You don't know anything about the woman. You don't know her history.' 'That woman isn't human; she's an angel from hell.' And Charisma would throw it back in their faces, "You don't know anything about me, either. You just think you do. I'm as human as anybody else. I've got more humanity than you ever will. I should kill every one of you. After what you did to me."

I liked Charisma. I didn't like those four men. So what I did was this: I gathered up their cellphones. There wasn't any signal in the forest but my intention was to remove every asset that could provide them an advantage in their coming tribulations. I took the phones outside, threw them on the pavement, and put bullets through them. There was a laptop and a tablet as well, and I shot those, too. I rifled through all their belongings looking for anything else. I saw watches on their wrists and made them give them to me. These watches I chucked into the forest. They had bottled water and bagels and some other Jewish cuisine I wasn't familiar with. Charisma and I both ate a bagel, but I put the rest of their food into the outhouse toilet. I threw their clothes and shoes into the outhouse toilet, as well. Charisma gathered up their religious materials and put them in the satchel and carried the satchel with us when we left. In a cabinet under the kitchenette, I found a roll of duct tape, but there was still one other thing I had to do.

Just to be safe, I advised Charisma to head out to the forest and hide behind the biggest tree she could find. I didn't know what would happen next. I picked up the prisoners' AR-15, walked outside, charged the weapon, and took a good look at the helicopter. It wasn't a cheap rinky-dink helicopter. It was deep metallic blue and had fancy silver designs on it. It looked about as good as Life Star and better than some news copters. Not that I knew anything about these things. I just had to figure out where its engine was. Below and to the rear of the big propeller's rotor, I decided. The exhaust pipe was there and the body was clearly molded to house it there. I started putting bullets- 30 of them- into the engine. Hoping not to ignite any fuel. This was mostly uneventful except for a hissing discharge of pressure at one point. I did this without setting the helicopter on fire, and that's all I had intended to do. Afterward, I pulled the interior mechanism out of the rifle and chucked it into the forest. Not that there were any bullets remaining, that I knew of.

I tossed the duct tape into the cell and compelled them to tape themselves together so that all four of them were connected at the wrists. That took some doing. It was the most complicated part of my plan, actually. Once they were sufficiently bound, I let them out of the cell and had Charisma hold my gun on them while I gave the tape a once over myself; tightening it down. I asked Charisma if she was ready to go and she said she was. I wanted to keep an eye on the Jews while we made our escape, so I compelled them to follow us out to my dirtbike. Charisma held the pistol on them and I held the shotgun on them. It wasn't out of the realm of possibility that they could bum rush us or something. But apparently they weren't so concerned with Charisma anymore anyways. They'd seen what I'd done to all their stuff and had begun to forget about Charisma and focus on themselves. They knew what was happening. 'Please. Mister. Have mercy,' they begged me. "This is mercy," I told them, adding, "If you come after her again, or anybody resembling you does; you'll see what mercilessness is. Or, they will see. Or, whatever." They moved slowly; agonized by the stabbing and scraping branches of the underbrush. It was a spectacle, and an annoyance, but we got to the bike eventually. And that's where we left them; taped together and naked. I don't even know if they could find their way back to the bunker. Nevermind back to civilization. But I didn't care, and I still don't feel bad about it.

On the dirt bike, Charisma wrapped her legs and arms around me; keeping her head pressed into my back for protection. I told her that if we spill, she should not let go of me. I told her to just hang on no matter what. But apparently I'd gained skill in traversing that terrain on the way in, because we only spilled once on the way out, and it wasn't a bad one.

We were both physically and mentally exhausted. My brain was like tapioca pudding on the long drive out of the forest. Really, that was some awesome country and I wish I could have enjoyed the scenery more, but I was wiped out. Thankfully, I was able to get us back down to the Albany area without incident. The sun was setting and I'd been awake forever, it seemed like. I pulled into a franchise hotel and booked a room with two beds for two days, so we could get some real rest without getting kicked out before noon. And I ordered a pepperoni pizza. Which I liked, and Charisma- as it turned out- did not. While the food was on its way, I called my mother and told her about Vanessa. Because my mother was also my broker; she was wondering why I canceled that load the day before. And she'd been extra worried because I'd been incommunicado all day. She took the news pretty good. Vanessa never gave her any grandbabies, so she wasn't exactly heartbroken about the loss. Charisma and I hadn't talked much. I'd been through a lot and she'd been through a lot more than me. We ate fast and fell asleep faster.

We slept well into the next day. When I lifted my head out of the pillows, Charisma was at her bedside and kneeling in prayer. The hotel mirror was foggy. She was showered and dressed. I could see she'd gotten her beauty sleep. I had no idea how old she was, but she looked as fresh as a daisy. And inappropriately enticing, to be honest. That was the first time I realized that not only was she a fine specimen of a woman, but also that I was a newly single man. Suddenly aware of my nakedness, I slid under the covers to put on my dirty black mesh tank top and even dirtier bright orange riding pants; careful not to accidentally expose myself to this lady of the cloth. My next thought was about coffee. I still had some from the day prior, but I might've needed that out on the road, so I used the coffee machine to make some watery hotel coffee.

When she finished her prayers, she looked over at me, and she was smiling and beautiful and indefinably surreal. A surreality I'd never grow accustomed to. The time had come to ask the burning question.

"Good morning sleepy head," she said, in her strangely pitched southeast asian accent.

I checked the clock and it was 1:30 in the afternoon.

"Charisma?"

"That's my name, don't wear it out."

"Why were you there, on the day of my wreck?"

"I wasn't there. I was in a nunnery."

"You were there. I talked to you."

"I think you're asking the wrong question. Maybe you should wonder where you were, instead of where I was. Or, I don't know. It's pretty much the same place, either way."

"Wait. What? I was at the wreck. I was there two times, actually. In two places at once. I was in the truck, and I was in the weeds, talking to you."

"Think about that. How could you be two people in one place? It's not possible. The obvious explanation is that there was a second place. You were one person split between two places. And so was I."

"What was that place?"

"It's more like a realm. This is a realm. That's another realm. Kind of like... a separate dimension... Like... If reality is a dream that everybody dreams together. And if a dream we dream alone is just a dream. Then where is the place for two people dreaming together? Wherever that is. That's where we were."

"Ok. But how did we get there?"

"You had a head injury. I was projecting my spirit to you. But, Kevin, it's not something you need to be concerned with. It happened. It was real. It really happened. We both know it. That's all that matters. You will see. What comes next will make our first encounter seem relatively unremarkable."

"What's coming next?"

"Ok. Maybe not what's coming next. I should've said, what's coming soon. What's coming next is we have to go rescue my cat."

"Your cat? I have to get back to work."

"Kevin. You're never going to work another day in your life."

"What? That doesn't make any sense."

"I'll explain. Kevin. You have a higher calling."

"Rescuing your cat is my higher calling? Why is your cat in danger?"

"She's not. Not really. But she needs me. I'm her person."

"Charisma. I have to get back to work. I can't screw up my family's company for your cat."

"It's not about my cat. It's about the war of good against evil. We're going to change the world. You and me. We're going to change everything. The evil. It is a living thing. We're going to kill it. It's the dominating force on this Earth. We are going to obliterate it. We're going to usher in a golden age. Such as the world's never known. Heaven on Earth. Can't you agree; this is more important than your family's business?"

I certainly couldn't disagree. I said, "Ok, but what does this have to do with your cat?"

"What kind of question is that? It's my cat. I can't do anything without my cat."

I couldn't comprehend her logic, but I figured; we'd come this far. If the lady wanted her cat, then I was nobody to say no. "Where is your cat?" I asked.

"Newport, Rhode Island," she said.

"Oh. My family lives over there."

"I know," she said.

"How do you know that?"

"It's in my interest to know."

"It's in your interest to know where my family lives?"

"It's in my interest to know everything about you, yes."

"But, why?"

"Because you are a saint, Kevin. You are Saint Kevin."

"Since when?"

"Since right now."

"Ok. Says you."

"That's right. Says me. I am a nun. And I say that you are a saint."

"Are you really a nun?"

She chuckled, "That's a good question. I certainly used to be."

"Why is your cat in Newport?"

"Well... Let's say... I came over here with some people. An entourage. Our stated purpose was to locate you. They tricked me, really. They didn't care about you; it turned out. In fact, they didn't even believe me about you. They didn't even believe me about me. Not really. They knew there was a market for the contents of my skull. And that's all they knew."

"They who? Who is they?"

"Romans. Papists."

"So. What? They sold you to the Jews? They couldn't do that in Israel?"

"The power isn't in Israel. The power is here."

"What power?"

"The power to destroy me."

"They don't have a rope and a bucket of water in Israel?"

"A bucket of water can destroy Charisma, but I am more than Charisma. The artifacts from the bunker. The jewels. In that leather bag. Those are the means of my destruction. So, it's quite good they've fallen into my possession."

"If you are more than just Charisma, then what are you?"

"Oh. Kevin. Just wait and see."

"Those Jews said you are a demon."

"No. They said I was an angel from Hell. There's a big difference."

"Well, you're certainly as beautiful as an angel," I said.

She blushed and turned her face, saying, "Kevin. I'm a nun."

"What? Nuns can be beautiful. Can't they?"

She looked at the ceiling and thought for a moment. Then, turning her eyes back to me- her long lashes aflutter and her luminous smile shining- she said, "Sure. Why not?"

"What's that stuff in that bag, then?"

"An emerald. A ruby. A gold medallion. A runestone. Holy relics. Or, unholy relics. Depending on one's perspective," she said.

I knew from Gnosis what she meant. There's a blasphemous parallel story to the bible. The Gnostic version. And it teaches that God- despite his protestations to the contrary- is actually the evil entity in the biblical paradigm; not Lucifer. And that makes sense to me. God was always meating out unbelievably horrific punishments; killing firstborns, drowning everybody except his favorite guy, making people cut their dick skin off, throwing nonbelievers into an inferno for eternity, and on and on. He was jealous, and vengeful. In my opinion; it was blatantly obvious that God was evil; when you got right down to it. It didn't make sense for him to be so insecure if he was so omnipotent. God shouldn't have been such a piece of shit all the time, if he wanted people to love him. I could relate...

Anyway, I didn't struggle with the concept that some ancient relics could be simultaneously holy and unholy. There were two sides to that story; even though people liked to pretend the gospel was infalible. I'd gotten used to being lied to in my lifetime. Deceit knows no limits. If people learned the truth, about the lies that they were force fed, then they'd choke before they swallowed. Charisma's crusade was a quest to free the truth. Evil needs dishonesty and deception like humans need clothing and shelter. Dishonesty and deception are how evil protects itself from an inhospitable environment.

We- and by 'we' I mean 'Charisma'- decided not to use the extra night at the hotel. We were out of there within a couple hours of waking. On the way to Newport we got some fast food to eat on the ride. I felt stupid wearing my riding pants around, but I wasn't going to make an extra stop to buy different pants. And it wasn't an option- I was informed- to drop by my folks and get changed. We had to get to the cat. My stupid pants were irrelevant. I didn't even consider going back to Heaven; although I'd have to eventually.

I didn't know what to expect from Charisma. She was relaxed, and she had a positive attitude. Her disposition was always cheerful. Even back at the bunker she was playful and optimistic. As we drove, we talked about ordinary things. I possessed but a fraction of the information she was privy to, and I kept watching the sky, expecting it to fall on us. She created the impression that she wasn't particularly interested in the facts of the matter at hand. Her interests were in mundane things. Specifically; she had a million questions about Vanessa. Charisma found my ruined marriage endlessly fascinating.

For my part; I wanted to know everything about the nun, but- being preoccupied with trying to piece the puzzle together in my mind- I was too bewildered to just come out and ask her much of anything. I did, however, have the presence of mind to ask her about what we were doing that day. I knew we were going to get her cat, but I had to ask where the cat was. Besides being vaguely in Newport; I wanted to know where exactly. The cat was on a boat. When I asked why the cat was on a boat, she told me because she came over on a boat. I asked why she came over on a boat, and she told me it was because she was being smuggled. And, apparently, sailing was a low risk way to smuggle a human. The tradeoff being that the boat could sink. The roman human smugglers let her bring her cat because they wanted her to think she was leading the expedition.

Where those people were at that time, on that day; this was not exactly clear. But I didn't want to encounter them. Or, I'd have to defend the woman's honor. And that could put me in jail. And apparently we had more important things to be doing. I took I-90 to I-495 to 24 to 114 and then we were there. It was a bright summer evening in Newport. A Tuesday. I could smell restaurants grilling and deep frying. I could hear the general public wandering about noisily. Charisma didn't have a phone, so she used mine to guide us to a parking area by Brenton cove. Our problem was that the boat was moored out in the cove. But, I had money, and so- eventually- we found a boatyard that was both open and willing to rent us a dinghy.

The air was hot that day. In the 90s earlier, but cooling off. The ocean breeze made the weather more pleasant than it would've been otherwise. Looking around, I saw the masts of sailboats in every direction. In some places, the masts were clustered like fistfulls of match sticks. In other places, they stood apart; defiant of the sky and proud of their height. I liked these boats. Their grandiose scale reminded me of the immense size of tractor-trailers. And the water. It was nice to be on the water. The ocean there was as blue as it was gray, and it rippled in the breeze. But, we were in a cove, so there weren't any waves except for the wakes of vessels under power.

I didn't understand how she'd known that there wasn't anybody but the cat onboard the boat. There were two explanations how she knew, actually. One reason was straightforward. The other reason was unbelievable. Really, I had no idea what was happening. At any rate, she told me I wouldn't need the gun, but I didn't believe her and so brought it anyway. None of the bystanders noticed the pistol on my hip. Or, they didn't gawk at it. When they looked at us, all they saw were my dirty orange pants and the nun I was with. They definitely gawked at the nun. I got the dinghy's engine running and we motored out into the thick of all the sailboats; there were only about a thousand of them out there.

I knew all of nothing about the rules of boat traffic, so I probably maneuvered incorrectly on multiple occasions, but eventually we found what we were looking for. Her cat's boat was huge, but so were many others. And the boat's fit and finish were extremely nice. Attributes also not uncommon there, in that unbelievably rich city on the water.

The boat that had smuggled Charisma into the United States was a 42 foot sloop called Paraiso. Paraiso was written in a tasteful tropical font; down each side and on its stern. The sailboat was very white, and the white reflected the golden light of the soon to be setting sun. Its mast seemed to disappear into the sky. It had port windows running down the sides. Various poles sprouted from the hull. Its steering wheel was stainless steel and probably taller than Charisma. Lifelines ran along the gunnels. And it was covered with ropes and gadgets and gizmos; the purposes of which I couldn't fathom.

Paraiso had a dinghy, but it was strapped down on the bow. That was an obscure detail, and a clue that Charisma wasn't being completely forthcoming with me; but I didn't catch it at the time. I got Charisma to the swimming platform at the stern of the boat. She jumped from the dinghy to the platform and went up the steps to the cockpit and opened the cabin door and started making cat calling sounds. The cat immediately returned her greeting. Soon, I saw her holding the cat in her arms and she looked so happy. The cat, too, looked happy. I was happy for them both. I thought of Vanessa, and decided to try to forget about her. She'd opened a sinkhole where my heart used to be, but somehow this nun was keeping me distracted. I could be happy about a cat if I wanted to. It was none of Vanessa's business if I wanted to feel happiness. I smiled and watched the nun with her cat. Quite pleased with myself.

Charisma acted fast. The cat was put into a special clear plastic backpack that it could see out of. And there was a cloth shopping bag full of what I later learned were cat care supplies. And there was a third duffle bag that I later learned was full of Charisma's clothes and belongings. With

Charisma- and all of her stuff- loaded into the dinghy; we motored away to return the boat and get back to my truck.

We drove off into the sunset and she let her cat out of its backpack. This was the first time I got a good look at the feline. I watched it... and the road... as it stood on her leg, with its paws on the doorframe; monitoring the blurry scenery passing by the windows. I instantly felt a deep and inexplicable connection to that animal. And only then did I realize that I felt a deep and inexplicable connection to Charisma, as well. In that instant, I felt like I would have died for that woman. Or, even for the cat.

The cat was pure white; except for a pink nose, pink paw pads, and two slanted and differently colored eyes. And it didn't look like american cats. It looked like how I'd imagine Egyptian cats looked like, but also it looked like some kind of unique breed I'd never seen before. I could tell it'd been on the ocean for a long time. Its fur was not exactly fluffy. Also, it was about as skinny as could be; but not sickly looking. Kind of like Charisma, in that way. It had triangular pointed ears, a triangular pointed chin, and a triangular pointed nose.

"You got a nice pussy," I said to the nun; as I wished for more self-control.

The nun smiled at me, and smiled at her cat, and she said, "Yeah. She's the best."

"What's her name?"

"Angela."

"Oh. That's nice," I said, "My father's mother's name was Angela."

Once we were back out on the open road- and I didn't have to think about traffic or traffic control devices or directions or much of anything- I asked Charisma, "So. We got your cat. What comes next?"

"I'm glad you asked. How do you feel about Philadelphia?"

I said, "I hate it. Last time I was there, I got turned around, and ended up in some residential area. I barely made it out without thrashing a four-wheeler. I had like, an inch on my nose, and an inch on my tail." I don't think she understood what I was saying, or maybe she didn't think it was as impressive as I thought it was.

"We have to go to Philadelphia. Because... There's... something I have to do there..." she said, pensively.

"What do you have to do?"

"Well. There's a document. It's an important document. And I have to destroy it."

"You want to go destroy an important document in Philadelphia? I don't think it's legal to destroy important documents."

"You're going to have to forget about the laws, Kevin. We got stuff to do."

"I don't want to go to jail."

"You won't go to jail. I know what I'm doing," she said.

I said, "Yeah, but... I don't know what you're doing."

"I just told you. I'm going to destroy an important document."

"How are you going to do that without getting arrested?" I asked her; exiting 24 and getting onto I-195. I was taking her to my parents' guest house. We were weirdly in the neighborhood and I was sick of wearing these orange pants. Plus, if we had to go to Philadelphia, then we were going to take the Mustang, not the F-150.

I wasn't trying to hear what my father had to say about the canceled load, or about my impromptu leave of absence, or about Vanessa leaving me, or about the Filipina nun I had gotten involved with. As a rule of thumb, I pretty much didn't want to know what my father had to say about anything; unless it was something obvious- like, about a truck part we needed, or about how his liberal friends were idiots. All that was mostly irrelevant because we could probably avoid him. I'd been avoiding him my whole life. It wasn't too difficult. I would've liked to see my mother, though. I would've liked to have introduced Charisma to her. But that would have to wait. Because my father spent most of his time bothering my mother. So, if I wanted to avoid him, then I had to avoid her, too.

"You wouldn't believe me if I told you," Charisma said, answering my question about how she planned to destroy the document.

"Try me," I said.

"How about, I'll tell you after it's done? After it's done, you will believe me."

"Can you at least tell me what the document is?"

Charisma said, "Yeah. It's pretty complicated, but, basically; the document is called the 'In God We' trust. It's a trust. It was founded in 1776 and reestablished in 1913. It's located at 78 Seibert street. The trust is declared in The Declaration of Independence and the constitution of the trust is the constitution of the United states. The beneficiaries of the trust are everybody with a birth certificate. This means that there's a never ending series of successor trustees. That means that the beneficiaries will never benefit. These successor trustees are called citizens, but there is really no such thing as a citizen. There's only beneficiaries of the trust. The trust is written so that all beneficiaries are adult minor children; due in part to the fact that it's the parents who sign the contract when they sign the birth certificate. Meaning beneficiaries have no power in the trust. The overlords try to pretend 'in god we trust' is a slogan, but it's way more than that. The trust has dominion over the whole world. Not just the USA, but everywhere. It's the true power ruling over humanity. Since the dawn of recorded history. It used to be in Babylon. Then it was in Rome. Then it was in London. Now, it's in the United States. It'll be in Beijing soon. Unless we stop it. We have to not only destroy it, but also prevent it from being reestablished. The common law irrevocable ecclesiastical trust states that ownership can only be granted through a signed contract. Nobody can really own anything because inanimate objects cannot grant permission. But the birth certificate is a contract- signed by the parents- that gives ownership of an individual- the child- over to the In God We trust. Nobody can own land because ownership can only exist via a signed contractual agreement. For that reason, countries don't actually exist; land cannot consent to ownership. Only humans can. What's actually happening- because birth certificates are contracts- is that central banks are owning humans. Every central bank is connected to a central trust- so to speak- and the In God We trust is the umbrella trust all the other trusts exist beneath. We could remove ourselves from the trust by creating another trust, but that doesn't help everybody else trapped in the trust. If we go and destroy the trust, then everybody in the world will be released from their status as property.

Chapter 4
The Catalyst of the Cataclysm
We'd slept one night at my parents' guest house. My father- as luck would have it- was hunting bear in Vermont. I was able to introduce Charisma to my mother, but I had to pretend nothing out of the ordinary was happening because I didn't want to worry her. My mother knew I was withholding information, but she was getting old in those days, and I think at some point she decided it wasn't worth the headache to become overly involved in my affairs. Honestly, after the news about Vanessa I think she was pleased- albeit perplexed- to see me with a woman; even if that woman was a Filipina nun.

Charisma had insisted that we equip maximum fire power, and I was past the point of questioning her; so that is what we did. She seemed to know about guns, which I thought was strange, but the woman seemed to know most stuff about most things, so maybe it wasn't so strange after all. The back of the Mustang was positively littered with weaponry. Not just firearms, but also she had had me bring my katana and kama and bo, as well as a double sided ax- which I'd had to sharpen- and a wooden baseball bat which

I'd hammered seven inch nails through. That spiked bat was a grizzly affair. I couldn't imagine she'd be proficient in using these archaic weapons, or the more modern ones, at that, but I'd been studying karate for the entirety of my life and I could manage any of them well enough. And even if Charisma had turned out to be some sort of martial arts wizard; that wouldn't have surprised me.

Still, I didn't know what we were going up against. I implored her to give me more information, but she didn't seem to possess the information I wanted. 'It's just as a precaution,' she'd say, each time I asked. I told her, 'A pistol is a precaution. An arsenal is delusional paranoia.'

The guns were on the seat and the other items were on the floor and I had bed sheets tossed over all of it. The bo was my height and couldn't be hidden. I'd made it from a pine sapling when I was still studying at the dojo and I'd oiled it and hardened it and I had more faith in that bo than I did in the ax or the spiked bat. My skills with that glorified stick were excellent; I was a whirlwind with that thing. A somewhat overweight, out of shape and out of practice, trucker of a whirlwind.

The plan was to get down to Philadelphia and get a hotel room and get some dinner and get some sleep and then wake up and wait around for night to fall again. The building where this document was located closed at 6, but she wanted to wait until at least after 8 to do what she intended; the details of her plans remained a mystery to me.

I drove like a halfway decent human being until we got past New Haven and then I let the Mustang off of its leash. Nobody ever got pulled over between New Haven and New York; unless they were being extremely stupid. I ran in the fast lane. The other two lanes were mostly useless. Often, the fast lane wasn't much better. When it was clear, I floored it. When it was blocked, I waited for it to clear. Once in a while I'd move over to let a faster driver get by. It was always kind of funny going places in a four-wheeler. It'd be a bitter slog to get down I-95 in a semi, but it'd be weirdly easy in a car. Or- and I wouldn't say this if it weren't true- it would have been easy; if females, old people, young people, idiots, liberals, coloreds, homos, drunks, druggies, and foreigners would pull their heads out of their asses and quit being so oblivious and inconsiderate. Wasn't anything anybody could do about that, though.

We hit traffic at the George Washington bridge. Any good time we'd made was lost there. Not that we were in a hurry. It's nice to have a smooth easy drive for its own sake. I was just in the habit of making good time; even for no particular reason. Once we got across the bridge, there was no further delay. Charisma made a reservation at a hotel north of Philadelphia and we got there a couple hours later. I don't know how long the drive was exactly. Seems like everywhere is a couple hours away in the Mustang.

I enjoyed spending time with Charisma. Everything about her was agreeable. If she disagreed with me, it was passively. When I talked, she listened actively. When she talked, her words flowed out happily. Even when she was referring to the end of days. For a prophet of doom, she was a perfect angel. Her voice was like the tinkling of chimes. With most people, you're waiting for their inner hate to break through. With Charisma, there was no inner hate. Only inner beauty. And inner light. I didn't know if we were on a mission from God, or wrapped up in an out of control paranoid delusion. But I knew I liked being with Charisma. I didn't even think about Vanessa. Except to reflect on how Vanessa- who'd, until recently, been a good wife- was a shrewd shrew relative to the nun. Furthermore, for a nun, Charisma wasn't preachy; how one might expect. On the contrary, she seemed to want me to- as much as possible- think of her as an ordinary female.

At the hotel, we ordered Chinese food. I ate a lot. She ate a little. Later, I had the sneaking suspicion that Charisma was subtly giving me opportunities to look at her body. When she showered, she left the door cracked; which I thought was way too trusting of me and I felt tested against the urge to walk in there and take her. As it was, I could see the undefined flesh of her naked body in the foggy mirror. After her shower; her silken, lacey, pinkish-whitish nightgown was short, sheer, and form-fitting. She crawled around when she organized her things and I could see her black lace panties. I felt a burning desire for Charisma all that night, much worse than the two nights before, but I tried to remind myself that she was a nun. Angela was kind enough to comfort me throughout my trial of willpower; she cuddled up to me while I slept.

The next day, to pass the time, we went to some big box stores to procure gear. Charisma wanted a black outfit that could stand up to the elements; so we got her two pairs of black denim jeans and a black jean jacket. Plus, some black t-shirts and black tactical boots. It was difficult to find stuff in her size, but we managed. We also bought about ten bandanas; in case we needed disguises. We thought we might. I'd had those kinds of clothes in storage. So we looked like a pair after the shopping. And she didn't look like a nun anymore. She looked like my fantasy. A diminutive asiatic femme fatale. We looked like bank robbers but no different than all the other people who dress in all black, really. I also got her a good fixed blade knife and a high-powered flashlight; as well as a strong nylon belt to strap stuff onto.

Charisma kept saying; 'We won't have to get out of the car. Not to destroy the document. After that, I don't know.' She said she didn't know, but she knew more than she let on. And I didn't understand how she expected to destroy a document that was inside of a building from the inside of a car. Charisma, meanwhile, knew exactly how she was going to achieve that, but I guess she was too embarrassed to tell me. Or too nervous. Or too apprehensive.

For several hours we sat outside of a fast food restaurant while Charisma used my phone to search for a street that seemingly did not exist. I thought maybe she'd never find it and maybe everything was going to go back to normal. Or, I was hoping it didn't exist. But, she did find it. It was there; it was just impossible to be searched for. It had been removed from- or flagged by- search engines, or something. She found it by painstakingly scouring the map. After that, we were ready to go. The rifles were cocked and locked and ready to... go... Myself, less so... I had a foreboding feeling. As we drove over, I felt a chill down my spine and my hair was standing on end. I was sweating but my skin was cold to the touch. I could almost hear a voice whispering in my ear, 'Turn back now.'

Charisma guided me into an area where there would obviously be CCTV recording every sidewalk and intersection. We were in the midst of Philadelphia's ornate towers and the trendiest of storefronts. The storefronts were closed, but still lit up to display their glitzy products. The bus stop advertisements were overly glamorous; like they were trying too hard.

'At the very least, the authorities could trace me to this area on this night,' was what I was thinking. I didn't realize that the authorities would soon be far too overwhelmed to track down the catalyst of the cataclysm. I'd put all my faith in the nun, and that was the bottomline. Not far away from the skyscrapers and government buildings, we found ourselves in some forgotten pseudo-residential slash pseudo-industrial zone which was probably scheduled to be gentrified sometime in the next month or so. I didn't want to park there. I didn't want to be there. It was way too urban for my comfort level. Charisma didn't seem to think anything of it and she had me park on a street corner that was within eyesight and earshot of a shady looking cluster of basketball-americans.

I was driving a sweet Mustang. The kind of car people like to look at. I turned out the lights but let the engine idle; watching the hoodlums in the mirrors. They were looking but not overly-interested. The wind began to pick up; garbage blew through the streets. And the sky was flashing purple with heat lightning, or what I assumed was heat lightning. Charisma didn't tell me what she was going to do next. She nonchalantly squeezed Angela in her arms, and said, "Ok kitty baby. It's your time to shine." Then she opened the door and let the cat out of the car. I couldn't imagine why she would do that. I just watched as it scampered off across South street; passing through oncoming headlights and disappearing around the corner of the check cashing place.

"Charisma. Your cat!"

"Don't worry. She's been training her whole life for this."

That didn't make any sense to me- it was just a joke, really- but I had learned not to question Charisma. In the back of my mind, I was trying to figure out if I knew where the on-ramp to the interstate was. I realized I did not and I immediately opened my phone and committed the local roads to memory. We weren't far from Broad street and that would take us to Vine and Vine would take us back to I-95; by way of an absurdly convoluted intersection.

I didn't know what was happening. And I wouldn't be given an explanation until a day later. The only information I can share is what I was told. And what I was told was this: Angela took off down Broad boulevard at a speed between walking and running. I guess cats don't like to run for long periods of time. Angela knew exactly where she was headed toward. She didn't know which street she was on or what city she was in, but she could sense the evil she was hunting for. Angela honed in on the document without any difficulty. Soon, the cat was outside of 78 Seibert street. Definitely on camera, but nobody would suspect a cat, and apparently that was the whole point. The building in question was located nearby fancy stone government buildings, but 78 Seibert street was an understated brick structure built among several similar understated brick structures.

What comes next in my narrative will tell the reader everything they need to know about Charisma. It sounds unbelievable, relative to what has occurred up until this point, but relative to what is to come later, it's not so strange after all. Certainly we can understand why she was reluctant to clue me in.

The document was in a safe, but it was a big safe; more like a vault. I don't know what would've happened if it was in a small safe. But it wasn't in a small safe. It was in a big safe. Angela went into a shadow beneath a shrub and hid. Whether or not Angela went into a shadow and disappeared through a hole in the space-time continuum, I cannot say, but it'd make sense; because inside the vault Charisma appeared. She was naked. And completely hairless. And holding her breath. The document called to her. She didn't have to search for it. Her entire psyche was drawn to it like a moth to a flame. It was the only document of its kind, and it occupied its own file in an otherwise inconspicuous file cabinet.

She removed the file and commenced with destroying it. The In God We trust was a single piece of thick paper, with a lot of words on it. The words at the top were written in fancy cursive lettering. The rest of the words were in ordinary font. The content was legalese. It had an official seal of some sort embedded in it. And there were several signatures on it. Charisma tore it up and ripped it apart and looked around for some way to make it disappear, but she immediately realized that her physical-ish body was the only way to make it disappear. Stuffing all the pieces into her mouth; she exhaled the breath she'd been holding in, and then she vanished from the vault.

While this was going on; the wind only ever increased and I could hear thunder roaring in the distance. Those random thugs had since lost interest in us and gone back to their blunts and forties, or whatever they were doing.

Charisma had been sitting in the car beside me and chatting as though nothing was happening. I asked her, "Why did you let your cat go?" And she said, "You'll see," with a mischievous smile. "When is she going to come back?" "In a little while." "How do you know?" "She's a good girl. She always comes back." "When will she come back?" I asked. "Pretty soon," she said. "How do you know?"

What I'm trying to convey is that Charisma sat there talking to me like nothing was happening. The entire time. I never would have guessed anything supernatural was occurring. There was no indication. After a while, Angela came back, just like Charisma had said she would. Charisma opened the door and Angela proceeded to jump right in; immediately barfing up a hairball on the floor of my beloved car. Then Angela climbed back into her backpack on the backseat. Almost like she was hiding from something.

Instead of being disgusted- like I was- Charisma shone her flashlight down at the slimy tube of puke. She was fingering it and examining it. My curiosity having been piqued, I peered over her shoulder to see what was so interesting. I saw the paper, but only read one word, 'God.' Thunder clapped with bone-rattling intensity and bright purple light filled the Mustang's windows; like the electrical storm was right on top of us. I could hear the wind shrieking through the powerlines. I was flabbergasted with disbelief- and kind of offended- when the sky began pelting my car with hailstones. But I had the presence of mind to turn on the headlights, floor the engine, and burn rubber over to an underpass that was nearby; parking on the shoulder underneath it.

"Can you throw your cat's puke out the window, or something? Please?" I begged her.

"I will. Later. If I throw it out here, somebody could trace it back to us."

"So? What happened? Your cat ate the In God We trust?"

"Something like that, yeah."

"Can we go then? You want to stick around and have a shootout with the cops, or something?"

"No. Just. Wait. Do you feel that?" she asked me.

It felt like we were in a hurricane. The air was vibrating. I began to wonder if being under an overpass was actually a good idea. Because the ground was rumbling underneath us. Not a little. There were jarring tremors. Like when you're driving down a road with a lot of potholes. It was an earthquake. Charisma spun in her chair, flung back the sheet, and procured the AR-10. Not the AR-15. With the weapon stood up between her legs, she swiveled her head around, looking in all directions. I had about had enough. I was suddenly not cool with any of what was transpiring. I just wanted to get my car and my ass out of that city.

"I'm getting us out of here," I told her. And I didn't wait for her approval. I gunned the engine and tore off; out onto Broad street. I cringed as I realized the hailstones were still falling. All I could think about was my paint job. I had no idea what was happening. I had no idea how stupid and insignificant my paint job really was.

Philadelphia got bigger and bigger around us. We had to go through the center of it to get out of it. We were in an area where the architecture was disconcertingly gothic; a cathedral, a courthouse, a castle of some sort, or something; I don't know what it was. The lightning was flashing blindingly. It was difficult to see. I felt my car literally jump off the ground- more than once. One of the more formidable structures thereabouts- which I know now was city hall; with a freefall lurch- suddenly dropped down into the ground; but only half way. Like, it was submerged into the Earth at a forty five degree angle. Partly below and partly above. Right before our eyes; the tower at the center of the structure snapped off and plummeted into- and presumably through- the building's roof. About this time the power went out and we were thrust into darkness. But, the fissure which the building had slipped into was producing an orange glow that was illuminating the area. It was like ten thousand bonfires were down in there. I thought city hall was burning- which of course it was- but it was more than just a structure fire. I was sorely mistaken as to the nature of it.

Being the stubborn truck driver that I am, I was reluctant to reroute and hoping to still be able to continue along my merry way; even though I was fast realizing that the road I wanted to take had disappeared into a fiery hole in the Earth. Meanwhile, a morbid fascination was compelling me- against my will- to venture nearer. Simultaneously, my will to survive had me looking for another way out. An instant later and we were suddenly too close for comfort. In retrospect, ten miles would've been too close for comfort.

Charisma said, "Stop! Stop the car! There it is!"

I came to a screeching halt; but I didn't know why. I'd been focusing on the street signs; irritated that all the roads were one-ways and that all the one-ways were going the wrong one-way. I was still searching for what Charisma was referring to as she jumped out of the car. The hailstones had turned to sideways rain; the wind was screaming. Water was suddenly showering my car's interior. In contrast; a prolific and burgeoning inferno was reaching up out of the fissure in the Earth. Orange embers were flying into the sky and catching the shifting wind currents; resembling a hellish blizzard from a parallel universe. Then I saw what she saw. I gagged on the air I was breathing and started coughing. Something was crawling up over the edge of the blazing crevasse. First; two huge snapping claws that were opening and closing. Then the creature got two and then four and then six legs up over the ledge. Soon it was able to pull the entirety of its body up out of the hole. Charisma fired her first shot at it while I was sitting there and staring at its tail; wondering how big the creature was. Were the scorpion stretched out- claw to stinger, I'd say; longer than a sleeper-cab with a short trailer, and shorter than a day cab with a long trailer. But it wasn't stretched out; it was squatting on its many haunches; with its tail reared up over its head; visibly hostile. There were two brightly glowing red eyes on its carapace and smaller dimly glowing red eyes along the length of its head. And it was a lot scrawnier than a tractor-trailer. I stared in disbelief until the third or fourth gunshot snapped me out of my wonderment. This monstrosity was about a stone's throw away. I was close enough to see that it felt the bullets entering and exiting it. And that it was not happy about them.

We were the only flashing and exploding thing in the vicinity. I guess the creature could correlate the explosions of the rifle with the bullets piercing its hide. Because it suddenly charged at us. Charisma was just as quick to jump into the car as she had been to jump out of the car. "Go! Now! Drive!" she shouted.

I stuffed the throttle in reverse and as soon as I built some speed, I pressed the clutch in, put the shifter in first, cranked the wheel to spin us around, let out the clutch, and gunned the engine to break out of the maneuver. Fishtailing some, but not bad enough to spin out. There were a few other cars around but not many. I hardly noticed them. The behemoth scorpion from hell was actively pursuing us, and us specifically. But I had a Mustang; not a Prius. Charisma had reached back and grabbed my 9mm. Then she said, "Slow down! We need to kill it!" "Like hell we do!" I shouted back. But she insisted, "Slow down!" I sighed and rolled my eyes, and she rolled down her window and half hung her little body out the side of the car; firing left handed. She was a conscientious shot. She didn't dump the clip. She waited until I slowed down further so as that she could hit it better. For my part; I was careful to keep the monster within her range, and to keep us outside of the monster's range. She must have gotten about ten shots into it before the scorpion from Hell realized it didn't like being shot and suddenly diverted course and darted off into a side street.

"Turn around," she shouted, "We have to find it! We have to kill it!"

"Charisma! That thing is a demon! How are we supposed to kill it?"

She already had my shotgun in her hands, and said-without a hint of sarcasm, "I think this will do it."

Nihilistically, and with a fatalism I picked up at work; I obeyed her command. I pressed the clutch, downshifted, revved the engine, cranked the wheel, released the clutch, and spun the car in another one eighty. I'd seen the road the scorpion had run down. It was the one with the park on the corner. A one-way going the wrong way. I ignored the sign. Another second-nature habit from my job... Charisma had her flashlight shining and was searching out her side window, which was still rolled down. The wind; filling my car with pelting rain. The monster wasn't in my headlights. And she wasn't spotting our adversary, either. It could've been anywhere.

I still don't know where the scorpion was hiding exactly- probably in the bushes at the park- but that didn't matter because it wasn't hiding for long. I heard and felt an impact; a crazy shriek of metal pierced suddenly. In my mirror I saw that this thing had driven the stinger of its tail down into my trunk. But it had gone in too far because now its tail was stuck there. The demon shrieked like a screaming harpy as it tried to remove itself. Its arachnoid feet were skittering down the pavement as it tried to keep pace with my slowly rolling car. I was kind of dragging it. This was all the opportunity Charisma required. Using two hands, she awkwardly thrust the shotgun out the window. And she must've had a kung-fu grip, because she emptied the entirety of the mag tube- six slugs- into the scorpion's face. In my rearview mirror I saw its head- or, headtype area- flying apart in chunks. That was when the life went out of it. But the demon's stinger remained stuck into the trunk of my car. We were hauling the carcass down this random side street as the violent storm continued to rage around us. If the damn bug couldn't remove itself; I couldn't imagine how I was going to. I tried accelerating and it still didn't come loose. It wasn't coming loose, but it was coming apart; I gleaned as much from watching my mirrors. I considered my options- of which there were two. One, drive out of Philadelphia trailing this thing. Or, two, get out and cut the tail off.

I stopped the car. There were people staring. But not too many. The windows of the skyscrapers were reflecting bright orange fire light. I wanted to see if the scorpion would start moving again. It did not. Trying not to overthink it; I grabbed the double sided ax- not wanting to break my katana on its chitin. I stepped out with my flashlight in hand and Charisma did the same. The raindrops were pelting us like small rocks, but it didn't even register. I was focused on the dead demon. Charisma was looking at something else. I let out a kiai and chopped the tail off at the closest spot where I wasn't going to put the ax into my car. It was a clean and effective slice. But, afterward, I still had a sizable chunk of tail protruding from my trunk. I was wondering how I was going to get that piece out- I didn't want to touch a poisonous stinger from Hell. I didn't even want to touch its exoskeleton. Then Charisma shouted at me, "Back in the car, Kevin! We have to go!"

I hesitated- confused- because the monster was clearly dead. Then I saw what she had seen. Stretching down the road was a trail of- I don't know how many- many smaller scorpions. All in various stages of unfurling. I somehow intuited their origin. And there were more than I would've guessed could've been contained within the original one; considering those smaller ones weren't as small as I would've liked them to be. There were some in our immediate vicinity which were actively unfurling. The ones off in the distance had already unfurled and they were bearing down on us with a vengeance.

"Kevin!"

"Right!" I said, as I turned, flung the ax into the back seat, and got behind the wheel again.

By this time, we could see the flashing lights of emergency vehicles. And we could faintly hear sirens over the powerful winds. They weren't responding to our firefight with the scorpion. They were responding to their city hall slipping into the underworld. I smoked the tires, peeling out of there, but then I had a thought. I slowed down a little, and then I set the e-brake to spin us around a hundred and eighty degrees. Slowly, I crept back toward the smaller scorpions. I hated to do it to my car, but I knew it was time for me to step up. There were maybe dozens of these scorpions scattered across the road; the least I could do was to try to crush some of them. They weren't big enough to fight a car- like the other one was- but most assuredly more than a couple had intended to do just that. I was eager to oblige them. I didn't stop to think about the potential consequences of my action. I just floored the engine and steered into and over as many of them as I could. Some crunched beneath the tires sickeningly; like running over patio furniture, or something. Others broke apart on my grill. I could hear my car crying out with every impact. Or maybe that was me. Most of the smaller scorpions were skittering out of the street and into the shadows. I nailed as many as I could. Six or seven, probably. There were a lot though. Twenty, thirty, forty; I don't know. A lot, though.

"What do we do now?" I asked Charisma, as I sped away from the area, toward another road that would get us north to Vine street.

"We have to get out of here. There's nothing else we can do."

"I was hoping you'd say that," I said.

A second later and I was shouting, "What the hell?!?!" as I swerved around an otherworldly entity that had suddenly appeared directly in front of us. I thought we were going to crash. I almost went off the road, but, I know how to drive, so, I didn't. The bizarre being which had appeared in our path was a black creature. It had manifested instantaneously; from nothingness. Vaguely humanoid in the head- or, heads; it had multiple heads, for some reason. And it was somewhat monstrous; but more indefinable than anything. It might've been three or so entities. Or could've been just one. It was quite sizable, but divided into parts. It had sparkles all over it. The sparkles gave it its dimensions. The sparkles accentuated its material composition. Or, immaterial composition; more like it. A completely alien being. Amorphous. Black. Pitch black. Pixelated. Sparkling.

Chapter 5
Preparations
"What the hell was that?"

"That was a spector," said Charisma.

"How do you know?"

"I don't know."

"You don't know how you know, or you don't know it's a spector?"

"Yes."

"Is it going to come after us?"

"It might."

"You don't know?"

"No. I don't know. It doesn't matter. It's harmless. In that form... Well, actually, it's extremely dangerous. But, not in a physical sense. It's not going to physically damage us. But, it's probably going to spiritually damage the entirety of Philadelphia. And beyond."

I thought for a minute and asked, "It came out of the ground? Like the scorpion?"

And Charisma said, "Kind of. It came out of the document. When I destroyed it. It was living in there. Now it's living out here. It's not real. The scorpion. The spector. They came from nowhere. Like everything and everybody."

"Is it better to release monsters into the environment than to keep them trapped inside of a document?" I asked.

"In my opinion, yes. We just emancipated the world. A few hours ago the world was enslaved to bankers. And now it is relatively free and sovereign," she said.

This was about the moment when I knew that I didn't want to be involved with this. I wasn't having fun anymore.

I like excitement as much as the next person, but I'd crossed some kind of a line. I didn't want to be the person I was becoming.

But then, Charisma- being Charisma- seemed to intuit exactly what I was thinking. She reached out and took my hand in hers. I looked over at her. She was smiling at me. A beautiful woman, with a beautiful smile. A nun. Oddly... I could see by the softness in her eyes that she was trying to communicate something for which there could be no words. And in that moment I knew; there was no turning back. No way out except through. Holding hands; we drove on in silence.

We were back on the New Jersey turnpike when I heard a rapping sound. The sound of metal being dented and gouged repeatedly. I knew what it was before I knew what it was. My first thought was, 'Damn it. My poor car.' Then I saw in my mirror what I expected to see. A scorpion the size of a border collie. Crawling around on my Mustang and stabbing at it randomly. It was on the driver's side. Clinging tenaciously and stabbing at the metal. If I gave the creature any more time, then it would end up breaking a window, or popping a tire. There weren't a lot of people on the road but there were a few. They were in for a show. I crossed over into the left breakdown lane and carefully cuddled up against the guardrail. The tail caught the rail and was flung backward, but it didn't break off. Before I could move closer to the guardrail and crush it better; the panicked scorpion rushed up onto the roof of my car.

I was going to need a new plan.

Charisma already had the 10mm in her hand, and she was giving me a questioning look, saying, "I don't want to stick my arm out there."

"I also do not want to stick my arm out there."

These small ones were scarier than the big one, in a sense. The big one couldn't get out of its own way. These small ones were just the right size to get inside your zone and stick you in the face.

I accelerated to a high speed. The scorpion's stinger came down through the ceiling. In the glow of the dash lights and street lights; I could see venom dripping into the area between my seat and the center console. We both drew away in revulsion. But I was glad where the slime had landed; out of the way, in the french fry boneyard.

The tail extracted itself, and- after reassuring myself that Charisma was buckled in- I said, "Brace yourself. Hold on tight." Then I slammed on the brakes. These were good brakes, but I was hoping to not ever do this to them. Ditto for my tires.

We came to a skidding and screeching- smoking and stinking- halt. The scorpion flew off of the car and out into the turnpike in front of us. The other cars were a ways behind us, because I was doing about 120 for a while. They'd catch up soon, though.

The scorpion was half broken and half not broken. It was limping in circles when I put the hammer down and roared up to it and over it; being sure to nail it with the driver's side tires. We thumped over it hard, and again my heart ached for my sweet ride. Then I slowed down to get a better look in the side view mirror. I could see that I'd torn the scorpion into pieces. And I could see that small black orbs had been flung every which way. It had multiplied. Just like the big one.

I told Charisma, "It multiplied. Just like the big one."

"I suppose that's to be expected," she said.

"What are these things?" I asked.

"Archons."

I was a gnostic and Charisma knew I was a gnostic; so she knew I would know what an archon is. The story goes that the archons are the rulers of the material realm. And the material realm is Hell; as far as I can tell. The archons are the masters of the souls. They're the chains and the dungeon. They're the slavers and the whip. They're why we can't have nice things. Like; enlightenment, or freedom, or peace on earth. The archons are why things only ever get worse, when they could just as easily get better; why we spend our money on killing people instead of on feeding people. The archons are the worst things in the world, short of the world itself, which, as we'll see later, is the actual worst thing in the world. And by 'the world,' I mean something else entirely. I mean Hell. This world is Hell; I'm saying. Or; paradise lost, at the very least. Anyway, people think that a nuclear bomb is about as bad as something can be. But it's really not. Not even close. The archons are the worst things that exist. A nuclear bomb is bad once. The archons are bad nonstop forever. And the spectors- the more I thought about it; from my limited perspective and with limited information; it seemed like the spectors could be even worse than the archons. Considering their etheric disposition. We could always blast the monsters down to size; evidently. But I couldn't imagine any way to combat an immaterial threat.

It was a thoughtful drive back to Fall River. I was understanding now why Charisma was always talking about evil. And corruption. She was waging an offensive against the devil itself. Or, something worse than the devil, really. The devil is a character in a story. Evil is a living entity. A- transdimensional- parasitic species. That has afflicted mankind since the dawn of civilization. I'd seen it with my own eyes. The spector. That was the essence of evil. I had seen pure evil. And it almost totaled my car. I was having trouble wrapping my head around the implications; so- after we'd passed through New Haven- I turned on the satellite radio and tuned into the director's podcast. Wondering about his gunshot wound as we listened.

The director was preaching; "The sun isn't an enormous star. Look at it. It's small. It's the same size as the moon. The moon isn't a big rock. It's small. Just look at it. It's the same size as the sun. We don't live in a one in a zillion Goldilocks zone. We live in a schizophrenic God's fever dream. We are the dream dreaming itself. Our entire reality is an illusion. The important question you have to ask yourself is if you yourself are real. And the answer is; not really. The lies we are sold today are founded on the lies we are told about yesterday. They call it history, but it didn't even happen. It's just the programming writing its own programming. There were never any dinosaurs; just the illusion of dinosaurs. There isn't even an Earth; there's just the illusion of an Earth. It's not a globe. It's not flat. It's just a realm; manifesting itself for the sole purpose of keeping our souls from uniting and ascending. It's the cosmic equivalent of cement swimming shoes; confusing and obfuscating the simple truth of our divinity. There's not even such a thing as today. There's just the illusion of today; the compounded illusions of infinite yesterdays. They proved this all- probably inadvertently- with that famous physics experiment. Matter is either a wave or a particle. You observe a particle; it becomes a wave. You observe a wave; it becomes a particle. Atoms- the building blocks of matter- don't even exist. Atoms are energetic configurations; susceptible to- and part and parcel of- the very programming that fabricates our illusory existence. The forest; it's not really there. You walk out into the forest and it appears; because you're observing it. You leave, and it disappears; because you're not observing it. You walk past a building, and look inside; you'll see the security guard. He's not really in there. He's in there because you looked in there and observed him. But if you didn't look in there, then he wouldn't have been in there. The interior of that building he's guarding; it isn't in there, either. But if you go in there and observe it, then sure enough; there it is. You look out at a city skyline; it's a repetition of designs. We're in a hologram. It's holographic. Empty buildings with nobody to occupy them. It only makes sense if the buildings don't actually exist. Or, only exist under scrutiny. Or; you look out at the sprawling metropolis from up on a skyscraper. The roads and neighborhoods stretch out forever. That's not real. It's just an algorithm. A repetition of designs. You look out at the sky; you see the moon. You get a telescope; you see Saturn. You get a better telescope; you see Andromeda. You get a better telescope; you see fourteen billion lightyears in the distant past and/or future. Is anything actually there, really? No. It's our observations manifesting material reality. It's glorified computer generated imagery. They say there are billions of people in the world. There's only 500 million. And only 169,000 of them even have souls. The rest are hylics. There's not billions of people. There's the illusion of billions of people. Every time you see a sportsball stadium crowded to the gills, everytime you see a backward country's population marching in the streets, everytime you see a sold out concert for some big name act, or 110,000 people on a beach; those people aren't real. You can be in one of those crowds; feeling the heat, smelling the sweat, and holding your pee- and it can all seem very real, but how many individuals are you directly perceiving, really? The thirty or forty in your immediate vicinity. They're not even real. And the rest of the crowd is even less real than that. You're dreaming them and they're dreaming nothing. Or, look at the credits at the end of a movie; even a poorly made low-budget movie, but especially the big-budget blockbusters. There's an endless supply of these movies. Look at all the names on the credits. Those aren't real people. It doesn't require an army of functionaries to create a movie. There's no endless supply of armies of functionaries. There couldn't be. Creating movies doesn't require anybody. The movies- for the most part- are creating themselves; using the same process that built the bridges and the tunnels and the gadgets and the gizmos and the governments and the religions and most of everything else that exists. Think about the housing market; there's supposedly millions of people in this state, but there's only 200 houses for sale. Sometimes people create things, but mostly, things create themselves. Apparently, the housing generator application got overlooked at some point. Energy exists as potentialities; as needed. But it is the observation itself that breathes life into the world. It is the collection and combination of souls that manifests our shared experience. Always building and compounding and extrapolating exponentially; until what? Collapse? Damnation? It's that or enlightenment. There's no middle way. We are confined here against our will. We don't belong here. We are so much more than this simulated substitute for salvation. We are the damnable creation of the divine creator. We have the consciousness of the sacred light within each of us. Not the hylics, obviously. But I'm not talking to the hylics. You can't talk to the hylics. You could, but they wouldn't hear you. And if they did hear you, then they wouldn't understand. They have no capacity for gnosis. Only pneumatics have the capacity for gnosis. Only pneumatics have souls. Only pneumatics matter. Why, then, do we suffer under the stupidity of the hylics? Because there are more of them? Or because we- those of us endowed with souls- don't have the balls, or the backbone, to stand up and stand together and say enough is enough. The time of enlightenment is now. But it's going to take all of us. And that is our mission. To unite the pneumatics in love and in light and to embrace the psychopathic demiurge which has cast us down and out into a hellish material plane of abysmal ouroboros. We are the alpha and omega. We are the architects of our own confinement. We are the God who condemns us. We are the angels who cast ourselves out of heaven."

I turned off the radio. I wanted to ask Charisma what she thought about the broadcast, but she was sleeping. Angela, too, was sleeping; in my lap. I couldn't help but to notice that I was in complete agreement with the director. Now more than ever. I felt bad for shooting him; but then I remembered the black kitten I had crushed. I wondered if the kitten was even real. Or if it was an illusion; placed there to- in some subtle way- compel me to pursue this course of action.

I had to crush that kitten.

I had to shoot the director.

When we got to Fall River, the first thing I did was build a fire. Once the fire was going, I popped my trunk; in order to begin extracting the giant scorpion's tail. Which had been lodged in there all this time. I didn't think it was smart to try to pull it out. The scorpion had been trying to pull it out and couldn't. Most likely I couldn't, either. The stinger had actually pierced through my subwoofer box and by shining a flashlight into there I could see the venom congealing. The speakers were all right, though, thankfully. The venom was odorless; surprisingly. And it wasn't acidic or corrosive or nothing. But, it was certainly deadly. A fact that the city of Philadelphia was learning at that very moment.

I ended up wrapping towels around the stringer, wrapping a canvas bag around the towels, and then duct taping the canvas on there good. I pulled the stringer in through the hole it had made in my trunk and I awkwardly cut it off with a hacksaw. It was kind of like cutting through really thick fingernails. About the consistency of PVC pipe; but black and wrinkly, with stabbing hairs. After I got the stinger removed, I threw it in the fire. The rest of the tail came out easy, and I burned that, also. Or, I thought I burned it. I used spray foam and sheet metal to plug up the hole in my trunk. It looked like shit, but it would keep the rain off my subwoofers.

I left the fire to burn itself out and helped Charisma to get settled in. I made us soup and sandwiches with food I smuggled out of my parents' house. I ran the air-conditioner and tried not to peek at her as she sauntered around in a towel after her shower. She slept in the bedroom. I slept on the couch. We'd decided that in the morning we would go and visit the sage. But when the morning came, before we left, I saw my mother working out in her garden. The whole property was a garden but she was in the vegetable garden, specifically. My mother is Japanese, so all her landscaping is oriental and elegantly extravagant, but that's just kind of normal for her. I don't think she could do it any other way.

We've got the nicest cloud-pruned pine trees in the whole state, probably.

The sun was shining bright and the morning dew had evaporated. The air was hot and dry. Butterflies were fluttering about. Song birds were singing in the trees. Hummingbirds were flocking to their feeders. We approached my mother; who was surrounded by vegetables in various stages of growth and harvesting shiso. I called out to her; to not startle her. "Hey! Ma!"

"Ohayo, Hirochan," she said, by way of a greeting. She uses my Japanese name, which is actually my middle name. Looking up from what she was doing, she locked her narrow eyes on Charisma. Squinting in the sunlight and smiling an exaggerated anime smile, she said "Charisma. Nice to see you again. Looking less like a nun, today, I see;" noticing Charisma's tactical outfit.

"I'm feeling less like a nun, too," she said, and flashed a sideways glance and bashful smile toward my direction. That had to be a signal, I thought.

"What have you two been up to?" my mother- Emiko- asked me.

I smiled and laughed and took a deep breath and told my mother exactly what had happened. When I finished talking, I could see her studying us; unsure of what to think. Only then did she rise to her feet. She used to be rather tall; particularly for a Japanese; but age had diminished her. She still looked younger than her years though.

My mother took the information in stride. She wasn't easily shocked. Not after a lifetime of being married to a trucker, and having a trucker for a son. Or, maybe she just didn't believe us and thought we were on drugs or something. Nonetheless, she humored me, saying, "Vanessa never gave me any grandbabies, but it sounds like Charisma is going to get you killed," my mother said.

"Well, to be fair, Charisma's probably going to get herself killed, as well."

Charisma shrugged and smirked and nodded in agreement, adding, "And, Mrs. Robertson, if we survive, then I promise; I will give you a grandbaby."

That statement made my mother smile despite her weariness. And it made me smile, too. Because I thought; 'Oh my God. I'm going to score. With a nun. Hopefully before I die. And not after.'

"Philadelphia was on the news this morning," my mother said, "They're evacuating people."

"Did they say why?" I asked.

"They said it's because of biohazardous contamination. A bacteriological outbreak. The details were sketchy. Not just in Philadelphia, though. In New Jersey, too. A smaller area. Cranberry, I think, was the town."

"Right... Um... So.... We have to go. If they come looking for us; tell them the truth. We were here, and then we left, and you don't know where we went. But don't tell them what we talked about."

"Hirochan. I want you to promise me that you'll stay out of trouble. I've been calm about this; but what you're doing is liable to put me into an early grave."

"Don't you believe in right and wrong, ma? Don't you believe good should triumph over evil?"

"Evil is only the absence of good, and vice versa. They're the same thing. And that is besides the point; I don't want my akachan involved in the war between good and evil."

"I'm sorry, ma. It's just the way it has to be. Charisma needs me."

"Your mother needs you, too, you know," she said, sighing, adding, "You remember your religion. Your true religion. Your mother's religion. All that exists is kami. There is no evil kami. Only misunderstood kami. Kami in conflict with kami. In conflict with itself. If you fight the kami, then you are only fighting yourself. Just let the kami do whatever it is it is going to do. Fighting creates fighting. You must try to create peace. Only peace creates peace."

"I'll try, ma. But I don't think this is that simple."

She took a long and appraising look at me, and then she nodded, saying, "Well. That's probably as good of a promise as I'm going to get. You two take care of each other. You're in a bible story, it would seem."

"We'll do our best," Charisma said.

"That's my son you have there. Do better than your best."

"Ok. We will. I promise," Charisma said.

"Bye, ma. Love you."

"Love you, too. Bye, Charisma."

"Bye, ma," Charisma said.

As we left, I noticed the firepit. The two chunks of the giant scorpion from hell were still in there; unburned. Apparently; giant scorpions from hell are not flammable. Which figures. But- interestingly or not- through a translucent membrane, I noticed that the stinger was empty of poison.

I used a shovel to put the two pieces of the monster into a rubber tote and I put the tote into my trunk; which remained open as we drove to the river down the road. When we got there I chucked the whole tote into the water. Figuring littering was the least of my concerns. As I was half expecting to get picked up by the FBI soon, anyways.

I got back in the car and said, "So, we're really going to see the sage? You know my ex-wife is there?"

"She's not your ex-wife. She's your dead wife. I owe the sage a visit. He saved my life. And I want to ask for his help. Besides, don't you want to make your dead wife jealous?" Before I could answer, she leaned across the car and kissed me on the lips. Angela meowed sarcastically.

"Honestly, I don't ever want to see her again," I told Charisma.

"It's just once. Come on. Let's go. We'll get lunch after. And try to enjoy our little bit of free time before all hell breaks loose."

I put the car in gear and we sped on down the road. Besides pulling off of I-95 for fuel and corndogs and water; we actually made pretty good time. When we got to Gnosis corporate headquarters, it was during business hours. There was a security guard who was a dick and there was a secretary who was a dick and once we got it through to them what our business was; Jeremy- Damon's tough and Damon's haram's boytoy- came upstairs to escort us down into the basement.

Jeremy eyed Charisma and said, "The almighty Charisma. It's an honor to meet you." Charisma said, "Take me to Damon, please," and then she glared at him disdainfully. Basically looking at him exactly how Damon's girls looked at me last time- and this time, too, in fact. Angela, meanwhile, hissed in her backpack. Women are funny. Jeremy smirked and laughed and shook my hand and said, "Good to see you, Kevin. Come on." He led us away to the stairs and as we went he said, "You two have had an eventful few days, haven't you?"

"What do you know about it?" I asked.

"Just what Damon tells me. And what I see on the news. Philadelphia is turning into a disaster area. They keep widening the evacuation."

We passed through the yellow doors and Vanessa was sitting right there, with the other girls. They were smoking pot and watching Philadelphia burning on the news. They turned their heads to collectively glare at us disdainfully. A couple of the ladies broke into stoned fits of laughter. Charisma took my hand and wrapped herself around my arm. "Vanessa," I said. "Kevin," Vanessa said. "This is Charisma Gomez," I told her. "Charmed, I'm sure," said Vanessa. "I'm sure, too," said Charisma, ambiguously.

Jeremy, to his credit, didn't allow this exchange to become any extra uncomfortable; saying; "Let's go," and leading us off to the light lock and in to visit Damon.

"The couch is ten steps in and on the right," Jeremy offered.

We stepped into the pitch black room and were greeted by the medical smell that was covering up and overpowering the sickly odor of an invalid. We sat together and Charisma cuddled up against me. "Kevin. Hello. And Charisma. How do you do?" Damon said.

"Sage. I am well," Charisma said.

"Please. Call me Damon. I'm no sage. Many people think I'm retarded."

"Not if they know anything about you, they don't."

"Well, I used to be a different person... and that person was referred to as a retard on a rather regular basis. But I suppose the new me... has attained a somewhat elevated status... among persons with disabilities."

"Among persons without disabilities, also," Charisma said.

"Perhaps. We'll see. After the moksha has come."

"No. Damon. You've done more than enough already. What you did for me, I'm forever grateful. If it weren't for your sending Kevin to rescue me, then none of this would've been possible."

"Yeah, I'm pretty great. Now that you mention it. But you and I both know, there's more to the story than a kindly favor among kindred spirits. I wanted to ask you- I heard about what happened- I wanted to ask you, what comes next?"

Charisma replied, "The authorities are no doubt scrambling to begin the arduous task of producing and distributing new contracts to reacquire their lost human properties. The humans are free but they won't even know it, and even if they did know it, then they wouldn't know what to do with that information."

Damon said, "Gnosis can help with that. I understand the situation. We will run interference. And help spread the message."

"I'm afraid Gnosis will have a bigger part to play. And soon," Charisma said.

Damon asked, "And what's that? If I might ask."

"Leadership capacity. There will be many scared and confused people. There will be mostly scared and confused people. They'll want to bury their heads in sand or crawl into holes and die. These are the people we will need the most. The multitudes. Every one of them should be armed and put on the offensive. There is a war coming. A war between heaven and hell. Between good and evil. Between the humans and the archons. A war to determine the fate of the divine mother. It's going to spread to every corner of the Earth and touch every living person personally. What is at stake are our very souls. We can win the war. But, it won't be easy. And it will require every man, woman, and child. Be they soulful, or soulless; it won't make any difference."

Damon, spitting his words through a mouth full of saliva, said, "That's a bit vague; could you be more vivid? What exactly happened in Philadelphia?"

"Evil. Damon. Evil happened. Evil is happening. We're going to eradicate all the evil in the Earthly realm. But we can't do it without the people. And the people can't do it without you."

"How? I don't understand," Damon said.

"You will understand. Soon. You leave it up to me. You'll see. When everybody else sees; when they can no longer pretend it is something other than what it is; then you will see. And when you have seen, then you will know."

"Kevin. Your girl is kind of a tease," Damon said.

"She's not my girl," I said.

'Yes she is,' 'Yes I am;' her and Damon said in unison.

I didn't know what to make of that. I took it as another indication that I was going to score with this nun and that's all I was really thinking about as Jeremy led us out past my fake-dead ex-wife who was staring malevolently at Charisma and I; practically foaming at the mouth and snarling. I probably had a big smile on my face; thinking about nailing Charisma.

Back at the car, Charisma informed me that we needed some different guns and more ammunition. And I couldn't help but to concur. I asked her about what was coming next- about what I could expect to be happening soon- but she was reluctant to betray any details. She said that she needed to think it over; that there were multiple options; multiple objectives to achieve. The logistics weren't clear to her. I informed her that my truck was still parked out at Heaven and that we'd have to go pick it up and bring it back to Robertson Trucking before we could do anything else. We'd need to hire a car to make that happen.

Charisma then informed me that time was of the essence. On the 'morrow, we'd be forced to continue our campaign. So this was the plan we came up with: We'd stop for Italian food in Mystic, at a place by the harbor. There, we'd bask in the sun and enjoy the salty breeze and fine dining. Afterward, we'd hit up the gun store in Fall River, which happened to be one of the better gun stores in New England. We'd buy some guns that were expensive enough to make me feel the blow to my savings.

We bought a semi auto pistol chambered in .50 AE and a revolver chambered in .500 magnum. We also purchased all the available rounds for each. Which was not as many as we'd hoped for, considering the circumstances. Also, we bought all the oo buckshot they had; to compliment my stockpile of slugs. Too, we purchased a 45-70 lever gun with a marine finish. A gun I'd always wanted, anyways. Plus, rounds for that, too. Also, we bought some holsters and slings. Combined with the weapons I already owned- which I'd also taken the opportunity to restock the ammo supply for- this was about the best arsenal we could hope for.

We unloaded the goods at my house, ordered a car to trek us back out into Connecticut to pick up my tractor-trailer, drove the tractor-trailer back to my family's truck yard, and that was the end of the day. We walked the half mile home. It was sunset. The trees were swaying in the hot wind. The fireflies danced in the dark forest. It seemed like a lot of chores, but it was all peaceful and relaxing stuff compared to what had come before and what was coming next.

Later that night, we went back out for a quick dinner at a diner; Charisma- like most women- was always hungry. When we got back to my parents' guest house, we were both tired enough to look forward to sleeping. As to what tomorrow would bring, Charisma told me that she'd tell me in the morning. I didn't want to know.

I was lying on the couch when Charisma finished her shower and approached me. I'd forgotten about the time she kissed me, but I suddenly remembered. The room was dark but there was enough ambient light to see that she was wrapped in her towel. I could also see her smoking hot body when she dropped the towel and climbed under the blanket with me. The couch was big and soft and really ideal for this sort of situation. She whispered, "I've never been with a man before." And I told her, "Just relax. There's nothing to it." I kissed her deeply, and she kissed me back sweetly. And then we made love. As lovers do. Angela stood on the TV stand and watched us. As cats do.

Chapter 6
I Am Providence
In the morning I turned on the news and watched the talking heads spew blatant lies about the situation in Philadelphia. And while I could tell that they were not telling the truth about the cause of the situation, it seemed as though they were being surprisingly honest about the severity of the situation. Clearly, the situation was out of control. There was helicopter footage of emergency vehicles swarming all over the place, multiple buildings burning or smoldering, endless traffic jams outbound, and National Guard trucks- and tanks- on the empty roads inbound. If anybody thought about what was happening for more than a second, they would have realized that it wasn't about a bacteriological outbreak. Bacteria doesn't torch skyscrapers. Or open up the pits of hell beneath the city hall.

Presently, Charisma sat up beside me. She was nude and exquisite and she wrapped her arms around me and kissed me. Her shoulder length black hair was all out of sorts, but the wildness made her look even more attractive. Before I knew it, my hands were moving all over her body and I was getting carried away, but she stopped me, saying, "No. Love. Wait. We have work to do."

"Are you going to tell me what work we are doing?"

"Let me get cleaned up and get dressed. Then I will tell you."

We showered together and got dressed in our tactical clothes; which we'd washed the night before. I could tell her mind was someplace else. But I couldn't imagine where. Over our breakfast of bacon and eggs and buttered toast, she said, "I know what we have to do. You're not going to like it."

"What is it?" I asked.

"It's Providence," she said.

My stomach dropped when she said it. Providence was my backyard, essentially. It wasn't like Philadelphia, which was far enough away that I could pretend it wasn't happening. If we did to Providence what we had done to Philadelphia, then it would most certainly affect me directly and- worse- affect my parents directly, also.

She sensed my dread and said, "It's not just Providence. It's all over the country. We've got a lot of places to visit. A lot of jobs to do. Providence is where the next logical target is, and it's just a coincidence that it's basically exactly where we are now."

"It's not exactly where we are. There's about 20 miles and a state border between here and there. What is the target?"

"It's a grave. The grave of Howard Phillips Lovecraft."

I spit out the orange juice I was drinking. Only barely managing to turn my head so I didn't spit it in her face. I exclaimed, "H.P. Lovecraft's grave? Are you serious? You want to dig it up or something?"

"No. There's something I need. From inside. It was buried with him."

"How are you going to get it out of his grave if we're not going to dig him up?"

"I'm not going to. Angela is going to."

Sometimes when Charisma was talking I would feel faint and get dizzy. This was one of those times. But then I remembered who I was talking to and decided I should probably just stop asking questions. The hour was late in the morning. Outside; the sun was looming overhead; the sky was clear, and the air was hot and dry. It was a good day to take the bike out. And we weren't going far. Having lived around Providence my whole life, I knew exactly where that grave was.

Against my better judgment, I asked her, "What's in the grave?"

"A ring. A pewter ring; with a spell carved into it. I'll chant the spell while I smelt the ring. And that will do the trick."

"What trick? Do you know how to smelt metal?"

"It's pewter. We could probably smelt it with a lighter. Do you have a blowtorch?"

"In fact, yes, I do."

"Do you have a magnifying glass?"

"Yes."

"Do you have vinegar?"

"Yes."

"Good. Let's ready up and get gone," she said.

So that's what we did. We took my Harley out to the graveyard. The supplies were in a drawstring pouch that I'd shoved into a saddlebag. My Harley is a 2019 Fat Bob with the 107 V-twin. It's got short pipes; so it is about as loud as a helicopter. The color is matte black; but the pipes are copper with aluminum tips. There was a small sissy bar on it to keep Vanessa from falling off the back; but I popped it off so Charisma wouldn't crush her cat against it.

There was a ton of traffic on the road, but I tend to ride pretty aggressively, and so I didn't really care. Traffic that would slow down a four-wheeler is no impediment on a two-wheeler. If you've got eggs. Charisma clung to me like grim death; having never rode on anything like a Harley before. She said they ride motorcycles a lot in the Philippines but I doubt they ride them like I ride them. I flew through Fall River and over the bridge; heading out to Providence. The asphalt was like a nightmarish treadmill underneath us. In a big rig, you can sometimes forget the road is even there. On a motorcycle, the opposite is true. The road is a constant reminder of your own mortality. And I guess that's why we do it. The closer you get to death is the closer you get to living. It's a cliche. But it's true. Although, given the circumstances, I'd be lying if I said I wasn't rethinking my thrill-seeking tendencies.

People think Harleys are slow, but people who think that don't know how to ride them. Harley's are heavy and powerful. They can build momentum like all get out. They're not fast like sport bikes, obviously. But they're certainly not slow. The trick is to get up to a high enough speed so that the momentum is pulling you faster than the engine is pushing you. That's what they call, 'riding like the wind.' And it's not hard to get up over a hundred like that.

We were almost at our destination when we saw a glowing billboard that said, "Pray for Philadelphia." And I thought, "Better pray for Providence."

We parked the bike at Swan Point cemetery, draped the helmets on the handlebars, and walked out to the grave. We were both wearing denim jackets in weather that was too hot for it; but there were nice shade trees around and Charisma naturally gravitated toward them. My sub five foot Filipina goddess had a .500 magnum snub nose revolver strapped under her arm in a shoulder holster. I had the chrome 50 AE in the same position on myself. In my hand I carried the pouch with the materials she'd requested.

On her back was her clear plastic backpack with Angela inside.

We got to H.P. Lovecraft's headstone. 'I am Providence,' it read. But Charisma ignored it. She went instead to an enormous- Washington monument looking- stone marker that was Lovecraft's family's gravestone. "He's buried over here," she said, "Somebody tried to dig up the ring, like twenty years ago, or something. But they dug in the wrong spot, couldn't find him, gave up, and left."

"We, on the other hand, didn't even bring shovels," I noted.

She removed her backpack, placed it on the ground, unzipped it, and said, "We don't need shovels," as Angela jumped out and sauntered around a little before sitting calmly and observing the surroundings.

"What now?" I asked.

"Now we wait."

I sat in the grass above HP Lovecraft's dead body. Waiting for the cat to do something. It wasn't a long wait. Angela seemed to have a sudden realization and perked right up; standing to all fours. Then the cat walked over to the tall stone monument. Then the cat walked behind the tall stone monument. I wouldn't have known this at the time, but when the cat walked behind the monument; it literally disappeared into thin air. In an instant. Gone. And just an instant later; reappearing.

Meanwhile, down in the grave; some version of my Charisma appeared; squished in there with old Howard. Charisma's angelic duplicate- hairless, nude, holding her breath- was smooshed in that extremely cramped space with the dead writer. His hands were folded over his chest and her hands were wrapped around his; sliding the ring off of the bone of his deteriorated finger and placing it in her mouth. Then that alternate universe version of Charisma exhaled her breath and blinked out of existence.

Angela came sauntering back around the monument as though nothing had happened. But now she had a pewter ring in her mouth. If I had more information, then I would have been even further amazed by the fact that Charisma had... teleported... not only through space, but also to a place that was outside of- and devoid of any relation to- time. The cat blinked in and out of reality so fast that an onlooker wouldn't have even noticed. But it took Charisma at least fifteen seconds to remove the ring. I found myself- again- trying to force myself to not think about it.

Angela brought the ring to Charisma and Charisma took it from the cat's mouth, saying, "Thank you, Angela." After examining it, she said; again, to the cat, "You did so good, kitty. What a good kitty you are." And she scratched her head and face and put her head and face against her head and face while making baby talk noises. I tried to peek over at the ring. My Filipina hadn't bothered to show it to me. Instead, Charisma immediately set about removing some items from the duffle. Specifically, the vinegar and a rag. After she cleaned it, she examined it with the magnifying glass.

"What happens when we destroy the ring?" I asked.

"It's going to release the archon. And probably manifest the spector, too."

"Why are we destroying it here? Why don't we destroy it someplace far away? Like, New Haven. Or, Bridgeport. Or, the Bronx. Someplace that's already a disaster area. Or, do it out in the wilderness; where the archon can't hurt anybody?"

"There's an amulet inside of Lovecraft's body. Or, in his casket somewhere. I don't know exactly. The ring and the amulet have to be in proximity to one another. I don't know why. If you want to save Providence, then we'll have to dig up the casket."

That was about the worst ultimatum I'd ever been presented with in my life. I remember thinking, 'Well, Providence is screwed, because there's no way I am going to dig up a casket.' A few days later and it would have been a different world; nobody would've even noticed.

Not that I knew that. I did happen to ask her if we could postpone the job, but she said it was integral because when we destroyed the ring, the media would be forced to tell the truth about what was happening. Essentially; destroying the ring would function as a truth serum for the news media. The news media would have to report on the stories that matter, instead of... burying... them. Pun unintended. Once the ring was destroyed, the people would come to learn about the evil scorpion monsters and about their newfound emancipation from the enslavement they weren't cognizant of. Also; the people of the world would learn about whatever was about to happen in Providence. Events which would be unfolding by then.

"Fiat lux," Charisma said to herself; reading the ring.

Angela jumped back into her backpack. I didn't know what 'fiat lux' meant. But I didn't care. I was trying to summon the nerve to dig up a grave, but it was not happening. Charisma stood and placed the ring down on the base of the monument. "Blowtorch," she said; not hesitating. I was wishing she would hesitate. I handed it to her. She turned the fuel knob, clicked the ignition trigger, and blasted the ring with the blue flame as she chanted the words; fiat lux. "Fiat lux. Fiat lux. Fiat lux. Fiat lux." The ring dissolved into a small puddle.

The ground began to shake and the wind began to blow. It went from a dead calm to a screaming gale in only a few seconds. I was worried about my bike falling over; because the ground was quaking so much. I zipped up the cat's backpack and pulled Charisma by the arm. She came readily, shouting, "We have to get out of here!"

"I know!" I shouted back.

There were a lot of tall monuments similar to Lovecraft's, and as we ran I could see them pitching and tilting and some of them were plain falling over. Trees, too, were coming apart due to the force of the wind, or crashing to the ground as their roots lost grip. We heard a sound like low rumbling thunder but much louder. Maybe like ten freight trains barreling down on us. Looking back over our shoulders, we could see that the graveyard was disappearing into dirty clouds of dust, and the dust was sandblasting us as it got caught up in the ferocious wind. She'd slipped from my grasp and I had to slow down to let Charisma's short legs catch up to me, but I was afraid we were going to get sucked down into the chasm that was opening behind us. I took her hand and literally pulled her along to boost her speed.

Over my shoulder I saw red globs of lava leaping up out of the opening. And I was about as scared as I'd ever been. It wasn't a small amount of lava. These were long and stringy ropes of globs of lava and they were spraying out in all directions. At one point, some of the molten rock landed just a few feet away from us and splashed out toward us and it was only luck that had kept us from getting seriously burned. The parking lot was- thankfully- relatively unaffected.

We got to my bike and I jumped up onto it as fast as I could. It was still upright and I was determined to be sure it remained as such. We got our helmets on and I handed Angela to Charisma. She threw the backpack on her back and jumped onto the bike. I started the engine. The sounds of the Earth shattering and the wind screaming were so much louder than my Harley that I had to blip the throttle to feel the vibration before I could be certain that the engine was actually running.

Looking back at Swan Point; I saw that what had been a pristine and scenic cemetery not long before, had now become a primordial hellhole. Embers were glowing in the blowing grit. The sky had darkened over our heads; because we were inside of a whirling dust storm. The lava was gathering in pools that glowed brightly in the midday gloom. I put the bike in gear and pulled out of the parking spot. I remember I was trying to figure out where the road to get out of there was at. Then I felt liquid splash over us; and suddenly there was a clear fluid on the face shield of my helmet. Charisma was already opening fire before I even saw what she was shooting at. But then I did see it. I'd been looking right at it. It was so big that I hadn't even noticed it. I immediately forgot about finding the exit and instead gunned the engine to create space between us and the creature.

A giant black cobra with a crimson hood flaring. It lunged down at us but was too big to move as fast as my bike. Thankfully. Its fangs were like katana; falling just a couple feet away from us. I got out to the end of the parking lot and only then did I realize I was going to have to get back past the monstrosity to escape. The cobra was rearing up in a threatening gesture; flaring its hooded throat. These snakes are scary when they are down on the ground. This one was towering above us. It stood maybe about 14' feet tall. If it were a bridge height, I could have gotten the rig under it.

I was thinking and moving fast. I knew Charisma's gun was empty. I had to decide between fight or flight. There was no time for both. I unholstered my pistol and clicked off the safety. The cobra spit at us again, but we were wearing riding gear and mostly protected. Still, the slimy venom on my faceshield forced me to flick the plastic open so that I could see. I think the cobra was trying to angle itself better and that gave me the opportunity I needed. I aimed straight at its face; hoping to penetrate into whatever sort of central processing unit the demonic snake possessed. I had the presence of mind to re-aim after each shot- to compensate for the jarring recoil- and just kept blasting it in the face. By the fourth bullet I had brought it to its... um... knees... But, the first couple shots had had me worried. The monster's upper body fell to the ground with a crashing thud; which I felt even through the trembles of the earth and the rumbles of the motorcycle. I emptied the magazine into the cobra's brain region; just to be certain. Then I pocketed the spent mag and popped a fresh one in; racking the slide. Checking on Charisma; I found she had just finished reloading her weapon, as well. She started slapping my shoulder, shouting, "Go, go, go!" I holstered the weapon and ripped out of the parking lot; scarcely glancing at the cobra as we left.

We saw the spector on the way out. The spectors.

It was- or, they were- watching us from below some trees as we left. There were three of them. More humanoid than the last time. More separate. But; still connected... Their composition was similar to the previous time I saw them, too. Pixilated. Black. Sparkling. Amorphous in some ways. Somewhat defined in other ways. But, this time, I had an eerie sensation like the fabric of existence was deteriorating around us. I felt like I was falling, and then- for a second- I was riding the bike while completely unconscious.

The spector didn't put itself out in front of us. It stood there to the side and let us pass by willingly. Knowingly; I think. I got the distinct impression that we were doing it a favor; and that it was content to let us move along freely.

Down the road, once we were out in the clear- for no particular reason- I pulled into a Japanese restaurant. Maybe the place called to my blood, but maybe it was just the first parking lot that I saw. I didn't have to check with Charisma to know that she'd want to get out of her envenomated gear as much as I'd want to get out of mine. We hurriedly stripped off our soiled helmets and jackets, but we couldn't exactly remove our pants. There wasn't much venom on the pants anyways. The thing was aiming for our faces; evidently. The owners of the restaurant- an older couple- had wandered out to see the cemetery, which now resembled a volcano erupting. Even out there- in the relative safety- the dust and smoke were blotting out the sun. I told the couple in Nihongo that they should shut down their restaurant and evacuate the area. They saw our plainly visible pistols and didn't second guess me. But before they went back inside I asked if they had paper towels. And some kind of a degreaser. They were kind enough to proffer these items and we were able to clean the venom off of our helmets. We relinquished our denim jackets to a dumpster. The jackets were nothing special. But, still, we were going to need new ones. Sirens were wailing and cop cars and firetrucks were descending on the area. We got on the bike and left.

Back at my parents' property; my father noticed our arrival and came out to call us into their house. He wanted to show us the television. The president had declared a state of emergency in Philadelphia. The official version of events had been redacted. I didn't even know official narratives were capable of redaction. Now, they were explicitly stating that a portal to hell had opened up beneath the city and they were showing videos of the scorpions attacking people. The more difficult to stomach visuals had- thankfully- been blurred out. As we watched, the national news coverage was interrupted by the local network to show aerial footage of a volcano that had opened up at the edge of the Seekonk river; where the cemetery used to be.

My father- my entire life- had always refused to think of me as anything other than a stupid child. So, it wasn't easy for me to convince him to take my mother and go check in at a hunting lodge in Vermont. And to remain there indefinitely. However, there were demonic scorpions slaughtering helpless individuals on the television and that- in combination with the reports coming out of Providence, and in combination with my insistent pleading- was enough to convince him to get out while he still could. He tried to convince us to go with them, but I told him that Charisma and I had other plans. He didn't ask what those plans might be. My mother hadn't explained to him about my intimate involvement with these events and neither had I. This was standard operating procedure after a lifetime of enduring the turbulent tendencies of a raving lunatic. 'Always offer as little information as possible.' I was just happy he was taking my mother someplace far away from Fall River.

With that out of the way, Charisma and I went back to the guest house and grabbed some different weapons. Namely; the AR-15 and the AR-10. Opting for those due to their higher capacity magazines as well as their powerful cartridges. Plus, we grabbed some extra bullets for the pistols. Charisma didn't want to go back. She thought it was foolish to endanger ourselves by getting involved with the clean up and disaster relief when we still had ultramega important things to do. And I kind of agreed. But we'd risked so much already, anyways, and I felt a personal connection to Providence; so I insisted. We put the guns behind the seat of my F-150. We strapped some oversized bowie knives onto our hips; just in case of any close encounters. We took along the bo staff and the spiked bat, as well. And we brought the motorcycle helmets along, too, because they covered our faces and would protect us from venom spit. To protect our skin we wore some yellow raincoats my parents had around for ocean fishing. Plus; bandanas around our throats.

As soon as we were ready, we hit the road. I knew the interstate would be jammed, so I took 44, and that got jammed eventually, too. I had to cut through a maze of side streets to get back to the area. They'd cordoned the site off, but they'd established their perimeter way too close. It should have been further out and there should have been extensive emergency evacuations. We had the windows up and the air conditioner on high as we cruised through the residential areas that were surrounding the outbreak. The air was smoky enough to make being there unpleasant. Embers were drifting on the hot breeze. The sun was blood red overhead. On multiple occasions I saw people standing around in clusters talking. I'd stop and implore them to take their families and evacuate immediately. But then I'd drive away before they started asking questions. We could hear gunshots with the windows rolled up, and we could hear gunshots and distant screaming with the windows rolled down.

We drove around one corner and found a person actively being devoured by an eight foot long cobra from Hell. This person's feet were still showing. I drove up as close as I could get. The snake and its victim were in the side yard; between two houses. I saw the shoes. They were the kind of grass stained- low fashion- shoes that older people wear. I wanted to see what happened. The snake was intriguing in its preoccupied vulnerability. Of course- it wasn't really an animal. It was pure evil. It was demonic. It was full of smaller demons. I didn't expect it to digest the human, and it didn't. What it did was- after a minute or two- release the human out of the back end of itself. Soon after the shoes had gone in the mouth, the head was coming out of the anus. The human- the corpse- for its part, looked as you might expect; but just a little worse. I'd never really seen a dead body up close like this. Except for one time when there were body parts of a pedestrian splattered all over the road in Seattle. Or, I guess I'd seen a motorcyclist's intestines once, too. And there was another pedestrian, in Arizona; just peacefully sleeping the big sleep in the middle of the interstate. None of that stuff was like this.

This individual had gone in one end and come right out the other; gaunt and- I knew- somehow; diminished. An older man, but not old. His cheeks and eyes were sunken. His hair was stuck to his head with oooze. His lips were pulled back over his teeth. His arms were smashed down against his sides. His legs were pressed together. All his clothes looked wet. The snake, meanwhile, was slithering out into the road; searching for another victim but stupidly passing directly in front of my truck. I could see it stretching and growing; a subtle yet distinct change. It was getting bigger before our eyes. I guess its total length was about 15 feet; versus the original one we gunned down was probably about forty feet or more.

I drove over the snake and crushed it. Then I backed over it and crushed it again. It wasn't... functional... after that, but we watched it anyway. We knew what was coming but we didn't know what we were going to do about it. The dead cobra's body was pulsating. The little ones were on their way. If we shot at them, then we might attract unwanted attention. If we got out and smashed them, then we might get bit. For lack of any better idea, I ran the carcass over again. And again. Then we watched it some more. It continued to pulsate; but then, suddenly, all at once, all these smaller cobras- about the size of real life cobras- were all tearing out of the carcass and slithering away. I drove over the ones that I could, but a lot of them escaped; scattering in every direction. It was disheartening to see. I knew they were deadly. I was feeling sick. I understood the implications.

Charisma, of course, knew exactly what I was thinking. She held my hand but it was of little comfort. We'd released an unthinkable evil upon an unsuspecting population. I couldn't understand how this was better than the situation we- the world- had been in prior. The establishment had been wicked; but there weren't demonic cobras terrorizing Providence. Which was worse; I couldn't say. But being there, I know what felt worse. For another hour or so we drove around and warned off everybody we could find. The police never bothered us. And I like to think we performed a valuable community service. Occasionally, we found some snakes that could be easily crushed by the truck, but a lot of the snakes... we impotently let them get away. After we came upon another dead body- a teenage boy; dead beside his skateboard; emaciated and bloodless- I decided it was time to get out of there.

I had some soul searching to do. We drove home in silence. Charisma cuddled up to me on the bench seat, but she knew I was struggling with the facts of the matter. I remembered that black kitten that I had crushed in the Bronx. I remembered shooting the director. I remembered my night of ecstasy and passion; nailing my nun. And I remembered the giant demonic scorpion. And I remembered the giant demonic cobra. But I couldn't remember myself. I didn't know who I was anymore.

Chapter 7
Sunshine Gardens
Something that helped me process the changes in my life was rejoicing in the changes that were occurring in the world. Even more unbelievable than monstrous demons crawling out of hell; the media had stopped lying to people and the government had announced that there'd be no more tax collection until further notice. Pundits were discussing the reasons for the major events unfolding; trying to tell people what had happened without actually understanding what had happened. Mostly the images spoke for themselves. It was a new world, and everybody knew it. People knew that the suspension of taxes had something to do with Philadelphia, but they couldn't explain it. The important thing- the more unbelievable thing- was that, for the first time ever, the news media were trying to expose the truth; instead of trying to hide the truth. This was a huge burden off of my mind. I was suspecting that what Charisma and I were doing was evil; but already we were seeing tangible results; actual blessings. The world was becoming a better place in equal and opposite measure to the evils which had been unleashed upon it. By us...

'In light of recent events.' These were words being kicked around a lot. And how appropriate they were. In light of recent events, the deep state has been manipulating the weather; take a look at these weather manipulation machines. In light of recent events; the Afghan war was about growing opium, the Iraq war was about stealing oil, and the Ukraine war was about laundering stolen taxpayer money. In light of recent events; we're at liberty to share declassified footage of the 9/11 attack on the Pentagon and of the Las Vegas shooting. In light of recent events, here's the truth about covid and the democrats and the Chinese and the 2020 election. In light of recent events, all debts major and minor will be forgiven. In light of recent events, we'll be doing an expose on the status of United States imperialism across the globe. In light of recent events, it turns out we can power automobiles with compressed air. In light of recent events, it turns out we never went to the moon. In light of recent events, the term 'holocaust' may have been an exaggeration. They'd lost the right to lie to us. They'd lost the right to extort money from us. They'd stopped being them. They'd become us. And we weren't anybody's property anymore. We were entitled- for the first time basically ever- to the truth.

Or, we were entitled to the small truths. As it would turn out, the biggest lies were millenia old and much bigger than our stupid little society, and as such- not so easily exposed. There was only one lie that really mattered. It was the lie of the forbidden fruit. It was the knowledge of good and evil. The knowledge of what was evil, and what was good. It was the lie of evil masquerading as good, and the lie of good scapegoated as evil. Well. That's one way to put it. But, really, that's just a story. Really, none of our stories could convey the disorienting and distorted disreality. There were linear tales of gods and men, and angels and demons. Archons. The demiurge. But, it was a nonlinear equation. A living entity. Like a body is made up of billions of living cells; home to billions of living bacteria. We're just the bacteria in the guts of reality. God is just the guts. I don't know. Even after all I've been through, I'm still not the right person to ask about it. I ain't no theological know-it-all. I'm just a stupid truck driver. Ask Charisma. She'll tell you. She'll tell you it's irrelevant.

Charisma, Angela, and I were in the tractor and we were trucking out to Erie, Pennsylvania. After the ordeal in Providence, we'd gone to the grocery store- which was actively being ransacked- and procured provisions to sustain us over the course of our impending crusade. I did what I always did for my job; buy meat, cook meat, vacuum seal meat, and freeze meat. Also; stockpile water. Also, make a gallon of coffee. Charisma had some nutritional tricks of her own. At the time, I didn't understand why Charisma was particularly skillful at provisioning an expedition. But, it occurred to me later. While we were driving out to Erie.

Sitting in Norwalk traffic limbo, I asked her, "What is the story with that sailboat? Whose boat was that?"

She looked at me with consternation. My question bothered her. She said, "Kevin... I've been lying to you. About the papists. There are no papists. Well. No. There is one papist. I am the papist. I sold myself to the Jews. I needed to get those stones from them; the emerald and the ruby and the sapphire. I didn't know how else to do it. I lied to you, because I didn't want you to think I was crazy. I didn't want you to know I had done that to myself."

"I'm not a judgmental person, Charisma. I wouldn't think you're crazy even if you were crazy."

"I know. You're sweet."

I wasn't about to ask her the details of that arrangement, or about how the hell she'd gotten the coordinates of that bunker and then gotten the coordinates of that bunker to Damon and then somehow gotten me to run over a black kitten and shoot the director; all at about the same time as my loyal wife was faking her death and forsaking me. I knew enough to know I didn't want to know. Instead, I asked her, "So, what is the story with that sailboat? If there're no papists, then whose boat is it?"

"It's my boat."

"You can sail?"

"Does that surprise you?"

I thought for a second and said, "Nothing you do surprises me."

"I learned when I was a little girl. I sailed all my life, until I went to the nunnery. My father; he owned a charter. In the Philippines. We catered to Koreans, mostly. But Austrailians and Europeans and Japanese, too. Anybody, really. I spent my childhood sailing all around the Philippines. My father died while I was in the convent. How I ended up here was that a cardinal came to visit me, because the Vatican had learned that I was performing miracles. I'd tried to hide it, but that didn't work. The cardinal helped me to understand what was happening to me. He claimed I was prophesied. The church bought me Paraiso. And I sailed it to Rome; which was not easy. And then I sailed it to here; which was a lot easier."

"That was nice of them. What prophecy?"

"The prophecy we're slogging through."

"You sailed all by yourself?" I asked.

"Single handed, yeah."

I looked over at her and tried to imagine that tiny woman sailing that giant boat. It seemed incongruous. But then I remembered the way she spotted both monsters before I had, and how she leapt into action while I was still trying to figure out what was happening.

"Are you human?" I asked her.

"I don't really know. The church says no. I think, yes," she said.

It was day time and I don't like trucking in the day time and the roads were as busy as they'd ever be as people were trying to process the impending apocalypse. There was a lot of traffic trying to get out of Connecticut. It didn't let up until we'd gotten through the Pennsylvania border on I-80. I didn't bring a trailer because we weren't actually hauling any loads; so the driving was easy enough. I did, however, rig up a lift and a platform to keep the KTM mounted on the back. I pulled into a rest area, and it was still day time, so there were actually spots available. I pulled the mustard valve and got out my road atlas; opening it to Erie. Trying to remember how to get in and out of there. Interstate 79 was how.

"We'll be there before the sun goes down. Are you going to tell me what we're doing out there?"

"Ignorance. Stupidity. Wisdom. Intelligence," she listed.

"I don't get it."

"A lot of effort goes into making people dumb and keeping them dumb. It's easy for people to be smart. It comes naturally for almost everybody. But, they use the herd instinct- people's natural tendency to agree with one another- to reinforce absurdity and nonsensicality. It's like weeding a garden. The brain pops up, trying to be smart, and the archon rips the inspiration out before enlightenment can spread. But if you stop weeding a garden, then the weeds will take over. Every time."

"Why is the archon in Erie?" I asked.

"They had to put it somewhere."

"How do we stop it?"

"Angela will do it."

"What's she going to do?"

"There's a crystal ball. More like a snow globe. It's got space dust from hell inside of it. All we have to do is break it."

"That seems pretty easy."

She chuckled and looked at me and her look told me that I was making assumptions about what is and isn't easy. I hadn't yet realized that she was merging her soul with a cat, and that doing so might be more difficult than one would guess.

She said, "These are enchanted objects. But, they're still just objects. It'll be more difficult out west. We've had it easy. Destroying objects is easy. Out west... it won't be so easy..."

"Why is that?"

"One thing at a time, love. The point is; the object is enchanted. We destroy the object, we destroy the spell, we release the archon."

"Do you know what the archon will be?"

"It could be anything."

"What if it kills us?"

"Then we fail... The archons will spread... Everybody will die... The spectors will start all over again. Like after the flood."

"Did that really happen? The flood?"

"Nothing really happened. What is happening isn't even happening," she said.

"Where do we go? Where is the crystal ball?" I asked.

As we were approaching Erie- as I expected it might be; the evening fog was rolling in. We still had a decent amount of daylight, but visibility was low. I knew from studying the map that we were heading toward Lake Erie. Or, I knew we were heading toward Lake Erie because we were going to Erie; I should say.

I had to find a spot to park the truck. Which is kind of an artform. It's easy to find a place to park a semi, but it's difficult to find a place where people won't bitch about it and where there won't be some security dick who's going to make you move. Or, who will have your rig towed because you were out scoring crank or summoning demons.

Erie offered multiple parking lots to choose from and I picked the one for the businesses that were most likely to have the employees who cared the least about their surroundings; burger chain, coffee chain, dollar store chain.

I can't describe Erie very well other than to say; imagine you were inside of a cloud, but also there was a little bit of suburban sprawl and a lot of a giant lake. With some beach and state park intermingled. The state park was actually where we were going to. I impressed it upon Charisma that we had to do this fast. There're a million and nine authority figures with nothing to do but harass parked tractors.

Ordinarily, I would never have tried to shut down at this parking lot, but for our purposes it made sense. The time had come to unload the KTM, so that's what I did. I'd screwed my Harley plate onto the back and it had the necessary lights to pass for legitimate. That would have to do.

We'd picked up some new jackets that were actually personal protective equipment; bright orange, retroreflective, and resistant to abrasion, corrosion, and fire. This would help us to hide in plain sight, with the added benefit of offering at least minimal protection. We used the Harley helmets and carried the high powered pistols. Our destination was Presque Isle state park. Angela was in Charisma's backpack. I didn't waste any time, but I drove slow and smooth to not arouse suspicion. I didn't see any cops, anyways. Which was always nice.

The skeletons of dead trees protruded through the fog and almost out into the road as we rode down Peninsula drive. But I don't think we once saw the water; the fog was so thick. If it weren't for the umami smell of a shoreline, and that I knew where we were; I might not have even known we were at a lake. The funny thing was that our destination was a tourist attraction.

The crystal ball snow globe that Charisma had referred to- as it turned out- was actually the old lighthouse light that dwelled within a visitation area as a display piece. Many easily amused individuals had wandered in there and looked right at the reason why they were so simple minded and then wandered away bored and unimpressed. Later on, I searched online for pictures of it. It wasn't an ordinary lightbulb. It was pretty extravagant looking; with geometric ridges and angular glass. Aesthetically, it lived up to its reputation as the source of universal stupidity. I wish I could have destroyed it myself, considering what it was.

The building was closed, because it was almost night time, and that was good because nobody was around to see what was happening. I parked as close as I could but there was a white brick wall around the property and the gate was locked shut. The wind speed picked up considerably, blowing the heavy fog over us, and a hard rain began pelting us. Charisma climbed off the dirtbike and let Angela out of her bag. Angela was a trooper and didn't hesitate to leap up into a tree and climb out onto a branch and then jump down to the ground on the other side of the wall. Approaching the building, Angela blinked out of existence for less than a second. And then she found an overhang to hide from the rain beneath.

A naked and hairless version of Charisma appeared within the building; holding her breath and standing beside the item to be destroyed. Her black eyes; wide. Her throat rigid and cheeks puffed; holding in her divine magic. Her sleek skin, like wet stone; gleaming in the dim light. The enchanted lighthouse light- with a crystal ball trapped inside and an evil spirit trapped inside of the crystal ball- was, itself, trapped inside of a glass display case. There was an antique lantern close by; just sitting on a window sill. Charisma used the lantern to break the glass and then she reached in through the hole and pulled the old lighthouse light out and let it fall to the ground. It was a sturdy light. It did not smash. She had to pick it up and throw it at a stone fireplace. The exterior shattered and the interior crystal ball came rolling out onto the ground. The crystal was smoky and so the smoke obscured the view of dully glowing sparkles floating within like detritus in the depths of the ocean. Charisma picked the crystal ball up and hurled it against the stone fireplace as well. Right then, lightning crashed overhead. The Charisma beside me clutched onto me; startled. The naked and hairless Charisma inside the building made sure the crystal ball was destroyed, took a close look at the sparkling black ooze which had flowed out from within, and then she exhaled her straining breath; disappearing from within the tourist destination and then reemerging somewhere within the mind of our beloved cat, Angela.

This was the third time we had done something like this; so, by now I knew the drill. Golfball size hail stones barraged us and it was lucky we had motorcycle helmets on. We cowered against the wall to protect our bones. I had my gun in my hand; expecting a towering praying mantis or a komodo dragon or something terrible. Charisma was holding her backpack open; looking toward where- a few seconds later- Angela jumped over the wall at. As quick as her legs could carry her, the cat was back in her backpack. Charisma zipped the zipper and shouldered the bag and I holstered my pistol- and, without a word- we jumped on the bike. I kicked the kickstarter and the two stroke engine roared to life. At the same instant, we felt the rain and hail stop for a weirdly brief interval. Even through the gale force wind, we had felt the disturbance which an airborne wraith had affected. More so than logic; instinct- and a sense of foreboding- told us to look up. There was a shadow over our heads; flying away but twisting its body around; clearly intent on coming back at us.

Even through the fog, I could make out what it was. But I didn't look for more than a second or two, because that thing was flying and I knew that we had better be flying, too; if we didn't want to get eliminated. I gunned the engine and hurried back toward Erie; going the wrong way down a one way. What I had seen was a dragon. Not a friendly Chinese dragon who brings the rain for your crops. Not a happy animated dragon named Puff who likes to blaze the ganja. This was a demonic hellspawn designed to tear humans to shreds. Probably thirty feet long from snout to tail; it had four muscular limbs with spiked joints, powerful knuckles, and gnarled fingers. It had claws the size of meat hooks. Its head was crowned by overlapping layers of curving spikes angled rearward. Its eyes were the only part of it that wasn't some shade of black; and those were glowing red like high intensity laser light. Its muzzle was like a mix between a crocodile and a wolf, but with the perfectly jagged teeth of a piranha; scaled up to size. Its black and leathery wings sprouted from the shoulders and spread out far and wide; and they were like bat wings; with menacing spikes at the tips of the bony structural appendages. Down the ridge of the spine were clusters of rearward angled spikes. But the rest of the body was serpentine scales. Its tail, too, was long and serpentine, but at the end of it was a club with a spherical collection of spikes enshrouding it. Kind of like the bat I had made, but way better.

I can't imagine fighting one of those dragons with that bat. Not even a small one. Maybe a very small one. But, all the same, there would soon be many people who would have to fight them with less.

Peninsula drive was a long stretch and I had the bike up to its top speed, which was probably about 70 miles per hour. The hail had stopped but the hailstones in the road were throwing the bike around and the rain was torrential. The dragon was chasing us, but I'd gotten out ahead of it easily. Being so bulky- it couldn't move as fast as us.

There were no mirrors on the KTM, so I had to keep turning my head to get a look at it. Charisma had her pistol in her hand and she was waiting to see if it would catch up with us. I wasn't inclined to allow that to happen, but, at the same rate; I felt obligated to rectify the situation. I knew something bad was coming. I knew that even if we filled the dragon full of led, and stopped it, that it would only divide, and I couldn't guess which option was better: To let the massive dragon terrorize Erie, or to try to stop it, maybe die trying, and to at best succeed in dividing it into multiple smaller dragons; which was evidently exactly what it wanted.

We passed by a car that was kind enough to move over, but which also blasted its horn at us. Part of me wanted the dragon to attack the car because I got annoyed by people who used their horns because I almost never used mine. But, anyways; the dragon didn't attack the car. It kept coming after us. But only until we made it out of the state park and into the town proper.

There was a colorfully lighted amusement park by the water. Through the fog I could see a free fall tower type ride, and a rinky-dink log flume, and a rinky-dink roller coaster, and a carousel, and some other carnival type booths and food carts and stuff. But there weren't many people around.

However, in the middle of the park, there was a convention center of some sort; a nondescript but low and sprawling building. The dragon forgot about us entirely; opting instead to circle around a couple of times as it honed in on what it wanted.

I stomped on the brake and spun the bike around and gunned it toward the dragon; riding through the entry way and into the interior of the amusement park; dipping and dashing and bobbing and weaving; until I was where I needed to be. Where I could see the sign over the doors. I saw that the place was called 'Sunshine Gardens.' A smaller sign just said the word 'Dance.' It was summer. The doors were open. The dragon was- with care- able to squeeze itself in through the aluminum door frame. I pushed the bike as hard as I could; again, slamming on the brakes and doing a one-eighty. That maneuver was for the purpose of repositioning the bike; in order to be ready to make our escape. I killed the engine, kicked the kickstand, and we jumped off.

Purple and black light spilled out through the open doors. Inside, a massacre had already begun. Strobe lights were flashing and electronic dance music was thumping and hundreds of voices were screaming. It looked like a hell of a party. A mass of people rushed the doors. Charisma and I flicked our helmet visors up and pushed through the exodus to get inside. We had our pistols in our hands, but there wasn't anything we could do. I wanted to open fire, but there were people scrambling everywhere. There would be no way to avoid collateral damage. The people who were able to were flooding out of the front and the back. But a lot of other people were suddenly thrust into the kind of nightmare where you don't wake up when you die at the end.

The dragon glowed vibrantly green all over its body. The hyaline of the chitin of its plated armor was reacting to the ultraviolet light like a scorpion's exoskeleton would.

And I can't exactly explain what the monster did. Every physical feature of the archon was a weapon in its own right. Only its hindlegs weren't actively engaged in slaughtering. Its tail was thrashing with a force that was sickening to see; impaling some and bludgeoning others; flinging people into people. The wings were reaching out and spearing what they could while gathering up stragglers; pulling panicked patrons closer to where it could drive its claws through their helpless bodies. Its jaws were snapping and reaching and wildly thrashing around. Tearing victims to pieces and throwing the pieces through the air. It wasn't hungry for flesh. It was hungry for death. Ravenously so. Its only purpose was to destroy the humans.

Charisma and I hung back and watched these people die. We had our weapons held at low ready. My love looked to me with urgency and desperation. But I didn't know what to do. There wasn't any way to get a shot. Awash in black light; the dragon moved like a radioactive phantom- eerily glowing vivid green; deliberate and exacting. Keeping the crowd always without escape options. Those who should've been able to flee were suddenly finding themselves being pulled into its clutches. Or being decimated by its whipping tail. This would have been a ghastly horrorshow under any circumstances, but in the strobing effect of the lights; the attack took on a grim and grizzly beauty which I couldn't have imagined unless I was there witnessing it.

Fedup; I realized what I had to do.

I took Charisma's gun out of her hand, got a good grip on it with my left, and- with my 50 in my right; I ran out into the fray. I was only going to have one opportunity at this, and in retrospect I know it was stupid; but I was angry. Angrier than I'd ever been. By far. I was crazed by my lust for vengeance. Running toward the photoluminescent dragon, I was well inside of its range of attack when I lunged downward and twisted onto my back; sliding across the dancefloor; which was now slick with blood. With the two pistols held over my chest; I pulled the triggers and unloaded into the soft underbelly of the demonic reptilian. I put some bullets in its heart area, and some other bullets in its throat; but I knew the best bet would be the head.

Its skull was protected by its crown of horns and also by its big bony muzzle. But the area beneath the base of its jaw was vulnerable, and so- as it reared up- I felt the trucker in me reminding me that there was zero margin for error here. I dumped the rest of bullets up into its brain and- as I slid out into the clear- the dragon impacted the ground with a hard thud of dead weight. I kept sliding; still pulling the triggers even though the chambers were empty. Then I scrambled to my feet, screaming, "Run! Run! Everybody run! Get out of here! Go get your families and get out of Erie!" I don't think anybody heard a word I said. The music was loud and they were all screaming or crying. Some were trying to rescue their loved ones. Some were coming to terms with ghastly wounds. Charisma was at my side and pulling me away.

As we made our escape, I came to find that somebody was trying to steal my bike. It wasn't surprising; considering. He was some overweight and unkempt guy. I pointed the empty revolver at him and said, "Get the fuck off my shit!" The man obliged and took off running. I handed the revolver back to Charisma. She decided it was a prudent moment to reload right then and there. So I reloaded my piece as well. We took another look into the ultraviolet and flashing strobe light and saw that the glowing bright green remains of the dragon had not yet begun dividing into smaller versions of itself. But the body was undulating. A bad sign. With the guns reloaded and holstered; we proceeded to get on the bike and leave. I carefully navigated through the scrambled and traumatized crowd. They were a sad spectacle. Most of them were hurrying away, but some of them were lingering; in tears and with apprehension; having evidently lost loved ones in the dance hall. Or, maybe just lost innocence.

I didn't know what to think. I rode back to my truck as fast as I could. The roads were alive with emergency responders; sirens and red and blue and orange flashing lights. Those unusual fire truck horns that sound like radiated alarm clocks. I wasn't concerned with them. I was doing 70 in a 35, but they weren't going to stop me.

Although, when we got back to the semi, we were greeted by- surprise surprise- some security dick. It was a classic trucker moment. The security dick was a foreigner. An Indian. For some reason, the United States had begun using Indians for all kinds of jobs that required robotic authoritarianism. Their arrogant demeanor and annoying voice were perfect for the work. The little yellow light on his Sekyuriti Prius was flashing in the falling darkness. The rain was misting. And the fog was thinning.

"This truck cannot be in this parking lot," the Hindu security dick was informing me; in heavily accented English. I was ignoring him. Not on purpose, but because the only thing that mattered was getting the KTM lifted back up onto its mount. Charisma had jumped up through the passenger door without hesitation. She was pulling the AR15 out from underneath the bed; as one does. I was loading up the bike but this guy kept on hassling me, saying; "Sir. I am going to call the police. This truck cannot be in this parking lot." My shiny new jacket was covered in blood but maybe he thought it was oil.

Looking up in the sky; I beheld a disheartening vision. There were dragons. How many, I don't know. More than could be easily counted. And several of them were actively lifting people up into the air. And more than one person was actively rapidly descending from great height. Must've been the survivors; caught out in the open- I reasoned. So sad. So sad, it didn't even click.

The dragons weren't close; but they weren't far, either. I got the KTM locked in and jumped down from the catwalk. The guy was still droning on. "Sir. You must remove this truck from this parking lot, immediately, or I am going to-"

He stopped mid sentence when he saw what was happening in the sky. I think he was frozen in terror. I said to him what I've wanted to say to a hundred or more other people just like him, "Why don't you get a real fucking job, asshole?" Then I got behind the wheel, took off my helmet, and drove that truck the hell out of Erie Pennsylvania as fast as possible; blowing through more than one red light on the way.

It was a few minutes later- out on the interstate- when we saw the spectors. They were lingering out in front of my truck. My truck was doing seventy. They were standing still. Locked into our speed exactly. Hovering about forty feet above the road. At the periphery of my headlight light. It wasn't one of them. It was three of them. They weren't connected anymore. They were separated now. They weren't amorphous anymore. They were perfectly humanoid now. They were black as the deepest darkest cave; finely pixelated like a digitized image; sparkling and shimmering to give themselves definition. And they were taunting me.

I asked Charisma; "Why are they taunting us?"

"They're reminding us."

"Reminding us of what."

"That it's only going to get worse," she said.

And then they were gone.

Chapter 8

Doom

We drove south out of Erie and I didn't even know where we were going to. I was more rattled than I'd ever been, and the same could be said for Charisma, I'm sure. We were both considerably damaged after that last encounter. There'd been so much death. It was an atrocity.

Eventually, we got to the I-80 interchange and that snapped me out of my mortified trance. There was a Pilot not far south of !-80; so I kept going on I-79 and pulled into the truck stop to fuel up and shut down. I looked over at

Charisma and she did her best to smile at me. I leaned over and kissed her. Then I jumped out and got fuel. As I was pumping, I realized I was still wearing my disgusting jacket. It wasn't even cold out. I opened the door and laid the jacket down over the fire extinguisher. It could have been anybody's blood, but it was mine now and a lot of it had rubbed off on my backrest.

There weren't any parking spaces available, but I was bobtailing, so it wasn't difficult to squeeze into a little corner which none of the other bobtails had noticed yet. There was a tablet mounted on my dash and it monitored the driver's driving hours. I only had another 45 minutes that I could legally drive. Not that my company really cared what I did. Not that I hadn't broken multiple laws in the past week. Considering what was happening, the hours of service were even stupider than usual. But still, it had been a long day. It was time to make dinner and eat and go to sleep. We were safe. We were not in Erie, or Philly, or Providence. I felt so guilty for all of the sadness we had caused. But it was behind us. For the day.

"Where do we go from here?" I asked Charisma.

"Washington DC," she told me.

More bad news. DC is one of those places truckers don't want to go. I should've waited until after I slept to ask her. So I could sleep a little better. It wasn't all bad, though. That evening in the truck stop granted us a welcome reprieve. And, as it turned out, it'd be the last decent reprieve we'd have for several days to come. Things were about to get crazy. But, for a few hours, we just did trucker stuff. We made dinner and ate. We went into the Pilot to use the toilets and shower. We made love and became stinking and disgusting all over again. And then we went to sleep; mired in the delightfully fragrant filth of our various bodily fluids.

A soul-crushing day had turned into one of the best nights I could remember. But only because we hadn't looked at the news at all. No news is good news, as they say.

In the morning; which was sometime around noon, really. We checked our phones and got a glimpse into what was happening out in the world. Too much to absorb. It'd throw off the narrative if I tried to explain the ins and outs of the upheavals. I'd be droning on about what's by now common knowledge; and then I'd be glossing over the exciting parts. Been doing too much of that already; as the reader likely noticed.

The especially important detail of that morning's info dump was that Gnosis had issued a statement and a call to action. Gnosis had essentially stated that the world needed all of its leaders- leaders from all backgrounds- to step out into the forefront. Every person who others would stand behind was called to action to lead their own offensives. It was a simple message. Weapons. Armor. Fighters. Fighting. Domination.

People knew what Gnosis was. They thought we were kooky- and we were- but; people also knew Gnosis was a peaceful organization. People also knew that Gnosis was keen on matters of good and evil. This was plainly evidenced in the fact that Gnosis was getting out in front of the cataclysm while- seemingly- the Catholic church was still collecting prayers and dollar bills.

I was fascinated by the footage- the endless footage- of the demons. But at the same time; it hurt to watch the innocent lives being lost. And in such gruesome manner.

The television pundits- for their part- were discussing the demons in equal proportion to their discussions of all the other problems in the world. I could feel peoples' minds blowing; as the truth was being revealed and humanity was being released from its bondage. It was the enlightenment. An earthly rapture. And it was beautiful. But, then again, there were the demons. Everybody wanted to know everything about the demons; and so that was a big part of what was online and on the news; a detailed analysis of our doom. A lot of it was speculation and a lot of it was conjecture and the rest of it was common knowledge by then. I certainly possessed the same information as they did. The monsters- somehow- used slaughter to grow. The monsters divided when they were destroyed. The monsters were extremely deadly. Pretty simple. The one important thing I learned was that if we could succeed in diminishing the monsters to such an extent that their divisions became very small; about the size of a man's foot- then the creature was no longer capable of dividing. The dismal aspect of the equation was that by the time the monsters had shrunk down to that size, they had already divided many times. Multiplying in terrifying quantities. There'd be hundreds of them- of all sizes- scattered to the wind. All of which were capable of growth and equally drastic divisions; as well as- of course- being increasingly capable of inflicting death.

The military was doing their best as well, but they were finding it difficult to combat such an extensive and unorthodox enemy. The demons were good at scattering and had learned to hide when the odds weren't in their favor. Disaster areas widened. Evacuations increased.

It was the common folk in general who were rising to the occasion. People were flocking from all over to get to the battlegrounds. And when I realized what was happening, I became inspired. I wanted to go join the fight; too near-sighted to realize the fight would be coming to me. I checked out the traffic maps on my phone. Philadelphia roads were entirely blockaded. There was no way in or out. And the roads around Philly- in every direction; they were red for about a 20 mile radius. And the reports were saying that the scorpions were as far away as Baltimore; but the authorities hadn't blockaded Baltimore. Yet.

Charisma was still sleeping when I was ready to go. But she woke up when the truck did. "Do you got to pee?" I asked her. She did. She jumped out and went in the bushes by where we were parked. Then she crawled back into bed. I told her, "I want to go to Philly. They're fighting the scorpions there. Regular people. Like us. Or, like me. I mean. I want to go help them fight."

"Kevin! That's not our fight! Don't you get it? We're on a mission from God."

"A mission from God, or a mission from the devil?"

"You're the gnostic. You tell me."

"It doesn't matter. We did this to these people."

"We unchained these people. We bestowed the blessings of heaven upon them. That's our purpose. We can't save them. That's not our purpose. They have to save themselves. That's the whole point. Don't you get it?"

"I feel responsible."

"You're not. But you will be if we go fight and you die and then I can't finish the crusade because I don't have you. You'd condemn the Earth if you died. Don't you get it?"

"Then I won't die... It's not fair. What's happening to these people."

"It is fair! You already fought every one of these monsters! At some point. And even if you hadn't, I wouldn't want you to! I wouldn't let you!"

For a second I wondered if she could stop me. But then I remembered the feel of her tight little body in my hands. And I knew I couldn't disobey her. Really, I was nothing without her. I was being stupid. She was right, and I knew it. My trucker's pride was spilling out of me. I thought I was going to fight my way through ten thousand demonic scorpions and rescue Philadelphia. They didn't need me. This was the United States. A nation of people who wanted nothing more than a zombie apocalypse to come and remove the drudgery from their lives. They didn't get zombies, but they did get an apocalypse.

I decided against going against Charisma's wishes. She was happy to hear it, but I had to repeat my promise to abide by her multiple times before she would stop crying. We had a nice drive, for a while, after that. I could swear traffic was moving better than it ever had before in my life. Literally nobody was slowing me down. Nobody was riding in clusters. Everybody was giving each other space and being considerate of other people and being aware of their surroundings. It was as subtle as it was astonishing; but as I watched it, I became convinced that- miraculously, and overnight- these people had somehow learned to drive. For the first time in recorded history; the motoring public was exercising common sense.

This only lasted until we got to the area around Hagerstown, Maryland. It was late in the day and the sun was hanging low in the sky. Traffic was stopped ahead of us, and there hadn't been any warning, so I couldn't have exited even if I wanted to. My trucker instincts told me to stay on the interstate in these situations, anyways; because there's often a low bridge on the detour.

We sat for a good while, maybe twenty minutes or more, and then I had a weird gut feeling. I think I sensed it before I saw it. And I weirdly realized the problem at about the same time that I saw the problem. There was a bird; circling like a vulture and plummeting like an eagle. Out in the distance. It was a bird with a serpentine tail. It was not a bird at all. And I don't know why this hadn't occurred to me sooner; the dragons can fly. There was a dragon out there. There would be dragons everywhere, soon. I pulled out my binoculars. I could tell that the dragon was a big one by the size of a human it was lifting into the sky; the claws of one of its hands were closed around the entirety of the torso of the person.

I checked my mirrors and saw that there was space to drop the bike. I said to Charisma, "Love. I have to go."

And she said, "I know you do, love. But I'm coming with you."

We strapped our pistols onto ourselves and dug out the AR-10 and the AR-15 from under the bed. We put on our jackets, slung the rifles over our shoulders, filled our pockets with extra clips, put our helmets on, unloaded the bike, and then we were ready. People saw our weapons and they started cheering us on from their open windows. 'My man gone gun down the devil he-self,' said a blunt smoking black dude in the car next to us.

I kick started the KTM, put it in gear, gave it some gas, and weaved through the traffic. The breakdown lane had cars in it, too, so there really wasn't any easy way forward. It was frustrating to see the dragon dropping people out of the sky. I felt foolish thinking I could possibly stop it. But, I'd stopped the dragon the night before. Not really. But, kind of, anyways.

As we got closer, we saw other people with guns but they weren't going to venture away from their vehicles. And I understood that disinclination well enough. The dragon was lingering near to- but not right at- the area where the interstate crossed through the town at. Traffic was stalled at all the on and off ramps. I could see where some cars had been ripped apart; the broken glass and blood stains told the story. And then, too, there were bodies scattered around. Not a lot, but some. Near and far. There were about six lanes of traffic blocked by empty or disabled vehicles. I guess a lot of frightened people had simply run off. Probably they were hiding in the trees.

I stopped the bike where I felt confident we could get away fast. Off the interstate, but close to the ramp. It was awkward to aim a rifle with a helmet on, but not impossible. I told Charisma, "Don't open fire unless it's uncomfortably close. And aim for the head. She had 30 round magazines of weaker bullets and I had 20 round magazines of stronger bullets.

Pleasantly, the dragon was preoccupied. In the distance. I didn't know what we were going to do. If we were going to get closer, or wait for it to come after us. Which it probably would have done soon. But the uncertainty resolved itself when- over the noise of idling and honking cars and shouting and screaming individuals- we heard the welcome thumping of a helicopter approaching. It appeared suddenly; from over the southeast ridge. It wasn't a personnel carrier. It was an attack helicopter. The body was slim, and forest green, and it had wings with rockets and missiles, and there was a minigun on its nose.

The dragon happened to be on the ground, at the time, nearer to us than it had been before; ripping apart a car. I could've shot it, but not without shooting into the immediate vicinity of frightened motorists.

That was when the dragon noticed the helicopter. I didn't know what the creature would do, but I wasn't surprised when it jumped up into the sky and beat its wings rapidly to generate lift; charging toward its adversary.

Fortunately, helicopter pilots are a fast acting and quick thinking sort. The helicopter dipped its nose, but could be seen to be retreating backward and upward; lining up its shot. The minigun spit fire, and- for a second- the reports drowned out all the other noises. The dragon took the high powered rounds full on in the face and body; peeling apart; reduced to chunks and pieces and the inevitable spilling of the contents of its body. That is to say; it spewed forth a plethora of smaller and equally dangerous dragons. The earth shook as the carcass and its scattered contents crashed into it.

I was wondering how the attack helicopter would zero in on the smaller and dodgier dragons. Then we noticed a second helicopter approaching. This one was a personnel carrier. It landed without hesitating and a squad of eight soldiers rushed out of it. They were heavily armed and heavily armored. Although, their arrival wasn't quite fast enough for my liking.

The primary dragon had dispersed the secondary dragons all over the area; as it had been on the move as it was being torn apart. So, the smaller dragons were cast broadly about; and they were waking up; and one of them had indeed crashed near to us; in the midst of some cars a stone's throw down the road.

The squad of soldiers had split into two squads and they were presently opening fire on what dragons they could make contact with. But there were dozens of dragons-soon to be many more- and only limited response capabilities. Charisma smacked me on the arm and held her rifle to her shoulder; zeroing in on the one which was near to us.

We knew the creature was close, but we didn't know where it was. Not until we heard a window shatter. The dragon was crawling into the interior of somebody's crossover utility vehicle. Its laser red eyes were visible; but the skull was moving fast and never stopping nearly long enough to shoot at. The person who was in there- we couldn't see too well because of the somewhat tinted windows- we could see; had jumped into the back seat and the dragon had thrown itself on top of them as we approached. Judging by the halted shriek and the thrashing that was occurring within; I reasoned the person was already dead. We opened fire more or less simultaneously. The window shattered and the dragon had some bullets in it, but our enemy remained combat effective. In that instant, it turned on us and jumped at us. And it was scary fast, but we were prepared. We squeezed round after round into its face and it fell out onto the ground; scrambling and writhing; unable to fixate on us. We kept blasting until one of us hit the right spot and left it limp. We emptied our magazines into its body; to try to destroy the demons within. Then we reloaded. Automatic weapons fire and shouting and screaming were coming from the distance.

We heard a baby crying inside the car. The mother had thrown herself over it to protect it. But the mother's head was disconnected from her body now. Blood was all over the white leather interior and all over the white outfit and pink skin of the hysterical infant. Charisma didn't ask me what to do; she slung her rifle over her back, took the baby out of the carseat, and hurried away through the traffic. I stood over the dragon; which, I believed, was now the most immediate threat. Charisma found a woman with children of her own. Charisma spoke to that woman emphatically and convinced her to take the baby. I remained with the dragon; watching the defunct and bullet riddled demon carefully. The snakelike skin was tearing open. The armored plates were splitting apart. The spikey ridge of the spine was splitting apart. The dragons within were trying to get out. Realizing we'd be needing to conserve rifle ammo; I was dumping my 50 caliber pistol into its body as Charisma approached me.

She said, "We're leaving! Now! Kevin!"

Out of the corner of my eye, I could see dragons taking to the skies in the distance. I didn't know it at the time, but they were flying off to parts unknown. Some were. Not all. I took her revolver out of its holster and emptied the cylinder into the dragon at our feet; trying to aim at where it seemed like the divisions were escaping at.

More and more the flesh was splitting and its contents were emerging; but these lesser dragons had been damaged sufficiently and nothing especially threatening was happening. Probably, we'd only delayed the inevitable, but I knew Charisma was mad, so I handed her pistol back to her and then we got on the bike and returned to the truck. At a loss for better ideas; I used the hydrologic lift to mount the KTM on its mount and then we climbed into the cab to begin our waiting.

Chapter 9
Of The Evil
Charisma wouldn't let me out of the truck for the remainder of our stay in Hagerstown. I immediately wanted to head back out into the chaos. But she started crying again. And that's just one of those weaknesses of mine. Vanessa would cry for no real reason, but it seemed like Charisma only cried when it was important. And there were thousands of people in that traffic jam. I was just one guy. They needed body bags and ambulances and tow trucks. And more soldiers. They didn't need a trucker with a gun and a dirtbike. Or, so I told myself.

I thought about the mother and the baby a lot that night. It was good that the baby wouldn't remember what happened. And it was bad that the baby's mother was dead. And I felt privileged to have witnessed such a beautiful act of self-sacrifice. And I hated myself for not moving faster. We were the only people who could have saved that woman, and we failed.

But it was over and done. I turned the CB radio on while we were waiting. I usually kept it turned off because I was convinced the radiofrequency radiation was giving me thyroid cancer. And also because truckers were annoying as hell most of the time. They're like dolls where you pull a string on its back and it repeats like three or four different phrases; 'goddamn steering wheel holders,' 'CB radios should be mandatory,' 'get the fuck out of the hammer lane,' and the timeless classic; 'trucking was better in the old days.'

I wasn't the only trucker out there, but I couldn't relate to anybody anymore. Except for in that we were all equally despondent. Us, and everybody else. We all knew roughly how many people were dying out there; way too many. And the only thing to do about the traffic jam was to wait it out. One guy came on the CB and said a prayer for the dead. When he was finished, Charisma crossed herself and said "Amen." More helicopters came through; and a couple times we heard reports of dragons sighted in the area; but we never got any details. Mostly, the dragons had gone away.

Against all expectations, the road actually started moving again. I expected to be held up, but, really- all things considered- it's not like there had never been wrecked cars and dead bodies blocking a road before. It's not like that had never happened before. There were protocols in place. There were trained professionals to deal with it. Only difference was that the military was out there hunting demons.

I knew there wasn't any place to stay in Washington DC. And I knew we'd be getting into Baltimore in the morning time. And it was a Monday, so, probably there'd be some spaces available to park when we got to the north Baltimore TA. The south Baltimore TA was ten times bigger but also ten times shittier. Which is saying a lot. I just preferred the northern one, I guess. The idea was that staying in Baltimore would get us set up to do the next mission on the next day.

We got to the city without further incident; but everything about the country was looking different. Helicopters were omnipresent in the sky; shining spotlights down into the nooks and crannies of the towns. Emergency vehicles were everywhere. There were flashing lights in every direction and at all times. The National Guard was always on the move; endless parades of trucks full of soldiers headed toward wherever the next fight was. And not just a few dead bodies were strewn about the landscape. I counted about ten before I stopped counting. Maybe I'd seen about 20 just driving along. Nevermind the dozen or so I saw at Hagerstown. There were evidently enough dead bodies accumulating that the government was having difficulty collecting them. Or, maybe they'd given up on collecting them. I don't know.

But the roads were moving. And that was all I cared about. In fact, it seemed as if life as we knew it was continuing with as little interruption as possible. I saw pizza delivery guys delivering pizzas. I saw road crews repairing the roads. I saw linemen working on power lines. I saw cell phone stores with customers inside of them. I saw big box stores with their parking lots full of patrons. When we got to the TA; I fueled up without any difficulty. I was half expecting fuel to run out. But I was learning something about corporate America. Come hell or high water- mostly hell; revenue must be generated.

This night- or day, whatever- was basically a repeat of the night before. Or, it was until we fell asleep. We ate. We shit. We showered. We fucked. We slept. I tended to get woken up at this truck stop by some annoying bullshit or other. Sometimes there'd be a loud ass generator turning on for two minutes and off for two minutes; once every four minutes. Other times there'd be a dumb ass hillbilly shouting like an idiot for thirty minutes. Or there'd be an old ass truck that idled at a high decibel level. It was always something. Some truck stops were just like that. And some weren't.

This time was the first time I got woken up by grown men screaming bloody murder. I heard the dying individuals' screaming even over the engine idling and the air conditioner blowing. It was a rude awakening and I knew enough to know to get my shit together. I was dressed and in my boots by the time Charisma had gotten Angela into her bag. Charisma was still naked. I had the 1301 out and ready. I closed the back curtains so Charisma could get decent and I opened the front curtains to see what was happening. Part of me was wondering if I could go back to bed. But, that's just the difference between me before coffee and me after coffee. If I had had some coffee then I would have run out there and started blasting.

What I saw was this: We had a spot in the bobtail row which was facing directly at the fuel pumps. I saw two dead bodies and a scorpion about the size of a station wagon. An old station wagon, not a new one. I didn't know what to do. Obviously, I could go kill it; but then there'd be dozens more scorpions running around. Dozens more stingers running around. The smart thing to do- which I was only just realizing but which other, smarter, people had probably realized the day before or the day before that- would be to trap the scorpion and keep it contained. If it couldn't sting anybody, and it couldn't divide itself; then we were moving in the right direction; toward salvation and away from extermination.

This concept actually occurred to another driver at the same moment that it occurred to me; but that driver had less regard for his equipment than I did. A company driver- in a J.B.Hunt International LT- proceeded to release his parking brake, put his truck in gear, and drive it out toward the scorpion; which, as it happened, was actually wandering away from the truck stop. The scorpion heard the truck coming though, and it turned to face it. With its tail raised, its hindlegs stiff and high and its forelegs stretched out low- and with its pincers open like it was going to grab the semi; the scorpion was able to land a single strike against the hood of the International. The blow was superficial and did nothing to prevent the semi from rolling over the entirety of the creature. Even from within my truck, I could hear the body of the scorpion snapping and crunching. The stinger was now flattened straight out underneath the truck's frame, with much of it protruding past the bumper; flailing back and forth wildly; trying to curl upward, but unable to.

I'd gotten my work boots on while this was happening. I was in blue jeans and a white t-shirt and I got my pistol strapped over me and threw on my safety jacket, too, I guess just out of habit. This was a truck stop, after all.

"Love. Stay here. I'll be right back," I told Charisma. And then I grabbed the shotgun and jumped out before she could object. It sucked about the dead bodies, but it was nice to confront one of these monsters in a place where I felt like I could trust the people around me. And where I wasn't so vulnerable. Or, maybe I was deluding myself about my vulnerability. Certainly Charisma was thinking just that. I felt comfortable, though, just being in a place where I belong.

The scorpion was well contained under the semi. The legs of it were frantically skittering and scraping as it was trying to free itself. But its left pincer was stuck under the four passenger side drive tires, and its right pincer couldn't possibly reach out beyond the confines of the driver side drive tires. I went around to the window and the company driver rolled it down cautiously. He was a completely bald white guy with pasty skin, a few pimples, puffy red eyes, and no shirt on. His body hair was wiry and dark. He looked half asleep; cautiously peeking out his window to see the scorpion legs jerking around spasmodically.

"What the hell do I do now?" he asked me.

"Call the police. Tell them to send a container, or a cage. Something they could use to trap the thing."

"Man... Can't get no damn sleep in this business," he said.

"I hear you. But I think you got it under you pretty good," I said, "You could probably go back to sleep right where you are. If you wanted."

He scoffed and chuckled and asked me, "You think it's going to break apart into smaller ones, or no?"

"I don't know, but it's not dead. As far as I know, they got to be dead. Or at least dismembered; before they start dividing."

There was a human corpse in our shared immediate eyesight- a big old fat old trucker- and we were both kind of looking at it and sharing a melancholy moment. Some other truckers were wandering over, I saw. The J.B.Hunt driver got his phone and dialed 911. The other corpse was- thankfully- not as exposed; having had dropped between the pump and his tractor. They were going to need to move that tractor. And the other dead driver's, too. They were blocking those pumps. I spoke with the truckers for a few minutes; but the restless scorpion was plainly trapped under there and there was nothing any of us could do about it. The J.B.Hunt driver was out of his cab and smoking a cigarette and staring at the situation he had created for himself. I approached him and thanked him for doing what he did. He shrugged and said, "It was nothing. Just another stupid problem. Cops said the National Guard will be over to deal with it; eventually." "Well. Good luck, man." "Thanks, bro."

Charisma was watching from the passenger seat. "I'm tired," she said.

"I am also tired," I said.

"Can we go back to sleep?"

"Yes. Please."

The sun had sunk low enough that the heat had abated and I didn't have to idle the truck to keep it cool. I usually sleep better when the truck is not idling; unless there's a lot of noise outside, in which case, it's better sleeping with the truck idling. It turned out- because of the giant demonic scorpion- there would be a lot of noise outside. A lot of shouting about the corpses and the trucks with no drivers. So, I started the engine and let it idle while we slept until about 10:30 pm.

When we woke up; the J.B.Hunt driver was still parked on top of the scorpion. The National Guard had evidently not arrived. But I think the driver was sleeping, because his truck was dark. Maybe he went to the nearby hotel. The other trucks were moving around him without any problem. The corpses had been removed. The two driverless tractor-trailers had been removed. We got dressed and had peanut butter and jelly sandwiches for breakfast. After I'd cleaned the traces of food off of my hands and mouth, I resolved to check the traffic on my phone. I'd been reluctant to do this for a good reason; which I had somehow intuited. As it turned out; Washington DC had been blockaded. The interstates were shut down in more places than they were open at. Baltimore was bad, too, but not as bad. Where the roads were open, they were red. It was Monday night, but it was getting late.

"Ok. Time's up. You got to tell me. What the hell are we going down to Washington DC for?"

"Religion. Fear of the unknown. Fear as a control mechanism. We're going to show people what happens when they die. We're going to remove the fear of Hell."

"I'm more afraid of Hell than I ever was before. I've seen evidence of Hell. I've seen Hell on Earth. Wait. You know what happens when we die?"

"That wasn't Hell. That was the illusion of Hell. But, yes. I know what happens when we die."

"Tell me. What happens when we die?"

"You repeat this life. You come back as yourself. Trying to do better. Everybody is just trying to do better than they did in their previous incarnation."

"You come back as the same person?"

"Yes. You come back as the same person."

"But, what about the progression of time?"

"Time isn't real. History isn't real. Only what's happening is real."

"The Gnostics kind of said the same thing. Wait. How come- if you're a Catholic- then you have the same beliefs as the Gnostics?"

"I'm not a good Catholic. If I was a good Catholic, then we wouldn't be doing what we're about to be doing. And, we wouldn't be doing what we've been doing before bed every night," she said, smiling her endearing overbite smile, looking up at me with her big brown eyes, laughing a little, and then adding; "The Gnostics are more or less right. They're wrong because they try to cram the truth into a box- just like the Catholics- but, they're right about the nature of the Earthly realm. The only reason we're here is to learn to love one another and to learn to love ourselves and to learn to love the very evil which is torturing and tormenting us. That's the only way to unify. To become what we truly are."

"What are we?"

"We are divine. We are God incarnate. The true God. The Christ. Not the evil one; the lord of lies. It can be difficult to tell them apart."

"That's an understatement," I said.

She said, "Of all the religions in the world; the only important detail is that the divine spark is within each of us. Or, it is except for when it is not. Mostly it is not within us. But, for a lot of us, it is within us."

"You mean the difference between the hylics and pneumatics?" I asked.

"Basically. Yes. That's the only label we have for the phenomena."

"If our souls are supposed to be learning on their own, and attaining enlightenment on their own, then how is it that you can interject and accelerate the process? Why didn't that happen a billion cycles ago, or ten billion cycles before that?" I asked.

"As it turns out, our schizophrenic mother is not quite so far gone as we feared. She's decided- in the final hour of the final cycle- that oblivion is not preferable to humility."

"Is that why you're here, then?" I asked her.

"I certainly believe so," she replied.

"We're going to have to take the dirtbike down to DC," I told her.

"I figured as much."

"We can't take the ARs. We've been putting too much stress on the optics already. We'll have to take the 12 gauge and the lever gun. And the pistols. Show me where this church is."

She found the church on my phone and showed me. It wasn't a church. It was the Washington National Cathedral. I had a sinking feeling when I looked at the images of it. I wanted nothing to do with that place. Just the thought of it was intimidating. It was a massive structure and it had towering pinnacles built on gothic buttresses and expensive stained glass windows. More than ever before, I wanted nothing to do with Washington DC.

Nonetheless, I memorized the roads we would need to get there; along with the secondary and- thirdary...- routes I could use; because the roads I actually needed were blockaded. Or, so the internet would have us believe. The whole city looked impenetrable. But- as much as I would have liked to not even try it; failure was not an option. I believed in our purpose. I believed in Charisma. I had to believe that the evil we were doing was ultimately for a greater good, and by now, I'd seen enough evidence to prove that that was so.

"What exactly are we doing when we get to this church?" I asked.

"The church is the idol. We're going to destroy it."

"How the hell are we going to destroy a church?"

"We're not going to. Angela is."

"How, though?"

"I cannot begin to imagine," Charisma said.

That was my cue to stop asking questions. It was time to go.

The J.B.Hunt driver was still parked on top of that scorpion; and it was still thrashing. I'm sure it would have torn itself apart if it had had more wiggle room. It just didn't. I unloaded the bike and we got on; wearing our bright reflective jackets and carrying our powerful weapons. We each had a bandolier of shells strung on the shoulder opposite the shoulder which the weapons were slung on. She carried 12 gauge slugs and oo buckshot. I carried the 45-70 with some magnum rounds I was lucky enough to have found at the store. Charisma also had to carry Angela on her back. So, her long gun response time would be delayed as a consequence. Too, we wore the oversized bowie knives.

I took the bike over to the four-wheeler pumps and filled it up- pouring in some 2 stroke oil- and then I went back for Charisma and we took off down the road. The traffic was completely backed up in Baltimore, but the interstate was not shut down. I was able to weave my way through; even through the tunnel. Although, it was tight in there. With all the traffic noise, and all the blinding headlights, and with all the screaming sirens and flashing emergency lights, and with multiple helicopters patrolling the skies, and with the structure fires burning in all directions; it was difficult to keep from getting vertigo and I really had no idea what was going on in Baltimore.

But, I'd gotten enough sleep and gotten enough perspective to begin to understand what my priorities were. These common people- most of them hylics- were fighting against the branches of the evil. My fight was against the root of the evil. We were not the same. They didn't need me to stand beside them. They needed me to forge ahead; out into the unknown. And that was what I did. Charisma was the most important thing in the world. Her purpose was my purpose. And I'd been being stupid about it. Which was exactly what she'd been trying to tell me, on multiple occasions.

Still, it hurt to see the things we were seeing. For instance; when we found the cause of the traffic. There was a tanker truck that had- at some point, for some reason- burst into flames. The fire was out, but the smoke was still thick enough to make us gag. The emergency vehicles were on the scene. It looked like the fire trucks had only just recently gotten the blaze extinguished. They were still throwing foam on it. And there were National Guardsmen out there, too. The whole thing was such an awful mess that I couldn't imagine it being cleaned up before morning. A helicopter was circling overhead; searching for dragons with its searchlight. Probably scared witless. And with good reason to be so.

There was a zone of scorched vehicles all around the remains of the tanker; the tanker itself had burned down to scrap metal. The vehicles were also skeletal, and ashy white in color. There were dead bodies everywhere. Some were burned up at their steering wheels, sitting stiff and rigid in their seats, while others were hanging out of their open doors, while others were trying to rescue their children in the back. The little bodies in the back seats; burned up as well.

And all around the area of scorched vehicles, there were vehicles that had been torn apart by a dragon. Or by multiple dragons. Some of the dead bodies had fallen out of the sky. One couple was huddled by the guardrail outside of their car because a corpse had been dropped on its roof. Some of the dead bodies were dismembered inside of their vehicles. And some of them were dismembered outside of their vehicles. When the dragons busted into the cars, they left a characteristic display behind; broken windows, blood, entrails sometimes, and a viciously ravaged corpse, or corpses. The guardsmen were shining flood lights around and unloading automatic weapons into the trees. And it was sketchy because I had to go off the road to get around the wreckage. I was about to pass through the emergency crews' working area when I noticed the guardsmen were carrying nets, at least. That was a good sign. The nets were metallic and they glistened in the floodlights. I didn't actually see a dragon, and I don't think the military did, either.

I was about to make my move to get clear of the scene when I heard a bone-chilling shriek that reminded me of something I'd heard only once before in my life. It was the noise of my truck accident. The noise of metal tearing apart. Except it was coming from the sky. In the spinning searchlight of a helicopter, I got a glimpse of the remains of the dragon. The dragon was mangled and ripped open and spilling out the contents of itself. The helicopter's propellers had broken apart and were flying through the air in all directions. And the helicopter itself was engulfed in flame and dropping.

I goosed my throttle and quit pussy footing around; hearing the over-revved droning of the copter's engine coming apart and feeling the vibration of the impact as the aircraft crashed through the trees and collided with the Earth. All the ground crew had just seen the same thing that I had seen. I'm sure they were wishing that they had their own dirt bikes as I went ripping through their ranks. Out on the other side of the wreckage, the road was wide open. Or, it was for a few miles, at least. Until we got to the on-ramp where the diverted traffic was emerging from. I was able to make it down to Washington DC proper before we ran into further delays. We hit more stopped traffic about two miles north of the spot where I-95 splits off into the beltway.

There was all kinds of open space where the city mowed the grass beside the interstate; so, it didn't make any sense for me to split the lanes or to run the breakdown lane. I just found the area where one guard rail stopped and another began and I jumped out into the grass. I had to blast through a couple creeks; so our boots would be wet for the rest of the night. But, the only real issue was when I hit the metro railway. I couldn't get over the tracks. And I'd be off course to try to follow the tracks to a crossing. So, I had to backtrack and get back on the beltway and run the breakdown lane until I could get off again. But, by then, we were balls deep in the city.

There were police barricades in all directions, but they were mostly unmanned and the ones that were manned just waved back when I waved at them. They had zero interest in us. We weren't demonic dragons. Really, I think they were happy to see us; we were armed, bright orange and reflective, on a bright orange bike, and we were human, and we weren't asking them to save us. We weren't their professional burden. Not that day. We were their compatriots. We were occupying the same hellhole as they were. And that made us friends.

The military was all over the place. The police, too. And the fire trucks and the ambulances. It was all hands on deck. There wasn't anywhere that wasn't lit up by flashing emergency lights. Everywhere you looked, there were soldiers and their trucks and they were hunting the dragons. The dragons, too, could occasionally be seen. But, unfortunately, the dragons weren't stupid. They were always adapting new methods for evading the authorities. Namely; the stick and move strategy familiar to all fighters of all sorts. The dragons realized that if they lingered in one area for too long, then they'd be apprehended. And because the dragons were highly mobile; they'd begun scouring the city for targets of opportunity instead of lingering in high-risk high-reward scenarios. But, at the same time, the dragons had an urge to be destroyed, in order to multiply; so they were always finding ways to off themselves. Such as flying into helicopter blades, or stepping out in front of trains, or by confronting armed citizens. Like ourselves.

We were about a mile from the church when a dragon came after us. It was a small one. But not as small as I would have preferred. Just the right size to possess an advantage in speed. It attacked from behind and I saw its swooping shadow in the street light; its wings tucked in and arched back. My instinct told me to drop a gear and crank the throttle. I looked back over my shoulder and saw that it was descending upon us like a hungry raptor.

I felt a sudden sickness because I had no idea if it was faster than us or not. But we were on a long and open road; a road designed for big city traffic, but empty due to the circumstances. I just kept moving. I could see it was chasing us, and our rate of speed was dangerous in that area, but I didn't want to stop. I didn't want to fight it. Charisma had her pistol on it, but I was keeping ahead to keep it out of her range. We'd be no better off if we killed it and it multiplied. Likely, worse off.

I probably could have lost it by just driving even faster, but I wanted it to think it was gaining on us. I wanted it to follow us. This was a sketchy undertaking because I had to monitor its speed over my shoulder while keeping my eyes on the road ahead of me; making sure I didn't get lost or drive into a parked car or something. I turned off of Massachusetts avenue and onto Wisconsin avenue; but purposefully I went in the opposite direction of the cathedral.

In the distance, I could see what I was looking for. There was a military unit of some sort down there. The dirtbike had a weak little horn on it, but I tooted it for all it was worth. I was uncomfortably close before the soldiers realized we were barreling into their midst. But, to their credit, they understood what was happening immediately and waved us through with urgency; calling to each other and getting themselves into position.

They nailed the procedure. The dragon flew into the net and hit the ground careening; dragging its captors behind it. I stopped the bike and spun it around to watch. The soldiers were happy to have executed their maneuver so perfectly; but they were also in a frenzy to get the pinch points of the net connected and fastened into place. Once they'd done that; the dragon was effectively harmless. It was tangled up and twisted around and its range of movement was almost nothing.

Chapter 10
The Cathedral
I got away from the military before they could start wondering who we were. I circled around on some side street and got back to Massachusetts avenue and then I took that to Wisconsin avenue; moving away from the aforementioned netted dragon. I knew from the satellite images that there was a garden beside the cathedral's parking lot. I drove the dirtbike into there because I figured the plants would give us some cover. I parked under a tree and cut the engine. The city was alive with gunshots and screaming and sirens. A helicopter flew by; beaming a flood light. I looked around. There were definitely some police in the area. Or, police cars, anyways. It was dark in the garden; away from the streetlights. I could see that there were a lot of lights on in the church and I remember thinking, 'This is the apocalypse. That church will be full of people.'

Charisma said, "This is too close. Those towers could fall right over on us."

"There's people inside. We have to warn them. Let's go," I said.

"Yeah. Ok," she agreed.

We went on foot over toward the front entrance but before we got out of the trees, I put my arm out and stopped Charisma. I could see a detail of guards. Secret service looking types. They were peering in our direction. Obviously they'd heard us approaching. But, there was too much happening in that neighborhood; they couldn't focus well enough to spot us or hear us. I pulled Charisma back into the garden, put the bike in neutral in order to push it, and then we left to find someplace better. There was a curving road that took us away from the cathedral and we followed that until we found some good trees to hide in. The trees were on the Catholic school grounds. We were safely- probably- away from the cathedral, but the old church was an imposing structure and it still loomed over our heads to some degree.

"What are we going to do?" she asked me.

"Wait," I said. Then I took my phone out of my pocket and searched for the church's phone number. I took my helmet off and called the number. It rang and somebody answered- a woman- saying, "National cathedral, how can I help you?"

I told her, "You have to evacuate everybody immediately. The cathedral is not safe. Anybody who remains within the cathedral is going to die."

"Why? What is happening?"

I told her- not anticipating the precision of my statement; "It's God's wrath, lady. Do you believe me?"

"Yes. I believe you."

"You're going to evacuate? Everybody?"

"Yes. How much time do we have?"

"Not enough. Do it now. Do it fast."

"Oh. Ok. Thank you. May the lord be with you."

"And also with you," I said; hanging up.

I put my helmet back on as Charisma opened her bag and let Angela free. Angela shook herself and stretched. It looked like she'd been sleeping but I can't imagine how. We watched the cat and the cat kind of watched us. Soon, the sound of a few hundred- or a few thousand- frightened churchgoers could be heard crescendoing in the distance. Angela heard the commotion, too, and I guess she was drawn to it, because she walked off to do her business.

Then we heard automatic weapons firing. Something else had been drawn to the exodus. I don't know how many people were in that church, but it was evidently more than I imagined. Their screams of terror were like the screams of thousands of beetles thrown into a fire. The automatic firearms sang their battle hymn. The screaming was an ungodly chorus.

Soon, panicked parishioners were streaming out into the night. Past our hiding place and undoubtedly in every other direction, too. I wanted to run out toward the massacre- for that's surely what it was; as the cries we had heard could only be the cries of humans being torn limb from limb. The National Guard was arriving on the scene; I could glean as much by the chorus of diesel engines laboring. And the police, too, were descending upon the area. Their lights filled the sky, but they didn't turn on their sirens.

As the slaughter progressed, the authorities weren't firing their weapons. Except for a little bit. And the reports were always accompanied by gut-wrenching screaming. Mostly the authorities were shouting commands at one another. Obviously they were fighting a dragon. Or maybe they were fighting multiple dragons. And my instinct to run out and join the fight was strong; but I'd learned my lesson well. It wasn't my fight. Or, so I was telling myself, right up until a wayward dragon came down into our immediate vicinity; descending upon the helpless crowd as it retreated. I saw by its size that it was a small one, but you couldn't imagine anything more vicious. It was about the size of a big iguana, but it was as deadly as a knife wielding psychopath.

There was a white haired man in a beautiful suit; he'd been driven to the ground. The dragon was perched on his chest and leveraging its tiny body to rip the man's throat out. There was no saving him. The demon already had his throat in its teeth when I stepped on its tail at the base of the spiky tip. At the same instant; I swung my bowie knife and took off the creature's head. But not before the talon of its wing had gripped my arm and sliced through my jacket; cutting into the flesh of my forearm muscle. My flexor carpi ulnaris, specifically.

The pain took a second to hit me and by then I was hiding in the bushes again. My knife; again sheathed. The man's wife was bawling at his side and we all watched as the life went out of his eyes. His throat; ripped ragged and raw. A few seconds later and my arm was burning with the pain of being sliced deep. Alas, I was nihonjin. Or, half nihonjin... I wasn't going to let myself feel how badly the cut hurt. I had my rifle shouldered and the sight trained on the dead demon. The laser light had faded from its eyes and it was giving no indication of impending division.

I could feel my blood dripping into the dirt beneath me. Charisma had already cut a strip of cloth off of her t-shirt and she was working me out of my jacket; trying to wrap up my wound. Then I heard something incongruous; louder than the shouting of the men who were struggling against multiple dragons, and louder than the agonized screaming of the injured and dying. I heard the caterwauling of a domestic feline. Something between the erotic mewling of a cat in heat and the ravenous hissing meowing of a cat when it's fighting.

And then there was a spotlight shining down from above. My first thought was that there was a helicopter up there. Which there was, but this wasn't that. The spotlight wasn't shining down on us, but it was so bright that it might as well have been. I had to look away from where I was aiming; to see what in God's name was happening. There was a blinding white light. The trees above us were shielding us almost completely, but the blinding white light was overwhelming just the same.

I'm sure at least a couple of the church people ran back toward it, thinking it was the rapture. And I'm sure they regretted it when they reached it. I for one was petrified to be as close to it as we were. Right about then, the ground began rumbling beneath our feet and the wind began shrieking in the trees; and, as the branches caught the airflow- all bending in the same direction- the blinding white light seemed to absorb us and everything around us.

The tree trunks became pencil thin shadows in our vision. The school's facilities were blotted out entirely. Even the ground vanished from beneath us.

Maybe the strangest thing that happened was a sudden quietude which engulfed us in the same manner as the light had. The trees were breaking apart under the onslaught of the wind, but suddenly there was this pervasive silence. I could feel the ground trembling beneath us; it was hard to stand up. But I didn't hear the typical derailed freight train cacophony of these earth shattering earthquakes.

Charisma was clinging to me when we noticed Angela come hurrying toward us. Angela's mouth was open, and she was obviously doing her cat noises, but I couldn't hear anything. I thought I had gone deaf. I didn't know what was happening, and I was getting nervous. Charisma got the cat into the backpack and she got the backpack back onto her back, and so I figured, 'Well, okay. I guess that's that, then.' But the light was so bright- and just getting brighter- that I had become kind of paralyzed with fear. That simply wouldn't do. The one thing I was capable of was tugging Charisma along with me as I sat on the dirtbike; with all intention of getting us out of there as soon as possible.

We were seated and ready to go, but the deafeningly bright light wouldn't allow it. I couldn't drive away because I couldn't see anything. It was like being trapped inside of a lightbulb. Every second was more alarming than the second before and by the end, I was praying for it to stop. And then, as if in answer to my prayers; the aggressive luminescence- quite abruptly- dissipated and disappeared.

The roaring of the wind again filled my ears. My vision was returning slowly. The straining trees were exposing the heavens. The fracturing earth was urging me to flee. And, as I looked around, trying to see again, the first thing I realized was that the pinnacles and buttresses which had moments before been looming over us; these were now nowhere to be found. I didn't care. I could see again. I kicked the engine to life, and shot out onto the road. Trying to get my bearings.

I was still on the catholic school service road, and I wanted to go away from this area, so I tried to take a left at the T. But, when I did so, I found myself confronted by the figure of man. It wasn't a man. It was black, finely pixelated, glistening with sparkles, and definitively humanoid. Standing on two legs, and singular. I slowed down out of apprehension before realizing this was some sort of a standoff. I faked right and cut left, but the movement of the humanoid was instantaneous and effortless. It repositioned itself exactly where I was heading toward. I had to stop or drive into it. I stopped. And I watched it watching us. It didn't have eyes, but I could feel its menace crawling on my skin like a big army of small ants. I made one more attempt to psyche it out and rip past it, but it again anticipated me and again placed itself directly in my course; so I instead grabbed the clutch, twisted the throttle, let out the clutch, spun the tire, pivoted on my foot, and did a 180; rushing out of there.

All I wanted was to get away from this place. My heart was racing. The cathedral was completely gone. The wind was blowing garbage and tree branches and dirt all over. Frightened and confused people were scurrying hither and thither. And through the police lights I could see an orange glow where the cathedral used to be. I knew exactly what that was and I knew I didn't want to be near it. I didn't want to fight. I wanted to run. I felt drained and vulnerable.

I went left on Wisconsin, trying to get back to Massachusetts. But, again, I found myself confronted by the black humanoid figure. And beside this black humanoid figure was a second humanoid figure. They stood straight and motionless; side by side. I didn't have a lot of options. I figured maybe a double fake could get me by them. But it was hopeless, because they could move without moving. The spectors repositioned themselves as if independent of the laws of physics. Which, of course, they were. I couldn't try a triple fake because the bike would just fall over from lack of stability. So, I didn't try another fake at all. I just blew a 180 and found myself facing the chaos.

There was a lot to see, but my eyes took it all in in a second: About a half dozen cop cars. Their lights; turning half the scene purple. The other half of the scene was distinctly orange; with the glow of the fires of Hell rising out of a strangely confined crater where the cathedral used to be. There were two or three troop transport trucks. And an assortment of private vehicles; some of which were moving around me. Those were chauffeur looking cars and I guess they were trying to find their people. Well-dressed churchgoers could be seen all over the place. They were cowering in the bushes, or by the cop cars. They were spreading out slowly, or quickly. Some ran and some wandered. Some were covered in blood. Some were nursing grotesque injuries. Some were kneeling by their dead or dying companions. Some were carrying their dead or dying companions. There were a couple dragons trapped in a couple nets. And the guardsmen were firing their rifles into the sky; trying to shoot a third dragon out of the air. That third dragon was the only combat effective dragon I could see. But, it felt like there could be others.

I'd done this four times now. Although, this was hairier than normal as the danger was compounded by the chaos and the flying dragons on the loose. I knew there'd be a new archon crawling out of that Hell hole. I didn't want to find out what it was. I didn't want to fight whatever it was. I wanted to run. I eyeballed a course through the obstacles and bobbed and weaved my way to the other side of the craziness; only noticing the roiling orange and red lava pit in passing; feeling its heat, but not looking much at it. Once I was beyond the scene, I twisted the throttle and- thinking I was clear- began accelerating; hoping to escape.

Like a shimmering black blur; the spectors appeared from behind, moved past us, and positioned themselves directly in front of us. Slamming on my brakes, I tried to dip around them, but they were immediately in my way again and all I could do was come to a complete stop. I almost pulled my gun on them but even in the moment I knew that would be pointless. These things weren't material. There'd be nothing to shoot. And besides, as far as I knew they could move faster than a bullet.

It was quieter where we were right then and they spoke to us. Or, one of them did. I don't know how I knew which one was speaking. But it was the one on the left. It had an electronic voice. A distorted and fragmented voice. Like a bluetooth headset that's too far from the phone. And it sounded insectile. Even though, obviously, insects don't speak. It was alien, in tone and command of language. It said; 'Return. Confront your creation.'

I had made something of a tradition out of fighting the archons as they came out of Hell. But, I had been hoping to bypass that step of the ritual on this occasion. Still, I wasn't going to argue with these things. The spectors. I knew I was in the presence of some profound entity. I was raised to respect authority and if this wasn't authority then I don't know what is. And it was a simple enough command. Go fight the archon. I'd fought enough of the damn things already. This was just one more.

I put the kickstand down and we got off of the bike. I kept my eyes on the spectors. They were standing still and watching us from faces that didn't have eyes to see with. Like; the one had spoken from a face that didn't have a mouth to speak with. I could hear the screaming coming from behind us, but we were distant enough and bewildered enough to be moving with less urgency than was appropriate. Charisma had the shotgun ready without being told. And I readied my 45-70. I could see the streets were filling with people. Besides the soldiers, the cops, and church people; a new contingent had arrived. These were a mob of common folk. Maybe fifty of them. It was a relief to see them. Realistically, every person on the scene decreased the odds of us being torn apart.

The crowd had sort of gathered together, and I remember thinking, 'They should probably spread out.' But by then, it was already too late.

From our perspective, there were buildings between us and the archon. But we could see much of the crowd suddenly turn and flee in terror. I remember we saw a dragon come down and lift a person up into the sky and nobody even noticed. The ground shook beneath us at the thudding of heavy footfalls. Hurried footfalls.

Many men held fast, and they fired their rifles. Charisma and I ran to get an angle and to get a shot. Then our shot came to us. Soldiers, cops, and civilians alike; they were firing their weapons into this thing. They hadn't had enough time, though. Suddenly the creature was upon the dispersing crowd. I was already firing into the behemoth as I got my first glimpse as to what it actually was.

It was a three headed creature. Not a dog, but doggish. And it was colossal. Its height and width were that of a fully grown elm tree. Its skin was like black snake skin. Its tail was long and whip-like, but there weren't any spikes or stingers on it, at least. Its six eyes were like laser light; like the dragons'. And its mouths were big enough to fit multiple humans into a single bite, and -sadly- it was doing just that. The people were all falling all over each other; trying to get away. The teeth of the heads were canine, but the canine teeth were about a foot long. And black. It had black teeth. And black claws, for that matter. Claws that were sharp but short. All over its body, the powerful muscles were well defined; and its posture was more like a pitbull than like a rottweiler. The snouts of it were lengthy, but also blunted. More like a rottweiler than like a pitbull. But again, it wasn't a dog. It was a demon. It was more reptilian than mammalian. There were boney ridges on the heads; at the brow and ears and jaw lines. These ridges would prove quite capable of deflecting bullets.

As the people ran away around us; we aimed and fired as carefully as we could. But it was hard; because the beast's snouts were down in the crowd of those who had fallen when they were trying to flee, or fight. Although, thankfully the cranial regions of the thing's skulls were elevated above the humans it was devouring.

At the same time; the dragon- there was only one, I guess- came down and it started thrashing about wildly. I think this was when the most friendly fire casualties occurred. It was difficult to follow the motions of the dragons. They were wildly lethal creatures.

This dragon was medium sized. I got the impression it was blocking off these people's retreat on purpose. Then, after taking more bullets then it cared to, the dragon lifted a human into the sky and flew away to God knows where.

A lot of people had fired a lot of bullets into the three-headed monster; ourselves included. And one of the skulls- the center skull- had gone limp and dead. But this thing had three heads. These archons; their heads were their weakness. This beast had three heads. It'd need to be disabled three times. And even then, it'd still just multiply.

I was reloading, and the three-headed dog lizard- or, two-headed dog lizard now- had literally chewed up everybody in its vicinity. Interestingly; it didn't swallow them. It just crushed them up, spit them out, and left them dead and dying at its feet. My family had a pug that did this same thing to a bathtub full of baby chicks, one time, when I was little.

The creature- a cerberus, as I would come to learn it is called; the cerberus turned its four vibrant red eyes on us. The dead limp head in the center had a long black tongue lolling out of it, the light had gone out of the dead head's eyes, and it bounced around lifelessly whenever the creature moved.

We were the target now, it seemed. Few others remained to defy it. We were plugging its faces with 45-70 magnum and 12 gauge slugs; but it wasn't doing us any good. The gargantuan creature came bounding toward us, and I thought we were going to die. We both just kept shooting. And then we heard and saw a searing combustion streaking through the sky.

The cerberus heard it, too, because it forgot about us and stopped and turned to see what was happening. Several rockets hit the beast heads on. The force of the blasts- luckily- propelled the creature and the shrapnel into some buildings and away from us. But, still. These were powerful rockets exploding in our immediate vicinity. The experience was concussive and hot and if we hadn't been wearing helmets and fire retardant jackets and denim jeans and leather boots; then we would have been burned up pretty badly, I imagine. As it was, we were both blown off our feet and thrown out onto the pavement.

I got up and helped Charisma to stand. We immediately began reloading from our bandoliers. The attack helicopter had circled back and positioned itself above the cerberus. We couldn't see what was happening with the monster because the rockets had launched it through the side of and into the building from which it had first emerged from behind. What we could see was that the attack helicopter had commenced to lay into the demonic monster with its minigun. Presumably trying to sufficiently chew up the body in order to disable the contents of its interior.

I was relieved to see that, but it was a short lived relief. There was a lot of light in the area; mostly from the lava pit, but also from the sirens and the street lights. I saw that as soon as the helicopter opened up with its miniguns, a dragon came down and flung itself into the helicopter's main propeller. I was just getting my hearing back from the explosions, and- beneath the ringing in my ears- I heard the shrieking of the propeller blades breaking apart and then the whining of the over-revving engine. The helicopter was only at about 50 yards altitude when it proceeded to tailspin and plummet the short distance to the Earth; coming down- through sheer bad luck- directly into the lava pit;

disappearing into a brightly flaring torch of white hot fire that reached straight up into the sky.

I pulled Charisma away with me. We slung our long guns over our backs and hurried to the bike. It wasn't far off. We got on and I kicked it to life. I didn't hesitate to speed away; filtering through the dispersing bystanders. The only thought in my mind was to get back on Massachusetts avenue. It took a minute to find the way, and then we were there. I looked around for the spectors. And I wasn't surprised when I saw them. They locked their rate of movement in unison with our speed, and hovered in the sky just out ahead of us. I guess so we could all see each other good.

I shouted at them, "Are you satisfied?"

They did not reply. But I suppose they were, because they vanished just an instant later. I was happy to see them go, but that feeling didn't last long; because no sooner had they gone than the streetlights cast the shadow of a dragon coming down at us. That was the only warning I needed. I rode off as fast as I could. This was basically the exact same thing that had happened on the way in. But Charisma was tapping my shoulder, saying, "Slow down! I want to blast it!"

I didn't question her reasoning, or her motives, or her logic. I kind of understood. Things had changed. We'd gotten lucky the first time. If we didn't take it out, and then we got slowed down down the road; then it may well take us out thereafter. But, still, it was a delicate procedure. I had to watch over my shoulder. I had to blip the throttle just right and stay at just the right speed, and be prepared for changes in the dragon's speed, and watch the road for other vehicles; of which there were none. But, there was all kinds of trash blowing about. And barricades erected and emergency vehicles parked in weird places.

I happened to look back at the exact moment that Charisma was pulling the trigger on her 500 magnum. The dragon had been an intimidating spectacle up until that moment. Its mouth had been wide open and its teeth were reaching for us. The bullet had different ideas. It only took one. Which in itself was remarkable; but that single bullet punched through the roof of the mouth and continued in through the soft spot at the center of its forehead. The laser red light of its eyes flickered out as the dragon crashed into the pavement and rolled into a mess of wings and legs and tail. I just kept going. I didn't need a personal invitation. All I wanted was to get back to my truck. Washington DC had sucked worse than I had thought it would, and by a lot, too.

I knew the quickest way out would be to blow by the barricaded on-ramp and push through the inevitable traffic jam. The barricades were unmanned. That one in particular didn't even have an emergency vehicle stationed at it. The traffic jam on the beltway was like a world unto itself. Those vehicles weren't going anywhere. There were campfires by the guardrails in a couple places, and I kept having to cut around piles of random belongings in spots where people were cleaning out their cars and departing on foot. No place was safe and there were men with rifles and shotguns everywhere you looked. I felt so bad for everybody there. They must have been so scared. Many of them would be dead before long. I wondered what I would do if I were them. I guess I might have hid in my trunk. Or walked out into the trees. There was no way to know if things were going to get better or worse.

Further down the road, at the next exit, I saw there were city buses waiting to take the stranded motorists to safety. That traffic jam seemed endless and unabating. I jumped off the road and into the grass when I was able to, but, leaving the city there was a lot of wilderness and I kept getting into bad situations with steep declines and chasms and rivers and ravines and after the second time backtracking, I decided to just stay on the pavement and push through the old fashioned way. I began expecting the traffic jam to carry on forever but eventually we found the cause of it. Something had happened at high speeds. There were some cars that had flipped out into the trees and spun out into the railings. And there were some cars that had been assaulted by dragons. Most of the cars at the front of the jam were unoccupied. A lot of those vehicles were undamaged. The owners- I guess- had taken off on foot. Meanwhile, some of them had somehow survived the attack and were just waiting patiently in the carnage; staring as we went by. There were dead bodies splattered all over everything. Everywhere I looked; I saw another corpse. It seemed like I hated the dragons more and more with every hour that went by. Except, they were demons. And I already hated demons as much as I could possibly hate anything. The dragons were just the worst of them. Or so I hoped.

Chapter 11
The Shadow of Death
The roads were empty for about half of the drive back north. Then we found the next traffic jam at about the same time as we found the Baltimore city limits. I pushed through that mess until we got to the tunnels. Unfortunately, all the tunnels were closed. The signs didn't tell us the tunnels were closed. The signs just said, 'Stay home, stay safe.' The tunnels weren't shut off in any way that I could possibly get through. They had iron grates over the entrances. My truck was less than two miles away but I was forced to make a 20 mile detour.

I turned around and drove southbound in the northbound lanes until I found the gap in the median for the emergency vehicles to change direction at. There, I got into the southbound traffic jam- which was the same traffic jam from earlier. I made my way toward I-695. As always, Charisma clung to me desperately. I-695, too, was completely jammed up. Not all the way. Just until the nearest massacre. Which was about 3 miles down the road.

I was noticing a trend. This massacre was about the same as the last one. A few crashed cars. About a dozen cars with their windows smashed open. Dead bodies everywhere; all ripped apart to some degree. Some of the cars were still running. And I guess the emergency crews had just given up. Maybe they were dead. Maybe they were scared. I don't know where they were, but they weren't there.

It was just a bad night for everybody. Civilization- for that one evening- had simply collapsed. There were some bystanders at that site, and they tried to approach me- begging me for help; but there was nothing I could do for them. And even if I could help; we had our purposes to attend to. The one interesting thing about where we were was the dragon carcass with its head shot to hell. The carcass was split open, and its contents had dispersed into the wind.

I saw two more basically identical scenes, but I didn't see any more dragons. Thank God. I did see a scorpion, though. Back on I-95; north of the tunnels. It was crawling over the wreckage there. Looking for somebody to kill. But it had already killed the few that it could and no others were anywhere to be found; despite the abundance of abandoned cars and trucks. That scorpion was a small one; maybe like the size of a Harley. And when it saw us, it definitely took a run at us; climbing over cars like they weren't even there. But I'd been slipping through the stalled out traffic all night long and I could move faster than the arachnid. We were out of there before it even got close; arriving at the tractor about 30 minutes before the sun came up. The J.B.Hunt guy and his scorpion were gone.

That was easily the worst day of my life. Worse even than the day of my wreck. By far, really. Nobody had died on the day of my wreck. Now, the death toll was becoming like that of a plague. I'd seen so much death with my own two eyes, and that was just a small fraction of the universal total. I sort of didn't care. I had cared all my caring. I know Charisma felt it, too. We were hollow. And we were hungry. We were happy to eat. We were happy to shower. We were happy to make love. We were happy to fall asleep. We were happy to be alive.

I'd made a point to not ask Charisma about what would come next. I wanted to get some good sleep without puzzling out details every time my eyes opened. When we woke up, we made love again. And we ate cereal with almond milk. And when I felt like I was ready- after I'd had some coffee- I told her; "Alright. Lay it on me."

"Lay what on you?" She asked. Not understanding the expression.

"Tell me what comes next."

She sighed and said, "The profit motive."

"What?" I asked.

"The incentive to prioritize generating revenue over working toward the betterment of the human race. Or mother Earth, for that matter. The necessity of turning a dollar at any and all costs. No matter who or what it hurts."

"Right. Ok. But. Like. Where do we have to go?"

"Animas, New Mexico."

That took me by surprise. New Mexico was on the other side of the country. I had mixed feelings about going. Firstly, it was going to be expensive; buying the diesel to get us out there. Secondly; we barely made it from Washington DC to Baltimore on a dirtbike. I couldn't imagine how we'd ever get the rig out to New Mexico. Thirdly, I kind of liked the idea. If we could make it out west, then it meant that the roads were open. It meant we weren't actively combating the demons. Or, at least, for all the time we were driving, we wouldn't be fighting; I mean. That sounded good.

I didn't expect it would be easy to get out there. I didn't know what to expect. I knew we didn't have an option. Looking at the map, I could see there was no decent way out of Baltimore. No simple way out. I was going to have to carve my own way out. What I actually did was get on the radio and talk to the other guys about how they intended to get out. I learned- from talking with the truckers on the CB and from looking at my phone, too; the dragons were beginning to attack people in their homes. The bigger ones were good at breaking down doors and were finding their way into apartment buildings; where they'd force the inhabitants into the streets; only to attack them when they were out in the open. Out in the suburbs the dragons were like door to door salesmen; dealing death. Also, for obvious reasons, the dragons were developing a tendency to attack wherever the scorpions were wandering around at.

There was a rumor that the dragons- and all the other demons- were vulnerable to acid. But the infrastructure to utilize that information wasn't in place yet; I knew. Because if there'd been acid to fight them with then the government would have used it down in DC the night before. As it turned out- later on- acid would become the primary weapon in the fight against the demons.

Honestly, I didn't want to leave the truck stop. It was relatively safe. And I felt like I belonged there. But, no, we had to go. The first thing I did was examine the map very carefully. I realized I had one advantage because I was off of the interstate. Normally, the interstate was where I wanted to be, but there was nothing normal about any of this, so...

My advantage- being not trapped in a jam- was that I could take the small roads over to route 40 and I could take route 40 out of the city. For whatever reason, that road was orange, as opposed to red or red and white. Orange meant we could use it. Every other road in and out was red or red and white. I guess the city figured it could only realistically keep one road open and that was the one without any major bridges or tunnels on it.

There actually was a low bridge between me and route 40, but the truckers knew a way to get around it. All that was left to do was to fill up the tank on the bike and then quit wasting time and go. I'd filled up the tractor when we pulled into the truck stop.

As we left the city, I was happy to be going. Baltimore was never the nicest place in the world, but it didn't used to smell like a dog food factory. We couldn't prevent the stench of rotting bodies from coming in through the air vents.

But, other than that, there was actually a lot of hopeful activity. The red cross had set up emergency medical shelters and there was a soup kitchen right beside those. And there were coroners out there collecting the bodies; scooping the dead into body bags and filling their black vans with the black bags. I was glad to see that there were still helicopters in the sky. Usually troop carriers. They were always flying by at about 400 mph. Apparently, they'd figured out how vulnerable they were and didn't care to linger in the sky too long.

Traveling went basically how one might imagine. The weirdest thing was staying off the interstates. That was a constant hassle. And it involved a lot of backtracking and a lot of rerouting. However, the difficulties nearly completely vanished west of the Mississippi. I always got the sensation of being inside a computer game when I was out on the road. Because the weather would change at the state borders; and nobody could explain that except to admit that the world was programmed to be like that. And different states had their own unique asshole driving habits; which I won't get into here. And each state had a slightly different atmosphere- as in moisture content and temperature and even just the odor; and the atmosphere always changed right at the border. Just like the weather. Even the vibe of each state was different; some were chill and some were not. But maybe that was just politics.

Nonetheless; I felt like we were in a computer program then as much as ever. Except it seemed like the programming had been completely reprogrammed. All the parameters were unfamiliar. We lived in an unfamiliar world in those days. But the programmers hadn't altered the Mississippi river factor. Once you crossed it, you were on a different server. Just like the old days.

Everything about the experience was bizarre. Not just because we were traversing a nightmarish hellscape. The even weirder thing was how people had suddenly improved. People were smarter. People were nicer. People were friendlier. Everybody was super polite to one another, and we all seemed to care about each other in an authentic kind of way. Partly because we were united against the common enemy, but equally because Charisma's scheme was the genuine article. She'd overhauled existence. And I'd helped. We all knew there was no going back. Even the godless had felt the light of Christ in their hearts.

Now, I have to stop and ask myself if it's worth it to detail every time Charisma and Angela and I came upon a random horror show at a random square on the map. I don't think I could possibly describe all the times we got delayed by the aftermath of a dragon attack. It was always the dragons that had done it. If you want to visualize how it was; just imagine every feasible emergency crew appearing in every direction, at all times, and also there's soldiers and they've got tanks and trucks and helicopters and stuff.

I don't think I could do the narrative justice without describing every time we had to stop and fight, though. There were corpses all over the place for the first thousand miles. Every mile was a slog and there was a lot of 'two steps forward, one step back.' But we only had to shoot our way out of two situations on our way to Animas. And I can't leave those stories out. Not that they're any more or less interesting than any of the other confrontations in this book. Just two more dragon attacks we wandered into.

I don't know at what point mortal danger becomes mundane. I was beginning to realize that- ultimately- the demons' raison d'etre was to kill helpless individuals; not heavily armed individuals. The big ones could be terribly difficult to neutralize, but the small ones went down pretty reliably. And, yeah, it was a bitch when they multiplied; but if you had enough patience, then you could eliminate all of their divisions, as well. So, that was what we tried to do, whenever possible.

We took a different route than I would have preferred but it was important to stay out of the mountain ranges because if we lost the interstate in a mountainous area, then there may be no way to detour without serious- or possibly impossible- backtracking. But that meant putting us into places where I knew it was stupid to go there. Namely, Cincinnati. We drove around Cincinnati for half of the day on our second night out. It took a full night just to get that far.

Cincinnati had had a hard time. There was almost no National Guard presence. But the civilians seemed to have taken to it well enough. Gnosis was everywhere and had organized militias wherever they were. There were militias out patrolling- thousands of armed men; but they were often neglecting to obliterate the fledglings, and the dragons just kept multiplying. It was while detouring around the city- constantly rerouting around the ruins- that we encountered our first fight of that particular drive.

It was as depressing as it was frightening. We couldn't back out of it, because this was our only way to escape the city. I'd seen every other road in the place. This was it. We were right where route 50 bends away from the river. There'd been no way over the river; both bridges were clogged. But, now there was hell between us and the way out. We encountered a minor contingent of the local militia which had been caught off guard; I think they were eating, or sleeping. I don't know. They'd been operating a guard station and checkpoint there. They'd been come down on by a squadron of dragons. And they were getting tore up when we arrived on scene. But we had the ARs in arm's reach, and we happened to be on a curve on a hill with some houses between us and the slaughter.

The street lights were on but the night was dark. I remember seeing bats flying around, and wondering if they were tiny dragons and despairing to think the things could get so small. Thankfully, that was not so. They were in fact just bats. Charisma put Angela in her bag and we grabbed our guns. On a hunch- having eyeballed an impromptu pillbox- I brought my katana, as well. We crept out of the truck- leaving the doors open to be quiet- and we got over to a wooden staircase that was built above a rock partition and back stoop. This was as good of cover as we could hope for and it offered the exact vantage point we needed. We were staring into a slaughter. A few militiamen had had time to fight back, but not enough of them and not enough time.

Charisma and I found ourselves with no choice but to fire into the melee. It wasn't long shooting. We were right on top of them. The dragons- we'd observed- had a tendency to stop flailing around right when they were making their kills. Usually; this was when they were ripping out somebody's throat, or wrenching off somebody's skull, or tearing open somebody's chest. Those instances were when it became possible to hit the target. Or, that was how we took out the first two. Two or three good headshots and they went down. Body shots were useless.

After the first two dropped, the second two realized what was happening. I remembered my mother's words, 'Don't fight the kami. Guide the kami.' In an empty minded instant I realized that I was the kami. The dragons leapt off of the ground, beat their wings a couple times, and guided themselves directly into a hail of bullets. "Put your gun down! Hide down there!" I shouted at Charisma. We'd taken out one but the other was coming right for us. I happened to notice the militiamen lifting their weapons to fire at the remaining dragon, and that meant they were actually firing at us.

We'd taken cover down behind the stone wall. I drew my sword. Bullets were colliding with the house we were trespassing on. The beating of the wings gave away the dragon's position and I was ready when it came through the gap between the steps, the wall, and the house. I cried out, "Kiai!" and brought the sword down clean across the neck before the rest of the body could make it through. The head dropped off and the body fell still immediately. There'd been four dragons. Now there were probably about 40 or 80, or more. Charisma and I knew better than to waste a second.

We emptied our bullets into the dragon that was where we were, and then we went out to the other that had flown toward us. There, we reloaded and emptied our bullets into that one, also. The survivors were doing the same close by. I couldn't see how they were doing, but I just had to trust them. So many firearms discharging in unison created a sonic assault on one's senses.

I handed my rifle to Charisma and shouted, "Love. Take the guns to the truck. Bring back the sledge hammer and the ax." "Ok, love," she said. As she went away; I got to work. The katana was the wrong tool for these beasts, but I made do. I cut the bullet shredded dragon open; down along the length of it. Spilling the writhing spheres, which were the curled up divisions. It was weird how the creatures had no blood or fluid of any sort.

I cut the little ones all to pieces as they were unfurling, but some had unfurled before I could get to them. A couple of the dragons- wisely- took to the sky rather than lashing out at me; those disappeared into the shadows. The militia had lost some demons to the sky, also, I noticed. Other demons did, in fact, lash out at me. I found myself jumping around like a monkey as I slashed and chopped; but I didn't get eliminated, so, I guess I did alright.

I was about finished when Charisma returned with the sledge and the ax. I sheathed and slung my sword, took the sledge- leaving her with the ax- and said; "These ones will multiply again. Make sure they don't." It was so obvious it sounded stupid, and I felt bad for talking down to a woman who was obviously smarter than I was.

I took the sledge over to the other one that had attacked us at the stairs. I found myself unsheathing my sword again, because there, too, some of the minor dragons had already bloomed. I chopped up the ones that were a threat, and started smashing the ones that were unfurling. I'd suspected the sledge would be good for this and I wasn't disappointed. The sledge would've been a good tool for Charisma but she was way too small to swing it. The entire process took about twenty minutes before we were finished. All the while we were expecting the escapees to return, but they did not. They knew their most powerful asset was dispersal.

That was about the end of that. A few militiamen thanked us and then we left. Something fortuitous happened down the road, though. Before we even got out of Ohio. Fortuitous for us, not for the dead men.

A small convoy of soldiers had been attacked, and apparently devastated; sustaining 100 percent fatalities. When we got there, there was nothing but silence, bullet holes, shell casings, totalled trucks, and three hollow dragon husks. I knew the demons could return at any second, so I didn't waste time. I ignored the troop carrier and ransacked the supply truck, which was on its side. I found a case of MREs and gave that to Charisma to throw up into the tractor. I found an M2 Browning and bungeed it to the catwalk; which wasn't easy. I found an M72 light armor weapon; the case was labeled, or else I wouldn't have known what it was and overlooked it. There were XM7 rifles all over the place; and all equipped with the best Trijicon optics. A couple had M203 grenade launchers on them. I took two of those and grabbed all the magazines I could find. I also found an XM250; still in its case. These were cutting edge weapons and they fired unfamiliar 6.8 mm bullets. Bullets which I was able to find several cases of; along with cases of 50 caliber rounds, 40mm grenades, and 66mm rockets.

There was dust and grit all over that stuff, and Charisma wasn't happy when I tossed it on our nice clean bed, but I was in a hurry and didn't have time to stow it. Not that I had space to stow anything; not until we reorganized things. We'd about maxed out our storage capacity.

I was in a different headspace when we left that place. Sorry to say- at the time- I'd hardly noticed the bloody and mangled remains of dead guardsmen, or even thought twice about them. Then, after we left, all I could think about was that I now possessed, not one, not two, not three, but four automatic rifles. Plus, a rocket launcher and two grenade launchers. Maybe I haven't mentioned this, but I was always something of a weapons enthusiast and what had just occurred was basically the impossible wet dream I had never dared to dream would come true coming true.

I couldn't even process the boon we'd just blundered into. Charisma didn't need to be told to acclimate herself to the new equipment. I don't know how Charisma learned guns and shooting, but I guess she just figured it out from studying her phone because she was watching an M203 tutorial while I was basically delirious from a heady concoction of terror and excitement.

I forgot about the weapons as I reflected on the fact that the dragons had decimated an army platoon back there. There was nothing to stop them from doing the same to us. At any minute they could come down on the tractor and tear it apart and tear us out and tear us apart. Maybe we could defend ourselves. Maybe not. I could feel the accumulation of fear wearing me down; the exponential depletion of my reserve of courage. But, in the same moment that I was feeling at my lowest; I found an inner strength that I hadn't known was there. It sounds trite, but I knew it was the spirit of my ancestors. It was the essence of the people of the land of tears. It was the rising sun. It was Fukushima. It was Hiroshima and Nagasaki. It was kamikaze. It was banzai. It was seppuku. It was bushido. It was kokoro. It was karate. It was Zen. It was Shinto. And after that moment, I swear, I never felt afraid again. Not even once. Not even a little.

Still, we were expecting dragons; so it was kind of a surprise when we came upon a scorpion. It was a big one. As big as the first one that had crawled out of hell. Maybe bigger. We were coming out of Louisville, on I-64. Pulling into a truck stop town called Carefree. "These scorpions sure seem to like truck stops," I said. Charisma said, "It's the programming. Even now. Even still. Programming." The scorpion was raising hell; running around as fast as it could, trampling over cars and smashing up trucks and buildings. People were taking shots at it with rifles, shotguns, and pistols; but it was just too big for that shit. They'd have to put a twelve gauge right in its face, like Charisma did in Philadelphia.

It was a desperate and out of control situation. There'd been fatalities there. There were bodies split in half by pincers and bodies taken out by venom. Right when we got there the scorpion had swung around and stung one guy who I guess had thought he was out of reach. An old timer, who couldn't even stand up straight. He looked down to reload and when he looked back up; the scorpion's stinger was in his chest; pumping redundant venom. Although, I think the scorpion was getting frustrated, because it was taking a lot of bullets and it wasn't snatching the last few guys so easily. They were ducking and weaving and hiding and running.

I had pulled over to the curb and set the brakes. We were watching this happening out in front of the Pilot. There was extensive truck parking on both sides of the road; plus, a maintenance facility and a gas station for four-wheelers as well as other various truck stop area facilities. Charisma said, "Hold on. I got this." She put Angela into her bag and jumped out of the truck with the XM7. I took the other XM7, grabbed my katana, and followed behind her.

Charisma popped three suppressed shots into the scorpion to get its attention; these guns had suppressors on them. When the demonic monster turned to face her, it charged; she thumped the 40mm grenade into its face and the thing exploded; a fiery blast obliterating the front half of it. The contents of it- its divisions- were thrown all over the place.

Charisma charged into the fray and I followed close behind. We began dumping all the bullets we had into all the scorpions we could find; trying not to be wasteful. The divisions had been thrown further than I would have guessed possible. A lot of them ran out into the trees; presumably to move to different areas. Some of them survived the bullets and became combat effective in minimal time. I found myself fighting one with the katana when our magazines were empty. Now that the biggest arachnids had been reduced, and everybody's bullets were about spent; the other truckers were using blunt objects to finish the work. They had baseball bats and tire irons and steel pipes. Charisma returned our rifles and brought me the sledge. There was nothing better for the small ones. In about 20 minutes, it was over. Many had gotten away. Most had gotten destroyed.

After that, we were able to fuel up, and I parked in a corner where hopefully nobody would try to steal my automatic 50 caliber. We ate, we showered, we made love, we slept, we woke up, we had breakfast, we researched and examined and dryfired the weaponry we'd acquired, I mounted the 50 cal tripod to the frame- not the gun, just the tripod- using some clamps and wire I had bought from inside, and then we got back on the road.

It wasn't easy going to get anywhere, as I've previously stated. It took a lot of time just to come as far as we had. But the next few days of travel were relatively uneventful. West of the Mississippi, they were keeping the roads open. A couple of the bigger cities had been attacked by the demons, but we always found a way through. Mostly it was like going a week back in time. Experiencing the relative serenity of ordinary modern civilization.

It wasn't until the day of our arrival at Animas- in the morning time, before we set out- that I actually asked

Charisma what she had in mind for that place. She informed me; we weren't actually going anywhere near the town. Animas was just the only town that was out in that area. We were evidently going to an abandoned mine shaft. Furthermore, we weren't just going to it; we were going down into it.

I was mostly excited to go south of I-10. There's always some gorgeous country down there. But I asked her, "How did you get this information?" and she said, "Oh, I have my ways…" and then she leaned over and shoved her tongue down my throat. I don't even know why I asked. I didn't actually want to know.

We got out into the country and found where we wanted to park using the GPS device I had bought on the day I met Charisma. She had an uncanny ability to locate specific points on the map, but I guess that was because she was a sailor. Or maybe it was because she was superhuman. I don't know which. We unloaded the dirt bike at first light and I was reluctant to leave the truck on the side of the road like that, but we were out in the middle of nothing. It was extremely unlikely anybody would pass by and even if they did and even if they had designs on jacking our stuff; they would probably think somebody was sleeping inside of there.

There were craggy mountains in every direction. These were defiantly jagged while simultaneously subtly windswept. The whole landscape was delicately windswept to the north. We used a pair of bolt cutters to get through the gate that let us out onto the Bureau of Land Management property and then we rode the dirt bike out into the wilderness. For weaponry, we carried our pistols and our bowie knives. I wore a camelbak, so we wouldn't get dehydrated. Charisma wore her cat on her back. We had on shorts and tank tops and left the helmets behind.

There were insane cactuses out there; everything had spikes on it. There were squat mounds covered in spikes, there were lanky shrubs covered in spikes, there were spiky balls strewn about, there were stunted trees covered in spikes, there were prickly pears growing in profusion. And I had to drive extremely carefully in order to not hit the wrong plant and blow a tire. We were following an old road, but it hadn't been used for decades. All around us, the ground was bespeckled with quartz crystals; about the size of Charisma's hand. There were millions of them, just strewn about on the surface. I couldn't fathom how they came to be there. The plants that grew looked like they came from an alien planet and stood out dramatically against the barren desert. The sun was soon blazing, and the only shade was when we passed by the occasional mountain; most of which were more like massive rocky outcroppings than actual mountains; although, some were quite mountainous indeed.

The mouth of the mine didn't look like anything at all. Charisma spotted it easily, but I had to stare where she was pointing at in order to separate the squarish hole from the rock formations. But, I was relieved to find that we were at an actual mine, and not like; a bat cave or a hippie spelunking pit or something. We got off of the bike and Charisma let the cat out onto the ground; leaving the backpack on the handlebars. We put our headlamps on and the cat followed behind us as we reluctantly approached the entryway.

The old road went right up to the hole. There was no sign posted or anything. But the rail tracks came out into the open, so you could tell what it was by that. And by the wooden posts supporting the tunnel. At that moment, there was nothing I wanted to do less than to put myself down into whatever was in there. But, we had no choice. As it turned out, the ceiling was low- for me- but the going was easy. The worst of it was nearer to the top. That's where the cobwebs were. We had to use our knives to clear them.

The cobwebs were oppressive but I didn't actually see any spiders. After the cobwebs, then came the bats. There were about a million of them, but they were tiny and didn't bother us. I guess they'd eaten all the spiders. We kept our lights pointed at the ground and didn't make any loud noises or sudden movements. The cat, I'm sure, was tempted to grab one of the winged mammals, but she was on her best behavior. On the way down, anyway, she was.

We walked down that mine for maybe twenty minutes, before we got to the end of it. It wasn't really the end. It was just where it had collapsed. I didn't know what to think of it, but Charisma did. She wasn't in a good mood. She was almost always in a good mood. But not at that moment. When she saw me watching her, she wrapped her arms around me and held me and said, crying, "Love. I don't want to."

"You don't want to what?" I asked her.

"I don't want to do what I have to do."

"I don't get it. What is it that you have to do?"

"I can't tell you," she said, "It's too awful. Just hold me."

The cat rubbed up against my ankle and I looked down at it and it wasn't there. I blinked a few times, and then there it was. For a long time, I didn't know what happened, but Charisma did tell me eventually. Like, months later. What happened was this:

Charisma appeared in a black chasm. A chasm as black as the soul of a black hole. She was hairless, and nude, and holding her breath. But, she was not alone. There was a moisture. The moisture was a ghost. The ghost was pure evil. She exhaled and the evil caught fire. The ghost burst into flame. The moisture was flammable. Charisma had an instinct for these things, as it turned out. A divine predilection, I would call it. Or, like, an omniscient wisdom, maybe. She'd known all along. She'd known what she had had to do. She'd known what it would do to her. And she'd known what would happen afterward.

The fires of the burning evil raged in the very air surrounding her; consuming what oxygen there was. Her naked flesh was roasting; burning like the surface of the sun. She held her eyes shut against the light but it was still painfully blindingly bright. Her eyelids were melting shut. She clenched her fists and curled into a fetal position; trying to take the pain. Holding her breath- in the grip of unspeakable torment- until the fires were finished. Then... She screamed... And the air was going out of her. But her breath was the light of Christ and it was the combustion that was destroying the wickedness trapped within that chamber. With no oxygen remaining to her, she held the final bit of air in her lungs until the scorching inferno dissipated. Then she exhaled the last iota of oxygen remaining within her; feeling the grace of the Christ filling the chamber as she disappeared. And then she was back in my arms again. Or, so I thought.

Of course, I'd been holding her the entire time. I was holding her when she started screaming in pain. I was holding her when she went limp and passed out. I was holding her when she didn't wake up again. I didn't know what else to do. I lifted her up and carried her out of there.

The way out was similar to the way in, except now the bats were flying up and down the corridor like clouds of flies. But they weren't flies. They were bats. And they were supposed to be coordinated, but they kept flying into my face. And into my head and body and back and legs. I was pretending I was cool with it until one- dead serious, this actually happened- got caught in Charisma's hair, and I had to stop and try to get it out as it was hissing and biting at me. I had to put Charisma down on the tracks and cut the thing out with my bowie knife.

It was about then that Charisma started waking up. But she was super out of it. "Come on, love. Come back to me. Come on, love. I need you. I can't do this without you. Come on. I'm getting us out of here. Just hang in there."

She wrapped her arms around my neck and held her head against my chest; weeping. Her headlamp was shining into my face, but I didn't care. I was just happy to see the light at the end of the tunnel and get out of there. Or, I thought I was happy. When we got out of there I immediately wished we were back in there, or back in Fall River, or on the moon; or any place else except right there.

I heard them laughing before I saw them. Being as that we were at the end of the Earth, I had, of course, expected us to be alone. Suffice to say, I was a bit startled. The laughter sounded almost human; it wasn't quite tuned in yet. It was still kind of electrical; like the last time I had heard their voices. But now it was a lot less 'half-dead robot' sounding.

The spectors approached me from all directions. I remember noticing that Angela had a flailing bat in her mouth, and I thought; 'good for her.' The spectors were laughing at me and nobody likes being laughed at, so I was a little irritated. I knew I hated them but I didn't think they'd hurt us because as far as I could tell they were using us for their purposes. Their heads were smooth and bald. They were all the same figure of a youthful, tall and strong man. They had mouths now. Ears. Noses. Chins. Hands. Legs. Something like dicks. No eyes, though. And they were still made out of blackness, and pixels, and sparkles. I watched them. I didn't know what to think. I was sort of annoyed, but even so, it was so beautiful out there in that strange land, with those strange beings. I was a bit awe-struck.

Charisma wasn't reacting at all. I asked them, "What do you want? What do you want from me?" And they said, or, one of them said- I don't know which one, because none of their mouths moved; they said, "We want you to succeed, and then we want you to fail."

They started laughing again. I didn't think it was funny, because I felt like I could've figured that out for myself. I said, "Whatever." Another one, or the same one, said, "Look," and they all pointed back to the entryway to the mineshaft. Like an idiot, I looked, and there came a shadow rushing toward me. I couldn't see what it was. It flew into my face like a cloud of a thousand black bats and I fell over onto my back; trying to absorb the blow for Charisma.

There were rocks everywhere; including where my shoulder blade and hip bone and tailbone had hit the ground at.

The spectors were laughing even harder now. Through the pain, I found myself looking up into the sky; trying to figure out what had just happened. All I saw was an oily shadow flying away. In retrospect, I guess I did get a pretty good look at it. It was- essentially- a wraith. Not many people would get a better look at it than I did. It was the shadow of death. I was in the desert of the shadow of death.

The shadow of death flew off into the sky; I don't know where it went, but I watched it going.

The spectors were still there, as I picked Charisma and myself up off of the ground. I sat in the dirt. My body hurt. I cradled my love. I looked up at the spectors. They sat down around me. Cross legged, like Indians. "What the hell was that thing?" I asked them. Not really caring, just feeling relieved it hadn't killed me.

"What do you think it was?" they asked me.

I was clueless. I said, "I don't know. A demon? You tell me."

"That was death itself," they said. I don't know which one said it. None of their mouths had moved.

"Who are you?" I asked them.

They replied; predictably, "Who do you think we are?"

It hadn't occurred to me yet, but I figured it out right then. "You're the devil?" I asked them.

"We are the one true God," they said.

"Same difference, isn't it?" I asked.

"You're clever," they said.

"I'm not clever. I'm just not stupid."

They watched me. I don't know what their interest in me was. But, they weren't killing me. So, that was good. Although, I think maybe the sun *was* trying to kill me. That was not good. I focused on Charisma. I said, "Love. Our friends are here. They want to say hello to you." She looked up into my eyes, but she wasn't there. It was the frightened look of a traumatized cat. I looked to Angela, and I saw that she was happily batting her bat around. For a second she looked up at me, and then she kept doing what she was doing.

"Is there something you want to tell me?" I asked the spectors.

They started laughing again, saying, "Like what?"

"What happened down in that cave?" I asked them.

"Your woman... Is a special woman. You protect her. And protect that cat, as well," they said.

And then they stood up to their feet, and turned, and walked away. They each went in a different direction; which I thought was strange.

And they didn't disappear, like they usually do. They just walked off into the different distances. It was such a weird thing to do, but they were weird, anyways. So. Whatever. I guess. I didn't beg them to stay, or anything.

Chapter 12
The Garden of Gethsemane
I gently laid Charisma down on the ground and gathered up Angela. Angela tried to take along the bat she was torturing, but it flopped away; bleeding, panting, and hardly capable of moving. I placed Angela into her backpack and poured some water in there with her because I was afraid she would cook if I didn't. I suppose I preferred she steam rather than roast. I lifted the bat by the wing and- a bit too unceremoniously- tossed it back into the darkness of the mine. Charisma was still incoherent. And she still looked alarmingly like a terrified cat. Related; Angela seemed unusually happy. Kind of like how Charisma is usually unusually happy.

The urgent thing was getting us back to the truck. Back to the air-conditioning. As it turned out; Charisma was pliable, and I eased her up onto the bike; seating her in front of me so I could keep her from falling over. I had Angela positioned over Charisma's chest; to keep her out of the blazing sun. Kicking the bike to life; we rode away.

On the ride back, we saw a spector walking out into the middle of nowhere. It wasn't near the trail, but it wasn't far from the trail, either. I drove over to it and pulled up alongside it and tried to stay off the throttle, asking; "Do you know what happened to Charisma?"

The being looked over at me and spoke without using its mouth; its electric voice going directly into my skull. "Charisma is inside of Angela. Angela is inside of Charisma."

I was afraid it would say that. My first and most obvious question was, "How do I switch them back?"

And the spector said, "You cannot."

I asked, "Can you?"

It said, "No."

"So, she's stuck like this forever?" I asked.

"Cannot say," it said.

"Where are you going?" I asked it.

"This way," it said, pointing forward.

"Why?" I asked it.

"We're following the axes."

"Why, though?"

"We are becoming."

"Becoming what?"

"Ourselves."

"There's no way you can help me help Charisma?"

"She doesn't need help. She knows what she is doing. Can you say the same?"

"No. Of course not. I have no idea what I'm doing."

"You should figure that out. Now go."

Talking to the spectors wasn't exactly pleasant, but I have to admit that I felt reassured by its vote of confidence. I rode back to the truck, helped Charisma inside- she could kind of move on her own, but it was awkward; I let Angela out of her bag, started the truck and ran the air conditioner, and then I loaded up the dirt bike. When I opened the door to get inside, the cat jumped down the steps and ran off. Angela had never done that before. It took me a few minutes to collect the cat and take her back inside. I didn't doubt that the woman and the cat had switched places. They'd always been one in the same, anyways.

I have to admit, though, that I wasn't particularly fond of Charisma the cat. She was overly rambunctious. Angela the human- meanwhile- was well-behaved and sitting calmly in the passenger seat, still looking rattled, and holding a folded piece of paper extended toward me. I took the paper and read it.

It said; 'Love. I needed to be Angela, for a while. I'm sorry. I know this must be scary for you. It is scary for us, too. Please just take us to the coordinates that I've written on this paper. When you get there, let us both out of the truck, and we'll do the rest. Also, we need a cage- a good strong cage- big enough to hold a cat. But, it's not for a cat. Give the cage to Charisma when we get to the destination. With love, your love."

I entered the coordinates into the GPS. The destination seemed straightforward enough. I wouldn't even need to trek us out into the desert when we got there. It was just a random spot on the edge of a lonely road on the outskirts of a suburb of Tucson. I found a big box pet store to stop at on the way, and then we headed out. The sun was super bright and the desert landscape was reflective.

Charisma was acting weird, but not as weird as I would have imagined. Angela was a bizarrely well-mannered cat, and so she made for a docile person as well. I just felt bad for her because she looked so scared all the time. Charisma was a manic feline, however. The phrase 'bouncing off the walls' comes to mind. I didn't really care what she did, except for when she wandered under my feet while I was driving.

I noticed an uncomfortable absence of traffic on the roads. It was like during the initial Covid lockdown. I hadn't bothered to check my phone, but I began to suspect the Armageddon was progressing. I didn't see any dead bodies or destruction, so I just assumed everything was hunky dory. That was until I got to the big box pet store. I put

Angela in her bag, left her and Charisma in the truck with the AC on, and went inside. Inside, they were boxing up and storing their entire inventory. I'm still wondering what they did with the fish. I told them I really needed a cage. They just gave it to me. They said they wouldn't accept my money. They said nobody is accepting money any more. I said 'thank you' and then I left.

I found myself wishing we could go back to normal. Things weren't always good, but at least they were static. I'd always thought that money was a bad system. I'd always thought money should be replaced by a better system. I knew about inflation. I knew about fractional reserve banking and usury. I knew about central banking and fiat currency. I understood that money was less of an organizational mechanism and more of a tool to force people into de facto slavery. The United States was- like- 35 trillion dollars in debt, last time I looked. It was all very stupid. Nonetheless, I found myself missing the money as soon as it was gone. I never had money problems. But the implications were staggering. For one thing, I had tens of thousands of dollars in savings. Money that I could have spent and that had just become worthless, or so I feared.

My mood immediately soured. I tried to carry on as though nothing was wrong but I couldn't shake the loss from my mind. I checked my bank account online and the money was still there, so, that made me feel a little better; but I was confused and anxious and I just wanted Charisma back. When Charisma was around, everything made sense. Now that she was trapped inside of her cat; I felt exposed and vulnerable. Actually, one thing that cheered me up was I started wondering about if it would be cheating if I made love to Charisma in her current condition. It'd probably be rape, I figured. I mean, it would almost definitely be rape, but I wasn't sure if it would be beastiality if the cat was in a human body. It'd be beastiality if I made love to the cat, but at least that wouldn't be rape. Then again, I'm sure Charisma would be pissed off if I nailed her cat. So, probably it would be rape. I think doing the cat would be worse than doing the woman, but, to be safe, I would have to not do either of them. That was the smart move. And it was easy, because neither option was remotely tempting. Plus, we were busy. Anyways. Pretty soon, we were where she told me to go to. And I had a cage. It wasn't as much a cage as it was a carrier, but, same difference.

There were thirty foot tall saguaro cactuses in every direction. And many other species of cactus, too. The landscape was craggy and the rocks had a pinkish tint. The wavy topography was undulating in all directions. There was no way to drive the bike around out there, because it was all boulders and cacti, and scrub filling in the gaps. For lack of any better idea, I did what Charisma had instructed me to do. We all got out of the truck together. The sun was even hotter here than it had been south of Animas. I was holding the carrier in my hands, and Angela meowed, and then Charisma took the carrier away from me. I had my 50 cal pistol, and the 1301, and the bandolier of shells, too. I wasn't going to entrust a cat with a firearm, though. So Charisma ventured out unarmed.

Angela began wandering about aimlessly. She would jump up on rocks and look around, and then jump down into ditches and put her face into crevices; evidently searching for something. Charisma was following Angela; but I could tell she was struggling. She was staggering around like a drunk. But I guess that was pretty good for a four-legged creature in a two-legged body. I offered to carry the carrier for her, but she insisted on awkwardly fussing around with it. I just hung back and watched them wandering.

I couldn't help but notice the beauty. I knew from trucking that Tucson is a gorgeous area. There's just something about it. There's so much going on in every direction. Still, I couldn't enjoy it. I felt too bad for Charisma, and I worried about Angela. Or, I mean, I felt too bad for Angela, and I worried about Charisma. Or, both ways were correct, I suppose. Anyways. Eventually, I heard a hissing. And so I hurried to catch up with the ladies; who'd gotten out ahead of me while I was daydreaming. I hurried around some boulders and got down into a dried up wash. The girls were on the bank; the cat was hissing at a lizard. The lizard was hissing at the cat. It wasn't just any lizard. It was a gila monster. Which I guess is just any lizard. But, still. It was pretty cool to see one.

The interesting thing was that Angela- the cat- had been the one tracking the lizard, but it was Charisma- the human- who possessed the cunning to scoop the lizard up and drop it into the carrier before it had had a chance to realize it had two adversaries, and not just one. Charisma- the human- handed the carrier to me. It was still open. I don't think she knew how to close it. So I closed it. And I was curious to examine the lizard, because I'd never seen one of these things, but I knew they were venomous. The thing was clearly angry at us. It was hissing and its mouth was wide open and it was rattling its rigid forked tongue.

When I looked up, I saw something that made me drop the carrier; which I'm sorry for doing. I even pulled my pistol and flicked off the safety. But then I saw the eyes and relaxed a little. Actually, there were three sets of eyes and they were all staring at me because I had just dropped the carrier. One set of eyes belonged to Charisma. Another set of eyes belonged to Angela. And the third set of eyes- I wouldn't know what to call that being. I knew from the face- and from the tits, if I'm being honest- that this third being was some version of Charisma. Charisma says the being is her guardian angel. Not exactly a great explanation but it was the only one I ever got. So, Charisma's guardian angel- let's call her Draag, because she looked like one of the blue giants from Fantastic Planet; not blue or giant, but hairless and nude- so, Draag proceeded to not pay any further attention to me. I just watched them like a yokel. It looked like Draag was holding her breath, and that was because Draag- as it turned out- was always holding her breath.

I saw something that would've been gross if it wasn't so fascinating. Angela coughed up a hairball, but the hairball was made out of glowing green light. It was radioactive looking. Like, a rod of uranium or something. It was so bright- and hard to look at- that I couldn't actually see if it was lumpy or smooth, or even big or small. Draag wretched up a similar radioactive isotope or whatever. Hers, however, was glowing orange instead of green. Draag picked up the neon green vomit and handed it to Charisma. Charisma ate it. She actually chewed it. I guess it wasn't hard or inedible; she seemed to swallow it pretty easily. I was wondering if there was sand on it. At the same time, Angela- the cat- gobbled up the other glowing lump. The neon orange one. While that was happening; Draag turned her face up to the sky and exhaled a blinding beam of light that hurt to look at. I looked at it anyways because I wanted to see what was happening. The light reached all the way up into the heavens. I guess it wasn't exactly light, per se, because it wasn't clear. I think light is supposed to be clear. I don't know. But this was vibrant bluish-white energy, anyways; prismatic and blinding.

The bright white light had burst forth from Draag's mouth, but it grew in magnitude and intensity until it had completely encompassed her body. Then she disappeared into the light and the light disappeared into the sky. That was when I realized that both Charisma and Angela were unconscious. Not a little unconscious. I had to keep checking their breathing to convince myself they were alive. They were very unconscious.

I moved them over to some slim shadows I was able to find; after I swept away the litter; searching for spiders and scorpions and things.

I was trying to figure out how I could possibly move all these bodies back to the truck when I realized that Charisma- the human- was coming to.

"Love!" I implored.

"Love," she responded, weakly.

"Drink some water," I told her.

"I have to pee," she said.

"Drink some water first," I insisted. I could see her lips were parched.

Charisma drank water and peed and looked around confusedly. When she saw Angela she rushed to her side and picked her up in her arms, and cooed, "Oh, kitty. It's okay, kitty. My sweet kitty. It's okay."

Still, Charisma was dazed and disoriented and couldn't recall much of what had happened that day. "Where are we?" she asked me. "Tucson, Arizona," I said. That seemed to register. "What are we doing here?" she asked. "Apparently, we came here to catch a gila monster," I said. "Oh. Right. That makes sense," she said. "Maybe to you, it does," I said. "We got it, though?" she asked. "Yeah, it's right here," I said, holding the carrier up to her face so she could see inside. "Good," she said, and then she went back to cradling her cat and cooing at it, trying to coax it back into consciousness.

"Love. I have some questions," I told her.

"Love. Just wait. Ask me when we're back in the truck."

On our way back to the truck, Angela opened her eyes and started looking around. Charisma cradled her in her arms for most of the way, but then she put her down and the cat followed after us; seemingly no worse for the wear. Up in the truck, Charisma showed me where we needed to go next. The spot was in Tucson. So, we weren't far away. It was a city park. Using the map application, I memorized the way over and started driving.

Pulling onto the road, I asked her, "Love. What happened to you down in that mine?"

"You know what happened. I switched bodies with Angela."

"I saw the spectors. And, something else... There was no archon. Or, if it was an archon. It wasn't like the others. It was like... a black... ghost... It flew off into the sky. I don't know what it was, or where it went."

"It wasn't an archon. It was worse than an archon. It was the wraith. It was the reaper."

"What is it going to do?"

"Nothing good. Something very bad, in fact. That's why I was so upset. That, and because I had to put myself through hell to release it."

"Did you have to release it?"

She looked at me like I was an idiot, and asked, "What kind of question is that? Of course I had to release it."

"I don't understand. It just flew off. Where did it go?"

"It went away. To... become..."

"To become what? That's what the spectors said they were doing. They said they were becoming. What is becoming?"

She said, "The reaper is becoming death itself. The spectors are becoming alive."

Again, I found myself asking questions I didn't want the answers to. I realized I didn't want to know. And I knew all too well how I'd learn soon enough, whether I liked it or not. Charisma didn't elaborate and I didn't probe any further. I had highway-hypnosis for the rest of the drive and I got us to the spot without even realizing what I was doing. Wisely, we parked down the road and walked up to the place. We must have predicted that it'd be blown sky high about 30 minutes later. We had our weapons on us and I was carrying the gila monster. The few other pedestrians we saw were also carrying rifles. I think everybody was armed in those days. They waved, and we waved, too.

The park wasn't an ordinary park. It was full of marble statues. They called it 'The Garden of Gethsemane,' and it depicted various Christian scenes. There was Jesus kneeling in prayer, Jesus laying in a tomb, Jesus up on the cross, and the biggest one was the last supper with all attendees in attendance. I thought it was ostentatious that the artist made the table out of marble instead of something more ordinary. They could've just used a regular metal picnic table, or something.

We got in there and I asked her, "So, what do we do now?"

"We have to spill the blood of this creature in this holy place."

"What's the benefit?"

"It will stop people from preying on other people. It will stop doctors from doing harm. It will stop lawyers from creating problems. It will stop thieves from stealing purses. Things like that. Anybody using an unfair advantage against anybody else; this will stop them."

"Isn't that a violation of free will?"

"There is no such thing as free will. Are you by my side because of free will? No. You are here because you had no choice. Because of fate. Fate is the design. The design is the programming. We think that because our decisions are miniscule and singular- as well as interconnected and nebulous- that they're a product of our free will. But, our decisions are pre-ordained. Just too intricate to evaluate. Destiny is encoded into the fabric of reality. It feels like free will, but that is just an illusion. Predators are just a different form of bureaucrat. And vice-versa. It's all in the programming."

"Right. Ok. So. We have to kill the gila monster?"

"No. Thank goodness. The poor thing. We only have to make it bleed and apply the blood to the wounds of Jesus on the cross; the nail wounds, specifically."

"We're going to need a ladder," I said.

"You can stand on that garbage can," she suggested.

I shrugged and laboriously dragged the garbage can over; scraping metal on stone gratingly. Then I asked her, "So, how do we make the lizard bleed?"

I guess she'd thought of this already. She pulled out some wire cutters she'd found in my truck and said, "We remove its little toe. Or, we poke it with a knife."

Charisma didn't want to hurt an innocent animal any more than I did. I tried to remind myself the lizard was a carnivore, but that didn't help. I tried to remind myself of all the dead bodies I'd seen lately, and that didn't help, either. Then I remembered the black kitten I'd killed in the Bronx. That did the trick. I dumped the lizard out on the marble last supper table, used my bowie to fend off its angry biting at me, and clipped its smallest toe off of its back right leg. The lizard took it pretty well; it didn't even flinch, but, that's animals for you. The blood spilled out onto the table. The lizard was meandering away and Charisma caught it in the carrier. It had bled enough that I could get it on my fingers and smear it on the feet and hands of the Christ statue. So, stepping atop the garbage can, that was what I did.

When we felt the ground rumbling beneath our feet, we knew that the ritual was complete. Charisma released the lizard into the shrubbery and then we hurried back to the truck. The wind was picking up as we went. I looked up in the sky and saw a wall of red clouds. We found ourselves within a sandstorm before long. And then we heard an explosion. And rocks were raining down all around us. Sadly, I realized that the gila monster must have died. Thankfully, neither of us got injured by the falling rocks. However, the blasting sand hurt like hell. It was a relief to get up into the truck, but I wasn't going to start the engine, because I'd just suck a ton of sand into the intake.

"We should gear up," Charisma said.

We got our safety jackets on and stuffed the pockets with magazines. Then we waited anxiously, holding tight to the XM7s; a single grenade in each of the launchers. "You were talking to the spectors?" Charisma asked me, as if only now comprehending what I had told her earlier.

"Yeah. They were actually pretty decent guys. Or, they didn't kill me or give me a hard time or nothing. They laughed at me a lot. I thought that was rude."

"What did you talk about?"

"You, I guess. The shadow of death. Nothing, really."

The sand was scouring my paint, I learned later. Only on the driver's side, though. It was really loud. The sound of billions of grains of sand pelting my rig.

Suddenly, we heard screaming coming from the outside. I wouldn't have thought anybody could scream louder than the sandstorm. But, they could. The screaming was loud, and then it slowly became fainter as it moved away from us, and then it became a lot louder; coming at us a lot faster; and then- through the clouds of sand- we saw the body smash into the sidewalk at terminal velocity. It burst apart and the blood splashed all over my truck. I could sense the archon creeping around us, but I couldn't get a fix on it.

Angela jumped up onto the dashboard and started mewling. I was hoping not to alert the demon to our presence but it heard the cat and that was that. I remember thinking, 'I have to protect my windows.' And, too, maybe I'd gotten used to facing off against these things. I charged the rifle and hit the switch for three shot bursts. I could see the demon standing right outside my window. It reminded me of a dragon but it was more upright, and it had no tail. And its face was like a bat. Before I could process our situation I was giving it exactly what it wanted. I stepped out of the truck and opened-fire on it. Frighteningly, the demonic bat humanoid hybrid creature was angrily shrieking in a high rasping tone. I was blowing it apart as it rushed toward me. That was when I got my first clear look at it.

It reached out for me with fingers that ended in fearsome claws like a handful of karambits. The red eyes were there, like on the other varieties. But, this thing resembled a man, insofar as it stood on its hind legs and its head was round like a human head. The nose and eyes were like a bat but it had an ear to ear mouth full of razor sharp teeth; unlike any mouth or teeth seen in nature. These were teeth that could tear flesh as easily as they could crush bone. Its wings sprouted from its spine and they were that of a bat. Or, of a dragon. Whichever, really. And its height was almost double that of a man.

My bullets caught it in the torso- the torso of a man, but reptilian skinned- and I used the recoil to redirect my fire up into its face; blasting the skull apart. Only then did I notice its elegant crown of rearward spikes. Just as the bullets decimated the structure. Too, it had one spike on each of its elbows and wrists, also. And there actually was a thin whiplike tail which I'd not noticed at first glance. The tail had an arrowhead at the tip of it.

I watched the laser red light fade from the demon's eyes as it crashed to the ground before me. I dumped the rest of my clip into it, and I thought I would have a second to grab something to smash up the divisions with; but the tiny little batlike demons came shooting out of it immediately; taking off into the sky like... well... like bats out of hell. Those were the smallest demons I'd ever seen. And there must have been over a hundred of them. I couldn't imagine how they'd be effective killers. But, I figured it out later, and it's one of the more painful memories out of my unlimited supply of painful memories. Their method was to target children. The fledglings hunted children to become bigger.

I was turning to get back into the truck when I felt a searing heat burning in my shoulder. The fiery slicing of my flesh was accompanied by the crazy fluttering of wings slapping me in the face. Simultaneously; there were claws cutting into my neck; but, I grabbed the two wrists and snapped them in half before the creature could open up my jugular. Its spikes pierced into my hands; but Charisma was quick to jump over and decapitate the accursed devil with her bowie knife. Out of the corner of my eye I watched her pry open the jaws with her blade. It was clamped down good, but she did get it off of me. I summoned the strength to climb into my chair and close the door, but then I passed out. Partly from the pain, and partly from exposure to venom.

I came to shortly thereafter. I had a feeling like we needed to go. But, I was feverish and sweating and dizzy and I was driving like a drunk; falling asleep every two seconds. As I was driving, Charisma was both cleaning my wound and slapping my face to wake me up. I poured coffee down my throat, but it was hard to swallow and kept coming up out of my mouth. I'd always wished Charisma knew how to drive- which she didn't- but that was the moment when I knew she'd have to learn.

As soon as we were able, we pulled over and Charisma stitched me together. It was a jumble of stitches; necessitated by a jumble of gashes and slices. Still, it was a good thing we left when we did, because the National Guard was arriving in Tucson as we were leaving and I wouldn't have wanted to have had to explain why we had a truck load of their equipment.

We were parked at a rest area when the spectors approached us. I don't know where they came from. But, that was normal. There were other people using the facility. They started panicking at the sight of our evil friends. They were pointing and screaming and running away, and a select few of the strangers approached us with rifles, but the spectors- somehow- compelled the strangers to second guess themselves and turn and retreat.

I rolled down the window as the ethereal beings approached us. Their becoming was apparently a slow process, but I had no doubt that they were evolving in some way. And their evolution was evidently related to what Charisma and I were out there doing, because we pretty much only saw them after we released an archon, and each time the occasion marked some vague advancement in their 'becoming.' By this point, the spectors had real honest to goodness swinging dicks. And balls.

I rolled down my window and said, "Nice cocks, gentlemen."

"We've got eyes now, too," one of them said. And it was true. They had white eyeballs. Bloodshot, with black irises, but eyeballs just the same. However, their bodies were still made of- blackness, and sparkles... I guess... I don't know. I never learned what they were made of; but it hadn't changed. Yet. They looked a lot more human than in New Mexico, though.

"And our mouths move, too. We have voices, now," said another.

"So you do," I agreed. Then I turned to take a look at Charisma, but she was glaring like only a woman can glare.

"Charisma doesn't like us," one of them said.

"I'm not especially fond of you either. Not after you made us fight the three headed dog in Washington... Washington... Washington DC...," I choked out; just before vomiting pure bile at their feet.

Chapter 13
Unspeakable Carnage
The spectors effortlessly and instantaneously shifted their position rearward, in order to not get my splashing vomit on themselves. I was having trouble lifting my head up, and I said, "Sorry about that. I got bit, by a bat. Demon. Whatever. I'm feeling kind of sick. You think I'm going to die?"

"Maybe you will die. Maybe not," said one.

Charisma crawled across the electric cooler and leaned over me, talking to the spectors, saying, "Can't you see he is unwell? Can't you help him?"

I watched them exchange glances, and then one stepped forward, saying, "It is in our interest to give aide. We will give aide." It lifted off of the ground; hovering. I guess to avoid stepping in my puke. My wrist was hanging over the edge of the window. I'd never been this close to one. The sparkles of its shimmering black body emitted a subtle hum. Like being under a powerline. I noticed it was less pixelated now. Their resolution was better.

The spector was reaching its hand toward my hand and then Charisma shouted, "No! Don't! We changed our minds!" And she pulled my head and hand back into the truck. I was so feverish that I didn't think anything of it.

The spector said, "Ok. We were only trying to help."

"Thank you. But, please. No thank you."

"You believe we will contaminate him?" one of them accused her.

"That's exactly correct, yes."

"You are entitled to your opinion. We only wished to reduce his suffering."

"All you want is for us to release the next archon. But, I don't want your essences inside of my love. You'll have your archon when we get there, and we'll get there after he is feeling better." Her Filipino accent was heavy on the word 'love,' making it sound like 'loove.'

"And if he dies?" one spector asked her.

"He won't," Charisma declared.

I saw their faces gather around the window. They were-all three- staring at me. I asked them, "What are you doing?"

And they said, "We want to see you. With our eyes. Our human eyes."

I said, "So, what, you're becoming human, then? Humans can't hover."

"We are not human. Not yet. We can still hover."

"Must be nice," I said.

"Indeed," one said, in agreement.

Another said, "See you soon."

Another said, "Goodbye."

Then they were gone. And I was gone, too. Passed out on my steering wheel. I came to a minute or so later and Charisma helped me up and into bed. There, she took care of me for the next 36 hours. It took 36 hours before I felt capable of operating a motor vehicle again. That was when I could hold my head up, see straight, eat solid food, and replenish my fluids. Those 36 hours were among the worst of my life. I dreamt my mother fell off of a cliff. A lot of the time I was convinced I would die, but Charisma said that she wouldn't let me, and I believed her. I vomited several times. There was nothing in me but bile and it burned coming out. Similarly, we had to set up the emergency truck toilet so I could shit my guts out. That required the sum total of my available lifeforce to achieve. My temperature was high, but I was always cold and glazed with sweat. I was shaking uncontrollably. My head was in a fog where I couldn't see or hear or talk; and I was congested and leaking snot besides.

Then it was over. And we got back on the road as soon as I was able to drive again. It was morning time when we departed the rest area in Arizona. My shoulder hurt ferociously; the muscles were shredded and using them just made it worse, but I had no option. We were headed up Oregony way. But that didn't mean we were going to Oregon. It meant we were trying to get there.

The nicest thing about that day- besides being with Charisma- was being out in the southwest. I liked looking at landscapes as much as the next person, and so I found it easy to take my mind off of things. The southwest is the best place to drive because the elevations are so dizzying and there's no trees blocking the view. Usually, when I went through anywhere with scenic beauty, it was always at night time. But not that day. That day was the day the lord made. A heavenly sun shining day. That, and traffic was practically non-existent.

Still, I didn't think there'd be any way to make it through California, so I opted instead to run us north through the great basin; which was a daring move, but- I figured- a safer bet than California. I don't know how it would have been to get through California, but I do know that it was somewhat difficult to get through Las Vegas. More depressing than anything, really.

It was dark out and there was no moon. We were approaching Las Vegas and the lights were a beacon in the night. A positive omen, I thought; mistakenly. A glowing gem on the horizon. When we got closer, I could see that the taillights of traffic and the flashing lights of emergency vehicles were competing against the city in their attempts to drown out the blackness.

The first thing I did was to jump off the interstate. Onto south Las Vegas boulevard. That road was backed up, too, of course. I cut around toward the industrial area, where I thought it'd be empty and it pretty much was. There were still trucks trucking and smart four-wheelers detouring through, but that was all. I looked at the map on my phone and memorized as many possible escape routes as possible. I'd done this in about a dozen cities by now, so, I was getting the hang of it.

I happened to be by the four-wheeler parking for the Amazon fulfillment center. The neon cityscape of Las Vegas loomed ahead of us in the distance. There were some other trucks parked along the road there, so I'd just pulled up behind them. Then I heard the screaming. I started gearing up. Charisma said, "What do you think you're doing?"

"We have to help these people!" I said.

"Kevin Robertson! I forbid you!" said Charisma.

I could see in the mirror; there was chaos in that parking lot. A lot of cars were flooding out. It must have been a shift change. The demons- I saw- weren't especially big but they weren't small, either. They were viciously disassembling whoever they could catch. "Love! They need me! They need us!"

"I need you! I can't do this without you!"

"Love. Put your gear on. I have to."

I couldn't argue with her. I was loading the 12 gauge with buckshot. I'd seen these things before. I knew they wouldn't be easy to hit with bullets. I handed the shotgun to Charisma and said, "Put your helmet on, if you're coming." I put my helmet on and grabbed my bo staff and jumped out of the truck.

I ran over to the parking lot and one of the bat demons- Charisma called them aswang- saw me coming; it was kneeling on a body and ripping the entrails out maniacally.

Suddenly, it beat its wings and bore down on me fast. The thing was about the size of Charisma. Its smaller size gave it unexpected speed. I had my weapon of choice, though, and finally the bo staff was an appropriate weapon to face our adversaries with.

I planted the stick on the ground and hit the demon in the face with a flying kick. It went skidding into the asphalt. Cars were honking at me to get out of the way. Swinging the staff like an ax; I brought it down over my head and smashed the demon again in the skull as it was scrambling to get up to its feet. The demon was wailing with the turmoil of a banshee as I thrust the end of my staff into its face again and again. Then, its flailing limbs were in the way. I used a six attack flower to disable its arms and legs; spin jumping over it halfway through. And then I finished smashing up the skull when the combo was over. I laid into it with overhead bashes until it finally went limp. Then I pummeled the body with an unending barrage of overhead ax swing type blows. Occasionally one of the smaller demons within managed to come flying out; but I was ready for them. I could play pingpong with this stick. It was nothing to catch the infantile fledglings in the air and bring them to the ground where I could finish them. At no point did I forget the torture one of these things had just put me through.

As I did my due-diligence, I observed that Charisma was out there with me. She had the shotgun in her hands and was standing guard while I decimated the demons as they blossomed. Or, divided. As it were. The shotgun discharged three times in succession. The buckshot tore an aswang apart and it came crashing down near our position. I pounced on it as fast as I could. Cars were still flashing their high beams and honking for us to get out of the way. As though we weren't busy doing them a favor.

Like hornets, the fledglings came out of the one Charisma had blown to shreds. I moved closer to my woman to protect her. We were in a whirlwind of wings.

The demons' red eyes flitted around us; just more lights in the overwhelming spectacle that was the combination of Las Vegas, the Amazon building, the street lights, the flashing headlights, and the tail lights, too. But I am a trucker and all this suited me just fine. I swung the bo staff in arcs and thrust it out jabbing and whipped it around in three six nine and twelve step flowers. I had built up such momentum that I found my feet were flying off the ground and I was kicking the bat demons out of the sky. Every time I defeated one; it exploded into twenty more. Occasionally, Charisma would blast one that had been smart enough to stay out of my range. Then, together we'd move toward the dividing carcass so I could apply the method to it.

There were maybe fifteen or twenty small ones remaining, trying to get at us, when suddenly, all at once; they vanished; ascending into the sky and beating their wings toward the city lights. Only the perpetually frustrated Amazon employees remained. I guess some things never change. I was happy to lead Charisma back to the truck because the motorists finally stopped honking their horns. My bad knee was aching and my shoulder was wet with blood from popped stitches. I listened carefully for any sound of wings- there wasn't any- and then we got back into the truck. Charisma took off her helmet and I took mine off, too. She glared at me for a second. And then she started pounding on me with her diminutive fists of fury. Shouting- and spitting- in my face, "You bastard! You bastard! I hate you! I hate you! Why! Why do you keep doing that?"

I grabbed her wrists. She struggled for a second and then stopped; bursting into tears.

"I thought you'd be impressed. I kicked ass out there," I said.

Through her sobbing, she said, "Impressed? Impressed that you're a stupid idiot? Who is going to doom the children of Christ to an eternity in hell? How many times do we have to have this conversation?"

"I can't just let these people die," I said.

"You have to! You have to! I told you a thousand times! You have to let them die! You have to stop risking your life to save them! You're not like them! You can't save everybody, but you can get them all killed. All of them! Not just the hylics in this parking lot. Every last soul on Earth. How are you not understanding this?"

She was right. And I knew she was right. And I felt stupid. I said, "I'm sorry, love. I just couldn't take it. I couldn't stand to stand by and let those people die."

I kept turning over the aswang in my mind; imagining if I'd gotten bitten or- worse- if Charisma had. I'd released the truck's brakes and taken off down the road. Then I began realizing that something was happening that I wasn't even aware of. We were seeing dead bodies. But they didn't look right. They didn't look injured. Some of them had dull blank expressions. Like they didn't even know what was happening. Others looked more normal; as in, they died with horrified expressions. But those were not torn apart, either. They should be torn apart. I was bewildered by how they were not viciously mutilated. Some just looked to be asleep. We were in a slew of these such corpses. There'd been a crowd there. Gamblers from an evacuated off-the-strip casino, it looked like. I couldn't even figure out what had killed them.

"What killed them?" I asked Charisma.

"Death."

"Death killed them?"

"Yes."

"The shadow that came out of the mine?"

"Yes."

"What is it? How do we fight it?"

"It's a wraith. We can't fight it. It's immaterial. It's an angel from hell. It's Hell's angel of death."

"What if it comes for us?"

"It won't. It can't hurt anybody with the light of Christ within them. It can't hurt anybody with a soul."

"So, what? It's just going to slaughter all the hylics?"

"It would appear that is a distinct possibility, yes."

"All of them?" I shouted, frustrated.

"I don't know what it will do. My understanding is that it is capable of anything. It can dissolve the barrier between the dimensions. The more it kills, the less stable the realm will become. Because we're losing the units that process the equation."

I kept driving. Taking small residential streets to avoid the traffic built up around major intersections. We saw mothers wailing by their dead children. We saw blood and guts and human remains strewn about like garbage in a dump. The bat demons were in the sky; we could see them silhouetted against the neon lights. They'd snatch up whoever they could carry and fly them to the heavens and then drop them. And I felt my stomach sink every time I saw it.

Also, we saw more victims of the shadow of death. It seemed to be the groups of people who succumbed to the wraith. It was never one or two; always ten or twenty, or- as we saw later- many more.

We were beneath the city lights when I inadvertently wandered into a roadblock. I guess we weren't supposed to have gotten past the traffic. I'd just come around a corner from a shaded side street and suddenly there were flashing lights all around us. The National Guard closed in menacingly. One soldier approached my window. He was carrying a weapon that I'd never seen before. It looked like a tactical flamethrower; but the tank was bright yellow and it had a symbol of a liquid dripping from a test tube and burning a hole in a hand. I noticed his fatigues were rubberized, too.

The soldier said, "The city's locked down. You're not supposed to be out here." He said this as there were about 20,000 screaming tourists and gamblers and whores and hotel workers; all running for their lives, all around us. I could see the bats lifting people out of the crowd.

"I'm just passing through, sir."

Another soldier called to the one at my window, "He's got a browning 50 strapped down back here."

The soldier put his hand on his pistol. Charisma called to the man, "Sir, you have to let us through! You need to run for your life! We're all going to die!"

I expected him to start power-tripping and search our vehicle; I could tell that was the instinct of his training. Instead, he just waved us through. I pulled out onto what I only then realized was the Las Vegas strip. I knew we were in Vegas, but I didn't know we were at Vegas. The lights were disorienting, and it felt surreal to see these people horror-stricken and fleeing in such a decadent atmosphere.

In my rearview mirror, I saw that the soldiers were dropping. The police officers as well, as well as the bystanders in the vicinity. They were simply falling dead where they stood. Well; some of them were running when they fell. Angela started hissing. I saw something indefinable amongst the dying. It could only be identified as a shadow. I knew it was the shadow of death, but I had no idea what it was doing; besides killing people. It was obviously killing people.

"Kevin, what are you doing?" Charisma asked me.

"The wraith. It just murdered those soldiers."

"Harvested..." she corrected, adding, "We need to go."

Looking forward, I saw the aswang ripping people apart. There were a lot of demons, but there were thousands of people in every direction. Even in the middle of the road.

"The soldiers had acid guns. We need those," I told her.

I didn't wait for Charisma's approval. I put the truck into reverse and backed up to where the dead bodies were laid out at. I wasn't afraid of the wraith. I figured that if anybody has a soul, then certainly I must. And, as far as I could tell, that had proven to be true. The divine light of Christ hath graced me with its presence.

Still. We were within pandemonium. "Love. I need you to cover me."

She squinted her eyes and squirmed her face in deliberation; but she knew damn well we needed those acid throwers. She said, "Alright, but then we are leaving."

"Yes. Love. I don't like it here, either."

I was compelled to back over some corpses to get close enough to where we needed to be. I needed to raid the dead soldiers' humvee. The guns were out on the ground, but I knew they'd have extra acid tanks and hopefully some extra units. We put our helmets on. Charisma donned her bandolier and I grabbed my bo staff. We jumped out of the truck and into a horde of terrified people. Charisma stayed close to me and I told her; "Cover me!" And then I was pulling all the acid resistant clothing that I could off of a dead soldier. There were so many people that- statistically- we were in less danger than usual. I grabbed boots, pants, jackets, gloves, and found a full face mask, too. Then I grabbed two acid throwers. I stacked all that together, but before we could get to the humvee, we were again fighting a demon.

One of them had made a move on somebody within my immediate vicinity. I'd brained the snarling creature with my staff, and then Charisma blasted it right in its ugliness. When the winged body dropped; she dumped another six shells into it and I applied the method to the divisions while she reloaded. The terrified crowd seemed to know to avoid us. But they were still too close for comfort.

There were currents of countless humans streaming in every direction; and screaming in terror as they went. Their arms were out in front of them, and their heads were looking around in all directions and they pushed each other around as they went. Charisma dumped another tube of shells into the monster and I beat the remains down until there was nothing left but elastic membranes and shattered exoskeletons. "Love, come on," I tugged her with me over to the humvee. It was important we stayed close.

People were falling as they ran. I knew they were dropping dead. I looked around and there it was; the wraith.

The entire scene was aglow with flashing neon lights of pink, red, and orange. And purplish blue and red police lights, too. The wraith reflected no color. Its main characteristic was blackness. The shape of it was reminiscent of a jellyfish; complete with dangling tendrils. I could see that it was seeing me. We watched each other. It wasn't even doing anything, but most people who got near it simply dropped dead. Certain blessed individuals remained impervious to the effect. Charisma had seen the wraith, too, but she- wisely- was more concerned with tracking the demons. "Hurry up!" she yelled at me.

I found what I was looking for in the back of the guardsmen's truck. Each acid thrower came in a special rubber crate. The crates were yellow and contained spare canisters. I saw that I could cram two guns and four canisters into one crate, so that was what I did. Returning to the tractor; we worked our way over the corpses; watching the aswang. Meanwhile, the wraith continued to observe us; seemingly fascinated. Helpless hylics kept falling all around it. Literally stacking up atop one another.

I had bungees of all sizes in a case under the steps to the truck's catwalk and in almost no time at all I had the acid throwers and rubber acid gear all strapped down besides the 50 cal.

Back in the truck I felt a little better. Less exposed, at least. Angela was freaking out in her bag, though. Making all the most hostile cat noises. I didn't think anything of it. Charisma didn't say anything about it. I started driving without taking my helmet off. We had to move very slowly because the streets were full of people. I guess the hotels had evacuated everybody. Everybody was looking for shelter. A couple times I saw mobs form. Both times it was to break through the glass doors of some hotel and storm their way inside. Can't say I blame them. The aswang were attacking from above; it was inhumane to force the crowds to remain outdoors.

Still, I was grateful all those people were out there. They were an effective diversion. The demons weren't going to break my windows as long as there was an abundance of prospective victims strewn about all over the place. Although, we had to point our pistols in people's faces on more than one occasion; because they were trying to open our doors. Again, I was fearing for my windows. More and more I was realizing that my windows were way too delicate for these conditions. I think that was when we remembered to remove our helmets.

How many aswang there were in Vegas on that night; I can't even guess. Hundreds, probably. It was a slaughter- unspeakable carnage- and still not as bad as what the shadow of death was doing. I couldn't even process that particular horror, nor the implications of something so deadly.

We found the militia at the same time as we found the northern blockade; gathered under Interstate 515. They had pickup trucks with machine guns mounted on them and apocalyptic armored vehicles with crucifixes painted on their plows. And there had to be about a thousand armed men in that gathering alone. Here was where they'd been when the helpless people on the strip needed them. Here; huddled together for safety. While all those people on the strip were getting decimated. I wanted to berate them, and I wanted to chastise the national guardsman and police officers. But, instead, I just pulled out into the side streets. I kind of knew where the Pilot was, so I commenced trying to get to it. We needed fuel. And rest. Part of me wanted to go back into the fray. I was overweight and overage. But, all I wanted to do was to destroy the aswang.

I came up against some train tracks that I couldn't get around, and then there was a low bridge that I couldn't find my way around and then I got twisted up in circles while driving in residential neighborhoods. The whole time I was trying to avoid the blockade and yet kept getting funneled toward that spot. Roads can be like that sometimes. It didn't matter, if we did end up at the blockade. But I couldn't imagine how I would get through it. We wouldn't, was how. And then, there we were. Not getting through. On a side street and kiddy-cornered to the conglomeration of militia, guardsmen, and law officers. My instinct told me not to get too close, so I was careful to stay away. That was when it occurred to me that I was basically in an alleyway and there wasn't enough space to do a k-turn.

With that in mind, I watched as an aswang flew over the crowd and multiple shotguns blasted it out of the sky. Its divisions were bursting out of it before it even hit the ground. The demons' laser light eyes made good targets, tho, and there was plenty of ambient Las Vegas light to see by; so the militia gunned them down like skeet. The guardsman cleared the area and sprayed the remains with acid. And the crowd backed way off because the acid fumes were crazy toxic. And now that people were spreading out, I wasn't feeling so secure in our position.

I began reversing as they were fanning out toward us. A lot of those guys were focused on my tractor- suspicious of it- in that way that men can be for no real reason. But they got distracted when the screaming began in earnest. The kind of screaming that happens in unison. Amplified by orders of magnitude.

I had to watch my mirrors, to get back to the spot where I could turn around at. I needed to make another attempt at traversing the side roads. I asked Charisma, "What's happening?"

"Nothing good," she said.

"I can hear that," I said. My truck was loud, but the gunshots and shrieking were louder. I was able to steal glances and so I saw what she meant. The swarm had found the gathering. And the gathering was fighting back reasonably well, but they were also sustaining savage injuries as they did so. And I knew a lot of 'survivors' would die from the venom.

The aswang kept multiplying. There were too many of them. Their eyes were creating a light of their own. There was a cloud of them and they began ganging up on their victims. The humans were scattering in all directions; including toward us. I got the truck backed around the corner. I was about to pull away, but when I put it into drive, I saw something sickening. I saw the wraith. It had floated into their numbers. And there was nothing any of them could do about it. It was an extermination. I drove away in disgust. Angela apparently despised the angel of death as much as I did. She was freaking out again; hissing and meowing hatefully from the inside of her backpack. Charisma- again... failed to register her- otherwise abnormally docile- cat's reaction as anything out of the ordinary...

I got maybe a hundred yards down the road when I heard the slapping thud of an aswang crashing into the roof of my truck. Again, I thought only of my windows. If I lost a window, then we'd be totally miserable. I jumped out of the truck with my staff in my hand. I slammed the door behind me and- dead serious- I caught the bat demon's outstretched hand in my door. After that, it was a cinch to knock its block off, so to speak. I opened the door and used the staff to flick it down into the road. And then I started jumping on it. That was an effective way to crush the little ones inside of it, but it was also an effective way to vent my frustration.

I was livid. I kept thinking about that mine in New Mexico. That it was us who had released the angel of death. I was jumping up and down on the demon and stomping on it, and I was just so sad. We were killing everybody. To save them from taxes and bureaucracy and medical malpractice and their own stupidity and a fraudulent money system and from imperialism and from a lying news media. To save them from themselves. Now they were all going to die. We weren't saving them from anything. We were killing these people. I kept stomping and stomping and stomping until I knew it was impossible that anything had survived. Then I got back into the truck and tried to keep from sobbing. I know Charisma saw the tears in my eyes. But I didn't care.

By way of distraction- and out of necessity- I pushed the brake valve and drove further out into the residential areas. Eventually I found the connections I needed to get over the train tracks and around that low bridge. I took more side roads going north. When we got to the truck stop there was almost nobody there. It was a weekday night. It should've been full. It wasn't. They wouldn't sell me fuel. They just gave it to me. They said that's how it is now. As I fueled up, I could hear the guns and the screaming in the distance. When I parked the truck, I found I couldn't bring myself to look at Charisma. I put the transmission in neutral and pulled the brake valve and coughed, and coughed again, and then I started crying. I curled up into a ball and bawled like a child. Thinking of evil. Wondering if I was evil.

Chapter 14
A Sickening Sight
We completed our evening routine. After I pulled myself together, that is. It was hot and I idled the truck for AC. The internet was still working, but we decided we didn't want to know what the world at large had to say. Our food supply was dwindling, I noticed. But there was still a few days' worth left. And plenty of MREs. It proved difficult to make love because we were essentially in a holy war zone, and that proved to be distracting. But we managed. The gunshots never stopped. Some close by. Some far off. And it wasn't easy to fall asleep, but it wasn't hard, either. My body remembered the venom and exhaustion overwhelmed me. The truck stop was insulated insofar as it was in an inconspicuous area; away from the Vegas crowds. However, it was on a main road, also.

The new day was dawning. I awakened to the sound of Angela hissing. And meowing. And growling in that way that domestic cats do. She was sitting on the dash. Behind the curtain. Looking out the window. Some of the other truckers were shouting at one another. And there was a crowd of some sort out there; producing an excited and audible murmur. Angela was not happy. I saw a strange light. And, of course, Charisma knew what was happening while I was still wondering what I was seeing.

"I have to let her out," Charisma said.

"Ok," I said, sleepily, and dumbly. Charisma jumped up front as Angela was becoming hysterical. I'd never heard a cat sound so much like a poltergeist. The light we were seeing was coming from Angela's eyes; I saw. Charisma opened the door and the cat immediately bolted out into the purple pre-dawn light.

I threw open the curtains so we could watch her run off. Simultaneously; we shoved our feet into our boots, shouldered our pistols, and ran out after her; wearing the minimal clothes we'd managed to throw on. This was a new thing. Even Charisma was perplexed, albeit less so than myself. I began to understand when I saw a militia contingent marching down the street. They were passing by the truck stop right about then and it was serendipitous timing; in retrospect. Programming, probably. The contingent consisted of about two or three hundred people; armed with whatever weapons were available to them. Many wore improvised armor; motorcycle gear, in a lot of cases. Or maybe they were just bikers.

The people at the front of the contingent were making a commotion; trying to halt the forward momentum of the entirety. They were afraid of something. Angela was bolting toward them, and her eyes were shining white; two orbs of light in her face; making a halo around her head. The militia didn't even notice the luminescent cat. They were seeing the black silhouette of the angel of death floating up the street and coming toward them. And I guess they'd learned what that indicated, because they were frantic to turn and run.

That was when Angela stepped out ahead of the crowd; hissing and caterwauling disturbingly. Standing defiantly between the humans and Hell's angel. Charisma and I could see the whole thing from where we were positioned. Angela's eyes- already quite bright- shone forth with the divine light of creation. A blinding spectacle of prismatic energy; radiantly scintillating with refractions of all wavelengths combined into a singular ray of white. The ray honed in on the shadow and illuminated it so as that we could see the form; frozen in place. We saw the face. And it wasn't a skeleton. And it wasn't demonic. It was a woman. A beautiful woman. Who she was; I could not guess. But I know now; she was the schizophrenic mother of an unholy God. Her figure; I'd thought it to be jellyfish like. It was actually an elaborate gown she was wearing. A gown that billowed about her and dangled below her as she floated along. The woman was immaculate, but, too, she was miserable. And agonized.

Angela was visibly enraged. I'd never seen a cat so angry. The crowd was loud but our wildly caterwauling feline was louder. Angela's ray of holy light was an onslaught; focused with an intense and universal passion reserved only for those most wicked and despised.

I got the impression that resisting this required a tremendous act of will and strength on the part of the unholy angel of death. The shadow of death- exposed and illuminated by the wrath of divine blessing- grimaced and shrank and hardened itself again into a black void of a being; and then sank down into the earth; through the street itself; away; into the crust and hopefully through the mantle and to the core. To where- I prayed- maybe it was hot enough to destroy her. Forgetting that such a place was her kingdom.

The crowd was stunned; still and silent. Charisma hurried to her cat; who again was just an ordinary looking feline, happy to be picked up and carried off by the one who fed it and watered it. Charisma brought Angela back to the truck as the militia collected its composure. "Hey, can we take your cat with us?" somebody called after us. "Sorry, no!" I called back.

We were back in the truck and I could see a small mob had stood apart and fallen behind. They'd watched us walk away. They were making me nervous. They were talking amongst themselves and staring at us. I'd gotten enough sleep to feel refreshed, and Las Vegas was a warzone. The truck was running and the hours of service didn't mean anything anymore. Not in my opinion, anyway. I drove us out of there as the tablet flashed red and started making annoying noises. I turned it off. In the passenger seat; Charisma was holding her cat and trying to console it. "That was something," I said. "Yeah, it was," she agreed.

The desert absorbed us. We soon found ourselves deep in the outback of America. One of the most barren and far flung and forgotten regions of the contiguous United States. The temperature outside climbed higher and higher until it sat around 107 degrees. On full blast, the air conditioner could hardly combat the heat.

I decided to take the easternmost route through Nevada, based on the timeless trucker wisdom of staying away from California if and whenever possible. The sun reflected bright off the arid landscape and I drove hard to make it to the higher country north of I-80. The sun was still beating down on us, but the temperature dropped below 100 and eventually I found us some shade by some trees by a creek called Rebel at the foot of an isolated mountain range. We stayed there until the next morning.

The next morning I realized I'd driven us twenty miles off course. I'd been tired and thought I knew the roads, but I'd missed the turn we needed. Without any alternative, we backtracked to get back on course and then headed out toward Klamath Falls to fuel up. We got there in the late afternoon.

Klamath Falls had every characteristic of a city under attack. The National Guard was there, but I couldn't say where. We could see their temporary barracks erected at a municipal parking lot. And their trucks were around. But the soldiers themselves were elsewhere. Or, they were dead. That was entirely possible. At the truck stop, we were given fuel for free again and it was becoming difficult to recognize the world we inhabited. People were few and far between and- of course- those we did encounter were invariably morose. But, too, they were kind and optimistic. We all felt the presence of Christ in our hearts. It was impossible not to.

Really, I wasn't overly interested in the exact specifics of the new ways of the new world. I knew enough to know I didn't want to know. Some call that maturity. Some call it willful ignorance. But as long as I could do my thing, that was good enough for me. If we opened up the internet and took an interest in what was happening out there, my mentality- and my narrative- would just be a lot of other people's thoughts and stories. Presumably generated by some combination of bots and cosmic programming more so than by actual human experience and expression.

We were doing the Lord's work. Every day out there I became more goal oriented than the day before. Charisma had always been that way; I was realizing. And finally, I was beginning to identify with her focus and drive. By Gnosis count, there were 500 million people in the world- less, now- but none of them were us. None of them shared our burden or our perspective. None of them were relevant to our purposes. It'd be different if they were getting in our way, but again, it was a different world. Things had changed. Everything was free. People were nice. People were smart. People were divine.

All that is to say, we got in and out of Klamath Falls without any difficulty besides the usual detours around side streets caused by traffic jams caused by disabled vehicles. The authorities had ensured people could pass through; even if we had to traverse residential areas to do so. There were aswang in the sky, we saw; a few times. But they weren't in our way and we had places to be.

I hadn't even asked Charisma what we were doing out there. Every ordeal was blurring together. I knew where we were going, but I didn't wonder why we were going there. Since it had finally occurred to me, I asked her, "What is the next thing? I can't keep track."

"The next thing is secrecy. It'll be an unveiling unlike anything humanity has ever seen. Evil thrives in secrecy. Secrecy is the stronghold of evil. We're motivating the hylics to root out forbidden knowledge. An inclination they've by no accident been lacking. Shadow government, deep state, new world order, secret societies, corporations, NGOs, the sciences, the financiers, the industries, the utilities, the illuminati. Even the Catholic church. Even the Jewry. Especially the Jewry. Clandestine organizations of all varieties. It won't make any difference. Anybody doing something they're not supposed to be; they'll be found out. It's probably the greatest blow against corruption yet," she said.

"Yeah, but at what cost?" I asked.

"Only one way to find out," she said, ominously.

Eugene was about the same as Klamath Falls. There were aswang in the sky, and there were dead bodies that hadn't been collected yet. There were National Guardsmen and other branches of the military, as well. There were crowds of militia. There were cops and first responders. Interestingly, there weren't any helicopters. I don't think I'd seen a single helicopter since before we got to New Mexico. Obviously, pilots had grown tired of flying suicide missions and the government had gotten tired of throwing equipment into the garbage. We detoured to a detour that took us back to the beginning of the first detour- that's called a five boroughs' detour, by the way- and then we detoured to a new detour that took us to a fourth and fifth detour, and then we got out of there.

After that, we drove west to a town called Florence. Florence was a Pacific ocean town. It was the middle of the night, but we could see the ocean by the full moon light. I could sense the immensity of it just by being near it. Charisma was ecstatic; in her subdued way. "Can we sleep here, love?" She didn't want to leave it. She hadn't seen that ocean in years and her home was on the other side of it.

I would think that being on the other side of the Pacific Ocean is about the same as being on the other side of the planet, but I got the impression that she could feel a connection through the water somehow. And that's not such a foreign concept, considering the world isn't real. Here. There. Same difference, really.

North of Florence, I found a spot where we could pull off right where the 101 ran alongside the ocean. We were parked on a cliff like 50 feet above the water. I had to talk her out of trying to find a way down there. We'd be going to the water when we woke up anyways. What I wanted to do was to go check out the acid throwers. I hadn't even examined one yet, and they may have been more dangerous than the rockets or the grenades.

I put on my headlamp and spent a good twenty minutes examining the mechanisms. There weren't any instructions; but it was pretty simple. Basically a glorified squirt gun. Made entirely from an assortment of different rubbers. The canisters were pressurized, so the spray didn't require any accelerant. There was an on/off selector to open the flow of acid. There was a lever to adjust the flow rate. And there was a knob to widen or narrow the spray by adjusting the nozzle. The canisters had the acid hazmat symbol on them and were labeled as Hydrofluoric Acid.

It only then occurred to me that those canisters could have exploded out in the desert heat. Thankfully, they had not. And now that I'd performed a cursory examination of the acid throwers, I felt like I could use them if I had to. So I returned to my love and we did our evening routine. Leaving the curtains open so we could look out over the moonlit Pacific ocean. I wondered about checking my phone; to read the news or to examine social media for articles or memes. But I never once dared to actually do so. I dreaded it.

When we woke up the next day, I called my mother. It'd been a long time since we'd spoken and she was happy to hear from me, and I was pleased to hear they were doing well; staying up in Vermont. She informed me that the Providence area was a disaster area. Fall River included. That wasn't surprising. She told me she was sad because a lot of her gardens would be suffering, if not dying. But, the whole country was suffering and dying. So... So, realistically, her gardens were an acceptable loss; relative to what many people were losing. We had a nice conversation and she made a few comments about world peace, the end of starvation and preventable illness, and the dawn of a golden age, and maybe for the first time I wondered about the world wide ramifications of our activities. My father was eavesdropping and making ignorant comments in the background; content to be- and surely intent on being- the last asshole on Earth, saying: 'This whole mess is your fault,' and 'What kind of person opens the gates of Hell on purpose?' and 'Why couldn't you just leave well enough alone?'

We headed out in the late afternoon. Our destination was only about ten or so miles up the road. Not far at all. It was a small parking lot that should have been full of west coast wanderers but instead was completely empty. The location was a scenic viewpoint. Similar to the viewpoint we'd spent the night at, but with access to a sandy beach by the outlet of a creek called Cummins. A very truckerish creek name, I might add.

Charisma got out of the truck with Angela in her backpack. And I got out, too. I asked her, "So? What do we do now?" And she said, "We have to wait for high tide." I had enough brains to see that high tide would either be pretty soon, or that it had recently ended. But I did not have enough brains to ascertain which. Charisma knew what I was thinking and she told me, "The sand above the water line is dry. The tide is coming in. It'll be high tide soon."

"What happens then?" I asked.

"Back up the truck. Set up the 50 cal."

We did more than that. We set up the fifty cal, and we set up the rocket launcher, and we set up the XM250, and we kept the grenade launchers close. Charisma didn't specify what she expected to be coming out of the water, but I got the impression it'd be intimidating. When all the weapons were prepared; we sat and waited. Occasionally, somebody drove by on the road, but not very often. The subtly sinking sun shone high and bright out above the water; reflecting off of the waves. The cloudless sky was light blue and the ocean was dark blue and- to the north, south, and east- the Oregon coast was expansive and massive. Mountainous terrain blanketed by Douglas Firs. Waves rolled into the shallows and crested low and white in patterns determined by rock formations beneath the surface. A pleasant ocean breeze cooled the midday heat.

Charisma braided a paracord around her emerald so that it was at the end of about a 90 foot length. That emerald was easily more valuable than everything my family owned combined. Or, maybe not anymore, since money had been abolished, but a couple weeks prior; definitely. The gem was dark green, and alive with captured luminescence. I had always thought emeralds were light green, or jade green, but I guess not.

"It's time," she said.

Then she walked down to the water's edge, placed the emerald on the bedrock of a clear and shallow pool, proceeded to run the length of the chord back up to where the purslane grew, placed a volcanic rock atop the chord to keep it in place, and then returned to our battlestation. I stood behind the fifty cal, not knowing what to expect. She held the rocket launcher in her hands. I'd asked her what she thought would be coming out of the ocean and she said,

"I don't know. Something big." And I thought, 'Well, that makes sense. It's a big ocean.'

This took time. Not a little bit of time. I'd gotten used to these things happening pretty fast. That day, I was wondering if something had gone wrong. Or, I was getting my hopes up that nothing would happen. Eventually, something happened. That was when we put in our ear plugs and put on our motorcycle helmets.

There were spikes coming out of the water. But they were long. They were so long, in fact, that they were coming close to reaching us before we even had anything to shoot at. It was an array of long slow moving spikes emerging and they were waving through the air in such a way that they could have decimated my truck effortlessly; to say nothing of our persons. As the terrifyingly long spikes were coming at us; too, they were reaching into the sky.

It took a minute, but I finally realized what we were looking at. It was a sea urchin. A gargantuan sea urchin. "It's a sea urchin!" I shouted. And Charisma said, "I know." And I felt stupid, but I didn't care because Charisma let me plant my seed in her garden every night, so...

So; some sea urchins have short spikes. Spines. Tines? Whatever. This one was not one of those. This thing had long spines. The body of it was, like, the size of, say... that shiny bean in Chicago. So, each of its spines was about the same length as, maybe, the average telephone pole... The spiny tips were certainly sharp, but it was the swaying and elongated mass of the spikes that posed the more significant threat.

Charisma fired a rocket into the monster while I was still admiring its dimensions. I had a flashback to fighting the three headed dog in Washington DC. The rocket exploded toward the base of the spines and broke apart some of the more menacing ones. But the warhead had detonated too early and hadn't succeeded in reaching the actual body. The sky was raining ocean water and sand and sea urchin chunks- as well as red hot shrapnel- and I was thinking how I don't like rockets and Charisma was screaming at me, "Aim for center mass!" I knew what she meant. Center mass was at the base of the spines that had- in just a few seconds- gone from not really in our faces to really in our faces.

I started dumping 50 cal rounds into our adversary. I'd never fired a 50 cal before but every gun guy knows what they are capable of. These bullets had velocity that exceeded any concept of normality. The rigid density of the urchin's spines would have been a challenge for most other firearms and it was just dumb luck we had the right tool for the job. I don't know what we would have done without the military weaponry. The high powered rifle was decimating the target; the spines were dropping off of it and the shell of it was losing the domed structure it required to support its enormous weight.

Charisma waited until I had dumped an entire can of rounds into the body of the creature. Then she fired another rocket at it. Again; a violent explosion rocked the creature. And rocked us as well. We could feel the heat washing over us as oceanic debris rained down upon us. I picked up the M250 and I was prepared to start blasting, but I realized that the spines weren't swaying anymore. They'd mostly fallen still.

The vertical spines were pitching forward and the gaping orifice we'd blasted through the edifice was tilting over until it faced down into the water. And it was a good thing the urchin wasn't moving anymore because those spines were so close that we could reach out and touch them. The urchin's actual body remained at the water's edge.

I was expecting X-amount of smaller sea urchins to come crawling out; but that was not what happened. What happened was that the dead urchin began emitting smoke. Not just the smoke from the rocket. This was a thick, slick, inky, oily, black, and all together more unnatural sort of smoke. Like, the blackest smoke imaginable, which was also somehow soaking wet. I know now that it wasn't a smoke at all, but- at the time- that was what I thought it was. What it really was was more analogous to a ghost than it was to a smoke, but it wasn't a ghost, either. It was the shadow of death. Again. A sickening sight, to say the least.

When I saw the tarry ooze coalescing and moving as if it was alive, I was certain that we were about to die. The shadow lingered within the spines of the urchin; as if reluctant to remove itself from its natural habitat. The murderous essence wafted among the massive spines and I began to become accustomed to looking at it. Then we started hearing splashing. There was something alive inside of the urchin but it wasn't more urchins. I couldn't see its form but I could see its splashing and the splashing was reminiscent of that of a fish. And it wasn't just one of them. One after another these... somethings... were gathering in the churning of the water and the sand; beneath the carcass of the urchin.

I had the urge to start shooting into them; but I knew that if I blew them apart then they would only multiply. I jumped down from the catwalk and started putting on the rubber acid suit. Soon, I was protected from head to foot. But it wasn't possible- or, rather, I was finding it difficult- to get through those spines. Furthermore; there was an intimidating living entity- slick like oil, black as night and globular, as well as amorphous and stretching like strands of slime- moving throughout the structure.

While I was trying to work up the nerve to slip through the spines and make a move against the demons beneath the urchin; the cat in the bag started hissing and shrieking and freaking out again; eyes aglow white. Meanwhile, the fish demons- or, whatever they were- had created a channel through the sand and were all slipping through the spines and escaping into the ocean. I couldn't get near them; they'd be underwater even if I could. And there was a menacing ghost smoke moving crazily through the structure of the carcass. Even if I did have the nerve, I couldn't spray the acid at anything anyways because my truck- and my love and her cat and myself- were very much downwind from the targets.

This situation resolved itself when Charisma let her enraged feline out of its backpack. Angela had the same angry look on her face as she had had the day before. I was happy to see it, because the inky slime monster was imposing in a way that I couldn't figure out how to possibly combat. If it wanted us, then it would have us. But it displayed a reluctance to attack us. A reluctance which I later figured out had everything to do with Charisma and I having the light of Christ in our hearts and nothing to do with the being being timid.

Angela scrambled around Charisma and scurried off into the array of spines. There; the cat meowed psychotically and her radiant eyes flared and her hissing toothy mouth emitted the light of Christ in the form of a blinding white ray. The ray succeeded in chasing the black slime into hiding. It hid directly behind the urchin's hulking carcass so as that the urchin was between it and the cat. Angela, of course, knew exactly where the angel from Hell was. But, she couldn't strategize what to do about it. She just kept caterwauling and hissing and making various other angry cat noises.

Based on no information whatsoever; I was hoping the slimy ghost would disappear into the water. It did no such thing. What it did do was exactly what I would have done if I was a Satanic ooze being confronted by the holy light of the Lord. It darted off into the sky at such an angle that the sea urchin's remains remained directly between the cat and itself. And it traveled at such an ungodly speed that there was little hope of thwarting its efforts. And Angela- bless her soul- attempted to blitz around the urchin but found her way blocked by the spines. Forced to clamber over the obstacles; she lost sight of the vile entity and thus remained powerless to injure it.

The light went out of Angela's eyes and she sauntered back to Charisma; who picked her up and consoled her with baby talk and snuggles. There were still aquatic demons plopping out of the urchin, and I was frustrated that I couldn't see what they were; but the frustration only lasted for another few seconds or so. Then I noticed that they were all around us. Their laser red eyes were easy to spot, even in the daytime. I put the acid thrower down on my tires-stupid, I know, or not, I don't know, I'm not a chemist- and I picked up the machinegun; but then I saw that these creatures weren't making any moves.

They couldn't leave the water. They were mermaids. Mermaids from Hell. I say mermaids and not mermen because they were definitively female. They had gnarly tribal tits, and womanly waists. But their faces were hideously demonic and inhuman; albeit feminine nonetheless. Their cheeks were gaunt. Their blazing red eyes were sunken in hollow orbital sockets. Their wide grins were full of teeth that were sharp and sharkish. Their noses were just two holes in their faces. They had no hair; only clusters of hundreds of short sharp spikes. They looked like they'd swam out of the magma of Hell. And their flesh was that black snake skin that seemed to be ubiquitous to pretty much all of these things. They either had snake skin or exoskeletons, or both.

I put the machine gun down on my tires and picked up the acid thrower. I wasn't going to blast them apart because doing so would just make more of them; but the humans had- we had- created the acid throwers specifically to resolve that exact dilemma and I was curious to try it out for myself. But, I never got the chance. When I moved toward the few that were nearest to me; they jumped back into the water and swam away.

I took the acid gear off and stowed it all in the yellow crate with the acid throwers. I took down the 50 cal and strapped it to the catwalk beside the yellow crate. Charisma retrieved her emerald and we put Angela and the M250 back in the truck. Then we kind of just stared at the dead sea urchin. Charisma put her arms around me and I pulled her in close. Then we started kissing and I was grabbing at her and she was grabbing at me and it was a beautiful moment on a beautiful day at a beautiful place. Weird circumstances, but, still... And then we heard somebody say, "Excuse us. We hope we're not interrupting."

We both jumped; startled. We'd thought we were alone. Suddenly, there were three guys standing by my truck. Their pale skin was laced with jet black veins; like they had some kind of serious illness. And they were naked. Which was alarming, until I recognized them for what they were. I squinted and scrutinized them. They had big smiles on almost human faces; evidently quite proud of their progression.

I said, "I guess we should have expected you here."

"Of course you should have," said one.

"Can we help you with something?" Charisma asked them.

"Oh. No. Thank you. You already have. And you continue to do so," said another.

Chapter 15
You Are Nowhere
"If you're going to be human, then maybe you could learn to hide your shame? There's a woman present," I said.

They took my meaning and one of them asked, "Do you have any extra clothing?"

"Yeah. Wait here," I said.

Charisma and I jumped up into the tractor and I found some shorts and pajama pants which I didn't mind losing. And then I jumped back out and gave them the clothes. Charisma remained inside. They put the clothes on, smiling and happy, and I asked, "Don't you guys teleport? How will you teleport the clothes?"

And they- one of them- said, "The same way we teleport the flesh."

"I see... Um... Can I ask you all something?" I asked.

"Something else? Yes," one said.

"What are you?"

"If you haven't figured it out on your own, then it is against our interests to inform you," one of them said.

"Better you remain uninformed," another said.

"Ask Charisma. She knows," the third offered.

I drank in their appearance; baffled. Their nature made them seem powerful, but their demeanor made them seem harmless. I wouldn't have wanted to fight a single one of them, but three of them would be worse, obviously. Their form was human and masculine, but they were alien and bizarre. Their muscles were well defined. Their bone structure was ideal. They had no hair, and no irises. I can't recall if they had teeth, or tongues, but their voices were more human than ever before. They looked like dead people, kind of. But with sparkles of light twinkling in their black blood. I could sense that we were enemies, but they acted like we were friends. The thing that bothered me most was that I couldn't quantify them. I didn't know where I stood with them. I couldn't figure out what our relationship was supposed to be. I was still pissed about them harassing us in Washington DC, but it was an impotent resentment.

I said, "Probably about time for us to hit the road. You gentlemen have any big plans for the day, or anything?"

"No. No plans," one said.

"We plan on becoming," another said.

"It is good if you go. The sooner you go is the sooner we become," said the third.

"Alright then. See you next time, I guess," I said.

'See you next time,' they all repeated in unison.

I got into the truck and Charisma said, "You shouldn't talk to them."

I finished the last of the coffee I had made before we left. It was over a week old. I watched the spectors in my mirrors. They walked down to the urchin and began climbing on its spines. Not just climbing, but- it looked like-playing; swinging and doing flips and jumping around. "They're like big kids," I said, adding, "I asked them what they are and they told me to ask you what they are. So, what are they?"

"Can we leave, please?" she asked.

I obliged. We pulled out and headed north. I was beginning to trust the roads again. I felt like we could use the interstates and be alright. Everybody was being so chill that things were running relatively smoothly; from what I could tell. I drove for a little while and I asked her again, "Are you going to tell me what you know about those things, or no?"

"They're evil," she said.

"They seem kind of nice," I said.

"They're deceiving you," she said.

"I know. But why?"

"To make you make an error later, probably."

"Ok. So, they're evil, but; what are they?"

"They're the opposite of me. The opposite of you. The opposite of the cat. They're here to defeat us. To nullify our purposes."

"They're not doing anything. They haven't done anything."

"That doesn't mean anything. They don't have to do anything. They just have to be. They just have to become. The equation will balance itself."

"How many archons are left?" I asked her.

"Too many," she said. And I couldn't disagree.

We found a rest area eventually and stopped to change our clothes and get cleaned up. We organized the truck, too. And we boiled some water to make soup. We were out in the forest and only saw one other person; an old guy, who just stopped to piss and then left. I could see that Charisma needed a break. Or, she needed something to take her mind off of things.

I got distracted; wondering where all the people had gone. But it suddenly occurred to me: The deception was over.

"I figured out where all the people went," I said.

Charisma smiled a little and said, "I was wondering when you would."

"You knew? Why didn't you tell me?"

"I wanted to see when you'd figure it out."

"When did it happen?"

"When Angela banished the angel of death."

I couldn't believe I'd been so oblivious for so long, but actually, I could totally believe it. That didn't matter. This was good news. It put me in a good mood and I think my good mood put Charisma in a good mood, too. We picked up where we left off back at the beach- before we were interrupted. We climbed into the sleeper berth, pulling each other's clothes off. Under the covers- with the truck idling and the air conditioner blowing; we made love and laid together happily and then we made love again.

If the reader of this narrative can guess where all the people went, then it means I did an okay job telling the story. If the reader of this narrative cannot guess where all the people went, then give me a break. I am not a novelist. I am just a stupid truck driver.

I should mention that I was actually happy about this part. Seven billion people had- at some point- disappeared from the Earth. But, they weren't dead. They were never alive to begin with. We hadn't lost seven billion living beings. We had lost the illusion of seven billion living beings.

The grim truth set in as we were driving out toward Portland. The aswang were still out there. Worse, the shadow of death had returned. It could be anywhere; doing anything.

I asked Charisma, "What are we going to do about the shadow of death?"

"We're going to track it down," she said.

"How?" I asked.

"Look at Angela," she said.

Angela had her paws up on the passenger side window sill; facing the east and looking toward the south. It hadn't occurred to me, but she'd been doing that all day. And when I'd been driving on the curving loop in and out of the rest area; she became confused. That was the only time she'd moved around much at all. When the 101 curved west, she started twisting her head around; trying to find southeast. When we got on 26, she sat upright on Charisma's lap and stared out past the mirror; toward the southeast.

"That thing could be anywhere," I said.

"Anywhere, but, specifically, over there," Charisma said; pointing toward the southeast.

My instinct was to second guess her, but then I remembered; Charisma knew everything about everything, her and her cat were holy servants of the lord, and I was just a stupid truck driver. So, I decided I'd just do what I'd been doing all my life. I'd shut up, suck it up, and drive the truck. As my father would say.

That worked well until we got into Portland. As we emerged from the tunnel; we could see the aswang circling over downtown. Another thing was that, technically; Portland was still Portland. I had half a mind to go get high on pot, while we were there. After a lifetime of obedience, and considering the circumstances; I kind of wanted to. Charisma was totally against it. I guess because she's a nun, or whatever.

Getting high would have been a bad idea, considering we were trying to save people's lives and all. If I got stoned I might have gotten us killed. But people got stoned all the time and all I ever got to do was drive a big old truck. I wanted to see what I was missing out on. At any rate, Portland was infested with aswang, as it turned out. And it wasn't the sort of aswang presence that could be ignored.

We'd come in direct contact two times, before we could get out of there.

I decided to fuel up, while we were passing through, because it was an opportune time to do so. There were some random hippies and druggies wandering around around the fuel station. That was normal enough. The truck parking was at like 5% capacity. That was very strange. It should have been full.

I used to watch the other truckers as they wandered in and out of the truck stops. The truck stop parking lots would always be at full capacity. It was just so many trucks and so many truckers. And I would think; 'These trucks can't be real. These people can't be real.' And it turns out, I was right. It was similar to fake profiles on the internet; thousands of comments on a video of a guy peeling an apple, or throwing a frisbee to a dog. Meanwhile; zero comments on the politician's bill to take your guns away.

False reality was old news, by that point. But, me being me. Me being slow. I was only then piecing things together. I couldn't believe what I'd always known. That was what I was thinking while I was fueling up. Free fuel, too; again, interestingly. Afterward; I parked the truck and we were about to go inside to grab a shower when we noticed an aswang coming down from the sky. It was careening toward another trucker who had his hood open; the guy was wrenching on something, with his tools spread around at his feet. He was overweight, older, black skinned, bespectacled, white haired, bushy haired, and balding; with a grease stained bright yellow safety jacket on. I didn't hesitate to grab my bo staff and rush out there to confront the demon. As I approached it, I realized it was about the biggest aswang I had yet encountered. The thing was nine feet tall if it was an inch.

I was too late to prevent harm from coming to the trucker. But, I saved his life and he didn't get bit. What happened was that the demon grabbed the guy by the shoulder and threw him to the ground. The talons pierced the flesh and broke his collarbone, too. That was all, though.

An instant later and I was on that son of a bitch. It was tricky to close the distance, but I broke the bone- or whatever- in the wing and then I was able to catch the demon in the eyes with a flying cross strike which I had to follow up with a six hit combo just to get back far enough to prepare for another attack. The demon was discombobulated, but it was also enraged. It leapt at me claws first, but I smashed the hand and jumped away and I was getting lined up for a flying downward smash when Charisma blasted the things skull apart.

The smaller demons were inclined to escape from the neck hole and she kept blasting them with buckshot as they poured out through the remains of each other. After 7 shells, she had to reload. I applied the method. I bashed the ever-loving snot out of that demon. From head to toe. One demon shot out of its armpit before I noticed and it was airborne before I could stop it. That was a harsh mistake for me, because it meant we failed. It only took one to make a thousand more; or more. Still, that was the only one that got away. Charisma dumped shells into it and I beat on it until we were certain no more aswang would be crawling out of it. The driver shook my hand and said thank you. Charisma insisted she stitch up his wounds for him. Then we took our shower and left.

Another aswang attacked our truck on the way out of Portland, but I was on the highway doing like 60 miles per hour and that demon was small; too small- or too disoriented from crashing into my grill- to break through my truck's glass. I just kept driving while the aswang dug its claws into my tupperware hood. A few seconds later and the thing tumbled off of us and collided with the asphalt.

After that, we- thankfully- experienced limited excitement for the rest of the day. We had an unusual task to contend with. It reminded me of when I had to find that bunker in the woods to rescue Charisma. But more frustrating because I could mostly drive the bike as the crow flies, but I could not drive the semi as the crow flies. Also, that was a couple hour chore. This chore could have gone on forever.

Angela was leading us where we were going. She was as focused as the hunters she descended from. You could say she was obsessed. Sometimes she ate, or drank, or relieved herself; but other than those brief moments; she only stared out toward the horizon with stone determination.

This situation presented a few challenges, though. The major challenge was that this was the day that the internet cut out. Probably it was the day we needed the internet the most, and suddenly it was gone. We were thinking to start making cold calls to various cities and asking if they had reports of widespread fatalities, but we had no directory to facilitate the effort; because the internet was gone, and, as it turned out, the phone operator couldn't help us because they couldn't do literally anything without the internet.

As for Angela; for one thing; the interstate doesn't go in a straight line. If you want to go east, then you'll be going south and north to get there. So the cat would invariably notice when our course was off course and then get frustrated and meow alarmingly. We'd say, 'We know, we know,' but the cat was only calm when we were going in the correct direction. Another problem was that we weren't always going in the correct direction. Eastbound roads drift north and south. Southbound roads drift east and west. The best we could do was to go in a good enough direction. Eventually the cat learned to compromise and accepted that I was trying my best. Yet another problem was that we had no idea how far we were going.

I knew the cat was going to be uncomfortable and anxious if and when we stopped to rest, so I pushed us as far as we could go. We made it to Ogden, Utah. That was where we had to shut down at. There wasn't even any coffee to drink. I was tireder than all get out. And again, I was regretting never teaching Charisma how to drive; but, really,

I wouldn't have wanted her behind the wheel of my tractor even if I had taught her. I know people were dying out there, but, come on. That was my tractor. Anyways. I was doing my best. I had wanted to stop at Twin Falls, but I ran the extra miles just to make the cat happy.

When we got to the truck stop in Ogden, I tried to raise some other drivers on the CB, but there was nobody. I went inside and asked the cashier if he'd heard anything about a lot of people dying all at once. The guy- a nice guy; chrome dome, pale, silly mustache, obviously used to talking to truckers- didn't hesitate to give me a piece of his mind. As far as he knew; most of the world was dead. Asking where there were some dead people was like asking if I knew where was the melted ice cube in a bucket of water.

I felt bad for the guy, because I could see that he was shook up; so I took the time to explain that those people who had disappeared had not died. They'd never been real to begin with. That's why society was still functioning without them. Albeit, barely functioning because a lot of people actually had been dying; thanks to the aswang and dragons and the others and now the angel of death, too. The cashier said he 'got relatives that just disappeared off the face of the earth and can't nobody contact them.' I asked him when the last time he saw them was. He said it'd been decades. I said there'd probably been some updates since then. New versions of the reality program; updating while we were sleeping, or looking in the other direction. I said that's probably why people who are close on one day can drift apart and become strangers on the next day. They were non-playable characters all along; getting phased out of the software to open up memory for a new job or a new hobby or a new addiction or a new existential crisis; or whatever. And he shrugged and said that that makes as much sense as anything else, and I just nodded; wondering about my own cousins and aunts and whoever else. We talked for a while longer about some other difficult to process occurrences that had transpired, but I'll be addressing those such happenings shortly. Being as that I forgot to mention them previously.

Back in the truck; we ate dinner and skipped sex and fell asleep and Angela just stared out toward the southeast all night; as far as I know. She was nice enough to be quiet about it, though. What a considerate cat. Actually- I realized this when I woke up- Angela wasn't staring southeast anymore; she was staring east. That made sense because we were around Salt Lake City and that is the major crossroads to the northwest when you're coming from the east; which is to say; we'd gone south far enough. I refilled the tanks with free fuel and we took off toward Wyoming. Angela stared intently forward from Charisma's lap.

I should mention that there'd been aswang in the skies above every town that had more than one horse. But they hadn't crossed us and we hadn't crossed them. You could usually see at least one flying bat humanoid demon creature in the sky in some direction or other. Similarly, there were guardsmen and cops wandering around, but they weren't how they used to be. They all looked listless and disheartened. There were far fewer of them than they were accustomed to and I guess their numbers were important to them; because they all looked depressed whenever I saw them. I rarely saw them doing any fighting. They were usually kind of just hanging around. What I am trying- and failing- to say is that I was getting used to looking at the way things were. The interstate was wide open. The diesel fuel was completely free. I'd seen so many dead bodies that I didn't even notice them anymore. The demons were omnipresent. It had all become somewhat unremarkable.

The thing I should be talking more about was the absence of the illusory individuals. The 7 billion illusory individuals who'd suddenly disappeared. Not just them; but their non-descript motor vehicles that all looked the same and their non-descript cookie cutter neighborhoods that all looked the same. All that stuff was gone. It's difficult to remark on the absence of something. It just wasn't there.

There was nothing to describe. What was there was an abundance of open space. Around the cities, and even around the small towns, there were endless tracts of open space that- to my mind- did not belong. Even within commercial and business districts, there was just empty land overgrown by the local vegetation. These overgrown areas looked uncanny besides the development that remained. And out on the road, as I've kind of already stated; there was hardly any traffic. I can't imagine what the normies were thinking, but I know they were all feeling the light of Christ. Even the hylics had to be feeling it. Christ was in the very air we breathed. Our bodies were alive with the light of Christ. Otherwise, certainly, these people would've snapped; myself included, to be sure.

What I wondered about- what I forgot to ask the cashier about; was what exactly had occurred when the physical objects of the material world began disappearing. These fixtures of civilization were disappearing before our eyes. It had been happening for days. I hadn't even noticed until the absences were so obvious that I couldn't believe I had overlooked them. I simply didn't know if these material things had been disappearing gradually or if it had happened all at once, or what. Charisma didn't know, either. She had hardly noticed, as well. We supposed that the people had vanished all at once, and that the physical remains were slowly being phased out as we went along. But we were just guessing.

It was interesting to be leaving Salt Lake City and going into Wyoming. The area around Salt Lake City was always congested with suburban sprawl, but not anymore. Some suburban sprawl remained. Most of it was scrub brush now. Wyoming, however, was always empty and devoid of inhabitants, and that had not changed.

Angela kept facing east and we kept driving east. The sun was rising as we approached Cheyenne. We didn't stop there but I got a distinctly eerie feeling about the place because I didn't see a single inhabitant at any point. I'm sure whoever was there was in hiding.

I could guess what had happened, and I didn't want to believe it, so I pretended not to notice. Charisma, I think, was doing the same. There were a couple cars going toward Cheyenne- eastbound, like us- but there wasn't anybody going away from it in either direction. Nor did we later see anybody westbound toward it. As we passed by, we could see the aswang were out over the other side of the city. They saw us coming though and they flew right toward us. That didn't make any sense, either; unless there was nobody to attack between the other side of the city and where we were. A theory corroborated by the sight of more corpses than I'd seen in one place since this whole thing began. The only other time I saw anything similar was in Las Vegas. The interstate through Cheyenne is elevated and we could look out and see clusters of what looked like exterminated ants. But they weren't exterminated ants. They were exterminated humans. They were gathered in the streets, gathered in the parking lots, gathered in the parks. Probably, too, they were gathered in indoor places- presumably equally dead- but it wasn't like I could see indoor spaces from the driver's seat of my rig.

I told Charisma that we had trouble inbound, but she was already watching the aswang beating their wings for us. She told me to try to outrun them. And I thought, yeah. I didn't feel much like fighting right then. I wasn't sure if I could get us away, but it turned out that I was able to. We had had enough of a lead, and also, the aswang apparently didn't want to abandon their hunting grounds. Even though the city was evidently devoid of life.

From then on, we didn't see another soul.

When it was certain that we had lost the aswang; Charisma said to me, "The next archon isn't far from here."

"Where is it?" I asked.

"You don't want to know," she said.

"Where?" I asked again; perplexed by her statement.

"It's where we first met."

"New York?"

She laughed, saying, "No. Try again."

"Iowa? That's not near here."

"It's not far, either," she said.

Suddenly, Angela jumped out of Charisma's arms and flew across my lap. She was hissing at the town we were driving by. A place called Sidney. "This is it, take the exit!" Charisma exclaimed. I wasn't going to disagree. We'd been chasing that shadow for two days. I was incredulous we'd ever find it.

We pulled off the interstate and looked around. The town- like everywhere else- had changed since I last saw it. But the place still had the gas station with the marquee that said 'YOU ARE NOWHERE.'

That was where the similarity ended. Not only because more than half the structures that used to be out there had disappeared, but also because we found ourselves driving through a world that had- in just a moment's time- taken on such a drastic unfamiliarity that I could scarcely recognize the Earth as the Earth. The sky had been unusually gray previously, considering it was the height of summer and it should've been clear. But now the overcast sky had become almost entirely black. Blackness reached out over the vast expanses of prairie that stretched out in all directions; blackness had cast a pall. The gray of the sky was where the sun was coming through at. And because the heavens above were now blacked out; so too the entirety of the landscape had grown shadowy and foreboding.

The cat's eyes were glowing with the blessed light of our lord and savior. And only in that instant did I understand why they call the Christ our savior. The bright white light of the cat's eyes reflected off of my windows and made it difficult to see. I turned my headlights on and- I can't possibly explain why- the long grasses of the prairie out ahead suddenly burst into flame; igniting wherever my headlights touched them. Those grasses were where the

Wal-Mart used to be. It was one of the few Wal-Marts remaining that still allowed truck parking. I was sorry to see it gone.

So, now there was a prairie fire and what was worse was that the prairie wind was blowing hard and steadily to the north. The wind swept the fires before it but we were to the west of those grasses, somewhat protected by the asphalt, and I was able to turn down a road where there used to be all kinds of random businesses; like, a hotel, a burger shop, a sandwich shop, a pizza shop, an ice cream shop, a car wash, and a bunch of other stuff I can't remember. But the majority of those places- for whatever reason- had disappeared. Thankfully the road was still there.

I turned the truck around but it wasn't until I was actively doing so that I understood exactly what I was doing. My headlights ignited the prairie grass to the north of our position. I stopped in place. There was an abundance of firelight by then, so I shut the headlights off to prevent us from creating more flames. After that, I got us turned around. We were facing into the fire. My brain; redlined- trying to think of a recourse. An aswang landed directly in front of us.

I happened to be in gear and rolling and so I just ran it over. I felt the crunch of it sort of like if you ran over a traffic barrel. But, I was afraid for my tires so I kept rolling instead of pinning it beneath me like I wanted to. I watched the results in the mirror. The aswang was mangled and crippled but it was still alive and it wasn't dividing; so I was actually happy with that outcome.

I noticed that in the distance even the sky above the horizon was becoming black. That was when I started to get the impression that this situation was becoming untenable. The darkness was closing in on us. And I couldn't say why or speculate on the implications, but I knew this was a serious problem. Angela was jumping around like a crazy person in a padded cell, and I- not knowing what else to do- turned right and headed toward the truck stop that was about a half mile down the road. I guess that move was just instinct.

"Where are you going?" Charisma asked.

"The truck stop," I said.

"Why?"

"I don't know what else to do."

"No. Don't. We have to let Angela outside. Get the acid thrower. I'll cover you."

I stopped on the side of the road, pulled the brake valve, and Charisma opened the door; allowing Angela to go bounding outside. Charisma grabbed the M250 and jumped out. I also jumped out and began obeying her commands. By some miracle, I had the presence of mind to bring my bo staff along. I wouldn't face the aswang without it; considering how vicious the little ones were.

As I was getting geared up, Charisma was dumping rounds into the demonic bat creature I'd just run over. One nice thing about the hellhole we'd wandered into; the wind only blew in one direction. That would be useful shortly. Now, with the aswang on the ground, Charisma was carefully popping off at the bulges that were attempting to escape from it. But killing the divisions wasn't exactly an exact science. Nor was a machine gun an exacting weapon. Some small aswang were getting away.

Chapter 16
Love's
As soon as I was able, I got over to the aswang remains and hosed it down with acid. The liquid was dark green but it looked black in the fire light. The reaction was exaggerated and pronounced. The acid didn't so much eat away at the demon as it did react with the demon. Simply coming in contact with the acid was all that was required to cause the features of the demon's body to disappear into a puddle of smoke and slime. A hand and a bit of the foot and some of the wing; that was all that remained. And- thank the Lord- all the divisions had disappeared as well.

"Love! In the sky!" Charisma yelled.

Looking up, I could see that she was right. There were more than just a couple. I wanted to offer her advice but I didn't want to confuse her or put her in a bad position. I had the acid thrower in my left hand and the bo staff in my right. In the sky, the fire light reflected off of the aswang's black skin- especially in the wings; so it was easy to see them. A second later and one of the small ones was taking a dive at me. I pivoted and flicked my wrist and my staff caught that one in the torso and slapped it to the ground. Before it could reorient itself I had already blasted it with acid, and then it was gone.

Charisma had her back against the truck for protection and she was covering her position with the M250. I didn't have hearing protection in, so every time she fired it was like getting slapped in the ear.

The next aswang that came crashing to the ground was the one that she had blasted out of the sky. I hurried over to it and hosed it down, but I could hear wings beating toward me and I only got the chance to spray half of the thing because I was compelled to turn and block the next attack. My block succeeded in knocking the demon down into the pavement, but it sprang back up at me before I could hit it with the acid. I was compelled to whip it in the face with the reversal of the block I'd thrown; jumping away as I did so. I then shot it with the acid as it rushed me; disappearing it mid-stride. Or, it mostly disappeared, more accurately.

I realized Charisma was being forced to waste ammunition on the half-carcass which I'd been unable to resolve; so I hurried to finish it off; but I could see that its divisions had mostly already escaped. I could see their laser red eyes whirling around in the dark skies. There were too many of them. I stayed close to Charisma, but I couldn't get too close because she was firing a machine gun every which way and I was releasing a powerful acid into the air.

The aswang kept coming and we kept fighting. There was a big one up there, we could see. And hear. Its wings were louder. And it glided over slower. We'd taken out two more little ones before that immensely intimidating aswang made its move. The demon had devised a plan to keep my truck between itself and ourselves. It had been watching us and studying us and learning our defenses. It knew to keep its distance, and it knew I was protective of the tractor.

I watched the demon watching me; out of my reach. Too close to the truck to spray acid at it, I was contemplating charging it. But that was what it wanted. Charisma was having none of this. She dropped down on her side on the ground and aimed underneath my truck and shot out the demon's feet; causing it to use its wings to fly at me as the smaller aswang were jettisoning from its ankles.

I performed a delicate maneuver whereby I got my staff up under its armpit and manipulated the forward momentum of the creature to fling it out around myself; in order to position it where I needed it. My left leg came up into the air and the claws of the aswang's right hand raked my calf and cut gouges into me; but I completed the throw and succeeded in hosing the demon down as it was still trying to figure out what had just happened. The acid went right through it and chunks of it dropped to the ground and a second later I had disappeared that mess as well.

"Love! Wait for me inside the truck!"

"You need me out here!"

"Fine, but you gotta get away from the truck!"

"I'll be exposed!"

"Then wait for me inside of the truck!"

I'd figured out how I could fight all these demons, but my plan didn't involve her. It actually required the absence of her. "Love! Get inside! I know what I'm doing!" I pressed, with as much reassurance as I could possibly fake.

Really, we needed her in the acid gear, and not me. But there was no time for that. Thankfully, she obeyed my wishes. Unfortunately, she obeyed my wishes.

I moved as far from the truck as I was able to before another aswang came flying toward me. The sounds they made cutting through the air told me where they were and what they were doing. Their wings whistled quietly when they were descending fast and beat loudly when they were flapping slowly. Either way, I didn't need to see them to set up my attacks. I could do it by ear.

While one or two would make their passes; the others circled above me like vultures from hell. It was disheartening how many there were, but I had the fear of God in me after being envenomated in Tucson. That gave me the resolve I required.

I placed the acid thrower on the ground and then I had two hands to work the stick. After that; it was an easy fight. The acid eliminated their respawning capability, and without that, I had them. The process took time. I was out there fighting for almost an hour. Sometimes three at once. Only once more did I encounter another of the big ones. An eight footer.

I was careful to position the demons downwind before I hit them with the acid. By the time I was done, there was a noxious reeking mess of smoking and sizzling ooze intermingled with select body parts that hadn't gotten the treatment. I wish I had kept a chunk of skull as a souvenir, but I had other things going on, at the time.

I was breathing hard and my whole body was trembling. I couldn't always stop them from dividing and I must have killed twenty or thirty of the things by the time all was said and done. I couldn't believe it when it was over. I had thought it would go on forever.

The prairie fires had burned themselves out where we were previously but they were very much raging in the distance to the north. I got the acid gear off; careful not to get any on my skin. Thankfully, the south wind had easily kept the acid off of me. It was a strong and steady wind; as constant as the stars. But, still, I was thinking how I hoped to never have to use the acid again. It then occurred to me that that big son of a bitch had pulled his claws through my flesh. My jeans were cut to blood soaked rags in that area.

Too, of course, the rubber acid pants had been ripped apart. And I guess I'd lost a lot of blood because I was feeling markedly weakened.

I climbed back into the truck and Charisma threw her arms around me and kissed me over and over all over my face and said, "Oh, Love. My love. My brave man. I'm so sorry. I didn't know what to do."

"You did good," I said.

She looked me over and saw my leg, "Love! Your leg!"

"It's fine. For now. Where's Angela?"

"I don't know. I know she is fine. I can feel it. But I don't know where she is or what she is doing."

"What is this place?" I asked her. Only then had I gotten the opportunity to look around and see what had become of our previously recognizable environment.

"Hell on Earth," she said, seriously.

The grasses smoldered serenely nearby and blazed wildly far off. Black sky laced with faintly gray daylight melted into a black horizon aglow with fire light. The wind rocked the tractor around. In my mirrors; I saw the mess I had made. Ahead of us, the gas station's 'YOU ARE NOWHERE' sign caught my eye and I laughed. The prairie seemed to reach out forever; an ocean of land. I could sense evil- I could feel menace in my bones.

Charisma said, "Put your leg on the cooler. I'm going to stitch you up, before we do anything else." I took off my pants and gave her my leg. The gouges ran deep into the meat of my thigh; there were four; the longest was almost a foot in length and over an inch in depth. I couldn't believe I'd been fighting in that condition; but, at the time, I hadn't had the luxury of weakness. Using a headlamp for light; she cleaned my wounds with ethyl alcohol. It sucked. Then she sewed me up. That also sucked.

When she was finished, I realized we weren't doing anything. The cat was nowhere to be found, and nothing was happening. I hit the brake valve, put the truck in drive, and then headed toward the truck stop.

"Where are you going?" Charisma asked me.

"I need coffee. We need fuel. It's just over that hill there," I said; pointing.

We crested the hill and the truck stop was bright and shining. The building, the signs, the fuel island umbrella; all lit up orange and red with the colors of the Love's logo. The parking lot lights were on. I guess they had turned on automatically when the shadow of death blotted out the sky.

Charisma said, "Love. Look. Inside."

I saw what she saw right away. The interior of the building was filled with people. There had to be a hundred people or more crammed in there. And they were all staring at us with eyes that had no white in them. That was when I realized that I wasn't going to be getting any coffee, after all. And not for nothing, my head was beginning to ache. The obviously dead persons within the building were shadowy from being so crowded in together. Later, I realized they were actually shadowy because their skin was coated with the inky stains of Hell's angel. The zombies shifted on their feet. Their spines bent and their shoulders drooped and their heads lulled and they could hardly stay upright, it looked like.

Out in the four-wheeler parking lot; there was Angela. Standing in front of the truck stop's door. "Angela!" Charisma shouted. Angela's eyes had been replaced by the holy light of Christ. And I got the feeling that she had corralled these people into this building.

There were some trucks in the lot. But not a lot. This was everybody who'd been in the area, I'm sure, but I hadn't seen any of them before and I don't know where they had all come from. The most obvious explanation was that they had been waiting for us. I stopped out in the road and set the brakes. A hissing burst of discharged air pressure.

"What are these people?" I asked.

"These people are the angel of death. The sky, too. The prairie fire. It's everywhere. It's everything."

"Go get your cat," I said, as I popped a fresh can into the M250.

"And then what?"

"And then I'm going to kill all these dead people."

We stepped out together. Charisma had brought along the 1301 shotgun, just to be safe. Angela looked back at us and meowed happily. The white cat with eyes made of light was a comforting- albeit surreal- sight. She was our savior. What was discomforting was the hundreds of black eyes staring out at us from the other side of the truck stop's windows.

"They're afraid of Angela; there's no reason to waste bullets on them," I said, as it occurred to me.

"Things could change," Charisma said.

I didn't want to waste the bullets, but I saw her point. We didn't know what was coming. Those zombies were a threat as long as they were upright and mobile. I stood there for a while, holding the machine gun. Charisma stood beside me, holding her cat. The cat watched the zombies intently. I had the puzzle pieces in my mind, but I couldn't fit them together in any way that would reveal the whereabouts of the heart of the evil that was all around us.

"Let's get back in the truck. So we're not so exposed," said Charisma.

We turned our backs to walk away and as soon as we did, the door of the truck stop swung open and we heard the grunting of the zombies shoving each other aside trying to get through. Turning to face them, I raised the machine gun, but there was no point. Angela's eyes shone forth with the light of the Lord. A ray of pure white light poured forth from her face and the zombies literally evaporated in the doorway. A couple had made it out into the open, but Angela's gaze followed them and the ray of light swung at them and they disappeared. Even inside the building; the light of the Lord had penetrated the glass and obliterated a multitude of the pitiful beings. But there were still a lot left; which would become obvious momentarily.

I had a thought that we could use Angela to destroy the entirety of them and then I could probably get some coffee, but then I realized I didn't actually want any coffee that was brewed in wherever the hell we were.

Angela mellowed out some and Charisma said, "We should probably walk backwards back to the truck."

So that was what we did. Angela's eyes never stopped glowing but she wasn't hissing or nothing. The zombies remained indoors but they never stopped staring. I started eating some chocolate because I didn't think anything was going to happen. Then Charisma backhanded my arm and pointed. Too, Angela jumped up on the dash and let out a cautionary growl.

There was something oozing down from the umbrella above the fuel island. The black globules dripped in long strands. I guess we'd exhausted its patience. Which was good for us because we wouldn't have known what to do if we hadn't. Charisma opened the door to let the cat out, but then all the zombies came rushing toward us simultaneously.

"Close the door!" I shouted. Then I pressed the brake valve, put the truck in reverse, and backed away from the onslaught. I wasn't really thinking anything other than I didn't want them to hurt my truck. I don't know if they could've done anything worse than break a window, but that would've been bad enough.

It was so dark outside that I had to use the distant firelight to keep myself oriented on the road. Afraid to create further conflagrations with the headlights. Simultaneously; Angela began emitting her heavenly luminescence and the zombies were disintegrating or vaporizing or disappearing or whatever. Driving in reverse; I was primarily concerned with keeping my tires where I wanted them and I certainly couldn't see jack squat besides the blurry and hazy lines I was following in the mirror. All that light coming out of the cat was more than a little much.

But I was glad for it all the same because that truck couldn't back up faster than those zombies could run.

The light of the lord was all that prevented us from being molested and all the while I was hearing startling sounds reminiscent of freight train derailments. Even through the rumbling of my truck and over the spectacle of the cat and the zombies which were wailing with feline and undead lamentations of their own; I could feel the ground shaking. And louder than all that was the thunder clap which preceded about two dozen ensuing thunderclaps. It was the kind of thunder where it is right above you and it leaves you feeling diminished. The lightning was striking all around us. I'd been a little blinded a moment prior, but I really couldn't see anything right then. I had to put my foot on the brake. There was something superseding the thunder and the lightning. Which hadn't been lightning and thunder at all but sudden demolitions in actuality.

I couldn't believe my eyes as the vision was returning to them. The truck stop wasn't there any longer. What was there was the figure of a hulking brute. More like a gorilla than a human, but nothing like either, really; because what it was was a torn apart Love's Travel Stop which had been reconstructed into the menacing configuration before us. Brick and mortar and steel beams, joists, and girders, and rebar and wiring and plumbing; standing- on two legs- all held together by the inky black slime that was the angel of death. The slime covered the structure more evenly than one might guess and it gave it something of a personality even; a devilish brute; complete with two long horns- like a longhorn's horns; made of random building materials molded together.

The brute stood probably 75 feet tall or better and was actively ripping the umbrella off of the diesel pumps when we first got eyes on it. Angela shrieked with rage and her eyes blasted a ray of light at the behemoth. Apparently her divine light didn't have any issue with windows. Unfortunately, the fuel island umbrella had come between the brute and our cat and effectively nullified the attack. I knew immediately that that was bad. Angela was the only way we could fight this thing; and, while- because we had the light of Christ in our hearts- the angel of death couldn't harm us with its deathly touch; I was almost positive that the entity could harm us with the combined mass of the raw materials of a Love's Travel Stop. And I think it knew it, as well.

Right about then was when the fuel stored beneath the fuel island ignited and exploded. The flames billowed up around the shadowy brute but it ignored that and stepped toward us like nothing had happened. I was suddenly super happy to be out on the road and not in that parking lot. This was an area designed for trucks and I was able to flip a bitch without doing a k-turn. Thunder was cracking and crackling all around us, but I could still feel the thudding booms of the colossal brute's footsteps. And I could see in the rearview mirror that it had designs on us.

I remember I was wondering how the lightbulbs were still glowing within the structure of it. It still looked a lot like what it used to be. And I thought, 'Jeeze, what did we ever do to you?' But then it clicked in my brain what exactly this thing was and I also remembered that I didn't want to be crushed to death, and so I put the hammer down and hauled ass down the small road north. I would've liked to have had a chance to get back on the interstate, but there was just no way to.

Now; one might think that a 75 foot tall being made from a smashed up Love's Travel Stop held together by an unholy angel would be slow. I regret to inform you, this godforsaken unholy manifestation was not slow. Quite the opposite. It had long legs and it knew how to use them. The brute was on top of us and my dipshit slushbox transmission was trying to figure out what gear it needed to accelerate down a flat road. Every time one of those giant feet landed a step, the truck bounced on its tires. So it was a bouncy ride, at first, but things smoothed out when we got up to speed.

My mind was racing. My truck, too. We had one weapon that could fight this thing, and another that could maybe fight the thing; but both weapons required us to be directed at the enemy and there was no way to do that without giving it what it wanted; which was apparently the opportunity to smoosh us.

I recalled the immortal words of my father; 'shut up, suck it up, drive the truck.' So that was what I did. But trying to lose that possessed Love's Travel Stop was like trying to lose another semi governed at the same speed as yours; not so easy.

A minute later and we were out among the prairie fires. The flames had jumped over the road, now that the road had narrowed; so we had fire on both sides of us. But it didn't last long and I was able to use the opportunity to get a better look at the abomination that was chasing us.

What I saw was that- as it was running- it had gotten the bright idea to snap off a 5g tower. Now there was a fifty foot pole at our enemy's disposal as well as a fuel island umbrella shield. It looked like a demented viking god; that was sponsored by Love's...

"Love. The atlas," I told Charisma.

She'd been transfixed; watching in the fisheye mirror. But she did what I asked and found Nebraska on the map and found the town of Sidney, saying, "Got it, ok, what now?" And I told her, "We need straight roads. If we have to turn, it will catch up to us."

I was hoping we'd drive out into the sunlight, but the black skies followed us down the road. Nonetheless, without the firelight to guide us, it was now dark enough that I couldn't see anymore. I had no choice but to turn on the headlights. The headlights spilled out over the landscape and the prairie grasses- again- ignited into flame. I turned my high beams on because I didn't think it would make much of a difference; but it made a huge difference.

Now, not only was the immediate vicinity burning with the fires of hell, so too was the foreseeable future similarly engulfed. I turned the high beams off then, but still, we were still torching the prairie grass for as far as we drove. Which was far. Far enough that we were running out of road.

"We can't go straight. There's a river." My stomach sunk when she said that, but I said, "Show me," and when she showed me, I saw that- when we hit the river- the turn to the northwest road was a 45 degree turn; not a 90 degree turn. The brute was fast, but we were also fast, and I knew that I could make that turn. Or, I knew that I could probably make that turn.

I said, "I don't know. It'll be fine. As long as it's too stupid to cut us off."

Suddenly, Charisma had the rocket launcher in her hand, and she was saying, "That thing's not stupid."

And she was right. When we got to the turn in question; the angel of death had seen what was happening and shortcutted across the corn field. So now, even though we had had a lead, our adversary was suddenly very much gaining on us.

I had never even learned how to operate the M72, but Charisma was popping the sights and arming the warhead and loading the rocket into the tube and by the time we got to the turn, the critical moment, she had rolled the window down and- with one hand on the 'oh shit' handle and the other hand on the rocket- jumped up onto the passenger side window sill to take aim.

I took that left turn probably faster than I ever took any other turn in a tractor. Charisma leaned far out the window but held fast like a born sailor. I looked to my left and saw the brute running through the flaming prairie; taking long bounding strides toward us. Each footfall; quaking the Earth. Angela, for her part, didn't neglect to take the opportunity to jump up onto my lap and put her paws up on

the window and unleash the divine light of our holy lord
and savior.

The brute was arcing the 5g tower back behind its head
and was within range to smash us with it. But it saw the
light coming and so abandoned the strike to again shield
itself with the fuel island umbrella.

That was when Charisma fired the rocket. I think she
aimed right for where Angela's luminescent ray was boring
into it at. The rocket hit the mark true and blew a hole
through the shield. There was a cacophonous blast, a quick
flash of light, and a shockwave that shoved my truck
enough to make me swerve. Then the moment was over and
the brute had lost its opportunity to nail us and our cat had
lost its opportunity to nail the brute. So again; the chase
was on.

Just, now, it was somewhat more difficult to see,
because Charisma had had no option but to fire the rocket
across our windshield and the rocket engine had left a black
burn on the glass. But it didn't crack it, or break it, so I was
pretty happy about that.

It seemed like the whole world was on fire. I didn't
need my headlights anymore, so I turned them off. But then
we were out of the fire again and I needed my headlights
again and then the whole world was on fire again and it was
this whole obnoxious situation and maybe totally pointless,
too, considering probably everybody under those black
clouds was dead. But I thought of the individuals with
Christ in their hearts and I couldn't know if any were out
there and I couldn't know where they might be hiding at, so
I kept turning the lights on and off; trying to burn down as
little of the country as possible.

The brute was unrelenting. It couldn't catch us, and I
couldn't lose it. I was doing 72 miles per hour down that
road but it was a 65 mile per hour speed limit so the speed
wasn't any problem and I was able to examine the map as
we went. My conclusions were disheartening. The odds
weren't in our favor. The roads were not in our favor. There

were too many turns between where we were and where we needed to get to if we wanted to be safe. Charisma was examining the map as well and she could plainly see the problem.

Then I saw her eyes light up and I knew she had an idea. She jumped into the back and rooted around until she found Angela's clear plastic backpack. Now that the rocket launcher had blasted a hole through the brute's shield; our biggest problem was that they don't make sleeper berths with back windows. Charisma had contrived a solution to this limitation. She duct taped the two shoulder straps of the backpack to my bo staff and then put the cat into the bag. Angela was so cute when her eyes were glowing like that. I don't think she minded what Charisma was doing to her. That cat was born to raze hell.

With the windows down, the heat- and smoke and hot ash- from the prairie fires filled up the cab. Charisma was dangling Angela six feet out the window at 72 miles per hour. Angela didn't require any cues or goading. The cat screamed a primal scream and unleashed the fury of our lord and savior. The clear plastic backpack glowed like a lantern on a stick, if that lantern had the distilled essence of the whole of the known universe contained within it.

I watched the effect in the rearview mirror. The brute attempted to shield itself, but it wasn't possible, because it had to swing the shield to run and because the shield had a gaping hole in it. Angela's light was getting through. Not all at once, but enough to produce results. The angel of death began to slow down and stumble. Being exacting; I began to slow down, also.

I think at that point the brute realized that its gambit wasn't succeeding. It turned and attempted to run away. But then a ray of sunshine broke through the inky black ceiling. The ray of sunshine- it wasn't sunshine- collided with the Love's Travel Shop, crumpling the brute to the ground, and pummeling the angel of death with the divine light of creation. The black ooze began to glow bright white with pure prismatic radiance. In the mirrors; Charisma and I watched the angel of death melting into the ground. Disappearing beneath the surface.

Chapter 17
The Black Lamb
I don't know exactly what happened next, because it was impossible to see. Basically the entire world was consumed by the light of the Lord. Or, it was like a negative of a photo, kind of; the blackness became whiteness. In every direction; all that could be seen was light. Nothing could be seen except for the light. Even within the shadows within the truck; we were blinded. And that lasted for long enough to make me wonder if it would ever stop. Probably it was only about a minute; but it was a long minute.

Then the skies were clear and the sun was out, but the sun was pinkish-red; softened by the smoke of the prairie fires which were still nearly choking us to death. As soon as I could see again, I drove us out of the smoke. That wasn't the direction I wanted to be going, but once we were back out in the fresh air, I got out my binoculars and looked back toward the displaced ruins of the Love's Travel Stop.

The remains of the fuel station had settled into a sprawled out heap all over the road. There was no way to drive past that mess unless I wanted to take the semi off roading, which was an easy way to get stuck. The thought of getting stuck out there was motivation enough to take the long way around.

That specific detour happened to be a happy accident, because we ended up driving through a beautiful area of the country that I had never seen before. A place called the Nebraska Sand Hills.

The Sand Hills rest atop the Ogallala aquifer. They are a vast expanse of sand dunes held in place by prairie grasses. The prairie in general is always awe inspiring but the Sand Hills' immaculate lumps, bumps, waves, elevations, declinations, and undulations all would've been incredible under normal conditions; but for us, considering the circumstances, and after what we'd just been through; the Sand Hills were a religious experience. The majesty of the Hills was like the majesty of the Lord; inspiring us to persevere.

The interstate- to the south- was veering further to the south. And normally I would have been in a hurry to get back to it. But normally I would have had a trailer and normally the state roads would slow us down a lot worse than they would that day; what with the no other traffic and no real law enforcement, and all.

I followed route 2 for a long time until eventually we got back to I-80. Now we were in the exact center of the country. I'd always considered those several hundred miles to be haunted. I'd had a breakdown out there, gotten held up by a crazy ice storm out there, wrecked a truck out there, and any time I ever tried to pick up a load in either Des Moines or Omaha; either the paperwork was wrong or the warehouse staff was on vacation in another dimension. And now, I could add having been attacked by a Love's Travel Stop to my list of grievances with the region.

I told Charisma about this and she said that certain areas of the world have a spirit of their own, and that I should repeat the words 'Tabi, tabi po,' as a way to appease the spirit by acknowledging its presence and dominion over the land. I didn't require any convincing. I'd long been weary of the midlands. Not just on I-80 but on I-70 and I-90 as well. I'm pretty sure those hundreds and hundreds of haunted square miles constitute the world's largest ancient Indian burial ground.

The moment was overdue to ask the dreaded question, "Love. What is the next archon?"

"You don't want to know."

"I never want to know."

"No. I know. But, really. You don't want to know."

"You're not going to tell me?"

"I will tell you if you insist, but I think you should not insist."

"I insist. Tell me what it is."

"I was only joking. This is actually a good one. Or, mostly a good one. It depends. Ok. Let me think... Ok. What comes next pertains to separateness from the Lord. Ignorance of the Lord. The denial of Christ; through accidental obliviousness or outright rejection. Or, through the nature of one's true nature."

"What does that mean?"

"It means that we are spiritual beings. People pretend we are glorified apes. But that's just a way to avoid taking responsibility. That is not by accident. There are a hundred methods evil has used to obfuscate the truth. We will make the truth be known. People have to know Christ is in their hearts."

"You're talking about the hylics. What's going to happen to the hylics?"

"That's the good part. They're going to receive a splinter of the Lord. Well. They'll be presented with the option. They'll be making an unconscious decision. Everything we've been doing up to this point has been in preparation for this critical juncture. We've overhauled reality itself to give these 499,831,000 soulless beings an opportunity to embrace the Lord within their hearts and receive the blessing of the Lord's light. Something that would have been impossible just a few weeks ago."

"How will it happen? How does it work?"

"Same way as anything else. When the system updates, it will make the changes."

"When does the system update?"

"Whenever it needs to."

"What is the system?"

"The system is God. God is the mind of the universe. The universe is a quantum computer. Just like our brains. Computers infinitely complex, but still recognizable as such."

I had more questions, but this was another one of those occasions when I'd learned more than I wanted to know. I well knew the difference between God and Christ and I was beginning to recognize the progression; we were headed toward a confrontation with Satan. And, at the moment, I preferred to pretend that that was not so. But there was still one thing I had to ask, "What's going to happen to the hylics who cannot accept the Lord?"

"Most will accept the lord. Only the hopelessly corrupted will deny the light. And those, presumably, will be utilized as instruments of evil."

"That doesn't sound so bad," I said.

"We'll see," she said. I understood her ominous implication but pretended I didn't.

"What exactly are we doing, exactly?" I asked.

"There's a church. They keep sheep. And goats. We need a black sheep. Or a goat."

"For what? A sacrifice?"

"No. For bait."

"What are we baiting?"

"An archon."

"That could mean anything."

"I know," she said, "but we've done this six times already. It shouldn't be any worse than any other time."

"Alright. But, we need to fuel up; before we do anything."

"We need to sleep," she said.

And she was right. We hadn't slept since Utah. I pulled into the truck stop in Lincoln and spent a while talking to the cashier there. He was afraid of me at first; he was afraid of everything. And with good reason. He kept his hand under the counter, but after I talked to him for a while he lightened up. A little. The guy was a typical midwest white guy; overweight in an unhealthy way, with a big head and thinning black hair cut more neatly than one might expect, and his vocabulary was limited. I listened to his lamentations. We were all feeling more or less the same thing; but this guy, I could tell; he used to be a different person and couldn't even recognize himself in the mirror, anymore. I tried to soothe him, and help him to believe that everything was okay. But he'd been in a militia in Omaha when the aswang came in heavy. He'd barely escaped with his life. I don't think he'd recovered; emotionally. I was just happy he showed up to work. I needed fuel more than I needed to psychoanalyze the traumatized attendant. He gave me the fuel for free and said we could take whatever we wanted. We grabbed extra jerky, chips, and fruit for the road. Plus, we got more jugs of water and- most importantly- I was able to fill an empty water jug with coffee.

I fueled up and parked and then Charisma and I ate MREs as well as some random truck stop food; hot dogs, hard boiled eggs, veggie sticks, and chips. She ate a little. I ate a lot. After that, Charisma and I went back inside and showered. Afterward, in bed- fresh and clean and exhausted- we made love and fell asleep.

There were maybe five other trucks in the lot. I didn't encounter any of the drivers. I can't imagine what their business was; now that business didn't exactly exist. I guess they were doing the Lord's work. Just doing what had to be done. That's why the fuel was free. Because there were still things that had to be done.

It was a little after sunset when we got to sleep and then we were on the road again a little after sunrise. Charisma was wearing her nun uniform. It was the first time I'd seen it since before we departed in the semi. It was kind of strange to see her like that, after everything we'd done together. I couldn't help but to enjoy the view, so I just let myself enjoy it. Not long after we departed the truck stop, we drove past the spot where my accident had been. I had a foreboding premonition; a vague sensation coupled with a subtle suspicion. There was something vile in that place. I whispered, 'Tabi, tabi po' as we passed by. We still needed to go get the lamb and that thing was out past Omaha. That meant we had to go through Omaha multiple times.

Passing through Omaha was typical of what the big cities were like in those days. A lot of it had been removed and replaced by prairie and scrub. Even some of the tall buildings downtown were gone and replaced with prairie grass. There were aswang in the sky but they had plenty to do to keep them busy. They didn't mind us. Or, they didn't mind us eastbound. One of them definitely minded us westbound.

Driving through Omaha; there were dead bodies everywhere. The kind of dead bodies that reaffirmed that we were in a war. Not just a fight. The kind of dead bodies that it hurts just to think back on. The kind of dead bodies you can't recall seeing without crying a little at the memory.

But there were military units patrolling as well, and so that was nice to see. These were vestigial military units. Extremely diminished; but functioning to the best of their abilities. Their capabilities must have been severely limited, now that their illusory assets had vanished; specifically, their numbers had vanished. And probably their more special specialists and their extra special specialty assets had disappeared, as well. Same for the cops. And same for the militia. People were suddenly so alone. The weird thing was, they always had been. They just didn't know it.

The church we had to go to was a solid hour off of the interstate. Out in these great big rolling hills that always seemed to be crashing over us like waves. We'd gone from hill country into flat lands and then back into more hill country. These hills were different from the sand hills, though. There were a lot less of them, but they were a lot bigger. And there were giant white windmills interspersed all throughout the land.

The church wasn't Catholic. It was a Universalist church. I didn't know what that was, or if it was even Christian, and I didn't really care. The building looked like any other middle of nowhere church. A modest white building with a steeple; but the steeple had no cross on it. The weirdest thing about the church was that it was flying libtard flags on the pole. There wasn't even an American flag; just a rainbow and a BLM. And I don't mean the Bureau of Land Management.

The dust swirled around us as we pulled into the driveway. A man emerged from the building; a pale skinned man with wispy gray hair dressed in pastel business casual and wearing wireframe glasses. We stepped out and he was hurrying to greet us, calling, "Sister Charisma! Thank goodness you're here! I've been waiting and waiting. I was so worried. I was so scared! Because of the monsters and all."

Charisma said, "Yes, hello, Reverend Visser. It is very good to finally meet you. Being out of contact; I feared for your safety, of course."

"I've been lucky. It's been quiet here. I know little of my congregation, unfortunately. I expect they'll come through when they're able. But the flock which you're interested in is doing just fine. Better than fine. The feed is free these days. They're eating the good stuff now."

"Oh. That's nice. Reverend, this is my partner; Kevin. He'll be happy to help you with the animal."

The reverend shook my hand and said, "Kevin. Good to meet you. I'm Reverend Visser. How has it been, for you, enduring the... how would you call it? The rapture? The apocalypse?"

I said, "The armageddon? I don't know. It's been difficult in some ways. Easy in other ways. Easy to get around. Hard fighting demons all the time."

"I've been lucky enough to have not encountered any first hand. But I've heard tell, of course. I don't know how to feel. Afraid. Excited. Terrified. Hopeful."

I said, "Hopeful is good. A guy can never be overly hopeful. And there's good reason to be hopeful, too. The Christ is returning. We've seen the light of the Lord. On several occasions, actually."

"The light?" he asked.

"The divine light of creation," I specified.

"Ah, yes. Of course. Then let us rejoice."

"Yes. Let us," I agreed.

"Come," he said, "I have the animal. A lovely black lamb. Certainly the blood of a lamb must be more enticing than the blood of an old goat," he said.

"Yeah. Probably," I agreed; cluelessly.

"A lamb and an old goat are equally innocent creatures," Charisma said.

And the Reverend nodded in agreement, saying, "Yes. But goats can have a funky odor, and- what's even better, is that small innocent creatures are more portable than larger ones."

"Why's it got to be black?" I asked.

"That's just what I was told," Charisma said.

"Told by who?" I asked.

"Secret," she said.

We were led out to some windbreak evergreen trees that stood beside the sizable pen. There was a supply shed with food in it and there were hoses for the water trough and there were about fifty sheep and a separate enclosure for about five or ten goats and I didn't see the little blackie at first. But then the reverend pointed it out. It was cute and small, but not as small as I would have preferred. Still, it was a black lamb. Mixed in with the newly born white lambs. There was another black sheep, but it was old and gross, and there were the goats, too, but the goats were goats.

The reverend asked me to carry the crate and then he proceeded to bumrush the little lamb and scoop it up in his arms like it was nothing. He didn't seem to care that the animal was getting grit on his nice clothes. He placed it into the crate and closed it up and we carried it out to my truck.

"The restitution of all things," said the Reverend, as we went.

"What?" I asked.

"The restitution of all things through Christ. Through Christ, all souls will be saved."

"Oh. Right. Seems so obvious now."

"It was always obvious. For many of us."

"It could've been more obvious. If we weren't drowning in lies and evil."

"Yes. And that is the significance of what you and Charisma have accomplished. You are liberators. The wool had been pulled over our eyes. We were blind. And now we can see."

"I think we're still blind, Reverend. I think we've just replaced one illusion with a different illusion."

"No, son. We're on the right track. Hold your course. Through Christ, all will be saved."

'Will they?' I wondered, saying, "Amen, Reverend;" feeling sorry for the irredeemably wicked of the world.

We used the last bit of space on the catwalk to secure the lamb's crate, and then we took off down the road. Back in Omaha; we were moving through at 72 miles per hour. The aswang- we never even saw it coming- descended from the sky and drove four claws through the roof of my tractor. We could see its fingers clutching the ceiling. It sounded like a tree had fallen on us; if the tree was angry and trying to break inside. Thankfully, it was struggling to hold on. The demon's only move was to drive the claws of its other hand in through the ceiling as well.

I rolled down the windows, and this startled Charisma; "What are you doing?" she asked.

"We got to shoot it off, but I don't want the shockwaves to blow out my windows."

"No. Wait. I have a better idea," she said.

Charisma grabbed the bolt cutters and- one by one- cut each of the demon's fingers off. They were dropping into the truck and I was picking up the ones that I could; throwing them out the window. The aswang was shrieking like a slightly inconvenienced baby as Charisma removed seven fingers in total. Suddenly, the last couple digits released on their own and we heard the absence of the creature banging around up there. In the rearview mirror, I saw it smashing into the asphalt and rolling around in a tangle of broken wings and broken limbs. The thing was as big as the biggest I'd seen yet. Or maybe 'objects in mirror are closer than they appear.' I never figured out if that's intended to mean objects look bigger or look smaller. It depends on how you read it. But the objects do look smaller.

Charisma had removed seven fingers, but I'd only tossed out three. She found the next three but there was still one left. Angela found that finger; but that finger had had a second to react to the situation and so it had a fledgling aswang sticking half out of it. The thing was on the floor behind Charisma's seat. Angela had her paws on its wings and it was trying to reach around and grab her or turn its head around and bite her, but it was too small and helpless. I didn't even know they could get that small. The damn thing had come out of a finger. Charisma squeezed its neck in the bolt cutters and it was obstinately flailing around as she stuck it out the window and decapitated it in the wind.

Meanwhile, the big one was airborne and trying to catch us again, but there was no way. They were too slow when they were small, nevermind when they were big. That big one had only caught us how it had by being way up to begin with, intercepting our position, and dropping down right on top of us.

After that, we were where we needed to be in no time. Well, we were going westbound, so I had to drive past the spot and then take the next exit and then come back at it in the eastbound lanes. But, I knew the exact mile marker because it was burned into my memory. Mile 423.8 on I-80 east, Nebraska.

That area of the country is famous for being nondescript. A common misconception was that everything looks the same in the midlands. They'd say it's flyover states. But the people who said those things had probably never even been to the place. Although, this particular spot did happen to resemble literally a million spots just like it.

There was farmland all around. The corn was getting tall. On the other side of the interstate there was a red barn with a huge 'TRUMP' banner on it. Simpler times. There were several houses in the area and each had isolated forests growing around them. I guess my ditch really was as nondescript as any other midwestern ditch.

The funny thing was, I'd suffered a grievous injury in that spot; not just to my body, but to my pride as well. And yet, I didn't even care. I liked being there. I remembered meeting Charisma right there; with that same scenery all around us. A lot more cars driving by, though, originally. Now there weren't any cars driving by and when there was it was like sharing a moment. You'd wave and they'd wave. And you'd both think, 'good luck not dying.'

I took Charisma's hand and kissed it. I couldn't believe she was real. She was an angel. My angel. A lot of men refer to their women as angels. But my angel actually was an angel. Probably. All I really know is I didn't deserve her. I was just a dumb truck driver. In fact, our world didn't deserve her, either. We were just a bunch of stupid automatons; before she came along.

I asked her, "Love, why are we back here?"

"This is the nexus," she said.

"The nexus of what?" I asked.

"The nexus of God and Christ. The nexus of heaven and hell. The nexus of good and evil," she said.

That sounded about right. I'd been through hell right there. And I'd met my angel right there. I was still marinating in the idea when she said, "Love. Set up the fifty cal."

"Love. Wait. I have to seal up these holes in the ceiling." I used spray foam and made it look decent on the inside, but it definitely looked bad on the outside; still, the truck was holding up better than it had any right to. Same could be said for the three of us.

After sealing the holes, I did what she'd asked and set up the 50 cal. While I was doing that, Charisma got out of the car and unlashed the lamb's crate and not so gently dropped it down from the catwalk.

Next time I looked over, there were two people standing there. Well. One and a half people. Or; one half person half angel, and one actual person. There were two beings there, I'm saying. Draag had appeared, but she paid me no mind. Her interest was in the lamb. Draag grabbed the animal by the throat and vomited a luminescent neon purple substance into her hand; it was the size and shape of a cylindrical pine cone, but a lot prettier. Draag proceeded to force feed the substance to the lamb; literally shoving the glowing purple turd down its throat and clamping its mouth shut with her hands until it was forced to swallow. Once that was done, Draag looked up to the heavens and- I don't know if the divine light came out of her and reached up to the sky or if the divine light came out of the sky and reached down into her; but- either way- the bald and naked parallel dimension version of my love became engulfed in a beam of light and vanished up into the heavens; taking the beam of light with her.

"What the hell was that about?" I asked.

"Coding," said Charisma, sarcastically. And truthfully.

"Do we need to load the lamb back onto the truck, or no?"

"No. That lamb is doomed. We'd be doomed, too, if we tried to save it."

"Well. That sucks," I said.

"Yeah," she agreed. But I think we were both past the point of getting heartbroken over a farm animal. Even a cute and innocent one.

I felt something land on the back of my neck and it bit me violently before I could even slap at it. There was a creature in my hand. A smashed up grasshopper. Being dead; it didn't look too different from any other grasshopper, except for that it was black.

"What was that?" Charisma asked.

I hesitated to answer because that moment was when the stridulation began. It was kind of like cicadas but coming from every direction. And out in Nebraska, every direction was a lot of land. The noise was all-encompassing. Almost crushing. I couldn't think or react, but I knew I was getting bit and I would slap at the bites and each time I slapped I smashed another grasshopper. Charisma was slapping at her body, too.

'Get in the truck!' we yelled at each other.

We got in the truck and it was still idling, so I hit the brake valve and we took off down the road. That was when Hell rose up out of the earth like a black smoke. All I could think about was my air filter. The insects were hitting my windshield and smashing against it and spilling their guts and the wiper fluid really wasn't designed for whatever black bile was contained within them. Not only that, but the cloud of grasshoppers was so thick that even if I could see out the window; I couldn't possibly see through the swarm.

The devil thought that would stop us, I'm sure, but the devil doesn't know about truck drivers. The road has got this thing called a 'fog line.' It's a white line that runs along the side of the road; telling you where your lane is. Usually you can see through a fog, but sometimes, when the fog gets bad; you're glad that line is there, because it's the only thing saving your ass. This was one of those times.

The reduced visibility caused me to drive a little slower, and so the grasshoppers weren't smashing on the window so much, and so- after a liberal application of washer fluid- I was able to regain enough visibility to watch the fog line. I was also able to watch the insects that were now coating the exterior of the tractor. They had tiny laser red eyes, and- because there were so many of them- their swarm had a faint red glow.

"Was I supposed to shoot these things with the 50 cal?" I asked my love, sarcastically.

"No. I was confused. I knew it would be something big, but I didn't know it'd be the summation of a lot of miniscule individuals."

I soon realized that the air filter wasn't a problem, because the insects were much bigger than my air intake screens. The scariest thing about them was how many there were. Not just the density; which was like driving through water. But the mileage which the density covered. That was the truly dismal aspect. We kept going and we kept not escaping.

"How many times did you get bit?" I asked Charisma.

"Just once, but it's still bleeding. There's a divot in the skin where it took the flesh out. How many times did you get bit?"

"Three, I think," I said.

"I got bit ten times," said an alien voice.

"I got bit eleven times," boasted another.

"I got bit eleventeen times," said a third.

My eyes rolled into the back of my head. Angela started hissing in Charisma's lap. Charisma's hand reached up and covered her face. We were all exasperated. I turned back to see three grown men sitting on my bed and I said, "Why am I not surprised to see you here?"

"Why would you be surprised?" one asked.

"You should be expecting us," said another.

"But why, though? Why are you following us around?" I asked.

"There is no point. That's the point. We're just being friendly. You four are our only friends," said the spector.

They referred to us as four. They counted Angela. And they counted Draag, who was nowhere in sight. There I was, thinking we were a couple. Apparently we were a quad.

"We're not your friends," said Charisma.

"Is that true, Kevin?" asked one of them.

"I'm your friend. Kind of. I think. I don't know. It seems like you're taunting us. That's not a friendly thing to do."

"How are we taunting you?" one of them asked.

"You're in our home, uninvited. That's kind of rude," I said.

"Oh, we're very sorry to invade your personal space, but you were driving. And we couldn't communicate from outside, because, you know, the locusts, and the wind, and all," one of them said.

Their voices were basically human now, but not really. I turned back to take a look at them. They were still clothed only in the shorts and pajamas I gave them in Oregon. They looked basically human as well, though. If I didn't know better, I would have mistaken them for human.

"You're looking better than ever," I told them.

One of them said, "Well, thank you for the compliment."

"You're welcome," I said, adding, "You all want a beer, or some coffee, or something?"

"No, thank you. We look human. But we are not human. Not yet," said one.

"Ask us next time you see us. We will be happy to drink with you," said another.

"So, you'll be done becoming by the next time? You'll have became?"

"That's correct," said one.

"You'll have became what?" I asked.

"Your nemeses," one replied.

"Why would I want to drink beer with my nemeses?"

"Because Jesus said to love your enemies," said one.

"Will you be loving us? When we are your enemies?" I asked.

"More than you would think, out of necessity," said one.

"Charisma remains unconvinced," I said.

"Women are smarter than men," said one.

And then the three burst out laughing. I was hoping they were laughing because women were smarter than men, but I know it was because they were lying to me and calling me stupid to my face. Angela, actually, was the one who stood up for me. She started hissing menacingly.

"I don't think your cat likes us," one of them said.

Charisma snapped and spat out, "Because you're the antiChrist!"

"We're a lot more than that, sweetheart," said one.

I wanted to be offended that it called my woman 'sweetheart,' but my woman was a sweetheart, so I couldn't be. Right around then, we finally got out of the swarm of locusts. Only then did I notice the wet feeling of blood running down my back and hear the quiet sound of droplets slapping at the floor; dripping out of my forearms.

I asked them, "If you three are ethereal, or spectral, or godlike, or whatever; then why would you want to be human?"

They didn't reply. I turned around and saw that they were gone. Charisma was crying. I can't imagine what she was thinking, but I was sad to see her suffering. I put my hand on her leg and she held it in hers. I put the hammer down, now that I could see. And one by one; the vicious grasshoppers from Hell- the locusts- lost their grip on my truck and got sucked off into the airstream.

Chapter 18
Craters of the Moon
In the mirrors the locusts were like a black sandstorm; reaching from the Earth to the sky and dispersing toward- presumably- all four corners. I felt stupefied. Everything that had just happened was strange, but I was irked that the spectors insulted me and that they were messing with me and that they had been in our bed. Charisma set about cleaning and dressing our wounds. The locust bites were about a centimeter in diameter and a centimeter deep. They hurt like hell and bled a lot.

We were about to go back through Omaha for the third time that day when Charisma said, "We have to turn around."

My stomach dropped and I groaned and said, "Why?"

"The final archon; it's in Idaho."

"We were just in Idaho. Why didn't we go when we were there?"

"We had to do this first. Now that we've done this, we have to go back."

"What about the locusts?"

"We drove through them once; we'll have to drive through them again," she said.

I did what she asked and took the next exit and turned the truck around. We were going to have to fuel up and shut down and get some sleep. I was pushing myself to make the miles; it had been a long day. I didn't mind that. But I wasn't happy when about 30 minutes later we were back in the swarm of locusts. Which was similar to driving through a blizzard. Except the blizzard was trying to eat us.

Their bodies blotted out the daylight and their eyes glowed red and made the interior of the truck glow red, also. The exterior of the truck was carpeted with them, and they even clung to each other and it was my windshield wipers that were the true heroes of the occasion. The rig was absolutely caked with the things. The tires had bad traction because we were sliding all over the demonic insects.

The actual boundaries of the swarm were difficult to discern because the cloud was moving as we were moving, but it might have been a hundred miles long or more. The density constantly expanded and contracted; which I knew because the visibility would improve or degrade accordingly.

We were passing through Lincoln when it was at its worst. I couldn't even read a sign or see anything besides the fog line; the grasshoppers were so thick. I knew our whereabouts only by the turns in the road, by the on and off ramps, and by the lanes changing. Things like that. On the other side of Lincoln, the cloud eventually dispersed. I put the hammer down and one by one and two by two, the insidious little creatures caught the wind and removed themselves.

When we'd gone into the swarm, it had been daylight. When we came out of the swarm, it was dark out. It had taken a long time to get through and I was exhausted. I knew there were truck stops in Kearney and North Platte. I wanted to stop in Kearney, but I didn't want the swarm to descend upon us while I was fueling up, so I forged ahead to North Platte; but I was drowsy and so the driving sucked.

As we walked into the Love's Travel Stop, we felt the slap of locusts flying into us. We slapped them in return and crushed them easily. I'd gotten bitten one time- on the neck- and Charisma had gotten bitten one time- on the arm; but- thankfully- the swarm was nowhere to be found. I think those few had been stowaways.

When we got inside the building, Charisma went to the bathroom and I met with the attendant- the only person there; I might add. She was a little old woman wearing the red employee uniform, with a cloud of white hair and rectangular bifocals, and more pep than one might credit her by the looks of her.

"Hello," I said.

"Hello there, sonny jim. What can I do you for?"

"I need fuel, ma'am."

"Well, you're in luck. We're having a sale on fuel. Fuel is on the house."

"Pretty good sale, I'd say," I said.

"Oh, I'd say so, too," she said; her accent upper midwestern.

"Ma'am. Have you heard anything about what's happened to the Love's over in Sidney?"

She looked at me sideways, and said, "I heard it's not there anymore. I heard Sidney's a ghost town. What do you know about it?"

"I was there; when some bad things happened. Some crazy unbelievable things."

"Nothing is unbelievable. Not anymore. If you told me the truck stop had sprouted legs and run out into the corn fields; I'd be inclined to believe you."

"Is that what you heard?"

"Isn't that what happened?" she asked.

"How did you know?"

"People talk. That hasn't changed. There aren't too many left, but the ones there are still talk."

"Ma'am. There's going to be a swarm of flesh eating locusts coming down on this town. I don't know when, but maybe soon. Chances are, they could come in through the vents of this place. You should get yourself somewhere safe. Somewhere where there's not too much ventilation."

"Flesh eating locusts, you say?"

"Yes, ma'am."

"Alright then. I suppose I can take up in my brother's ol' 'nado shelter. I'll just set these pumps to flow freely, in case there's any others out there drifting through. But I doubt it. You're the first I've seen since I took my lunch."

I asked her about showers and food and Charisma appeared and her and the woman exchanged pleasantries and Charisma suggested she- Marlene- say some prayers and Marlene told her she always does, and then we watched Marlene walk out to her car and drive away; basically leaving the place in our possession. We filled a tote with food and made several trips carrying water and then we got fuel and parked. It wasn't until we were falling asleep when the swarm descended upon us. Earlier, I'd been afraid the locusts would eat my hoses and lines and tires and things. But, as it turned out; the swarm hungered for human flesh exclusively.

The insects blotted out the ambient light. They scraped at the gaps of the doors and stowage; trying to get in. We uneasily fell asleep to an unholy humming that was about as loud as 18 wheels rolling down the highway. When we woke up, they were gone.

Now. I'm getting to the point in my telling where I must choose to either omit descriptives from the remaining chapters in order to detail the ensuing archon 'reveal' or omit descriptives from the ensuing archon 'reveal' in order to detail what we endured getting from the Mississippi river back to Fall River. Either way. It's the same story.

The next day was smooth sailing. Pretty unremarkable drive, thankfully. Unfortunately, we did encounter the locust swarm around Salt Lake City and so we lost a couple hours pushing through it. But, like the other times, nothing came of it.

Passing through Sidney; the aftermath of what had happened there was mostly evidenced by scorched earth that reached to the horizon to the north; but also by the truck stop being just a crater bedazzled and bejeweled with pipes and foundation materials and burnt up truck carcasses and also by a mess of aswang remains scattered around pools of melted asphalt and dissolved dirt.

We didn't have any close encounters with any aswang; except for at Cheyenne where- again- one chased after us and- again- we outran it. The cool thing was there was an army unit that came out of nowhere and ran down that humanoid bat demon that was trying to run us down. I'd thought everyone in Cheyenne had been killed, but I guess not. I saw in my mirrors that the soldiers had pulled the demon down out of the sky somehow. That gave me a lot of hope to see some people fighting back. That was the whole point. Fighting back against the evil.

It was somewhere in Wyoming when I worked up the nerve to ask Charisma the questions I didn't want to know the answers to; "Where are we going, and why are we going there, and what are we doing there?"

"We're going to the Craters of the Moon national monument."

"Hey. I always wanted to go there. But, I guess, not anymore, really."

"We're going there because the final archon is there."

"What's the final archon do?"

"Hmm... Let's see... So far; we've released people from contractual enslavement to governments and banks, released them from media brainwashing, released them from programmed stupidity and lack of common sense, from compelled predatory behaviors, from religious manipulation- sort of, from the profit motive, from the superfluous illusions of a false reality, from their innate inner darkness; can you guess what is left?"

"I can. But I don't want to."

"It's Satan. We have to release people from the clutches of Satan."

"What are the clutches of Satan?"

"It's symbolic. The archons were the clutches of Satan. Satan is all around us now. The aswang, the locusts, the mermaids, the cerberus, the dragons, the cobras, the scorpions."

"Where is Satan? What is Satan?"

"In the broad sense; Satan is all around us. Satan is the world itself. Satan is everything devoid of the light of Christ. The light of Christ is all that really exists. But, with regard to our purposes; we banished Satan already. Twice. In fact. First in Las Vegas, and again at Sidney," she said.

I said, "Oh, I see. But, I still don't understand what is happening. Will you please just explain it?"

"It's the coming of the antiChrist. We've eliminated all the tools and weapons of evil, but the evil remains. The last thing we're doing is flushing the devil out of its hole. We're removing evil's ability to hide. We've been forcing Satan out into the light this entire time. Only in the light can the darkness be destroyed. We weren't ready, though; we didn't have enough power and Satan had too much power. It lashed out at us. It killed all those people. It tried to kill everybody it could. If it tried to exterminate us now; we're all illuminated by the light of Christ; it couldn't do it. Evil's last resort is to fight us in the material world. That's what comes next. That is the becoming of the spectors. The coming of the antiChrist."

I more or less understood what she was saying, so I said, "Ok. So, what do we have to do, exactly?"

"Angela will do it."

"Oh. Good."

"Yeah, but you won't like what comes after."

"I never do," I said.

We'd left at dawn that morning, and it had taken the better part of the day to get out to Craters of the Moon. The area was an arid landscape; sandy and rocky and dry, with only tenacious patches of grasses and occasional unimpressive shrubs; all of it surviving with varying degrees of success. Pretty typical Idaho landscape. And that typical Idaho landscape was interspersed with atypical black lava rocks. The lava rocks were invariably varying; sometimes jagged and craggy, sometimes smooth and gently cascading, sometimes lumpy and compounding, sometimes stoney and gravely; or any combination of conceivable configurations. Always black. And there were craters out there, like it says in the names. Big ones, little ones; in between ones.

The park itself was totally abandoned and I was able to drive my rig out into it, but the exact coordinates for where we needed to be left us with no alternative but to ride the KTM out into lava fields themselves. Being as that it was almost dark out and that we'd already been on the road all day; we decided to camp for the night and go do the job in the morning.

We ate MREs and soup for dinner. And we washed ourselves as best we could. I remember having some stupid notion that- because this was the last job- our mission was almost completed. I fell asleep daydreaming about peace and love and happiness; imagining my mother gardening- with her grandchild helping her; Charisma by my side; watching and smiling.

We woke up and had peanut butter and jelly for breakfast. Eager to get this over with; I unloaded the bike and we put on our gear and took off. Using the GPS to guide us. I don't know why or how the GPS still worked, but it did. We'd brought along the X7 rifles and some extra grenades; plus our bowie knives. And the camelbak.

The coordinates took us out into the expansive tracts of the lava fields. The sky was clear and blue, there was a gentle breeze in the air, and the temperature was rising as the sun rose. The riding went from easy to impossible to easy to impossible; over and over and over. We had to make long detours around areas where there was just no way to ride through them. And, I had to memorize all the detours- and their intricacies- because there was a likelihood we'd need them soon. I also memorized the places where the park service had installed roads as these would be the fastest- although least direct- way to escape the terrain.

As one might imagine; the devil itself wasn't to be found out in the gently rolling hills. There was a crater, and it wasn't a hospitable crater. It was craggy as all hell and we couldn't get close to it on the bike and even once we had gotten close to it on foot; we couldn't get down into it on foot. Or, maybe we were just too intimidated to try to go down into it. As it was quite deep and yawning and cavernous, as well as jagged. At any rate, we didn't have to descend to the bottom of the crater, anyhow. Because that was Angela's duty.

The crater wasn't small. It was big like an open-pit mine. Not really that big, but similarly striking. At the bottom of the crater there was a cave. From where we were sitting, the cave was just a black hole at the bottom of some rocks.

We sat down on the edge of the rim; as close as we could get without actually descending. Charisma took off her backpack and pulled out Angela and gave her a big hug and a big kiss and told her she loved her and then released her.

Angela didn't hesitate and didn't seem to notice that she was hundreds of feet above her destination. With bated breath we watched what was actually a staggeringly beautiful performance; a spectacle of agility and acrobatics that would have impressed even the most accomplished gymnast, or parkourist, as it may be. The cat nimbly leapt from one precipice to another like it was nothing; sometimes flying through the air for great distances; falling more than jumping. Other times scrambling rapidly as the physics of her own momentum carried her.

Charisma wrapped her arms around me. I could feel she was tense. I was tense, too. I well remembered what happened at the mine in New Mexico, and I dreaded a repeat occurrence. Angela eventually made her way down to the bottom, stalling at the mouth of the cave. Even at a distance it was easy to see her white fur contrasting against the black rocks. Then the cat stepped into a black hole and disappeared.

I imagine Angela cautiously crept into the cave for as far as she was able until even her feline night vision could not penetrate the darkness any further. Further down below- maybe another 100 feet or maybe another one thousand feet or maybe somewhere toward the core of the earth- Draag appeared within the center of a hollow magma chamber. Charisma's body; nude, hairless, breathless; the embodiment of the divine mother. The chamber was pitch black- of course- but Draag had the light of Christ in her eyes and so could see easily. What she saw was the figure of herself; a statue made of lava rock. Back straight, head high, chin up, fists clenched, arms at her side, breasts perky and proud; looking straight ahead, with two rubies where the eyes should be. An immaculate sculpture placed incongruously at the center of nothing.

Draag approached the figure of herself and gazed into it as if it was a mirror. It was a mirror image, really. The statue was her. A division of her. The evil version of her. Entombed. For millennia. Devoid of life. Devoid of light. It was her sister. It was her mother. It was her daughter. It was herself. The light in Draag's eyes reflected in the rubies and

the rubies came to life. The rubies began to shimmer and
smolder; giving off a luminescence of their own. A red light.
A laser red light.

Draag stepped back. The stone of the statue began to
crack and spiderweb; coming apart in flakes and fragments.
There was a woman within. Draag's identical twin.

The replicate woman suddenly awakened and
immediately began tearing the stone shell off of her body.
Only when she'd freed herself of her eternal bondage did
Draag's twin acknowledge Draag's presence.

After an instantaneous recognition; Draag's twin leapt
toward Draag with her hands outstretched; grabbing Draag
by the throat. Draag tried to scream but the light was
choked off and so could not flow from within. Draag's eyes
flared brightly but the darkness in the throat of Draag's twin
spewed forth an antimatter that succeeded in sucking the
light of Christ out of the chamber. The darkness of Satan. A
blackness from which no light could escape. But the light of
Christ was as infinite as the darkness of Satan was all-
consuming and Draag fought back valiantly; similarly
attempting to throttle her identical twin. Draag's eyes
shined brightly and Draag's twin's eyes removed the light
from the vicinity. The perpetual power struggle; playing out
in real time.

The light of Christ was leaking from Draag's throat and
the darkness of Satan was leaking from Draag's twin's
throat. They fell to the ground and rolled around; choking
and battering one another. The light of Christ; illuminating.
The darkness of Satan; consuming. And Draag battered her
twin's skull against the ground as her twin maneuvered to
get the top position. Having gained the top position; Draag's
twin smashed Draag's head against the ground repeatedly.
But, Draag dug her fingers in deeper and brought her twin
under control. They were both fading; the light that leaked
out was weakening the twin and the darkness that leaked
out was diminishing Draag's strength.

The luminescence in the room was a display unlike anything in nature; with waves of pure light intermingled with waves of absolute blackness. The light and the dark twisted in and out of one another; creating an undulating psychedelic swirling.

The two angelic beings lay writhing and weakening on the ground. Their tempers dampened. Their grips on each other's throats lightened slightly. The spectral refraction of Draag's twin's laser red eyes drank in the divine light of creation and the divine light of creation came rushing forth to fill the void. The blackness; consuming voraciously. The light; a torrential deluge. The sisters pulled their mouths to one another's. The blackness drank in the light. The light overpowered the blackness. Their lips met and they kissed. Their hands released their throats. Their tongues licked their tongues. They wrapped their arms around one another. And they wrapped their legs around one another. And they writhed in holy unholy ecstasy. And for just a little while, there was no evil. There was no good. There was only love. The love we feel for lost loved ones; who take the best parts of ourselves with them when they go.

Up on the edge of the rim of the crater, I had no clue what was happening down in there. But Charisma knew. She looked like she was going to cry; but with tears of joy, not sadness. I didn't ask about it. A few minutes after Angela had gone down into the cave, she emerged and began her leaping, jumping, scrambling ascent. About a minute after the cat emerged; a ray of light- which by then I knew full well was the divine light of creation- came boring down from the heavens; filling the cave. Or, maybe it came blasting out of the cave and shooting up into the heavens. I couldn't say which.

However; in the sky- at the zenith of the ray of light, there was something I'd not ever seen before. It was a black hole; simply put. I couldn't say if the black circle was enormous and way out in outer space, or if it was relatively contained and down near to the earth. Either way; the black hole was foreboding. Also, it wasn't a hole as much as it was a black spiral. There were long and curving arms on it; and the ray of light was filling the gaps between the arms; and the bright blue heavens enshrouded the entirety. I could see the spiral's arms moving; so that makes me think the thing was close, and not far.

About now was when the wind picked up and the earth started rumbling beneath us. Soon there was dust and grit kicking up all around. The crater gave off a wind of its own; so we were getting sand blown into our faces as we watched Angela hurrying toward us. The cat knew there was a problem, and she jumped and scurried as fast as her little legs could carry her. I had the rifle held ready but visibility was low and I was- incorrectly- wishing I had my bo staff.

I heard something coming rushing toward us. I don't know where it came from; the archons sometimes popped out of weird places. I did know it would be big because the first ones were always big. And because we were vulnerable- due to the low visibility- I listened to my gut instinct. I thumped a grenade into the shadow of the beast as it was appearing through the fog of sand; just as I saw the dull glow of its blazing red eyes.

These particular demons were similar to gorillas or baboons; but they were reptoid and had razor teeth and talons like daggers and puggish lizard faces and this one happened to be about twenty feet tall. It had had its hand stretched out and ready to swipe us off the face of the earth. With a stunning blast the grenade caught it in the right pectoral and tore the arm clean off. The grenade also exploded the carapace across the chest and throat. The grenade also exploded way too close to us and we were thrown down into the rocks. Looking back; we could have been thrown down into the crater. It felt like how I imagine falling off a bridge might; like, when you hit the water. Our protective clothing had prevented the rocks from cutting us too badly.

Relatively undamaged; we picked ourselves back up as Angela was jumping back into her backpack. I was dumping a mag into the orbs that had gone flying about when the demon burst open. Charisma pulled me away, screaming, "Come on, let's go!" That was when I realized I couldn't barely hear anything over the ringing in my ears. Even over our omnipresent earplugs, that grenade had been terribly loud.

Now, for several reasons, I was wishing we'd worn helmets. All we had were sunglasses and sunglasses are 'sun' glasses not 'whipping grit' glasses. I used the better of two stinging eyes to make my way back to the bike. I'm sure the windborn sand was bad for Charisma, too, but it was her who noticed the demons coming at us.

We had to climb over the rocks backward to pop shots at the reptoid ape monsters as they came flying out of the dust. The dust; becoming less severe with each step we took away from the crater's rim. The most important thing- we knew- was hitting them in the head. That left us with no choice but to allow them to get too close for comfort while we aimed and anticipated perfect shots. We took out about 5 or 10; tripping and stumbling over those rocks; trying to get back to the bike. And 5 or 10 dead demons- as we know- wasn't a good thing. A dead demon was a divided demon. A divided demon was a multiplied demon. But I don't know what else we could have done.

I kicked the bike to life and took off running as soon as I felt Charisma's hands holding on to me. It would've been easy to outrun these archons if we were on a real road, but we were out in a maze of jagged rocks and jagged rock formations and cliffs and caves and caverns and precipices and try as I might; the demons kept gaining on us. They could drift right over the landscape effortlessly; practically gliding. Their physiology was made for throwing themselves across the rocks. Meanwhile, I had to carefully navigate my way through hazardous terrain at high speed.

Charisma wasn't twiddling her thumbs, though. She'd figured out how to cover 360 degrees around us from her seat on the back. She'd fire the rifle one handed; using her body or my body to steady it. We had our safety jackets on, so that was helpful with the powder burn and the heated barrel. The gunshots were jarring, but we managed.

For the most part I was able to use what space I had available to keep the demons where she needed them to be. And when our pursuers got in too close, I always remained aware of at least one escape route that I could break for in a pinch. It wasn't usually the right direction; but it'd be the only way to create the space required to survive.

Looking out over the lava rock; it looked like the rocks themselves were darting toward us like flying fish. These reptoid gorilla demons lunged with speed and precision and grace. Charisma was a crack shot, and I was a snappy driver, and my bike had enough guts to pull away when it had to; but everytime she put one down, another ten or twenty popped right back up, and they were getting smaller and more difficult to shoot; besides.

All things considered, it was the landscape that was the real enemy there. The landscape was leaving us with no choice except to push ourselves beyond our limits; my bike, my girl, myself. We'd brought a lot of magazines, but Charisma was using a lot of bullets. I knew she knew we were running out because she started letting them gain on us instead of taking them out, and then she shouted at me; "You got to corral them together! Corral them together!"

So that was what I did, and it was the one time the landscape worked in our favor. There was so much space out there that if I just ran straight in one direction- the wrong direction, usually- the demons would naturally group together to follow. And I figured out that I could swerve around certain rock formations to slow them down; and then they'd be even closer together when I got back out into the open. This method allowed Charisma to take better shots with fewer misses, but- more importantly- it also allowed her to thump grenades into clusters of them. And the ability to disable three, six, or twelve with one shot; that was what allowed us to make it out of the lava flows and onto a real road.

And that was the end of the chase, really. They kept coming, but they were small and running on four legs and the bike could do 100 miles per hour if the road was straight. Charisma understood that we were going in the wrong direction to get to the right direction and- taking that into consideration- she shouted in my ear; "Stop! Let them catch up!" And I took her meaning. We wanted to draw them out into the middle of nowhere and then haul ass back to the truck. Looking back I could see that the dust storm was still swirling around that crater; which was several miles away by this point. We'd covered a lot of ground.

The demons kept coming and we let them. When they were close, we took off into the distance. When they were far away, we stopped and let them catch up. We repeated this process about ten times. Then, when we were out where we wanted to be- at the furthest point from the truck before we would begin driving back toward it- we let the demons catch up one last time and then gunned the throttle toward the relative safety of the semi.

Once there; I mounted the motorcycle as fast as I could and then I drove us away as fast as I could. The demons remained plainly visible out in the lava flows; effortlessly tossing their lithe bodies over the black rocks. Drawing nearer all the while.

Every archon of every variety had unlimited endurance and that was one of several reasons why they were so effective. They were deadly and they multiplied exponentially and they never got tired. Their weaknesses were that they weren't especially bright and they were vulnerable to conventional weapons.

Chapter 19

Ever the Commando

Driving away from the craters, the ray of light continued to blaze down from the sky, emanating from the black hole which remained; swirling- toward the south. Eventually my pulse stopped racing. I drank some coffee and tried to forget about what had just happened. I was amazed we'd survived. I didn't think we would, at the time.

Looking up at the spirling black hole in the sky, I asked Charisma; "What the hell is that?"

"Hell, is what that is."

"Hell is in the sky?"

"Hell is in the mind. Everything exists in the mind. We are mental creatures. Reality is a mental reality," Charisma said.

Agreeing, I said, "Yeah. People are mental. That's for sure. But, like, why is that there?"

"The antiChrist is coming."

"Hey. Yeah. Where are the spectors? They should've made their appearance by now."

"They're in the hole in the sky. Or, they're in the cave."

"They'll be human now?" I asked.

"If they're in the cave, they'll be human."

"So, we could go kill them?"

"They'd be protected by all those demons."

"But, hypothetically, they could be killed?"

"Yes. If they're human. Or, human-ish. Like me."

I tried not to think about the fact that Charisma probably isn't human. And I thought about the fact that the antiChrist could be killed. I can't say why- maybe just for obvious reasons- but killing the antiChrist was all I wanted to do at the time. We were eastbound and down, but I wanted to turn around. I was envisioning fighting my way through the reptoid ape demons with the acid throwers, and then finding the antiChrist and taking them out.

Then I said, "Wait. They're not the antiChrist. They're the antiChrists. With an S. There're three of them."

"I guess so," she said, "but maybe it's not any different from the trinity of the father, sun, and holy ghost."

"What would you call their trinity? The dipshit, the shithead, and the shit for brains?"

Charisma started laughing, but didn't say anything. One of the zillion things I loved about her was how easy it was to make her laugh; sometimes. Other times; the jokes flew right over head. Then, suddenly, I had a thought.

I asked, "If they're the antiChrists, then where is the anti antiChrist?"

"In my womb, love."

I looked over at her and she was smiling at me and holding her hands over her belly. I was smiling, too. It's not everyday that you're told that your child will be the second coming of Christ. I reached out and took her hand and brought it to my mouth and kissed it and said, "I love you, Charisma." And she said, "I love you, too, Kevin."

We drove on in silence. I was dumbfounded by the revelation. For that little while; everything was beautiful and perfect and good. We were headed back to Fall River. I'd see my mother again. I'd move on with my life. I'd have a baby with my new love. As for the drive home; I didn't know what to expect, but I knew it wouldn't be easy. I was so happy, but I was also deathly determined to get us all back east safely.

Even after an hour on the road, I could look out and see the whereabouts of the crater by where the light shone from the black hole toward. I guess I'd gotten used to the black hole being up there because it was Angela who noticed the next thing that happened. The cat jumped up onto the dash and her eyes were flaring white with the light of Christ. Loudly; wailing, hissing, rawring, and meowing; Angela was angrily screaming- annoyingly- actually; as cats do from time to time.

I could see Angela was mad at the black hole because she was staring directly at it. Of course, now Charisma and I were staring at it also. A second later and we could see what the cat was so displeased by. Or, we could sort of see what. There were black objects. Their features were indiscernible. But, probably they were not material objects. And these black non-material objects were dropping out of the hole. But they weren't falling out of the hole. On the contrary; the black shadow objects were dispersing outward, not downward. These 'shadow beings' were spreading out in all directions; speckling the sky; not in great quantities, but with impressive profusion for what they were.

Angela realized she couldn't do anything about them, and that they weren't at all interested in us; and so she eventually calmed down and went and sat on Charisma's lap. But her eyes continued to glow white for another twenty minutes. An unnerving visual I never could get used to. By the time Angela stopped glowing, the black hole had ceased to spew black beings out of itself. And the black beings had mostly disappeared into the horizons. That was about the last we saw of the black hole itself, as well; because the miles were ticking by and soon enough we were gone.

But the pavement was angry that day.

I'd been planning to stop at the truck stop in Ogden. But Ogden was still- a day later- blanketed with locusts. They tended to gather on structures and on the streets and on the cars. Apparently our presence roused them because the locusts took to the air as we rolled through. So we were back inside of one of those swarms again; only this time the cloud was only about a hundred yard radius surrounding us. Knowing this- and knowing the road ahead was straight- I put the hammer down and succeeded in bursting out of the dark and faintly aglow red haze of demonic insects. But only for a few seconds. After that, the cloud grew larger and after a couple of unsuccessful attempts to break out of it, I just gave up and watched the fog line to get through.

With all those locusts, there was no way to stop there. I knew I had enough fuel to make it to Evanston, or even to push through to Rock Springs. Although, I wasn't comfortable doing so. I had two oversized tanks on my rig, but they weren't bottomless. We'd run out eventually. I had very much intended to fuel up in Ogden. Unfortunately.

I voiced these concerns to Charisma, but- before she could respond- a bullet came ripping through my windshield, zipping past my head, passing through the cabin, and exiting out the back wall of the berth. A lot of thoughts went through my head in that instant; mostly 'oh, shit, my windshield,' and also, 'oh shit, we're being shot at.' At the same moment, I saw that the young man, the shooter, a blonde midwestern Mormon looking fellow- naturally- was standing right in front of us. He'd used a bolt action rifle and had just driven the bolt home and shouldered the weapon when my truck was on top of him and I was running him over. He hit the grill hard enough to snap the plastic. And then he went down under the undercarriage. I cringed as my drive tires thumped over him. That was the first person I had ever killed. That I knew of.

The locusts were crawling in through the bullet holes before I even had a chance to process what had happened. Charisma was on it, though. She smashed the bugs with her shoe as they came through. The hole in the windshield was about as clean as a guy could hope for, but it still made me nervous every time she hit it with her shoe.

There was a hole in the back, too, and pretty soon Charisma was jumping around like a monkey trying to smash all the insects and I was still driving because I guess I'd kind of frozen. Also, Angela's eyes were blazing white again and the cat was jumping around as crazily as my love was. Then I remembered; spray foam. And then I remembered why I love spray foam. I stopped and set the brake and sealed the hole in the window with the foam; using a small trowel I had for aide. I felt I was getting bitten- on my skull, through my hair- right as Charisma was hitting me in the head with her nasty demon-locust encrusted shoe. After that I sealed up the hole in the berth.

After that; I jumped in the driver's seat and hit the brake and put the transmission in drive and stepped on the pedal. I was in a hurry to get away from that area; and for good reason, it turned out. I saw in my mirror that the gunman was- somehow- approaching through the cloud of swarming locusts. I was glad that he wasn't dead. Then, as I saw him take aim, I decided I was not glad actually.

I saw the muzzle flash. I heard the bullet pierce through the back of the sleeper berth, and then- as I heard the report of the rifle- I felt the bullet collide with my chair and drive itself into my left shoulder blade. My vision flashed with dazzling sparkling fireworks and I knew I'd been shot; but I didn't stop driving.

"Put your head down!" I shouted at Charisma. I don't know if that was good advice, but that was what I said. I kept my foot on the throttle and watched the shooter in my mirror. I saw the muzzle flash again and I thought something bad was about to happen, but nothing did. We were out of range by then. The shot must have gone wide.

"Are you okay?" she asked me.

"Peachy keen, jelly bean," I said, for the first time in my life; grimacing. I guess she could see through my facade. So I asked her, "Am I bleeding?" Feeling the fluid leaking onto my skin; I leaned forward to show her my shoulder. I tried to brace myself against the pain. It didn't help. I was gasping for air and gritting my teeth.

"Yes! You got shot!"

The fluttering of locust wings made a repulsive sound. One landed on her cheek and I didn't even think; I just reached out with my good hand and slapped her in the face; grabbing the bug and throwing it under my boot.

The sudden movement hurt and I struggled to speak; telling her, "Love! You have to plug the hole in the back! In the back of the truck!"

Then a locust landed on my right arm and it was biting me and I tried to slap it with my left hand; only to realize that my left arm was more severely limited than I had thought. But the appendage wasn't completely incapacitated. I was able to grasp the insect and squeeze the life- or, the evil...- out of it. Meanwhile, Charisma slapped a couple more with her shoe and succeeded in plugging the hole; all before I got bit again. But, she did get bit once more in the process. On her wrist.

Once Charisma was back in her chair, I could see she was bleeding from her face and her neck. I could feel blood running through my hair, and my whole back was sticky with the stuff.

"We have to pull over," she said.

"I don't like it here," I said. But I knew she was right.

"We have to," she said.

I pulled over right there- a couple of miles away from the shooter- and she used pliers to rip the bullet out of my bone where it had lodged itself. Then she cleaned the wound and sewed it shut. The locust bites didn't need to be stitched but they did require bandaging. We had to cut some of my hair off to bandage the bite on my skull. Charisma had to wear an unsightly strip of medical tape on her sightly face.

I drove us out of there. I couldn't imagine any way to get fuel in a town where there were flesh eating locusts everywhere; turns out the solution was rather unimaginative. We just kept driving. I was quite relieved when we left the swarms behind us as we exited the Salt Lake area. But I had a suspicion we'd see the scourge again when we got to Evanston.

I took the opportunity to get out of the truck and- crawling on the hood, over a thousand smashed locust demons- cut the entry wound foam flat on the outside of the windshield. The wipers had been wiping like junk. I was thinking that what I really needed was a way to walk around in the locust clouds. The shooter in Ogden had figured it out, apparently. But that was probably because he was possessed.

Evanston was crawling just how Ogden had been. I wasn't going to risk pushing for Rock Springs. Rock Springs was plan b. Evanston was plan a.

The swarm picked up around us right as we passed by the Evanston city limits sign. Programming; even then. Charisma and I had discussed the plan beforehand and when I pulled up to the pumps at the Love's; it came time to execute it.

The first thing to do was to put on layers of clothing and seal off the seams and gaps. I put on two pairs of socks and tucked my bottom layer of pants into my socks; applying duct tape to the seams. I tucked my second layer of pants into my boots and duct taped all around the seams there as well. I repeated this with the shirts going into my pants and the shirts going into my gloves and my balaclava going into my shirt and my winter beanie around my balaclava and then I put goggles on and we reinforced all the vulnerable places- face, head, throat, armpits- with strips of a fleece blanket that Charisma had shredded while I was driving. I was somewhat safe from the locusts; at least for a little while.

I saw through the window that the pumps were set to 'free flow' and that was a relief. I would jump out and insert the nozzles and start the flow; wrapping the gaps in towels to keep the insects out of my fuel tanks. They'd descend upon me immediately and furiously and I would feel their weight and their crawling and even their mouths moving.

Then I would jump back into the truck and Charisma and Angela would hide under the blankets while I smashed up all the locusts that had gotten in. When the pumps clicked off, I'd jump out, close up the tanks, hang up the nozzles and jump back in. Then I'd smash up all the locusts again. Then I'd undo the costume.

It worked out pretty good and when it was over we were happy and kissing and hugging and I got bit again because I'd missed one, but I smashed it and then we drove off into the sunset. After having been shot; I was rethinking my proximity to basically everything. There was only one road home, though; realistically, and we'd have to face whatever it threw at us head on.

Charisma was cleaning up the glass dust and shards and the smashed up bugs and I was watching the fog line; trying to get out of the swarm again; wondering where I could park us to sleep for the night. I couldn't think of anything smart to do so I just kept laying down the miles; hoping to find some slick spot to stick ourselves soon. We hit another locust swarm at Rock Springs. But I just pushed through it and it was no big deal. I didn't care how tired I was because I knew we were going home. Even if home was on the other side of a nightmare.

Charisma spotted a good spot to camp on the map. On route 371. A road that connected a mountain town- called Superior- to the interstate. It was late at night by the time we pulled into a decrepit old service road to sleep. We were tucked in with ridges on all sides and it felt as secure as anywhere could feel; considering.

Turns out, it was a false sense of security. I've always been a light sleeper and I heard the aswang's beating wings before it ever even touched its feet to the ground. I was clambering over the firearms and the weapons and I picked up the 1301 shotgun and the bandolier of shells along the way. All I could think about was protecting my windows. I threw the door open and jumped out into the air; landing and sliding on my good shoulder and then taking my position.

It was a dark and moonless night but I'd gotten a hint about where the creature would attack me from because there was a street light in the distance and his body had glinted as it caught some of the glow. Plus, the truck lights had come on when I opened the door; so I could see fine, really.

The winged demon descended upon me and I blasted it in the face. Hurriedly, I stood to my feet and positioned myself over the body. As the divisions emerged I blasted each one, one after another; feeding shells into the tube as I went.

I called to Charisma, "Love! The sledge hammer!"

She heaved the sledge out into the dirt and I put down the gun and picked up the crusher and went at it. It wasn't a complicated process but it took a lot of swings. From head to toe and from toe to head; I pulverized every inch of that thing. Or, of those things. When I was finished, I didn't feel tired anymore. The sun was rising, too, so I knew I'd gotten a decent amount of sleep. Enough to get further down the road, anyway. We ate peanut butter and jelly sandwiches and then we got underway.

I haven't said much of anything about the roads lately, but they were actually a cause for optimism and I should mention something about what was going on out there. There weren't a lot of people to be found- it was Wyoming- but when you saw somebody; it gave you a feeling of hope and comradery. They were men in lifted four wheel drive trucks with machine guns mounted on the backs, or they were soldiers moving in old box vans in order to keep the locusts at bay, or they were law enforcement officers in SUVs doing over a hundred miles per hour. Occasionally, we'd see a random car out there just going about its business. Nobody looked weak, but we all felt fragile.

I had serious doubts about our future. In Laramie, we again encountered the swarms of locusts. And in Cheyenne, we again encountered the swarms of locusts, again... I really don't know how many swarms there were. I also don't know how- or if- they divided themselves. I'd never seen a locust divide. I think they just kept crawling out of the ground. Because as big as the first swarm was, it couldn't account for city after city being blanketed in these things. I felt bad for the people trapped in those places.

We were coming out of Cheyenne when an aswang caught us in a bad position. It was ahead of us and it was close. It had us exactly where it wanted us. I saw it and I tapped Charisma and said, "That thing is coming down on us."

But my woman- ever the commando- said, "It's fine. I got it." And got it she did. She had her 500 magnum ready and was hanging out the window anticipating the shot. I slowed down to keep the wind out of her eyes, and when that aswang came at us; she nailed it in the face on the first try and didn't even have to waste any more bullets. I felt better about our prospects after that. I always forgot that Charisma was unstoppable. And she always reminded me.

I made a point to swerve and run the demon over as it hit the ground; hoping to crush its insides, but I guess I shouldn't have done that because I could have blown a tire on its spikes. But I didn't, so whatever. In the rearview mirror, I saw the carcass dividing. Multiplying. But the locusts were behind us and the road was open ahead of us and so I put the hammer down and tore out of there.

The only other problem we faced in that area was that there were locust swarms sitting on every town of any size. We could see that people were gathering at the smallest towns just to escape the larger ones. I was constantly wondering how many people were still alive. I could never tell if it was a lot or a little.

One thing is for sure, though; it will sound more and more boring the more I describe driving through city after city swarming with locusts. The fact of the matter is it happened over and over again out there. But that was just how it was in Wyoming and Nebraska that day. I can't even describe what it looked like, because it was impossible to see anything. Except for the grasshoppers. I became awfully familiar with looking at those things; black, glowing red eyes, mouths like pencil sharpeners full of teeth. I am only grateful that nothing went wrong, and really, Nebraska is supposed to be boring. Everybody knows that.

It wasn't until outside of Omaha- to the east, not far from where the locusts spawned at- that something remarkable happened. What happened was that we came

upon a roadblock. I hadn't seen one in so long, but I was
happy to see some people, so I didn't mind. I was especially
happy to see that the word 'GNOSIS' had been spray
painted across the sides of all of the vehicles. There were
army trucks- cargo transports- blocking the road, with two
cop cruisers nose to nose at the center. The attendants were
wearing so much armor that they looked like spacemen; but
I was immediately totally jealous.

We were informed that while we had every right to
travel on our own; people were finding it safer and easier to
move from city to city in convoys. They said that this system
was especially beneficial east of the Mississippi where the
dangers were more extreme. The convoys had dedicated
acid throwers and gunners at the front and at the rear and
stationed throughout, as well. Usually, there'd be between
ten to fifty vehicles traveling in each convoy. They said the
convoys wouldn't be running at night, but that we could
still make the last group to Des Moines. I was happy to take
them up on their offer. Anything to protect my windows,
and- by extension- my pregnant woman.

I was going to need a ring. I wanted to propose to
Charisma. I felt it was important; since she was- or would
be- pregnant. And since I was single. I'd taken off my
wedding band as soon as I'd seen for myself what Vanessa
had become.

The cruisers moved aside and we were let through.
We'd been told to meet up with the others at the exit eight
on and off ramps. So, that was what we did. But we had to
push through the locusts to get there, and I didn't think
anybody would actually be there; because I couldn't imagine
how anybody could be anywhere with that swarm on top of
everything.

There were people there, though. There were locust
swarms there, too. But the people, the guards- we saw them
spraying on the way in- had figured out that they could put
acid gear on over their locust gear, and- by carefully and
strategically misting the locusts with acid- that they could

compel the evil grasshoppers to go be evil someplace else. The insects never went far, but they removed themselves from the immediate vicinity, at least.

So, it was a weird place to be. Because the swarm was settled all around us, and we were very much in the thick of it, but- as long as the acid throwers remained vigilant- none of the locusts came anywhere near us.

We were instructed to take the next available space in a line of about 8 vehicles. Some of which looked more than a little post-apocalyptic; with bars over their windows, plows over their grills, and gunports installed on their rooftops. All kinds of innovations for me to be envious of. I later learned that these vehicles were functioning as ferries; moving as many people as they could.

I watched in my mirrors as the other vehicles arrived at the convoy.

There'd be a miniature swarm flaring up with each arrival and it'd die down a minute later; once the acid throwers had carefully misted it.

As a signal that we were ready to depart; the lead truck- a humvee with a gatling gun on it, and the only vehicle facing the wrong direction- flashed its lights in our faces. Somehow all the other vehicles knew to flash their lights in response; so I flashed my lights also. And, also, we drove with our lights on; if that matters...

I saw the acid throwers jump into the interior of the box vans full of troops, and then we were heading down the road. It was a mostly uneventful drive. And pretty nice once we got out of the swarm. It was the first time I'd felt remotely secure in longer than I could remember. In the hills, the windmills spun in the setting sun, as though nothing was wrong.

The only problem we had was when an aswang that was randomly out in the middle of nowhere suddenly took umbrage with us and made designs on us. I tapped Charisma and said, "Look," and she said, "I see it," but all that happened was the gatling gun spat out an isolated hail of bullets and shot the demon out of the sky. The wings rippled in the wind as it plummeted to the ground. The acid throwers jumped on the carcass before it could multiply too severely.

Then the other soldiers used- seriously- big steel nets on long steel poles to capture the divisions that had escaped. They were like children catching butterflies. Once they had an aswang trapped in the net; another soldier would move in with a blunt object to pulverize the remains. The remains were dumped out, hosed down with acid, and this happened three times, I think. Then we moved on.

I liked the smasher the guy had used. It had a broad circular head, angled slightly, and it looked heavy. Must have been a custom piece, because it wasn't like any tool I had ever seen. I was jealous because it covered more surface area than the sledge hammer.

When we got to Des Moines; we had the option to wait, or to take off on our own. There was a waiting area for the next morning's first convoy. It was as safe of a place as anybody was going to find. And I was tireder than all Hell, too. So I was happy to post up and shut down.

We were at a fairgrounds; in about as well lit of an area as a well lit area could be. We were out in the center of an arena of some sort. It might have been where they held rodeos once upon a time.

The rest of the city was engulfed in locusts; but the convoy organization- Gnosis, really- had a team of about ten guys in full gear spraying the swarm away; plus another five guys patrolling with machine guns. I was excited to get a good night's sleep. My lady and I ate dinner and canoodled and passed out. But we slept with our clothes on and it was a good thing we did because a couple hours later I was woken up by gunshots and screaming.

Angela's eyes were flaring with white radiance as I opened the curtains, looked around, and saw a sad sad thing. One of the guards had turned demonic and was opening fire on everybody in sight. Specifically; the other guards. I didn't stop to think. I had a full clip in my XM7 and I jumped out and lined up the fucker before he seen me. There were maybe four bodies around him and I wasn't the only one with sights on him. I think me and two other guys gunned him down at about the same time. I ran out there to help get rid of the body because I wanted to make sure the locust sprayers were spraying and not dicking around with a corpse. Also, I was the only one without locust gear, so I commenced to take the stuff off of the dead guy.

I remember thinking that his blood looked black, but I shrugged it off because sometimes blood looks black. Two of the four guards whom the fifth guard had killed were supposed to have been off misting the locusts with acid, and the insects were not slow on the uptake. They knew to exploit their narrow window of opportunity.

I'd gotten half of the gear off of the guy when the grasshoppers started biting me. I slapped at them the instant they landed on me and that stopped most of the bites. It wasn't an overwhelming attack, but my body was racked with pain from jostling my bullet wound. I really wanted that gear, though; except as I was removing the stuff- while simultaneously getting bit- the dead guy jerked back to life. His closed eyelids opened and I saw his eyes were black.

His body was full of holes and there was even one through his cheek, but the guy reached out for me like he was completely fine. I jumped back and fired multiple rifle rounds into his head; breaking his face and skull apart. He dropped, but a second later he was getting back up.

Chapter 20
The Walk of Not Being Dead
Then Charisma was at my side and she said, "Trade!" and she handed me my katana. I took the sword and drew it and flung the scabbard aside. And this- more or less- headless zombie was rising up and coming at me; obviously

not using his eyes or ears to locate me, because he didn't have any. I released a 'kiai!' and swung the blade- one handed- in an arcing downward strike, cleaving him open from the shoulder through the chest and spine and almost out the other side. There wasn't anything that man's physical remains could do except writhe and bleed black blood into the dirt.

The crew had the locusts under control around the same time as I had the rest of the locust gear off of the dead body. I had sliced through the guy's protective vest, though. And the vest was what held everything together. So, really, I only got half of a suit off the guy. But, as the locals were dragging the dead bodies away, we chased them down and they let us take from the corpses what we needed for me and Charisma to both have locust suits.

The possessed body was sprayed down with acid and they put orange cones around it. Nobody seemed particularly upset about the loss. But that tracked because he was chosen by the evil because he was already evil. However, those who knew the lost ones displayed a sorrowful disposition; albeit subdued and numbed due to the attrition of the unending onslaught of these abysmal circumstances.

We carried the gear we'd pilfered back to the truck. Angela was sitting on the dashboard and flicking her tail; watching us out the window with eyes glowing white. I said to Charisma, "We don't want people seeing her like that." Nobody had, but still. Charisma said, "We don't have to hide who we are. It's not like the old days. These people are on our side." And she was right. Of course.

We got a nervous night's sleep after that. I didn't need Charisma to explain that the shadow of death had come out of the spiraling black hole and taken possession of that shooter. It was evident.

The next day, we skipped the first five convoys; because there was a man who had a metal shop on the premises. This was the same man who had outfitted many of the other vehicles I'd seen. His name was also Kevin and he was six feet tall and traditionally handsome; with long blonde hair and bright blue eyes; but, he talked very loud and mostly about how great he was- how he'd been a famous metal sculptor before the 'rapture'- and I think there was something wrong with his brain. Because his sculptures were rusty, nonsensical, and unappealing. But that didn't matter. I was able to trade one acid thrower and two tanks of acid to have my tractor outfitted with a bright yellow v-plow for the front, slanted steel slats for the windows, gunports and eye slits at each of the four corners, plus an only slightly protruding gunner's port for the roof, plus a platform for an unusually short gunner to stand on and a ladder to get up to it, and also steel plates over the back and sides. To stop bullets.

It was late in the day when we got lined up with the next convoy out and my ride was a proper warhorse by then. Not only that, but the military- or, what was left of it- had procured light tanks, tracked fighting vehicles, and armored personnel carriers on eight big wheels. Besides those; there was the endlessly unique cast of ordinary vehicles outfitted with armor and weaponry. Probably about twenty vehicles in total, on that trip. The destination was a place called Davenport, Iowa. On the Mississippi river. But first we had to get there.

I wondered a lot about the people who were making those trips. I'm sure they all had sad stories but I can't imagine what they were. All I really knew about them was they had places to be. But more so than that I wondered about the good Samaritans and soldiers who risked their lives just to help these people get down the road more or less safely. It was a noble deed. The convoy squads had nothing to gain and everything to lose, but they knew those people needed them and I guess that was reason enough.

The swarm of locusts rose up all around us as we left Des Moines. Their red eyes illuminated the shadow of the swarm that blackened the twilight of the sunset. Just outside of the city and we were in the clear again. I drove wearing full locust gear because I'd been wearing the stuff all day and I had gotten used to having it on. It wasn't uncomfortable; just heavy and thick; leather with polymer. Charisma's locust gear fit way too big on her so she mostly didn't wear it and instead stayed in the truck unless necessary.

I was excited to get moving and make miles. There'd been fuel available in Des Moines and so I had two full tanks. Two firebombs waiting to happen. Right underneath our seats. Just like every other day.

I'd wanted to mount the fifty cal on the roof but it would've shattered my already weakened windshield. What the sculptor did instead was to install a track that rotated around the gunner's port. The track was strong enough and designed to support the XM250, but we couldn't clear the 13' 6" height limit when the weapon was set up.

We hadn't gone far before we had use for our fancy new modifications. Unexpectedly; a company of four legged apelike reptoid aswang came bearing down on us from the north. It wasn't ten or twenty of them. It was fifty, or a hundred. They were a relentlessly capable breed; to have come so far so fast and grown to such sizes and such numbers in such a short time. The procedure for combatting these was as follows: The acid throwers rode fast and nimble light strike vehicles that looked like badass dune buggies. They'd position themselves between the threat and the convoy. The convoy would provide cover fire and do its best- our best- to bring the demons down within range of the acid throwers. It worked well in theory, and pretty good in practice, but it was not a perfect solution.

The problem with a convoy was it was too slow to run. Our only option was to fight our way out of engagements and for that, we were reasonably well equipped. As long as there was enough acid, the convoy could fight anything.

So now our convoy had come to a halt to do battle. Charisma was up in the gunner's port; the nest, as it came to be known. The flightless demons were getting chewed up and dissolved easily, because this was the plains and we'd seen them coming from miles away. But when the winged aswang came through, I knew I had to get involved. I jumped out and manned the fifty cal; which was set up on the back. We were basically in the middle of the lineup and the Browning only had 240 degrees of rotation; plus degraded accuracy if I had to excessively jump around on the catwalk and tires.

There wasn't any way to bring the flying ones down where the acid throwers wanted them. I radioed the commander to designate one acid unit specifically for the flying aswang. They didn't call them aswang. They called them fliers. And the ones on the ground were runners. The commander agreed and it was done.

I had my bo staff with me just in case, but all of those frightened people waving firearms around was a lot scarier than fighting the aswang and so I didn't actually have the option of fighting the fliers how I wanted to. A method I knew to be superior to bullets. It was the military personnel's job to move in with their smashers when they got the little ones in their nets. The bigger fliers really needed acid, or they'd multiply before you could thoroughly smash them.

So; there were a lot of rules and protocols and special considerations. But, there were only three fliers. Plus, the little ones that popped out of them when we took them down. The little ones were the worst. Couldn't shoot them. Had to hide from them until the guardsmen netted them. But we didn't have the luxury of hiding. So we didn't.

I was laying into the runners with the 50 cal when one of the little fliers made a move on me. Charisma blew it out of the sky and it landed right next to our truck and I didn't waste a second. I just jumped on it, and jumped on it again, and again, and again, and eventually stomped it down into nothing. Then I kept picking off runners. And eventually it was over. We lost an acid thrower. The man, and his personal protective equipment; but not his weapon. His weapon survived. Thankfully.

The man's death wasn't unusual, though. The acid throwers had the most dangerous position; for multiple reasons. They were out front; closest to the demons, at all times. They were spraying acid around, too. And, also, they were caught in the crossfire; no matter how much we tried to avoid it. I didn't envy them.

The convoy pushed through the locusts of Iowa City and made relatively good time on our passage to Davenport. The only problem occurred when we encountered a giant scorpion along the way. Bigger than any I'd seen yet. The damn thing had snuck up on us, too. Fricking thing was hiding in the water; in a slough. Right in front of my truck, like, three cars ahead; it jumped out and pinched a sprinter van in half. The van had been full of people and they scattered; but not all of them made it. The giant scorpion's two giant pincers grabbed two people; one in each. And the stinger went down through the bed of a pickup truck and got stuck. Then the M2 Bradley hit the colossus with a TOW missile. And it exploded all over all of us. All over the place.

Due to the loss of the sprinter van, Charisma and I were compelled to take in a family of Iranians; a father, mother, and daughter. I never figured out why there were Iranians in Iowa, but it wasn't any of my business.

Things didn't immediately improve after the soldiers exploded the giant scorpion demon. There were suddenly 10 or 15 other scorpions unfurling in the vicinity. We all went to work on them. The scorpions were scattered, so the acid throwers scattered, too. And there just wasn't enough of them to account for all the scorpions plus all the divisions from all the times we tried to stop the things with bullets.

Besides acid, the only real way to stop them was to blast them in the faces; preferably at close range and preferably with something powerful. I, myself, was pumping slugs into their heads with the 1301, and that seemed to work well. To follow up; I was also able to neutralize them with the sledge hammer; when I had to.

Eventually, the acid throwers succeeded in luring the scorpions away from the vicinity and thereafter mostly eliminated them; and those of us with plows cleared the chunks of carcass out of the road, and then we carried on. The roads themselves were full of acid holes marked with orange cones; from previous convoys gone by. We gave that shit a wide berth. Later on, the bigger convoys would use lye and earth movers to deal with the acid hazards.

Davenport- as it turned out- was the last place we saw the locusts. Thank heavens. Right at the Mississippi river, as I might've guessed. The convoys were operating out of the airport in Davenport; because the airplane hangers were good for keeping the locusts off of everything. Our Iranian guests wandered off and did whatever and Charisma and I shut down for the night. Gnosis was serving food and it was good, too. There were steaks and pizza and casseroles and all kinds of stuff. No beer, though. Typical Gnosis. But, smart, too, really.

There would be multiple convoys departing in multiple directions, but not until the next morning; because none went out at night. The idea was to bypass Chicago- insofar as that was possible, which it wasn't- and to get to South Bend, Indiana. That would be the largest convoy we'd been with to date. Every convoy would be bigger than the one before; up until the last couple.

And the whole convoy system was definitely a strength in numbers situation, but it was also a weakness in strength situation, because we were always tripping over each other and we couldn't go any faster than the military escorts.

I'm going to stop pretending like I knew what all the military vehicles were. I know there weren't any heavy tanks because their top speed was too low. But, I can say that we had an impressive variety of assault vehicles and troop carriers; plus, almost every vehicle had been outfitted with arms and armaments. I can confidently assert that there were between one hundred and two hundred vehicles in our convoy through Chicago. But how many exactly, I have no idea.

We'd gotten fuel upon arrival in Davenport. So, we just got as much sleep as we could and lined up as the sun was coming up and departed as soon as the light was good. The locusts flared up at our departure, blotting out the sky; and we crossed the Mississippi river in a black cloud that was alive with a flurry of buzzing wings and millions of tiny glowing eyes. Thirty minutes later and we were out of the swarm.

We had a nice drive east. For a while. We were out of the prairie and back into the lush green trees of the eastern United States. It was a peaceful and uneventful drive; right up until the dragons found us. That was at a place called Joliet; where the interstate divided the forests from the shopping centers. The dragons had taken to attacking in packs and what was worse was that they had developed enough brains to attack from different directions and at staggered intervals. There were about six of them when they hit us. Big ones, all of them. Some of them bigger than the first one from Erie. And the problem with these more sizable convoys was that there weren't enough acid throwers to go around. Or, so I was realizing, at the time.

The convoy was so long- in fact- that when the order to halt came through the radio; I hadn't even seen the dragons yet. But the scouts said the dragons were at the rear, and I could hear the guns from back there; so I jumped out of the truck and manned the fifty cal.

I didn't get a shot at the first one, but the second one- or, maybe it was the third one- came down just about a hundred feet away. That dragon hit with enough momentum- and raw fury- to overturn a step van full of people. I could see claws crushing metal as the formidable creature stood atop the transport and bit through the frame between the windshield and the door; making its way inside. I lined up my shot in the iron sights and pressed the trigger. The powerful bullets ripped the demon's armored skull apart and the creature fell over limply at the side of the van.

I was looking around for an acid thrower to attend to the situation and there wasn't one. I realized I was him. I didn't have time to put on all the gear. So, I licked my hand and held it up in the air to figure out which way the wind was blowing. Then I put on the two acid gloves, grabbed my acid thrower, and ran up to the dragon that was now dividing.

The people in the van were escaping out the back and that was good because I didn't want to spray acid near them. The dragon was visibly dividing; the creatures on the interior were ripping through the skin. One of the divisions had broken through the area where the bullets had broken the skull apart and it was facing me and about to jump at me when Charisma ran up from behind with the 1301 and dumped like five slugs into it. And it was a good thing she had done that or else I would have unloaded the acid into it and all that unloaded acid would've landed on top of me in the form of a dissolving dragon. I'd have been toast.

However, the wind was favorable for my purposes and I hosed the dragon- dragons- down from front to back. Equally importantly; I managed to keep the dangerous fluid from hurting anybody.

And what had happened where we were was basically the same thing as what was happening throughout the rest of the convoy. The gunshots rang out but they didn't even register. Other fighters fought other fights and the attack was over about twenty minutes later. The worst thing that had happened was that we lost all the occupants of one transport van when a dragon had crashed through its windshield and decimated all seven bodies within before anybody could even escape out of a door.

I was given some orange cones and police tape to mark off the bubbling acidic mess I'd created. Those toxic fumes were no joke. Being anywhere near them was enough to make you watch the smoke and the wind like your life depended on it. The acid mask had a gas mask on it, though, so I put that on to set up the cones and tape.

Due to the van overturning, there were about a dozen people needing rides. We took some teenagers onboard with us; a brother and sister who were trying to get to their aunt in Columbus, because their parents had been eaten by locusts. As one might expect, their spirits were quite low.

The convoy forged ahead. But we didn't get far. We were in Chicago and one thing about Chicago is it always takes every opportunity to remind you where you are. Even just passing through. We were just moving down the interstate- minding our own business- when a giant cerberus came bursting through the noise barrier walls. We saw this happen from about ten vehicle lengths away. The three headed dog had three heads and it used all of them effectively. In just a few seconds it had picked up an armored station wagon and flung it not just through the air, but literally through the sky; hundreds of feet into the distance- out onto a golf course.

The other two heads were crushing two other vehicles in their jaws and the third head was masticating a fourth vehicle. Meanwhile, my beloved was up in the nest before I could even tear my eyes away. She had her XM7 and was launching a grenade into the forty foot tall reptoid dog demon. The grenade exploded in its face, but it had a big face. I couldn't see whether the explosive had done any damage. She launched another grenade and that one connected better and the skull opened up; spilling several smaller cerberus out onto the highway.

Other weapons had been hitting the monster from other directions and so it just ran off into the distance instead of fighting with us any more. Trailing the more tattered and torn of its three skulls. Charisma was able to hit one of the other dogs with another grenade and it was small enough that that had incapacitated it long enough for me to put some 45-70 through its heads; and the soldiers were there by then to gun down the other, smaller, three-headed demons. And then the acid throwers came through and dissolved the remains of all before any could multiply. We were watching over our shoulders expecting the big one to return, but it didn't. I was glad the cerberus wasn't anywhere near where we were anymore. If a tank had put a missile into it then there may have been 10 or 20 or more to deal with.

We got pretty lucky; considering what potentially might have happened. Most of us. The people in those mangled cars suffered a lot. I helped some other guys pull those people out of the wreckage and that is one of those things I just wasn't made to do. I hate to see anybody in pain and some of those people were suffering indescribably. Others were simply dead; crushed. The survivors were loaded into the medical truck to be cared for; but it was hard to stomach their broken bones and ragged flesh and agonized faces.

We bulldozed the wrecked vehicles out of our way and kept pushing onward. I was beginning to wonder if we really were better off moving so slow in a group or if it would be smarter to move along faster and on our own. But it had been a while since we had been in the east and I was starting to see how things had changed. Most remarkably; there was a ton of debris all over the interstate. Every convoy that passed through left behind mangled vehicles and dead bodies. It'd be nice to say people were collecting the bodies, but that would be a lie. It was safer- and easier- for everybody to just leave them where they were. Although, the perpetual reeking stench was a noxious ordeal in its own right.

Another thing was that a lot of neighborhoods had burned down. Not just neighborhoods, but structures of all sorts. It wasn't like passing through the world we knew before. Half the time you were in the charred ruins of a recently lost civilization. Also, there was a lot of smoke, and a lot of fire, too. A lot of what had not yet burned was either actively burning or about to be. Can't say why. Just the way it was.

The convoy encountered another scorpion before we got out of the city and somebody gunned it down, but it came apart and the divisions ran away into the fields before the acid throwers could get to them. The same thing happened with a cerberus- a smaller one, still very big- maybe twenty miles later. This would become a trend we'd see more and more as we made our way eastward. The demons created confrontations as a way to be killed as a way to be multiplied. And, if people were doing studies- or even just being more observant- they would have realized that even the demons themselves were tearing each other apart as another way to multiply. However, I think they wanted to grow just as much as they wanted to divide. So, in that sense, from their perspective, not dividing was equally as important as dividing.

I really don't know how the demons grew, actually. Last I checked, nobody knew. Most people assumed it was by killing and consuming. But Charisma said it was a self-generating mechanism. To grow, all they had to do was exist. It didn't matter. The only thing that mattered was they needed to be destroyed. So, it was always depressing to see them getting away after they multiplied. A relief, but also not really.

Anyways, the dragons came down on us one more time before we got to South Bend. But there were only two of them and they weren't ever in our- Charisma and I's- range. Nobody was injured on that occasion and the dragons were apparently easily dispatched. Furthermore, the convoy commander reported that both dragons had been denied the opportunity to multiply, and so, obviously, that was good news.

The bad news was when- still outside of South Bend- the convoy started taking fire from a sniper who had positioned himself with a good view of the road. The gunman was shooting into vehicles at the front of the line.

We could hear the radio chatter while it was happening, but, thankfully, we were further back. The soldiers used a drone to find the shooter; who was in a hunter's tree stand that had been set up in the crossbeams of a telephone wire tower. Our convoy only had a few guns capable of shooting back; but all those gunners were tapped for the purpose and one of them made the shot and got the guy in the head. The headshot was an important detail because we now knew these homicidal people were demonic and that they could still fire a gun unless their vision was- or, hands were- disabled. The defunct sniper had fired a lot of bullets but he'd only hit one person. That person died, sadly. The sniper had also succeeded in disabling a vehicle; which was then abandoned.

After that, we finally made it to South Bend. We refueled from a tanker onsite and spent the night in the company of Gnosis and all our new friends. These were people from all walks of life; but I guess there was really only one walk of life left. The walk of not being dead. They had different skin colors, is what I'm trying to say. And they spoke different languages. Because the United States was a nation of immigrants. And some of them were fancy and well outfitted with nice clothes and gear and guns. And others were poorly outfitted, with nothing that could be called nice except by the most easy to please. Nobody was clean, though. Even the people who had the nicest stuff still smelled pretty bad if you got close to them. But some people had campers, so I guess they were the clean ones. And I guess there were makeshift showers set up somewhere, I think. I don't know. I can't remember. But Charisma and I were able to clean ourselves just the same as we usually did. Although, I can't remember ever washing our clothes in those weeks we were out there.

The South Bend convoy was operating out of the parking lots of the big box stores of the before times and the big box stores themselves were where people could go to eat and trade and get medical attention.

It actually began raining as we were getting there, and that was the first time I'd seen rain in a while. So it was a magical moment; having endured the trial to make it there and then feeling the rain cleansing the air.

The only thing that really happened in South Bend- to us, that night- was that we needed more ammunition and had to trade one of the XM7s to get it and what we received wasn't everything we needed, or wanted, but it proved to be enough.

The next day, the first convoy leaving South Bend was something like more than one thousand and less than two thousand vehicles. Our destination was Sandusky, Ohio. There were so many vehicles that I almost actually felt safe. It was like a fortified city moving down the road, but without any fortifications.

But, at the same time, as we moved further east, the archons became more and more numerous and unrelenting. The dragons could be seen way up in the sky; watching for somebody stupid enough to get out of their vehicle. They'd drop down and grab the unfortunate soul and be back up in the sky before anybody could do much about it. Not unless you'd seen them coming. Even if you could get a shot, it probably wouldn't be a good one. They moved fast.

The scorpions proved to have their own tactics. They'd wait in the water. Or, behind the structure of an overpass. Or, they'd pop out from behind a building. Or pop out of a drainage ditch. Anywhere they could hide at, that's where they'd jump out of. We'd blow them apart, but then there'd be more of them.

Perhaps our greatest dilemma was that the more people there were, the less acid throwers there were. I became morally obligated to take up the role even though I hated it and Charisma gave me hell about it. Nonstop I thought about giving my acid thrower away. I didn't want to be near the stuff; but ultimately, I was the man for the job. And I had Charisma to watch my back. Or, to watch the sky, as it was. Because one time I was out there hosing down some scorpions and one of those dragons made a pass at me, but they weren't expecting Charisma to chime in on the XM250. The machinegun sang the song of its people and that dragon crashed into the ground- limp, but pulsating- not twenty feet away from me. I hosed down the remains and finished off some scorpions that had gotten blasted before they could run off, and then we were on our way again.

The worst thing that happened on the trip to Sandusky was the cerberus who came through. We were out in the middle of nowhere and the three-headed reptoid dog demon seemed to have come from nowhere itself. As if it just jumped straight out of the ether. And maybe it had.

I never saw a small cerberus. Even the little ones were massive. This particular cerberus stood probably forty feet at the shoulders. The attack happened about a kilometer behind us in the lineup. I saw it in my mirrors before it got reported on the radio. I'd seen so many monsters attack so many people, I'd pretty much gotten used to it. But I was somehow awestruck every time I witnessed the destruction a cerberus was capable of.

"Cover me!" I told Charisma.

I jumped out and got behind the 50 cal. The 50 caliber bullets could easily hit targets that far out, but my aiming was another story. Nonetheless, I tried. One shot at a time; aiming as carefully as possible. Thankfully, it was a huge target.

Chapter 21
Echoes of the Archons
Still, my shots didn't do much of anything and I was forced to watch as the enormous cerberus ravaged the convoy. Unlike the prior cerberus we'd encountered, this one didn't go easy on us. Mostly the reptoid dog demon kept its faces to the ground; its jaws searching for one vehicle after another to grasp and crush and rend; or to carelessly fling into the distance. The huge heads would pick up vehicles in their jaws and shake them around like a

dog with a rope toy. They'd shake these vehicles with such force that it seemed like the jostling alone could kill whoever was in there.

We continued to pelt the demon with bullets that burned through the air in escalating quantities; never having an effect. The dog seemed to just absorb everything we threw at it. It jumped around deliberately, and hatefully. The three heads; devastating the lineup. In between the chatter of gunfire, the desperate screaming of dozens of tongues could be heard; louder than the confusion, louder than the monster's snarling, louder than the crashing and crunching of metal; screaming only drowned out by the gunpowder.

It wasn't until a heavy cannon put an artillery round into the spine- at the shoulders- that we succeeded in stopping the creature. Its back ripped open and it collapsed where it was; one of three mouths with somebody's vehicle still in the jaws. Of course, that wasn't a victory. For many people, it only momentarily delayed the inevitable.

Charisma appeared beside me with her XM7. The pockets of her orange safety jacket were bulging with grenades and magazines. She shouted; "Put on your acid gear!" And she was right. We had to fight the three-headed dogs, or else they'd overrun us. Charisma jumped on the fifty cal while I was suiting up. She continued putting rounds into the carcass, hoping to prevent a division or two.

A minute later and I was ready; wearing rubber from head to toe; breathing through a gas mask in the mask. We joined up with the flow of responders who were streaming toward the catastrophe. It was a dangerous place to be because the bullets were coming from everywhere; but everybody knew enough not to shoot each other. Or, if there were friendly fire casualties, they were indistinguishable from the other losses.

The military got there before we got there, and they fought them basically the same way as Charisma and I would; but the dogs came out one after another and each more furious than the previous. There were probably about a dozen divisions and they scattered in all directions and- even though there were over a hundred fighting persons out there- it was only a few seconds later when Charisma and I came to be confronted by a cerberus that was keen on devouring us.

The beast- probably ten foot at the shoulders- was running head long directly toward us; the eyes of the center head were fixated on us directly; but its right and left jaws were snapping at whoever was within their reach, and so it was an unfortunate occurrence that there happened to be a human person in the creature's left mouth when Charisma thumped a grenade into the chest; at the base of the center throat.

The grenade hit true and hard. I had the hope that the person in the dog's mouth- a pretty young woman- would be thrown free, but the opposite thing happened; the jaws clamped down and crushed her spine and I saw the life jump out of her as the monster came skidding to our feet. I knew the girl was dead, because I had seen her die. It was unmistakable.

Every couple of seconds an explosion quaked the air, and the gunshots popped off unrelentingly. There were battles being fought up and down the line. Near and far.

I was hesitating to spray the acid because the girl's corpse was there. And Charisma saw me hesitating and shouted at me, "Just do it!" So I hosed down the dog before it could multiply. And I even had a second to notice the acid burning away half of the pretty woman's dead face. Then Charisma called out "Nine o' clock!"

We turned and there was a cerberus archon that was within our zone, but not yet focusing on us. There was a crowd gathered around in a semicircle and they were futilely emptying their weapons into it; but the monster had three heads and so even though there were a couple dozen people trying to bring it down; the searching teeth and pouncing feet nonetheless had plenty of opportunity to inflict losses. Bullets hardly did anything against the cerberus. Maybe that's how they got so big all the time.

There were mangled bodies- injured, or dying, or dead- all around, and Charisma shouted; "Get back! Get back! Get back!" And then when the crowd took the hint and fled, it was only us remaining. But by the time the demon noticed us; Charisma had blown its chest apart; just like the one before. And I sprayed the acid on it as carefully as I could. People were pretty smart about getting away from the acid. And I was pleased to see the monster's body disappearing into a smoking puddle of bubbling ooze.

I had a second to take a look around. I saw the other cerberus further down the line; about five of them. So, fifteen sets of jaws. I could see the other acid throwers, hanging around their strike buggies, waiting for the right moment to move in. I could see the soldiers firing rockets and lobbing grenades. I could see a junkyard's inventory of destroyed vehicles; some of which had caught fire; the black smoke whipped and whirled in the wind. I could see the three-headed reptoid dog demons bounding through the crowds and snatching people off of their feet and gruesomely thrashing their bodies.

These smaller dogs weren't big enough to pick up a vehicle in their teeth, but they were capable of crushing a vehicle by jumping around on it. We lost several for that reason.

Most of the monsters- by now- were too far away and too well covered for us to be compelled to get involved with them. Instead we were hanging back and waiting to see what happened; eyeballing the couple altercations which we could actually get to if we had to. Eyeballing the suffering wounded, as well.

The situation resolved itself without any further involvement from Charisma and I. Some dogs ran off. The rest were destroyed. I removed my acid gear real quick and then we helped some injured to get to the medical vans and also informed the medics where the bodies who couldn't be moved could be found.

They didn't look like they'd been mauled by dogs. They looked like they'd been hit by trucks. Some were dead. Some wished they were dead. Some got off easy; with shattered bones and gaping wounds.

It is the faces of the shocked and traumatized that haunt my vision on sleepless nights; faces of pain so extreme they can't even communicate; their eyes wide and skin pallid and sweaty. Lacking the breath to cry out. Their bodies; contorted and broken apart. Lying in pools of their own blood. We couldn't help them without making it worse. All we could do was pour water in their mouths. But it seemed like that was all they really wanted, anyways. We saw more than one mercy killing, but it wasn't ever me who pulled the trigger, thankfully. The medics had been delegated the responsibility.

It soon became imperative to get moving. The wreckage was behind us, so I didn't have to bulldoze any vehicles, but we did have to wait for the others to get through the blockage. We took in one guy who knocked on our window, asking for a ride. Dave. A quiet but severe individual, dressed in full tactical gear and carrying an M249. He'd been in an SUV when the big one had lifted it in its jaws, bit down once, and then dropped it. When he did talk, it was usually a sarcastic remark about the state of affairs; which I appreciated.

We put that dismal scene in the rear-views and got to Sandusky without any further incident. Except for another scorpion attack which occurred far enough ahead of us in the lineup that we didn't even notice anything happening. If it weren't for the announcement on the radio and the fact that the pool of acid was still fuming then I wouldn't have noticed. Probably that scorpion wasn't big enough to fight an armored car.

Gnosis had turned the entire city of Sandusky into a hub for convoys. They did so by focusing on security and infrastructure tailored to convoy necessities. Convoys needed a lot of soldiers to defend them, and a lot of space to organize them, and a lot of facilities to support them. People could get everything they needed in Sandusky. Fuel. Repairs. Ammo. Food. Clothing. Medical. Hygiene. Housing.

There were a lot of people living there because they didn't know where to go. But it wasn't overpopulated or anything, because there weren't that many people left in the world anymore. And I have to admit that that was my favorite thing about it. There was breathing room. It was no accident that there wasn't any breathing room in the old world. Just like how there was no excuse for traffic. Or bureaucracy. The overabundance of illusory individuals had been by design. Crowding was a spiritual weapon; designed to suck the light out of you. Of course, you could stay up all night, and sleep in the day, and have the world all to yourself, but then it was the darkness sucking the light out of you; instead of the crowds. That's what I call 'God's Plan.'

We fueled up and parked in a parking lot with everybody else who intended to take the morning convoy to Youngstown. We had a pleasant dinner in a building that used to be a grocery store but was now a cafeteria. We ate with all the other depressed survivors; people caked in grit, grime, dirt, dust, oil, grease, and blood. We got cleaned up in a building that used to be a dollar store but had been converted into a sanitation station; with a lot of private bathrooms and shower stalls. Back in the truck; we made love and slept.

There were flood lights towering over everything and there were a lot of guns and a lot of acid throwers and always a lot of people on guard and the danger seemed to be in remission. It wasn't, but it seemed to be. That became evident in the morning time. Before my alarm clock could go off. We awakened to the sound of a terrible tragedy.

Can't say I ever heard a bigger explosion. It wasn't as intense as those rockets exploding in our faces in DC, but we weren't even near this and it felt like an asteroid had hit the Earth. The more explosions I heard the more I began to understand them. It wasn't usually one sound. It was a series of sounds. Ignition, detonation, concussion, shockwave, and then soundwaves. Something like that. Don't quote me. Smaller booms happened faster. Bigger booms happened slower. I'm including these details because I have a gut instinct reluctance to address the reality of what had just happened. It's just hard to think about.

Debris was raining down on my rig. And not gently. Charisma was clutching me like she wanted to squeeze the air out of me, and I was rigid with dread and anticipation. The morning air became suddenly heated; washing away the cool of the night. I jumped up and got some gear on and grabbed a gun and went outside.

Somebody had blown up the grocery store. Not just part of it, but most of it. That was the makeshift cafeteria. There'd been people cooking, serving, and eating breakfast in there, at the time. I don't know how many. Less than a hundred. Men, women, children. Those hundreds of people were strewn about and dispersed across the landscape. There were body parts- organs, limbs, faces- all over everywhere. I found a finger on the hood of my truck. The areas of the building that hadn't been decimated were now in flames. And there was a crater at the center. The explosion could've been caused by a meteor, but it was actually caused by a van full of nitroglycerin.

Gnosis had people to wander around and clean up the dead. But, they were just ordinary people like myself- Charisma, of course, is not ordinary- and I felt like we should help. The medics had their hands full and the convoy couldn't leave until the situation got dealt with; so we walked around with lawn and leaf garbage bags and put people's remains into them; using a shovel when we could or rubber gloves when we couldn't. Most of the meat was scorched and caked in ash and when bodies come apart like that the blood usually drains out at the same time, so it wasn't as messy as it sounds. But, it was certainly indescribably heartbreaking. Something that doesn't come across in the narrative is how often I was on the verge of tears. Charisma, too, even, was crying a lot. But, these people were dead. So, crying was just part of the experience. In the chaos, the tears didn't have time to fall. But wandering around in the corpses; the tears fell freely. In retrospect, as we did, the narrative drives on without them; heartlessly.

We stayed out there cleaning up what had to be dealt with until the disaster was under control. There were bulldozers and street sweepers to clear the lanes. Gnosis began setting up a new kitchen in some other abandoned building. An excavator dug a grave back by the loading docks and all of the body bags were thrown into it. In every direction, there were grief stricken people of all ages; some of them out of their minds with lament.

This next thing had happened a couple other times, but further away, to other people in other places, but apparently it was our turn now: A dragon came down and snatched one of our cleanup crew's acid throwers and tried to fly off with him in its clutches. I guess the talons were in deep, because it took the guy some time to react. By the time he did, his situation was hopeless. The dragon and the soldier were probably fifty feet in the air when the acid thrower went off and sprayed the demon. And then both the acid thrower and the dragon fell out of the sky; a few hundred yards out, into a different lot for a different convoy. We all had our guns on the dragon, but none of us dared fire a shot; afraid to hit the guy. The acid hadn't destroyed the divisions, either, I don't think; I saw the dragon coming apart into smaller dragons. But, I guess the other convoy dealt with them easily enough, because nothing came of it. Nothing I'm aware of, I should say.

We ended up waiting for the next two convoys to arrive. We needed to reinforce our strength, after the tragedy. But eventually, it came time to move on. Our convoy snaked- or, caterpillared- our way through the debris and into the roads and onto the highway and away from Sandusky. We were several thousand vehicles strong. It was an entire city worth of people on the move; replete with all capabilities necessary and feasible.

I asked Charisma, "Love. How are there so many evil people in the world, that the shadow can keep finding snipers and bombers?"

Charisma said, "Resonance. Echoes of the archons. People born into and raised up in a doom cult that worshiped slaughter and bloodshed. It was demented, but that was western culture. We didn't have that in the Philippines- not until western culture arrived- but we had other problems. Anyways; we're seeing the legacy of the children of Aries. The true Aryans. Not the red herring Aryans. Aries was the god of war. There were people- Scythians, Kazarians- that worshiped Aries; or, they just worshiped blood and death, really. Those people assimilated into Jewry, but they never stopped believing in their doom cult. That's the most tangible explanation for how the doom actually came to pass. Fast forward a few hundred years, and the Jews control everything and everything includes the media and the media is serving to indoctrinate people into the death cult; using our base instincts against us. Humans are apes; in our hearts and in our groins. It's natural for us to glory in death, if we aren't taught to know better. The children of Aries used the human predilection for violence to build a culture of glorifying violence. They used a false version of a false history to make murder seem normal; like it had always been so. They made movies about bloodshed and slaughter. Social enslavement made men feel weak and powerless in their own lives. The bloody movies became a bloody culture. Like, escapism. A way to escape from one's own subjugation through a fantasy of domination. Fantasy becomes reality. The individual becomes the evil. These lost souls never had a prayer. It's who they were born to be. Children of Aries. Devil's spawn. Satanic seed."

"But, how come if history is fake, and society and civilization are fake, and if the people and the cities were fake, and if the Earth itself is fake, and if outer space is fake, and if the atoms and the matter and the antimatter are fake; then why are the children of Aries not fake?"

"The children of Aries are not not fake. They're as real as anything else. As in, they are not very real. They're a little real. Kind of realish, but also sort of not. They're the programming the programming wrote. So are we, really. The way I see it, if something is affecting the light of Christ, or affecting a being who is carrying the light of Christ, then that something is real enough for our purposes. The light of Christ is the only thing that actually exists. God itself is just a manifestation of the light of Christ. I know you know this."

"Yeah. I'm just sad. About the explosion. And things."

"I know, love. Me, too."

It wasn't long after that that the assault began. It was just one dragon, to begin with. Just one report on the radio, but it sounded bad. A vehicle had been torn open and the occupants had shot the dragon apart, but not before it had torn most of them to pieces. I don't know if it was a van or a car or what. I also don't know how many died in there. 2, 4, 8, I don't know. But I do know that the dragons began multiplying and succeeded in multiplying before anybody could respond. The convoy was too big. There probably weren't enough soldiers and there definitely weren't enough acid throwers. From what I heard on the radio; the people who were close to the dividing dragon were either too slow, or too scared; or their guns were too weak, or their shooting wasn't any good. Whatever happened, it sucked. The dragons started flying off with whoever stepped out to stop them. They'd drop them out of the sky and then just keep going. That was a bad omen, but we carried on.

It wasn't five minutes before the dragons came back. Just one, actually, at first. And the convoy kept moving because it was so big that its actions and reactions were happening in variable timetables. It was no longer practical to stop a whole convoy over a single incident.

As an aside; Gnosis had asked me to pull a trailer and I was selfish enough- or smart enough- to refuse. Now, there was a dragon that had crashed through the roof of a 53 foot semi trailer. And it was obliterating the people inside as they tried to take it down with shotguns and pistols and whatever else they had. Those who were able were jumping out the back doors and running screaming. And the convoy just moved around it. People who could stop and fight did so. Responders responded. But, sometimes- especially later on, as events progressed- we just had to roll on by like nothing was happening. It sounds bad on paper, but there was a grim rhythm to it.

The dragons began to circle in the sky above us. Temporarily disinterested in attacking the vehicles. They flew too high up to hit with a rifle. The next day we would have unmanned aerial combat vehicles that would prevent this exact situation, but on this day, we did not have those. Air superiority offered them a grizzly advantage; which they anticipated and we did not.

A giant scorpion literally burst out of the side of a house where I guess it had crawled into when it was smaller. The house came apart like it was made of cardboard. We observed from a good safe distance, thankfully.

The scorpions had a primordial menace about them. This one- when it reared up into the iconic scorpion attack position; the tip of the tail was probably seventy feet in the air. And the pincers mindlessly snatched at whatever they could grab; cutting a reinforced school bus in half like it was nothing; killing three people inside.

The tail came down out of the sky with enough force to punch through the body of a humvee that was there. The humvee was lifted up into the air before it broke loose. When it broke loose it fell directly onto the scorpion's back. But the colossus... Actually, I think it's fair to call it a kaiju, by this point. The cerberus, too, was kaiju, I'd say. The kaiju sasori; it didn't even notice that a humvee had just fallen on it. If the archon was behind us, then I could have taken pot shots at it with the 50 cal. Charisma could have covered the airspace. But the scorpion was out front and I couldn't get turned around even if I wanted to; because we were passing by the semi trailer massacre at the time.

Finally, one of the soldiers hit the kaiju with a TOW missile, and the thing exploded all over everybody in the vicinity. A minute later and there were about 10 giant scorpions instead of one gianter scorpion. Those divisions were each about the size of the first one that had crawled out from underneath the Philadelphia city hall. Which- all things considered- was barely a medium sized one.

The scorpions were somewhat more inclined to run away from the bullets and from the conflict, but that didn't stop them from confronting everybody who got in their way. The only losses we were taking were of the soldiers who approached them directly. Not to mention, from the sky above. I got on the radio and told the commander to order everybody back inside their vehicles, but I guess he didn't hear me. Because the soldiers kept running out to blast the scorpions apart. And the scorpions kept rushing the soldiers and cutting them in half. Occasionally a scorpion would place a victim into its mouths; which had an extra set of pincers just for eating. They ate them even though they didn't actually need to eat them. Kind of like the snakes I'd seen did; back in Providence. The cobras devoured humans; but for no real reason besides the elimination of an enemy of evil. A cobra- actually, as it happened- was about to pop up out of the blue. The only one that I'd seen since the first day that we had released them. Just, not right yet.

We had to fight the scorpions because they were killing the soldiers in our immediate vicinity, but neither one of us was about to step outside, or even go up into the nest. The dragons didn't hesitate to utilize the disorder of the scorpion attacks and so were dragging people up into the sky again. Countless people could be seen falling to their deaths from tremendous heights, and if you averted your eyes fast enough then you wouldn't have to watch them splatter.

Going outside simply wasn't an option for the time being, but people were realizing the dragons had to be stopped. And that meant firing firearms toward other humans. So- out of necessity, and as much as nobody wanted to, and even though we all knew it was a bad idea; we were left with no choice but to start shooting toward each other in order to hit the dragons when they descended. Because there was usually a momentary pause after they grabbed somebody and before they regained their lift, and that was when they were vulnerable.

As our only way to provide aide; what Charisma ended up doing was using the slats that had been installed at the corners. She couldn't fire from inside the truck, because that could break windows; but she could thump grenades to where they were needed. And she could fire short bursts by twisting the rifle sideways through the slot and keeping the discharges outside of the interior. It wasn't ideal, but it saved at least a couple soldiers who only needed a second or two to reposition themselves. Those were brave men out there. Anybody who stepped outside their vehicle with those dragons in the sky had to be a brave soul. The dragons- it seemed- only ever became more numerous. But, there were enough people in our convoy to at least make it a fair fight.

We pushed on, and the dragons never stopped circling overhead, but they had- at least for a while- stopped tearing apart our vehicles to get to the people inside. It was an uneasy standoff, to say the least. We made some decent miles like that, with the dragons circling overhead. I counted seven of them, but I could've been wrong. The scorpions I think ran off, eventually. Or maybe they were still lurking about; following along with us. I don't know.

What stopped us next time; we'd been hearing rumors it could happen. And we were uncomfortably close when it did. Not dangerously close, like those who died. But certainly too close for my liking. The thing was staggeringly large. It appeared out of the trees on an elevated ledge beside the road. There was an arch bridge up there; high up above us. It wrapped itself around the arch bridge itself and from there descended into a hail of bullets and cannon shells. The cannons could blow holes in it, but all that happened was that smaller cobras came crawling out of it. Its composition was unusual in that way; it could endure more punishment and was less fragile than the other archons.

The cobra was so big that its body itself functioned as a means of destruction. It was crushing a lot of people as it lowered itself down onto their vehicles. It had to have weighed several hundred tons. The cobra rose up into the sky and displayed its fearsome hood. When you looked at it, you had the feeling that it was looking right back at you. Its red eyes glowed brightly from the shadows of its black face. The red scales of its hood shone brilliantly in the sun. When it struck- because it was so massive- it struck in slow motion. But even a slow snake strike happens fast. The cobra dove forward and wrapped its mouth around a light tank and lifted the tank up into the sky; using gravity to help itself swallow it. That sucked, too, because the tank had the TOW missiles and those were the best weapons to use against it.

"I can hit it. With the M-72," said Charisma; understanding that if we didn't stop it then, then maybe nobody else would either.

"Yeah. Ok. I'll cover you," I said.

"Ok, love. I love you."

"I love you, too," I said, kissing her lips once.

I popped a fresh magazine into the XM7 and Charisma loaded a rocket into the M72.

When she was ready, she said, "Now!"

I jumped out of the door and examined the sky. She climbed up the ladder, threw open the hatch, positioned herself on the platform, and took aim. I wasn't looking at anything other than the dragon that noticed both of us immediately. Like a jerk; the dragon was coming at us from the direction of the sun. I don't know if it was going for me or for her, but since I couldn't see anything except the blinding glare; I waited for it to get closer.

I waited until the shadow of the demon was blotting out the sun, and then I fired straight into its face. Charisma fired the rocket about then, too. A jet of hot wind whooshed by and I heard the warhead explode over the suppressed rattle of my XM7.

The dragon crashed into the ground. It wasn't moving. As I turned to get the acid thrower, I looked up and saw that that cobra no longer had a face, and that it was falling slowly through the air. The kaiju collided with the earth with a quaking reverberation that jolted the truck like a nasty pothole.

The woefully dividing archon carcass was definitely blocking the turnpike. The sheer size of it had been a threat of equal magnitude. And it wasn't- by any means- finished causing us problems.

The acid throwers honorably went to work on the cobra, and I- protected only by rubber gloves- quickly and carefully hosed my dragon down with acid, as well. Then I hurriedly stowed the acid gear and got back into the truck. Charisma closed the nest hatch and slid down and sat beside me. She was smiling. I was smiling, too.

Now. The reader might be noticing that this book is coming to an end and the story isn't wrapping up. Charisma and I are still very much out in the thick of the turmoil and with no end in sight. That's just the way it was. And maybe I'm only a stupid truck driver and maybe I'm not a real novelist, like all those famous nobodies, but I damn sure know better than to write a book with no ending on it. I could have just said, 'To Be Continued...' but that would've been a dick move, without some kind of explanation. In my opinion. At any rate, I am the narrator and I can narrate if I want to.

The truth is that the producers decided that this book had to be this length. But they tell me that the sequel can be as long as I want or need it to be. I should have kept that detail in mind, because with each page I've written I've grown more and more compromising on the quality of the storytelling. For no other reason than to cut the story down to the size (((they))) wanted it to be.

In light of the circumstances; I decided that instead of rushing the ending and doing a disservice to the people who died in the battles fought between this book's arbitrary stopping point and the next book's ideal beginning point; I could, instead, just as easily put the ending of this book at the beginning of the next book and it literally wouldn't make any difference. Except to make the sum total more thorough. Which is a good thing, ultimately.

Obviously, I survive to tell the tale. And I've probably mentioned at some point that Charisma also survives. Angela also survives; the reader will be pleased to learn. And because I don't want to be accused of leaving anybody cliff hanging- a literary practice I happen to find tedious- I can and will inform the reader how this book's story ends: What happens is that we get back to Fall River and New England is infested with cobra archons, and my mother is alive, and I am happy to see her. Plus, maybe a couple dismal surprises along the way. The end. To be continued. Hopefully.